PENGUIN BO

Death's Mi

Karen Chance is *The New York Times* bestselling author of two urban fantasy series. *Touch the Dark, Claimed by Shadow, Embrace the Night* and *Curse the Dawn* all feature gutsy heroine Cassie Palmer, and *Midnight's Daughter* was the first in the Dory Basarab series. Karen Chance lives in Florida.

To find out more about Karen Chance's books, please visit her website: www.karenchance.com

KAREN CHANCE

Death's Mistress

PENGUIN BOOKS

PENGUIN BOOKS

Published by the Penguin Group

Penguin Books Ltd, 80 Strand, London WC2R ORL, England

Penguin Group (USA) Inc., 375 Hudson Street, New York, New York 10014, USA

Penguin Group (Canada), 90 Eglinton Avenue East, Suite 700, Toronto, Ontario, Canada M4P 2Y3
(a division of Pearson Penguin Canada Inc.)

Penguin Ireland, 25 St Stephen's Green, Dublin 2, Ireland (a division of Penguin Books Ltd)

Penguin Group (Australia), 250 Camberwell Road, Camberwell, Victoria 3124, Australia
(a division of Pearson Australia Group Pty Ltd)

Penguin Books India Pvt Ltd, 11 Community Centre, Panchsheel Park,
New Delhi – 110 017, India

Penguin Group (NZ), 67 Apollo Drive, Rosedale, North Shore 0632, New Zealand
(a division of Pearson New Zealand Ltd)

Penguin Books (South Africa) (Pty) Ltd, 24 Sturdee Avenue, Rosebank,
Johannesburg 2196, South Africa

Penguin Books Ltd, Registered Offices: 80 Strand, London WC2R ORL, England

www.penguin.com

First published in the United States of America by Onyx,
an imprint of New American Library, a division of Penguin Group (USA) Inc. 2010
First published in Great Britain in Penguin Books 2010

2

Printed in Great Britain by Clays Ltd, St Ives plc

A CIP catalogue record for this book is available from the British Library

ISBN: 978-0-141-03952-7

www.greenpenguin.co.uk

Chapter One

There was no sign on the abandoned church, but some-one had scribbled "Let us Prey" above the main doors. As a Catholic, I didn't approve. As someone bent on do-ing exactly that, it seemed oddly appropriate.

I pushed open the heavy wooden doors and went in. It looked like I'd guessed right in going with office chic when I'd gotten ready for the evening. There were a mi-nority of Goths and some tourist types in the church-turned-nightclub, but most of the crowd seemed to be composed of those recently released from corporate hell.

I fit in well enough, in a blue silk tank top I sweated through within five minutes and a short black skirt. The tank matched the new streaks in my short brown hair; the skirt matched my eyes. I got a beer at the bar and wandered around, looking for trouble.

It didn't take long to find it. The club was populated mostly by humans, but it was owned by a vampire. A group of the fashionable undead showed up every night for the all-you-can-eat buffet, and from the look of things, the owner was dining early.

He had a pretty brunette in a corner, his hand up her skirt and his fangs in her throat. That was frowned upon by the Vampire Senate, the ruling body for North American vampires, who preferred feedings to be kept nice and subtle. But then, this guy had already proven he wasn't too concerned about the Senate's point of view—about a lot of things. That was why I was here. They intended to teach a lesson, and to make it memorable.

The woman was facing out toward the crowd, and by the time I reached them, he'd managed to get her dress open all the way down. She wasn't wearing much underneath, unless you counted the scrap of black lace he had his hand inside. He did something that caused a quick, indrawn breath and a helpless shift of her hips. One of the bystanders laughed.

There were a dozen of them, all vampires, and at least a few were masters. I'd hoped to catch him alone, or at worst with two or three others. I hadn't planned on the show, and it complicated things.

He pulled the dress off her shoulders and it slithered to the floor, over skin already so sensitized that every tiny movement was torture. She began to breathe heavily through her nose, trembling like a fever had gripped her. He hadn't bothered to fog her mind, because it's no fun if they aren't terrified. And because his boys wanted to play.

Vampires have a limited ability to project thoughts, and because of my heritage, I pick them up better than most. She wouldn't meet their eyes, wouldn't raise her head. But she knew what they saw by the images they thoughtfully kept sending.

From a dozen perspectives, she was bombarded with images of her body, slick and shining under the lights, of the rivulets sweat had carved through the goose bumps on her skin, of her last piece of clothing being jerked down her thighs. And the pictures came in stereo, with every sound that was ripped from her throat magnified a dozen times and sent back to her. The watchers' emotions leaked through, too: arousal, anticipation and, most of all, rising bloodlust.

That was especially true of the monster draining her, yet still she writhed back against him. And when his hands roamed over her sweat-slick skin, she moaned desperately. She was trapped in the feedback loop of sensation that went with the feeding process. It was better than a drug as it coursed through her veins, tightening her nipples, shortening her breath and siphoning out her life.

I'd assumed that, with so many available donors, he wouldn't choose to drain her. Body disposal was messy and time-consuming, and prompted investigations that he had every reason to avoid. But he must have liked her taste, because even as her legs gave out and she collapsed, he followed her down.

It's crazy to interrupt a vampire when he's feeding, when he's at his most vulnerable and his most deadly. But then, I haven't been sane in centuries. The toe of my boot caught his wrist, tossing it away from the girl.

"You want to dance with me," I told him clearly, as he rounded on me with a snarl.

Odds were that no human had treated him that cavalierly before, and he clearly didn't like it. He liked even less that some of his vamps had seen me do it. But it intrigued him, too. I was suddenly a tastier dish than the one who lay gasping like a fish out of water, the velvet of her dress crushed beneath her.

"You know, I think you're right," he said, flashing me a winning smile with more than a hint of power behind it.

I ignored it and tangled a fist in his shirt so I wouldn't have to touch him. I dragged him onto the dance floor and he didn't try to get away. He just followed me with a glint in his eye that promised pain to come.

He had no idea.

He grinned, and his eyes dropped to my hips as I followed the beat. "You look hot."

Unfortunately, I couldn't say the same. His eyes were glued to my chest, maybe because it was directly in his line of sight. I'm five foot two inches, and the boots added another three inches, but that still meant he was missing a crucial element of the tall, dark and handsome stereotype. It didn't matter, since he was missing the rest, too.

Not that he appeared to know it.

"Thanks," I said.

He laughed. "I meant, you look like you could use a drink."

"If we can have it in private."

A blond eyebrow rose. "That can be arranged."

He took my hand, towing me across the sticky dance floor, scattering the crowd like peasants before royalty. The analogy amused me, considering that he'd been born the bastard son of a pig farmer. Not that I was in any position to talk. I was the illegitimate daughter of a serving wench and a vampire. It didn't get much trashier than that.

Of course, we'd both come a long way from our inauspicious beginnings. These days, he went by the name of Hugo Vleck and operated a successful club when he wasn't selling illegal fey narcotics. And as for me ... Well, I solve problems of the vampire kind, and Vleck was making my employer very unhappy. My job was to cheer him up. The fact that I was going to enjoy it was just a bonus.

The crowd was five thick around the bar, but we didn't have any trouble getting served. That wasn't too surprising since my date owned the club, but he shot me a look over his shoulder, checking to see if I was suitably impressed. I smiled and he put a hand on my ass.

"Cristal for the lady," he told the young vamp bartender, giving me a little squeeze.

"Will you be drinking, too, sir?"

Vleck grinned, showing off his fangs. "Later."

He and the bartender exchanged a look, while I tried to appear like someone who didn't know that a lot of vamps prefer their alcohol straight from a victim's veins. They say it increases the high they get from feeding, and is the only way to feel the burn with their metabolism. Vleck was clearly calculating how much more it would take to get me all the way to drunk. I could have told him there wasn't that much booze in the world, but why spoil his evening?

He had so little of it left.

The bartender sat a champagne flute on the bar but Vleck shook his head. "I'll take the bottle. Wrap it up."

"Where are we going?" I asked.

"My place. It isn't far."

Wow. He must really plan to get nasty. I draped an arm around his waist, and rested my chin on his shoulder. "I don't feel like waiting. Isn't there somewhere we could go here?"

"Naw. The office is too small—you can barely turn around in that thing."

"So? You're the boss. Make some space," I said, smiling seductively and pulling him away from the bar. Like with most crappy clubs, the bathrooms were down a dark hallway. I dragged him into the men's room and tugged his shirt off.

He chuckled and disengaged long enough to haul a couple of guys out of a stall and throw them out the door, one with his trousers still around his knees. I leaned against a sink while he instructed one of the vamps acting as bouncers to tell everyone that the facilities were out of order. Then he turned and grabbed me by the waistband.

"Let's see what you got."

"Thought you'd never ask." I smiled and shut the door with my foot.

Five minutes later, I emerged, a little out of breath but not too bad, all things considered.

The bouncer caught my eye on the way out. He seemed surprised, maybe because I was still alive. But then he grinned. "Have fun?"

"Loved him to pieces."

I stopped by vamp central, aka the East Coast Office of the North American Vampire Senate, to get my check. The vamps usually took care of fungus like Vleck themselves, holding each master responsible for his own servants' behavior. But the system wasn't as perfect as they liked people to believe.

Vampires could be emancipated from their masters' control when they reached a certain power level, freeing them from forced obedience. Others were under the control of senior-level masters on other Senates, who didn't always care about the rules laid down by their North American counterpart. And then there were the revenants, who had had something go wrong in the Change, and ended up answering to nobody but their own twisted minds.

When any of these types started causing trouble, the Senate stepped in. And luckily for me, the current war in the supernatural community had stretched their resources. It had gotten so bad lately that they were even willing to employ a dhampir—that hated cross between a vampire and a human—on the cleanup crew. But I always got the impression that they disinfected the office after I left.

The elevator opened onto a scene of old-world elegance. Shiny cherrywood pillars surrounded a polished table set with exotic flowers, dappled by the light of an exquisite crystal chandelier. Underfoot, an inlaid marble floor in a sunburst pattern in warm shades of gold and amber anchored the scene. It would have been an attractive room, if not for the strokes of too-white meanness propping up the walls.

One of them peeled off to block my path. Waspish and fine-boned, he was wearing a close-fitting coat and knee pants of midnight blue velvet and heels an inch higher than mine. His long, pin-straight blond hair was pulled back into a queue, and he had an honest-to-God cravat. He looked like he'd stepped out of a period movie—the kind where they don't stint on the costumes—and his expression said he smelled something bad.

"Who let you in?" he demanded.

Every time they changed the guards, it was the same story. And it was always worse with the older ones. They recalled the good old days when dhampirs were killed on sight, preferably slowly. Their attitude pissed me off, considering that I'd been working here for over a month now, and the nightclub scene had left me spoiling for a fight. Vleck hadn't been nearly enough of a challenge.

But damn it, I'd promised a certain someone to be on my best behavior. "I'm here to see Mircea," I told him, instead of punching the vamp through the pretty brocaded wallpaper.

"*Lord* Mircea."

"Whatever. I have a delivery," I said, pushing past.

And found my arm seized in a bruising grip. "You can wait in the alley with the rest of the garbage until sent for."

"I'm tired, I'm hungry and I have a head in a bag," I warned him. "Do not fuck with me."

He slapped me, hard enough to rock my head back, so I nailed his hand to the wall with a knife. He pulled it out, the slice through his palm healing instantly, and lunged. And ended up dangling off the floor like an errant puppy.

"Best behavior?" someone asked. I looked up to see the pleasant goateed face, curly dark hair and gleaming brown eyes of Senator Kit Marlowe. His agreeable expression didn't stop him from squeezing the guy's neck hard enough to make his eyes pop.

Since Marlowe hates me only marginally less than, say, bubonic plague, the smile made me nervous. I suspected that was why he did it, but it worked every time. I shrugged. "I didn't stick it in his heart."

"Perhaps you should have," he said mildly, and opened his hand. The vamp hit the floor, jumped to his feet and went for me again in a blur of speed. So I grabbed him by the neck and punched his head through the pretty brocaded wallpaper.

"Bring her in, Mikhail," someone called from off to the right.

Mikhail must have been the one with his head in the plaster, because nobody moved. I released him and he pulled out, pale eyes glittering with hate. I smiled. It's always so much easier when the vamps I deal with despise me. It's the ones who profess anything else that confuse the hell out of me. Mikhail and I understood each other; he'd kill me if he got the chance, and I'd make sure he never did. Easy.

"I'll take her," Marlowe said, while Mikhail stared at him.

"My lord. She attacked me!"

"If you are foolish enough to assault Lord Mircea's daughter while he is on the premises, then you deserve what you get," Marlowe told him shortly.

I raised an eyebrow. "While he's on the premises?" I repeated.

That disturbing grin widened.

I followed him through the open doorway. We passed through a sitting room and into an office with more of the same, decor-wise: hand-carved moldings, a soaring ceiling and a mural of fat cherubs that gazed down on visitors with smug superiority.

There was also a desk. It was a massive old mahogany masterpiece with carved this and original that, but it didn't draw the eye nearly as much as the man seated behind it. Unlike Vleck, Senator Mircea Basarab knew how to rock the tall, dark and handsome thing, and tonight he'd gone all out in full white-tie regalia. He gleamed, from the top of his burnished head to the toes of his perfectly shined shoes.

"All you need is a red-lined cape," I told him sourly, dropping my duffel bag onto the desk. It squelched a little. He winced.

"Your word is really quite good enough, Dorina," he informed me, as I fished out the remains. "I do not require a physical specimen unless I wish to question him."

"I'll keep it in mind." Vleck was dripping onto the nice marble floor, so I set him on the desk. But that didn't work either. He rolled and Marlowe had to jump to rescue some papers before they were ruined. I glanced around, but there were no handy baskets. So I stuck him onto the dagger-shaped memo holder. There was still some dripping, but at least he wasn't going anywhere.

I looked up to find two unhappy vamps looking at me. "Okay," I said, "it's all the same to me. I just want my check."

Mircea took out a leather-covered checkbook and started writing, while Marlowe regarded Vleck thoughtfully. "I've always wondered, how do you get out?"

"What?"

"Of the club or the house or what have you." He waved a hand. "As soon as a master-level vampire dies, every one of his children knows it. Even if they are old enough and powerful enough to have been emancipated, they feel it here"—he tapped his chest—"like a blow. Yet you regularly kill such vampires and escape the premises without your own head ending up on a pike. So I ask again, how do you get out?"

"I walk."

He frowned. "I am serious. I would like to know."

"I'm sure you would," I said sarcastically, as Mircea tore off the check. Marlowe ran the Senate's intelligence organization, and he'd probably vastly prefer to keep matters like Vleck in the hands of his own deadly little hit squad. But he couldn't afford to risk them in wartime on nonessential missions.

The conflict between the Silver Circle of light mages and their dark counterpart had been going on for a while now, and just to confuse the hell out of everyone, the vamps had decided to ally with the light. But it stretched their manpower, and they seemed to have more trouble taking care of the Vlecks of this world than I did.

I intended to keep it that way. This was the best money I'd made in years.

"Every vampire in that nightclub knew the moment their master died, yet you simply walked out," he said resentfully, refusing to let it go.

I put on my innocent face, which seems to annoy him about as much as those damn smiles do me. "Yeah. I guess I got lucky."

"You do it every time!"

"Really lucky," I amended, trying to take the check. But Mircea held on to the other end.

"Have you by any chance seen Louis-Cesare recently?"

"Why?"

He sighed. "Why can you never answer a simple question?"

"Maybe because you never ask any. And what would the darling of the European Senate want with me?"

Louis-Cesare and I had met only recently, despite being members of the same dysfunctional clan. It wasn't too surprising since we came from opposite ends of the vampire world. I was the dhampir daughter of the family patriarch, the little-known stain on an otherwise immaculate record. Dhampirs are feared and loathed by vampires for obvious reasons, and most families who accidentally end up with one quickly bury the error. Why Mircea hadn't done so was still something of a mystery. Maybe because I occasionally proved useful.

Louis-Cesare, on the other hand, was vamp royalty. The only made Child of Mircea's younger and far stranger brother, Radu, he had been breaking records almost since birth. He'd become a master, a rank many vamps never reached, before he'd been dead half a century. Another century had elevated him to first-level status, on par with the top players in the vamp world. And within a decade after that, he'd become the darling of the European Senate, feted for his looks, his wealth and his ability on the dueling field, which had gotten them out of many sticky situations.

A month ago, the prince and the pariah had crossed paths because we had one thing in common: we were both very good at killing things. And Mircea's bug-eyed, crazy brother Vlad had needed killing if anyone ever had. But our collaboration had had a rough start. Louis-Cesare didn't like taking orders from a dhampir, and I didn't like having a partner, period. But we eventually sorted things out and got the job done. He'd even learned some manners, before the end. And I had started to think that it was kind of . . . nice, having someone to watch my back for a change.

Sometimes I could be really stupid.

"Radu mentioned that the two of you had grown . . . close," Mircea said carefully.

"Radu was mistaken."

"You didn't answer the question," Marlowe observed.

"Have you seen or had any contact with Louis-Cesare in the last few weeks?"

"Why? What's he done?"

"Nothing . . . yet."

"Okay, what are you afraid he'll do?"

Marlowe glanced at Mircea, and they held one of those silent conversations vampires sometimes have, the kind I'm not supposed to know about. "I would merely like to ask him about a family matter," Mircea said, after a moment.

"As you're constantly reminding me, I'm family. Tell me and maybe I can help. Or does the family thing only work when you want something?"

Mircea took a deep breath, which he didn't need, to show me how much of a pain I was being. "It's about *his* family, Dorina, and is not my story to tell. Now, have you seen him?"

"I haven't heard from him in a month," I said flatly, suddenly tiring of the game. I didn't need another reminder that, as far as my status as family was concerned, it was and always would be second-class.

"Should that change, I would appreciate receiving word," he told me.

"And I'd appreciate receiving my check, or are you planning to hold it all night?"

Mircea raised an eyebrow, but he didn't let go. "I may have another commission for you tomorrow." He pushed a folder across the desk, careful to avoid the blood splatter.

"May have?"

"It has yet to be decided. Will you be available?"

"I'll see what I can do."

"And, Dorina, should I choose to go through with it, I will need this one alive."

"Will the handy-dandy portable size do?" If I didn't stake the heart, a master vamp could live in pieces anywhere from a week to a month, depending on his power level. And it was a lot easier to sneak out a head in a bag than a whole body. Plus, there was something about decapitation that made even the most obstinate vamp feel chatty.

"That will be sufficient," Mircea said, gazing cynically at Vleck. The ex-vamp's mouth had slipped open and his tongue was hanging out. At least he wasn't drooling, I thought, and snatched the check.

God, how I loved easy money.

Chapter Two

The gray weather we'd been having for the last few days was making an encore, but I made it home before it started to rain. I parked my latest rusted hulk—a Camaro that had once been blue and was now a sort of mottled gray—on the overgrown driveway to one side of the house. My key hit the lock as the first few droplets spattered down.

The leaden skies made the battered old Victorian look even more dilapidated than usual. It had been built by a retiring sea captain back in the 1880s, when Flatbush was Brooklyn's happening new suburb. It still sat on a decent-sized lot with old-growth trees, but its glory days were over. The paint was peeling, the porch was sagging and the gingerbread trim was missing a number of pieces. It made the house look a bit like an old person with broken teeth. But it was home, and it was glad to see me.

After a moment, a frisson of welcome spread up my arm, and the door opened. I hopped over a hole in the floor, set a couple of takeout bags on the counter and lit an old-fashioned hurricane lamp. On full power, the wards caused the electricity to go bonkers. And while it still worked okay for larger appliances, constantly blinking lights made me dizzy.

I snared a beer out of the fridge and stood at the counter drinking it, flipping through the day's mail. Someone had thoughtfully left it on the table, maybe because it was mostly composed of bills. My onetime roommate

Claire had inherited the house from her uncle, and when she went off to bigger and better things, she'd left it in my care. And it needed a lot of it.

Most important, it needed a new roof. There was a worrying stain on the ceiling of my bedroom, which had started out roughly the shape of Rhode Island, but now looked more like North Carolina. Another few days of rain, and it was going to be Texas. And then it wouldn't be anything at all because the battered old shingles were going to cave in on my head.

I filed the bills in the usual spot—the breadbox—and started to unpack the takeout when a clap of thunder struck directly overhead. It sounded like a grenade going off, and was near enough to shake the house. I froze, my heart in my throat.

Oh, please, oh, please, I begged, listening with all my might.

For a long moment I didn't hear anything, except the rumbling aftermath of the weather and my thudding pulse. And then a thin, tremulous wail filtered down from upstairs. My blood ran cold.

Within seconds, the cry had intensified to orchestra-like crescendos. A glass in the kitchen sink trembled and then shattered, along with what remained of my eardrums. I put my head down on the counter and thought about sobbing.

In my somewhat extended lifetime, I'd been through war, famine and disease. I was a strong woman. I was a warrior. But I'd never had to face anything like this.

I really, really wanted to kill something, but there wasn't anything handy.

There was nothing to do but pick up the shards of the tumbler and dump them in the trash. The horrible wailing that was threatening every window in the house stopped for a second, then two, and I took a cautious breath—before it began again with renewed vigor. I put the beer back and went to the liquor cabinet for whiskey.

I was cursing my roommates, who had cleaned out all

the liquor in my absence, when I heard the soft scrape of a footstep in the hall. It should have been impossible, even with my hearing, to detect anything over that din, but some desperate instinct brought it to my attention anyway. Maybe because it was so unusual.

There were a lot of creatures around the house these days, lumbering and stomping across the old wooden boards at all times of the day and night. But there was no one who just *stepped*. No one who was here by invitation, anyway.

I could feel the muscles bunching under my skin, ready to explode outward into motion. My breath started coming faster, and a bead of sweat slid into my eye. It could just be the house settling, I told myself sternly as I reached for the cleaver. Don't get excited.

Then the tiny sound came again, along with a squeaky protest from one of the boards in the hall. My mood lifted. Maybe I'd get to kill something, after all.

I crossed to the hall door and grasped the green glass knob, but didn't turn it. Normally, the kitchen door was left open because the hinges screamed with protest whenever they were used. But someone had closed it, and now I couldn't open it again without letting whatever was out there know I was coming. I was going to have to wait for it to come closer.

I expected to be able to tell a lot about the intruder even without sight. The weight could be guessed from the heaviness of the tread, the height by the soft susurration of breath, possibly even the sex if he or she was wearing cologne. But when I extended my senses, all I received was the shock of contact as my humanness brushed up against something Other.

My hand jerked back from the knob, but I still felt it: a fluttering sensation cascading along my skin, a sort of electric prickle. It wasn't painful, sharp or hot. It was like being caressed by fingers of water, a gentle, melting touch that soothed and reassured and calmed.

And made my skin crawl.

I didn't want to be reassured when there was a danger in the house. I couldn't afford to lose my edge. But I could feel it slipping away anyway, my heartbeat slowing, my breath coming easier, the sweat that had popped out on my arms a moment before cooling in the night air.

Even more worrying, the house itself wasn't reacting. The wards usually relished doing nasty things to trespassers. But the kitchen remained dim and silent, the only movement the flickering flame inside the lantern.

Its light danced off a row of chef's knives on the wall, some battered copper cookware hanging from a pot rack, and a broom with a solid wood handle in the corner. Any or all of them would have been useful against a large range of creatures, but probably not one who could so completely fool the house wards. And that went for anything I had on me, too.

I was contemplating sneaking out the back way and doing a Spider-Man impression up to my room, where I had a cache of much nastier weapons. But then the shrieking upstairs stopped. It didn't taper off; it just cut out between one breath and the next, like a hand had been clenched around a small neck. And suddenly I forgot about subtlety, tactics and strategy. I threw open the door and dove into the dark hallway, knife raised, a battle cry building in my throat.

And got slammed against a wall hard enough to rattle my ribs.

Rolling back to my feet, I threw a small table at my enemy, trying to buy myself a second to figure out what the hell I was fighting. But no such luck. I got a glimpse of huge, luminous eyes, with horizontal pupils like a goat's, and then a ball of fire came out of nowhere, reducing the table to cinders and sending rippling shadows up the walls. I leapt forward, looking for a vulnerable spot, but a massive clawed foot covered in gleaming scales slammed down on me with the force of a jackhammer.

My back hit the floor with my neck wedged between two curved talons the length of daggers. My own knife had lodged in the ball of the paw pinning me to the boards, between a couple of overlapping scales, but I doubted it was more than a thorn prick to the enormous creature. I thrashed and fought to free my weapon, but only succeeded in driving it a little farther into the thick hide.

And somewhere above my head, someone cursed, "Cut it out already!"

I paused at the very human-sounding voice, but I still couldn't see. And then a thin ribbon of flame shot out of the darkness and lit a row of candles on the wall, all at once. It was a good trick, but I was in no position to admire it. I was too busy staring at the sight of a large dragon wedged into my narrow hallway.

It didn't look very comfortable. Its small black wings were squashed against the ceiling, its huge legs were up around its neck and its elongated snout was sticking haphazardly out between them. The only part it appeared to be able to move was its foot, which was leaking a stream of black blood.

"That hurts like a bitch!" It bent its massive head a little closer to take a look at the damage.

I just stared.

An acre of pewter scales was broken by a ridge of gleaming amethyst down its back. Two horns the color of molten glass sat on its head, framing a tuft of absurd lavender hair. It matched the creature's eyes, which were creepy as hell, but had irises the color of pansy petals.

A nictitating membrane slid first across one great eye and then the other as the dragon regarded its wounded foot. After a moment, it transferred that alien gaze to me, and the whorl of scales across its cheeks took on a vaguely purple tint. "You stabbed me!"

"You broke in," I said slowly, in complete disbelief. Because I'd seen a lot of strange things in Brooklyn, but a dragon wasn't one of them.

"I did no such thing!" The huge snout grimaced, showing an awful lot of teeth. But the voice was melodious, almost hypnotic, sliding like a drug into my veins.

It soothed my racing pulse back to normal in spite of everything I could do to stop it. I needed the energy of anger to fight, but all of a sudden my body was contemplating having a snooze, and my muscles were going limp and noodle-y.

"I don't usually argue with anyone capable of crushing the life out of me," I said, fighting back a yawn. "But yeah, you did."

"It's my house!" A fold of skin that had been held flat against the creature's back suddenly opened, spreading upward like translucent fan to frame its long snout. "What are you waiting for?" it demanded. "Get it out!"

I assumed "it" meant the knife, so I resumed tugging on it. "It would help if you'd let me up," I said after a minute.

"Are you going to throw anything else at me?"

"Are you going to eat me?"

The eyes did the creepy sideways blink again. I was starting to wonder if that was the dragon equivalent of an eye roll. "Don't be ridiculous, Dory! You know damn well I'm vegan."

The foot rose and I slid out from between the gigantic toenails. They were black at the roots, shading to gray and then clear at the ends like the horns. Except for a few spots where flakes of bright red appeared. They looked suspiciously like nail polish, which was when I decided to stop thinking at all.

The knife finally slipped free, and the second it cleared the tough hide, a cold blue-white light swelled out from between the scales as if the huge body was cracking down fault lines. And then an explosion of light hit me like a fist, throwing me back a yard. I landed hard against the faded wallpaper, jarring a hanging mirror loose. It crashed against the floor, and the screeching from upstairs started up again.

"God, do I need a drink," a voice said fervently.

My thoughts exactly.

I sat up as someone pushed through the kitchen door and headed for the liquor cabinet. I got to my hands and knees and peered around the jamb, only to see a tall, naked redhead standing in the lantern light. She was glaring at the empty liquor cabinet. "Don't tell me you've gone teetotaler!"

"No," I said cautiously, sizing this new shape up.

It looked like Claire, my old roommate. The illusion was perfect, down to the little details that spells usually overlook. The creature's hair was a red fuzz ball, the way Claire's always got in rainy weather; there was a familiar pattern of freckles over the nose; and the arms were crossed under the breasts in an often-used expression of annoyance.

But there were discordant notes, too. This Claire had bruise-dark circles under her eyes, which kept darting nervously around the kitchen, and a sickly pallor beneath her freckles. Her lips were white and pressed tightly together, and she looked like she hadn't slept in a while, like she was running on nerves.

But the real clincher was that Claire wouldn't show up in the middle of the night, unescorted, barefoot and wild-eyed. When I met her, she'd been working a bad-paying job at a magical auction house and had needed a roommate for the extra cash. But that was before a real-life fey prince turned up at one of the sales and swept her off her feet—and all the way to Faerie. She'd been there ever since, presumably living the happily-ever-after that the rest of us just dream about.

"It's a damn good glamourie," I said, wondering exactly how one evicted a dragon, even in human form, from one's kitchen. "But for future reference, Claire didn't make a habit of running around naked. Not even in her own house."

"I was wearing clothes!" the creature said, snatching an apron from a drawer. It was the old-fashioned type that was more like a dress, leaving her decent as long as she didn't turn around. "I burst out of them whenever I change now. My dragon self has hit adolescence and it's growing like a weed."

I stared from the drawer with the aprons—I hadn't known we had any—to the woman shrugging one on. "Dragon self?"

She pushed limp red strands off her forehead with the back of her hand. "I'm half Dark Fey, Dory. You know that!"

"Yeah, but ... you never mentioned what kind!"

"I didn't know until recently, and anyway, it's not the kind of thing you just drop into conversation." She located a box of aspirin in a drawer and peered at the label myopically. Those pretty green eyes had always been nearsighted, and I guess going scaly would make it a bitch to keep up with glasses.

I got slowly to my feet, my head spinning. "Claire?"

"Who were you expecting?" she demanded. "Attila the Hun?"

Her eyes focused on the cleaver I still held in one hand, which was leaking blood—nonhuman black—all over the kitchen tiles. Dragon's blood was corrosive, which probably explained why half the blade was gone and the tiles looked like mice had been gnawing at them. I took what remained of the knife to the sink and rinsed it off, then put it back in the rack.

That seemed to reassure her, because she pulled something out from behind her legs and plopped it into a kitchen chair. It must have been behind her in the hall, because I hadn't seen it before. I slowly approached the table, regarding this new problem cautiously.

The small towheaded creature appeared to be human. He—at least, I assumed it was a he, judging by the natty blue tunic he had on—looked to be around a year old. But he nonetheless gazed calmly back, remarkably composed considering what he had just witnessed.

"What is that?" I asked, as he drooled a little onto his tunic.

Claire dry swallowed the aspirin. "The heir to the throne of Faerie."

"The heir to the throne of Faerie just spit up."

"He does that a lot. He's teething."

I blinked. "Teething? *Teething?* He's teething and you get *spit*?"

"Why? What did you expect?"

I waved my arms. "That!"

"That noise?"

"Yes! That horrible, screeching noise that goes on and on and—"

"That's a baby?"

"A baby Duergar. Well, half anyway," I amended. "The other half is Brownie, or so they said. I'm beginning to think it's more like banshee."

"You mean that little thing you picked up at the auction?" She located a box of Band-Aids and slapped one on her toe.

And okay, the apron thing could have been a fluke, but there weren't too many people who knew where I'd acquired my current affliction. The magical auction had been highly illegal and very hush-hush. That wasn't surprising, considering that they were selling illegal hybrids of supernatural creatures, some quite dangerous. I hadn't even known it was taking place until I accidently raided it.

As weird as it seemed, this actually was Claire.

"Yes," I told her, my head swimming with questions. I hadn't seen her in over a month. It seemed like she'd picked up a few new abilities while she'd been gone.

"But he already had teeth," she objected, frowning into the empty fridge.

"Those were his baby teeth. I've been finding them all over the house. Now the big-boy teeth are coming in and . . . Claire, I think I'm going crazy."

"You're not going crazy."

"I just saw you morph into a dragon!"

"Well, you shouldn't have startled me!" She opened the breadbox and stared at the mass of paper inside. "Don't you keep any food in the house?"

"I got takeout."

Her eyes latched onto the big white bags, which were spreading the smell of sesame chicken, veggie chow mein and fried rice around the kitchen. "It looks like you brought enough for three people," she said hopefully.

"Yeah. I don't know when we'll get to eat it, though. What with all the commotion."

Her eyes narrowed, and for a moment, she looked an awful lot like her alter ego. "Where's this baby of yours?"

I grinned.

Chapter Three

I led the way upstairs and Claire followed with her own quiet, well-behaved little bundle. The decibel level increased with every step, until I was sure the walls would crack with it. We opened the door to my old office and even Claire, who had seemed remarkably unmoved, winced.

Then she went in and the screeching abruptly stopped. A small, hairy head popped up from a nest of quilts under the bed and stared at her with wide gray eyes. Its owner looked like a cross between a monkey and a little old man: long, furry limbs, tiny squashed face and wild Muppet hair.

The unshed tears trembling on his lashes seemed to distill the moonlight filtering through the curtains, making his irises gleam like polished metal for a moment. Then he blinked and the tears coursed down his cheeks—and the noise started up again. Until Claire calmly walked over and picked him up.

He'd opened his mouth for another scream, but closed it again with a pop. A tiny hand with long, sticklike fingers grasped the frilly strap of her apron and he looked at her beseechingly, like I'd been beating him or something. "Why is he under the bed?" she demanded.

"He likes it under there," I said defensively. "Duergars live underground, and I think it makes him feel vulnerable, being in the open when he sleeps. I tried putting him on the bed, but he just drags everything down there anyway."

Claire didn't look like she thought much of that explanation, but she let it go. "What have you been giving him for the pain?"

"Everything. But he's like me—drugs don't work and whiskey only dulls it for a—"

"Whiskey?" Claire looked appalled. "Tell me you didn't just admit to trying to get your baby drunk!"

"I was just trying to rub some on his gums!" I said, offended. "He's the one who grabbed the bottle!"

"He's just a baby, poor little thing!"

"I know that," I said miserably. "And the alcohol didn't have much effect, anyway—"

"Dory!"

"I know what you're thinking! I suck at this motherhood thing!" It didn't help that I hadn't actually thought of Stinky as a "baby" when I took him on. Someone had been about to kill him, I'd objected and, the next thing I knew, he was mine.

I hadn't been too worried about it at the time, as he'd been more in the "pet" category in my mind. But experience had shown that there was a definite intelligence at work there—a fact I tried not to think about too much because it freaked me the hell out.

"You don't," Claire said patiently. "You saved his life. You've given him a home. You just need time to adjust, that's all."

"I don't think I'm going to last that long."

She smiled slightly. "Everybody thinks that way at first. They're these little people, with big, trusting eyes and an absolute confidence that we know everything, when most of the time, we don't have a clue."

Yeah, that was what worried me. I'd brought myself up, more or less, and look how that had turned out. I didn't want to screw him up, too, but there didn't seem to be an alternative.

There were damn few dhampirs in existence, since we could only be conceived in a very short window after a man was Changed. And despite what the movies would have people believe, most newly made vampires weren't thinking sex. They were thinking blood.

Mircea had been a little different, because he was cursed, not made. He'd failed to realize that the old Gypsy woman who'd been ranting at him had been the real deal for a week, until some nobles tried to kill him and he didn't die. In the meantime, he'd gone about his usual playboy ways, resulting in a bouncing baby abomination nine months later.

I could count on two hands the number of dhampirs I knew who were currently living, and I wouldn't even need all the fingers. But as far as I knew, there were no other Duergar-Brownie mixes at all. Stinky was in a class by himself, and I knew from personal experience where that left him.

It wasn't anywhere good.

Claire patted my shoulder. "Do you at least have a babysitter?"

I nodded to the small, huddled figure in the corner, who was trying to hide behind the rocking chair. "It's okay, Gessa. You can go."

Two tiny brown eyes peered at me myopically for a moment from under a fall of dark brown curls. Then their owner jumped to her full height of three foot two and scurried out the door. She never needed to be told twice.

"Olga was doing it," I said, referring to the very competent secretary I'd recently acquired. "But she's trying to start her business up again, and she can't stay all night. And the freeloaders downstairs scatter to the four winds every time I so much as look at—"

"What freeloaders?"

Oops. "Uh, well, when they heard she'd moved out here, some of Olga's old employees decided to come, too. And since they're also relatives, she didn't feel like she could say no. . . ."

"Are you trying to tell me that there's a colony of trolls living in my basement?"

"I probably should have worked up to it more."

"At least that explains the smell."

"That's Stinky," I admitted. "He believes in living up to his name."

"Well, maybe you should get him a better one!"

"I tried. There are no colonies of Brownies around here, but I located some Duergars who live over in Queens. But they just told me they thought he was already well named!"

"He's a half-breed," she said sadly, her fingers carding through his hair. "They probably didn't like him."

"They did tell me that their people have to earn their names. They just use a nickname before then."

"Earn them how?"

"They didn't say. But the elders have to award them, apparently, and you can guess what the odds are of that in his case. When he gets older, I'll let him decide what he wants to be called." I pushed up the window, letting in the night breeze. "And it's not so bad once you get—"

I broke off abruptly. For the second time that night, I saw something that had me questioning my sanity. More than usual, I mean.

The trees on the lot are mostly original, and the granddaddy of them all grew outside that window: a massive, old cottonwood that had to have been more than a sapling when the house was built. Its tear-shaped leaves were dancing as the wind swept along the side of the house, causing a rustling, shifting kaleidoscope of dark green, silver and deep black. And for a moment, in the contrast of light and shadow, I thought I saw ...

"Dory—" Claire touched my shoulder and I flinched. She frowned. "What is it?"

"Do you see ... anything ... in the tree?" I asked, trying to keep my voice light.

She peered around. "What? You mean the squirrel's nest?"

I swallowed. "I think I need a drink."

"Well, that's what I've been saying." She sighed. "Is there *no* alcohol in this house?"

"I may be able to come up with something."

"Wonderful. Let's sit on the porch, though. I could use some air."

Claire went to her old room to find some clothes, and

I went to the kitchen for a couple of glasses from the drying rack. I was just pulling up the trapdoor in the hall, where I keep the good stuff, when she clattered downstairs. She was wearing a green wraparound shirt that matched her eyes and old jeans, and she had a well-behaved baby on each hip.

"I don't know how long we'll be able to stay outside. It looks like a storm's blowing up," she told me, before catching my expression. "What?"

"You managed to get Stinky into clothes?" The fuzzy armful on her left hip was wearing a pair of bright blue running shorts, like it was no big deal. The last time I'd gotten him dressed, I'd practically had to have Olga sit on him.

"He did it himself."

I shot him the evil eye. Okay, now I knew he was trying to make me look bad.

I grabbed a couple of bottles from the small space, shut the door and carefully replaced the carpet runner. "I didn't know we had a smugglers' hole," Claire said, following me down the hall.

"There are hidden compartments all over the place. I think your uncle used them for storage."

Claire's late uncle Pip had been a bootlegger, and a highly successful one, at that. He'd purchased the place when the captain died and quickly realized he'd hit the jackpot. Two ley lines—the rivers of power generated when worlds collide on a metaphysical level—crossed directly underneath the foundation. The result was a rare commodity known as a ley-line sink, which generated enormous magical power.

It was the equivalent of free electricity for life. Only instead of lamps and refrigerators, he'd used it to power wards and portals, including a highly illegal portal to Faerie. It allowed him to bypass the heavily regulated—and heavily taxed—interworld trade system. And not any old trade either. He'd gone straight for the gold and started trafficking in the volatile substance known as fey wine.

The magical community's police force didn't catch on

because he didn't use any of the official portals. The fey didn't pay him much attention because he wasn't purchasing the wine directly, just the ingredients, and probably from many different sources. Once he had them in hand, he'd set up a still in the basement and started making magic.

"But why do you need it?" Claire asked. "There's plenty of cabinet space."

I glanced at her over my shoulder. "Have you ever seen trolls drink?"

She laughed, and suddenly she looked like Claire—the real one, not this pursed-lipped stranger. "They don't show up too often at court!"

"Well, if they ever do, hide the liquor." I bumped the back door open with a hip and stepped out into the sound of crickets and the smell of impending rain.

I paused to scan the yard, because I am not prone to hallucinations. But the only thing out of the ordinary was the weather. In the square of sky visible above the trees that bordered the right side and back of the yard, clouds hung low and ominous, seeming to glow from the inside. And above the neighbor's privacy fence on the left, near the horizon, a sheet of gray rain wavered in the wind like a billowing curtain.

"What is it?" Claire was peering into the darkness with me. Red curls whipped around her face, blowing across the lenses of the pair of glasses she'd dug up somewhere.

"You still need those things even though . . ." I made a gesture that encompassed the whole thing in the hall.

She shifted, looking slightly uncomfortable. "Yes. In this form, anyway. My other . . . Well, it actually sees better at night."

I usually did, too, but it wasn't helping right now. I leaned through the porch railing to look up into the branches of the massive cottonwood. Some of them overhung the porch, but all I saw were rustling leaves. I concentrated on the more sensitive peripheral vision, paying attention to any change in the light, any shifting forms. But the result was the same: nothing.

"What are you looking for?" Claire asked again, a little more forcefully.

"I'm not sure yet."

"We can go back inside if you think there's a problem."

"The wards protect the porch as well as the house. It's no safer inside."

"It's no safer anywhere," she said bitterly.

"Careful. You're starting to sound like me." I paused, listening, but my ears failed me, too. I could hear the wind snapping the tarp we'd put over a hole in the roof, the squeak of the weather vane and the creak of the porch swing's chains. But nothing else.

Claire hugged her arms around herself. "You scare me sometimes."

"This from the woman who just handed me my ass in there."

"I didn't mean I'm afraid *of* you," she said impatiently. "I'm afraid *for* you. You look like you're planning to take on an army all by yourself."

"Are you expecting one?"

"Not yet," she muttered.

"Well, that's something." I decided to let the wards do their job and concentrated on setting up the porch for civilized living.

It had been furnished more with comfort in mind than style. An old porch swing, with flaking white paint and rusty chains, sat on the left. A sagging love seat that Claire had brought with her from her old apartment, and which the house wouldn't permit past the front door, sat on the right. And a potting bench nestled up against the back of the house, next to the door.

I put the bottles and glasses on the bench and went back for the takeout. I returned to find Claire frowning at a small blue bottle and the boys hunched over a chess set my roommates had left out. They were sprawled on their stomachs near the stairs, happily watching the tiny pieces beat the crap out of one another.

The board was Olga's. The pieces were trolls on one side and ogres on the other, all equipped with miniature weapons—swords, axes and what appeared to be a small catapult half hidden behind some trees. The game was played on an elaborate board complete with forests, caves and waterfalls, and it bore, as far as I'd been able to tell, no relationship to human chess whatsoever. Olga maintained that I only said that because I always lost.

"I could make us some tea," Claire offered, as I put the bags on the makeshift bar. "I saw some in the cupboard."

"I don't like tea."

"But you do like this stuff?" She held up the rotund bottle containing her uncle's bootleg brew.

"I like some of the things it does for me," I told her, plucking it out of her fingers and pouring a generous measure into my glass.

"I thought you were supposed to be on some task force to keep that kind of thing off the streets," she said accusingly.

I smiled. "I assure you, I've been keeping off all I can."

"I don't think the idea was to stockpile it for your own use. It's illegal because it drives people crazy, Dory!"

"And it makes those of us who already are a little more sane."

She blinked. "What?"

I held up the glass. The crystal clear contents reflected the lights from the hall, shooting rays around the porch and making Stinky cover his eyes. "Here's to the best antidote for my fits I've ever found."

One of the fun facts of my life is frequent rage-induced blackouts. They can last from a few minutes to a few days, but the results are always the same: blood, destruction and, usually, a high body count. They are what passes for normal with my kind—the result of a human metabolism crossed with a vampire's killing instinct—and they are one of the main reasons why there are so few of us. And, because the problem is genetic, there is no cure.

Not that anyone has looked very hard. Like most human drug companies, the magical families who specialized in healing liked to make a profit. And there was little money to be made in devising something to help a scant handful of people.

Claire's eyes widened as she stared at my glass. "That really helps your attacks?"

"Stops them cold. And unlike human drugs, it works every time."

She picked up the bottle and took a cautious sniff. She made a face. "It's worse than I remembered."

"It's pretty strong," I said as her eyes started watering. In fact, it could double as paint thinner, which was probably why it was usually used as a mixer. But I wasn't drinking it for the taste.

"It isn't really wine," she told me, setting it down. "It's a distillation of dozens of herbs, berries and flowers, most of which have never been tested in any scientific way. And I don't like the idea of you as the guinea pig."

"I thought I volunteered." Claire was a scion of one of the oldest magical houses on Earth, one that specialized in the healing arts. She'd been working at the auction house only because of a dispute over her inheritance, which had left her on the run from a greedy cousin. Before then, research had been her specialty, and lately, she'd been experimenting on fey plants, hoping to find something that would help my condition.

"That's different! I know what went into everything I sent you. It was safe—"

"And ineffective."

She frowned. "Anything could be in there. I have no idea what ingredients Pip used. The recipes differ widely from family to family, which is why you get so many varieties of this stuff. And Pip never left any notes lying around."

"More's the pity."

"You don't get it, Dory. Drugs—and this can definitely be classified that way—often have a cumulative effect. Even the fey experience some mild side effects over time—"

I laughed. "Mild for them, maybe. I'm not a fey."

"That's my point! This is a controlled substance on Earth because it brings out latent magical abilities in humans. Before it addicts them and drives them insane!"

"I'm not human, either."

"You're half."

"Which is why I'm careful."

Claire's eyes narrowed; something must have come through in my tone. "What have you been experiencing?"

"As you said, some mild side effects."

"Like what?"

"Heightened memories, mostly. With sharper sensations, Dolby surround sound, the works."

"Like hallucinations?"

"Like heightened memories, Claire. It's no big deal."

She didn't look convinced. "And you can control them? You can snap out of these memories whenever you want?"

"Yes," I said easily. "Now, do you want to eat, or do you want to lecture me some more?"

The look on her face said this wasn't over. But her stomach growled, momentarily overruling her head. I flopped onto the love seat, passed around oyster pails, paper plates and chopsticks and we dug in.

"God, I missed this," she told me a few minutes later, her mouth full of chow mein.

"What?"

"Greasy human takeout."

"They don't have the equivalent in Faerie?"

"No. They also don't have TV, movies, iPods or jeans." Her hand ran over the threadbare denim covering her knee. "Damn, I missed jeans."

I laughed. "I thought you'd like being waited on hand and foot—"

"And having servants follow me everywhere, and having to dress up every damn day and having everybody defer to me but nobody *talk* to me?" She rolled her eyes. "Oh, yeah. It's been great."

"Heidar talks to you, doesn't he? And Caedmon?" Heidar was Claire's big blond fiancé. Caedmon was his father, the king of one branch of the Light Fey.

"Yes, but Heidar's gone half the time, patrolling the border, and Caedmon's holed up in high-level meetings deciding God knows what while I'm supposed to hang around and, I don't know, knit or something!"

"You don't knit."

"I've been so bored, I've been thinking of learning."

"Sounds like you need a vacation."

She chewed noodles and didn't say anything.

I tugged off my boots and chucked them by the door, enjoying the feel of the smooth old boards under my feet. They'd absorbed a lot of heat through the day, and were giving it off in steady warmth that contrasted nicely with the cooler air. A few moths fluttered around the old ship's lantern overhead, which was swinging slightly in the breeze.

"Are you going to tell me what's wrong?" I finally asked, when Claire had finished most of her whiskey and still hadn't said anything.

She'd been staring out at the night, but now she shifted those emerald eyes to me. "How do you know anything is? Maybe I decided to take that vacation."

"In the middle of the night?"

"You keep odd hours sometimes—"

"With no shoes, no luggage and no escort?"

She frowned and gave it up. "I don't want you involved in this. I only came this way because I didn't have a choice. The official portals are all guarded since the war."

"The ones we know about," I agreed.

"I mean on the fey side," she said, as if it were obvious that her own people would be trying to prevent her from leaving.

"Okay, back up. You came through the portal in the basement—"

"Because nobody knows about it. Uncle used it to bring in his bootlegging supplies, so he kept it quiet."

"And you needed to slip away unnoticed because . . . ?"

"I told you, I don't want—"

"I'm already involved," I pointed out. "You're here. You're obviously in some kind of trouble. I'm going to help whether you like it or not, so you may as well tell me."

"I don't want your help!"

"I don't care."

Claire glared at me. She had one of those faces that could really only be appreciated when she was animated. Ivory pale, with an aquiline nose humanized by a wash of freckles and a strong chin, it was pretty enough in repose. But with emerald eyes flashing, color high and that glorious mop of hair blowing around her face, she was beautiful.

She was also one of the few people I knew with more of a hair-trigger temper than me. It was always possible to get the truth out of her, if you made her mad enough. "I'm here to save the life of my son. All right?" she snapped.

Chapter Four

I focused on the little boy. He was the usual pink-cheeked, chubby-limbed baby as far as I could tell. He was currently poking at a couple of chess pieces, trying to get them to fight each other.

He had taken them out of the game and put them in the circle made by the round wicker bottom of the table. He was watching them avidly through the open side of his makeshift combat ring, waiting for some mayhem, but they weren't obliging. One had hunched down to clean his sword, and the other was having a smoke. Tiny rings wreathed its head for a moment, before the wind pulled them away.

"They're friends," I told him. He'd accidentally picked up two trolls instead of one of each.

Puzzled blue eyes looked up at me.

"They're allies," Claire said harshly, and a flash of comprehension crossed his features.

A chubby hand rooted around in the game and plucked out an ogre, its small tusks gleaming behind a metal faceplate. He put it into the ring and immediately both trolls fell on it. He frowned and pulled one of them off, making it an even contest.

"He doesn't know the word 'friend'?" I asked, a little appalled.

"In Faerie, you have allies and enemies," Claire said, getting up to get a refill. "Friends are a lot more rare."

Stinky had joined the little prince, and they had their heads together, one shining blond, one fuzzy brown with pieces of egg roll in it. I picked them out as Claire came back with what looked like a double. "He looks healthy enough to me," I commented. "What's wrong with him?"

"Nothing! And it's going to stay that way."

"Why wouldn't it?"

"Because he had the bad luck to be born a boy," she said bitterly.

"Come again?"

"The fey don't allow women to rule—at least, our branch doesn't—so a girl wouldn't have been a threat."

"A threat to who?"

"Take your pick! Everyone at court has had hundreds of years to make plans based on the idea of the king being childless. Then, a century ago, he had Heidar, but no one cared because he can't inherit."

I nodded. Heidar's mother had been human, and he'd inherited his heavier bone structure and more substantial musculature from her. It was the same blood that ensured he could never take the throne. The law said that the king had to be more than half fey, and Heidar was a flat fifty percent.

"But then I came along," Claire said, after taking a healthy swallow of her drink. "And I'm slightly more than half fey. So when Heidar and I announced that I was pregnant, everyone did the math and freaked out. Courtiers who'd hoped their daughters would snag the king realized that Caedmon had no more need to marry now that he had an heir through his son. The daughters in question, the male relatives who'd hoped to inherit if he died with no legitimate heir, the people who had spent a fortune sucking up to said relatives—they were all furious."

"But murder—"

"The 'accidents' started almost as soon as he was born," she said, quietly livid.

"What kind of accidents?"

"In the first month alone, he almost drowned in the bathwater, was set upon by a pack of hunting dogs and had the ceiling of his nursery collapse. And things only got worse from there."

"And Heidar didn't do anything?"

"The maid was fired, the dogs were put down and the ceiling was reinforced—none of which helped the fact that my son was surrounded by a bunch of killers."

I sipped my own drink for a minute, trying to think up a tactful way of putting this. It wasn't easy. Tact was Mircea's forte, not mine. "Is it at all possible that at least some of these things really were accidents?" I finally asked.

"I'm not crazy, and I'm not hallucinating!" she snapped, her spine stiffening with a jerk.

So much for my attempt at diplomacy. "I never said you were. You want to protect your child, and a mother's instincts are usually pretty good. But you were born here. Heidar was brought up there. If he doesn't think there's a problem—"

"Oh, he knows damned well there's a problem! Everybody does, after tonight."

"What happened tonight?"

"They tried again. And this time, they almost succeeded."

I sat up. "What happened?"

She took a breath, visibly steadying herself. "I was on my way to dinner, but at the last minute, I decided to check in on Aiden. He was fussy—he's teething, and he gets like that sometimes—and walking calms him down. So I took him for a quick stroll, and when I got back . . . God, Dory. The blood. It was in his *room*."

"Whose blood?"

"Lukka's," she whispered. "I found her lying across the threshold of the nursery. They'd cut her throat and the puddle . . . It had run down the tiles, into all the crevices. Almost the whole floor was wet with it."

"Lukka was his nurse?"

Claire nodded, her lips pale. "She was so young. I wasn't sure, when they first brought her to me, but she was really good with him. The fey love babies and she couldn't—" She swallowed. "She loved him," she said simply. "And he wasn't even there, and they killed her anyway."

"Who did?"

"I don't know!" She gestured tiredly. "It could have been anyone. There's no shortage of people who think they'd be better off if Aiden had never been born."

"But it must have been someone Lukka could have identified, or there would have been no need to kill her."

"That's what I realized, after. But then I just turned around and ran. I didn't stop until I got to Uncle's portal—"

"That's why you showed up with no shoes." That was one mystery solved, at least.

She nodded. "It's over a mile from the palace, in the middle of some pretty thick woods. I lost them on the way."

"Doesn't the palace have its own portal?"

"Yes, but I wasn't thinking clearly. I'd planned to come here anyway, and I guess it was stuck in my head, because I was halfway there before I even thought about it."

"You planned to come here?"

"Yesterday, when we found out about Naudiz." She said that like I should know what it meant.

"I hate to sound like twenty questions, but—"

Claire got up and started pacing back and forth along the porch. "It's this rune. It isn't even well carved, just a piece of stone with some crude scratches on it. Caedmon showed it to me once, told me it was part of a set that's mostly lost now. Nobody seems to know where it came from; everyone I asked just said 'the gods.'" She made a face. "But the fey always say that when they don't know."

"And it's important why?"

"Because it's been used for . . . well, pretty much ever, as far as I can tell, to guard the heir to the throne. He's supposed to get it in a ceremony on his first birthday, or as soon as he's able to withstand its magic. The legend says that whoever wears it can't be killed."

"But it's gone missing?"

She nodded. "Aiden's only nine months old, but he's a big boy. So I petitioned to have the ceremony moved up. There was some muttering about protocol, but considering the number of 'accidents,' I managed to get my way. And then, the very next night, the relic vanished, right out of the family vault."

"Who had access to this vault?"

"It was spelled. No one who wasn't a close blood relative could get in."

"And how many would that be?"

"Normally only two: Caedmon and Heidar. I couldn't even go unless one of them was with me."

"Normally?"

"Before Efridís came to court," Claire said savagely. "She's Caedmon's own sister, and yet—I should have known. She's Æsubrand's mother!"

I repressed a shudder. Æsubrand was a fey prince with a sadistic streak who had almost killed me the last time we met, playing what he'd considered a fun little game. I heal quickly—one of the few perks of my condition— yet I still bore the shape of a hand, faint and scar-slick, burned into the flesh of my stomach. His hand.

Of course, the fey hadn't given a damn about that, as human life, or what passed for it in their eyes, was hardly a valuable commodity. But they had cared very much when Æsubrand had tried to kill Caedmon. His father was king of a rival band of Light Fey, and I suppose he'd hoped to unify their two lands under one ruler someday. Or maybe Æsubrand was just tired of waiting for his old man to kick off and decided to go conquer himself a country. Either way, Caedmon hadn't been amused.

"Tell me they executed that little shit."

Claire shook her head. "The Domi—that's their council of elders—wanted to, but Caedmon vetoed it. Faerie is trembling on the brink of war as it is, and he was afraid that executing the Svarestri heir would tip it over into chaos."

"So what happened to him?"

"They put him in prison, if you think having about twenty servants and the run of a castle qualifies!"

"What the *hell*—"

"It's a hunting lodge, actually, but it's as big as a damn castle."

"Why isn't he in a cell somewhere?" I demanded. Preferably one with extra rats.

"Because the fey don't have prisons as we understand them. An offender is incarcerated for a short time pending trial, and then punished or executed. They really didn't know what to do with him."

"So they did nothing? He tried to kill you!" Æsubrand had hoped to eliminate his rival before he was even born by attacking Claire. He'd failed; we'd succeeded. So naturally he was the one sitting around in luxury, while I tried to come up with the money to get the roof fixed.

"They publicly flogged him, and as the wronged party, I had to watch. He stared at me the whole time, with this faint little smile on his face." She shivered.

"They flogged him," I said bitterly. "I'm sure that made a great—"

I cut off because the porch winked out, between one breath and the next, taking Claire, the yard and the softly creaking swing along with it. For a moment there was nothing but a boiling black void, like the color of storm clouds against a black sky. And then the scene was slashed with light, with color, with alien sounds and smells, and I was standing in the middle of an open field.

It was a glaringly bright day, the sun a hot coal directly overhead. Before I could get my bearings, rough hands shoved me up some crude wooden steps to the top of a platform. It was so newly built, I could smell the sawdust on the air, and see bits of it caught in the dry grass below.

In front of me were stands filled with people sitting under bright canopies. The air was still, the sun honey thick as it poured down, drenching us all in sticky heat.

Yet no one moved, not even to wave a fan. There was no murmuring, no jostling, no talking, none of the raucous behavior of every other crowd I'd ever seen.

But then, I'd never before seen a crowd composed entirely of fey.

He'd been left in the clothes in which he'd been captured for over two weeks, dirty, bloodstained and rank after all this time. They were finally peeled off him, leaving him naked before the crowd. Like a common criminal about to receive sentence.

His wrists were unclasped from behind him and secured to the top sections of an X-shaped rack. The muscles in his arms tightened and rippled as he jerked against them, uselessly. He felt the anger boiling up again, a fury no amount of shouting had been able to drain. That he should be here like this, while that thing *sat in the stands . . .*

His legs were pulled apart and secured to the bottom sections of the rack. The rough wood had not been planed properly, and splinters ate into his flesh. Gnats buzzed around his face, crawled over his skin, and he was powerless to knock them away. And on the boards before the rack, placed so that he could see it, the whip lay coiled like a leather snake, waiting to strike.

He ignored it and looked outward, slitting his eyes against the glare, searching the crowd. She wasn't hard to find. The pale skin of his exposed flesh was burning, but at least he wasn't sweating like the mongrel in the family box, perched next to that half-breed of a husband. The canopy over her head was not enough to keep her from staining her pale green gown. She shifted, looking anywhere but at him, her fingers curled tightly into her lap.

It was a testament to the High King's lust for power that he had brought such a thing into his court, polluting his line, sapping its strength. And now a full-blooded Light Fey prince was about to be whipped in front of a half-human, half–Dark Fey abomination. It was obscene.

Soldiers guarded the platform, barring any possibility of escape, watching. The armor on their shoulders and arms, the swords at their sides, the peaks of their helmets all glittered in the glaring sunlight. Pennants and flags of blue and gold hung limp in the breathless air, waiting like everyone else.

Drummers began a slow, measured beat that echoed around the silent grounds. From across the small hill separating the course from the castle, a parade appeared. The nobles of the court, lords and ladies clad in their glittering best, walked in lines behind the tall figure with the silver-blond hair and the golden circlet of office.

The king paused in front of the stands, speaking to the crowd. A pointless exercise. They all knew why they were here. But the voice droned on and on, like the sound of the insects buzzing around his ears. He ignored it in favor of staring up at the rotting pieces of flesh that adorned the corners of the stands, all that remained of the few this court boasted with the strength and will to act.

Vítus had been captured along with him, but he was not a prince. No war hung on the outcome of his fate, and there was no one to speak for him. His family had gone running like the rats they were, bowing and scraping and pleading with the king to save their own skins, to protect their lands and titles. They had left Vítus to the king's mercy.

He had been there to witness that mercy, while his own fate still hung in the balance. Had been forced to watch as the king unsheathed a plain battle sword, its water-marked blade gleaming mirror-sharp. It had caught the light, sending a spike of painful radiance into his eyes. But he'd refused to close them, refused to look away even for an instant, lest it be taken for weakness.

And so he'd seen the sword descend, the neck sever in two, a pulsing arc of pure fey blood shimmering in mid-air like a spill of rubies. It had all been limned in a flare of red, a slash across his vision, burning the image into his memory. It reminded him of the gleam thrown off by the setting sun just before it slips below the horizon. The difference between day and night, between what was, and what will be.

The crowd gasped at the first execution some of them had ever witnessed. But they quieted again as the king stepped past Vítus's body and stopped before Ölvir. He had been manacled kneeling, as the damage to his legs from the battle was too severe to allow him to stand. His hands were bound before him in cold black iron attached to heavy chains. The metal leeched his strength, and if left in place long enough, it would burn the skin.

It wouldn't have time to mar his.

He'd straightened as the king's shadow fell over him, first his back, then his neck, looking up proudly, tangled black hair falling over his shoulders and sticking to his cheeks. The damage to his face was ugly, and still only half-healed. Only one eye opened enough to see out of but he had stared up at the king without flinching.

He had not begged for his life or for mercy.

He had been offered neither.

The High King finally finished his platitudes and the nobles took their places, in a ring of special seats set close around the stands. They'd been there when the executions took place, too, ensuring that they went home with their finery splattered with the blood of traitors. It had been a clear message, as if any of the puling cowards had needed it.

The king stripped off his outer shirt, folded it and set it neatly on the thick gold grass next to the platform. His circlet of office went on top, and he smoothed his hair back over his skull, knotting the tail in a neat, quick movement that kept it off his face. Finally, he walked up the steps to the platform, stopping in front of the rack.

He bent and picked up the whip by the handle, leaving it to uncoil as he straightened, the braided leather slithering over the wood with a dry, scaly sound. He said nothing further as he paced to the required distance, as he drew back, as the whip snapped through the air with a crack. *It would be the first of many.*

Blood was soon dripping down the prisoner's back and legs, oozing from his tightly bound wrists, adding a new pattern to the reddish brown stains beneath him. The Domi had lobbied hard, or so he'd heard, for the maxi-

mum sentence: *five hundred lashes, likely deadly even for a fey. But the king had bargained it down to two, still trying to prevent a war.*

Fool. It was obvious to everyone but him. They were already in one.

Chapter Five

Someone slapped me. I flinched, and the brightly lit scene shattered and fell away, leaving me staring blankly at a cobweb on the underside of the porch's ceiling. I was sprawled on the couch with Claire standing over me, a hand gripped around my wrist, her face pale and frightened. Her other hand was raised, but I caught it in time. My cheek already stung enough.

"I'm all right."

"All right?" she demanded shrilly. "Your face went slack. You wouldn't talk. You were barely breathing! For over a minute, Dory!"

"I saw something—"

"I'm sure you did! You're lucky it wasn't the last thing!" She held up her uncle's little bottle. "How much of this did you have?"

"Not that much." I sat up, feeling too warm and vaguely nauseous. I could still smell the blood, hot on the air, hear the eerie silence of the crowd, feel the sharp bite of stripes I'd never taken. But that wasn't what had me struggling to my feet.

"Sit down!" she snapped, trying to press me back. "I'm going to get you some water, and you're going to drink all of it!"

"I saw Æsubrand being punished," I told her, pushing past to the railing.

"That stuff will make you see anything, if you drink enough of—"

"You were wearing green. An apple green dress. It

was hot and you were sweating. You looked like you wanted to be anywhere else."

She stared at me, her flame red hair glowing in the light from the hall. "How did you—"

"I see memories, Claire."

"But you weren't there! Dory, are you telling me you can see *other people's* memories? That you can see mine?"

"It wasn't yours I saw," I told her, scanning the yard. I concentrated on the distant rain, the metallic smell of it, its elusive, seductive whisper—and at the presence hovering just behind it.

Claire frowned. "Whose, then? Because Aiden wasn't—"

"Æsubrand?" It leapt out of me on a breath, curled at the end into a question.

Claire clutched my arm. "Dory! He's in prison in Faerie! He isn't here!"

"I didn't see the beating from your perspective," I told her harshly. "I saw it from *his*. And I only do that when someone is close."

"How close?"

"Very."

It was hard to tell what might be out in the garden, or in the darkness just beyond. The storm was almost here, and the breeze was increasing. I watched it run a circuit of the yard, high in the trees, slipping under the green leaves and turning them over so that their lighter undersides caught the moonlight. More leaves turned as the wind raced along the fence, until the yard became a silver flag unfurling with a rustle against the dark green storm clouds.

But if there was a person in all that, I couldn't see him.

Claire was shaking her head. "Nobody will be here for a couple of days at the earliest, I promise you. Even if he'd somehow escaped, he couldn't be here."

"The fey timeline differs so much from ours that there's no way to know how much time has passed there since you left. They could have had weeks to look for you."

"No, they couldn't."

"Claire! I saw you a month ago and you weren't even showing! And now you have a one-year-old—"

"Nine months."

"Whatever. The point is—"

"That time is running faster here right now, giving me a head start."

I turned from staring at the garden to look at her. "Come again?"

"The fey have the timeline variations charted out. It's one of their major advantages over us. They always know exactly when they're going to arrive in our world, and we never do in theirs."

"How the hell can you chart something like time?"

She pushed up her glasses, the old signal for nervousness. Or maybe it was just the heat. The air was thick with rain, muggy and hot like an encompassing blanket. Smothering. Like the day Æsubrand took two hundred lashes, and learned nothing but how to hate.

Like he'd needed the lesson.

"Caedmon has this room in the palace where they keep up with it," she told me, sitting back down. "There's this big thing on the wall. It looks sort of like a map with two rivers. One is our world's timeline; the other is theirs. And they each have their own riverbed, you know? Sometimes they go pretty parallel, while in others, one will bow out in a big loop, taking a lot more time to get back anywhere near the other."

"So sometimes time runs faster here, and sometimes it runs faster there?"

"Yes. I checked yesterday, and it will be a while before anyone can come after me."

"How long?"

"It depends on how long they look for me in Faerie before thinking that maybe I slipped through. The current bend in the river—if you want to call it that—isn't huge. So yes, a few more days. Maybe a week if I'm lucky."

I stared at the yard, unconvinced. "Then why do I feel like I'm being watched?"

"Probably because you are," she said sourly. "The fey have spies all over the place, and not all of them are human."

"Meaning what?"

"They can use elements of our world to spy on us. The Blarestri are descendants of the fertility gods, the Vanir—or so they claim. It allows them to connect with plants, animals, that sort of thing."

"What about the Svarestri?"

"They're descended from the other, rival group of gods—the Æsir, who influence things like the weather." She wrinkled her forehead. "I'm not sure what they can do. They weren't a popular topic at court."

"I can understand why!"

She shook her head. "It goes back a lot farther than Æsubrand's ambition. There was some war, a long time ago, between the two groups of gods. The Æsir won, and their followers ruled Faerie for ages. Then one day, they suddenly disappeared, with no warning, no explanation. It left everyone to sort things out for themselves. So, of course, there was another war."

"And the Svarestri lost."

"Not . . . exactly, no. Nobody really won that time. They were too evenly matched, and it just ended up being a slaughter. I don't know much about it because none of the older fey who were there want to talk about it. Anyway, after a while, the Svarestri settled in the lands they'd been able to hold, and the Blarestri did the same in theirs. And they've just gone on hating one another ever since."

"But Caedmon let his sister marry one of them?"

She rolled her eyes. "Not just *anyone*, the king. And I don't know about 'let.' Efridís was determined she wasn't going to marry beneath herself, and because she was princess, everyone at her own court *would* have been beneath her. Caedmon went along with it, thinking the marriage might improve relations between the two camps, foster goodwill and that sort of thing."

"But it hasn't."

"Nothing is going to do that! All the Svarestri care

about is getting back into power. It's like they're obsessed with it. I think they made the marriage because they thought if Caedmon died childless, their prince would rule everything. Only now Aiden is in the picture."

"And the Svarestri are scrambling."

"They don't have to—they have Efridís!" Claire got up again, like she just couldn't keep still. She'd always been the peaceful one between the two of us, but now her nervous energy skittered around the porch, like the distant lightning. "I don't know how that woman can be Caedmon's sister. She belongs with the damned Svarestri— she's as ice-cold as they are. And I tell you, Dory, if she comes after my son, I'll kill her myself. I swear I will!"

"Why do you think she's—"

"Because she stole the rune! She wants her evil son to inherit, and for him to do that, Aiden has to die. That's why she really came to court. She told everyone it was to visit Æsubrand, but that was just an excuse. She wanted Naudiz, and she knew no one else could get to it."

"How did she get out with it?" I demanded. "If only three people had access, it shouldn't have been much of a mystery."

"There was no damn mystery at all! The caretaker of the vault was suspicious when she just dropped by, unannounced and with no escort, but he could hardly refuse her entrance. But he checked everything as soon as she left, and Naudiz was missing."

"So everyone knew she'd taken it?"

"Yes, but not what she'd done with it."

"They didn't search her?"

Claire laughed angrily. "Oh, they did. And you should have heard the uproar over *that*! But Caedmon insisted, and of course they didn't find anything. Or in her belongings, either. Then she left in a huff, saying she wouldn't stay where she was insulted. And a few hours after she'd gone, after she was already to the damn border, they found out how she'd done it. She'd handed it off to a traitor in Caedmon's guards, probably one of the bastards who tried to kill him—they never found out who all of them were—and he took off with it."

"And met her later to pass it back. Clever."

"That's just it," Claire said, leaning back against the porch railing. Red curls blew about her face, bright with reflected light from the house. Framed against angry green-black clouds, she looked a little otherworldly suddenly. "He didn't."

"Didn't what?"

"Meet up with her. He also didn't take it to Æsubrand, if that was the plan. Caedmon thinks it might have been. A person who can't be killed can escape from anywhere, even the best-guarded prison."

I suddenly felt like buying this guard a beer. "Where did he go, then?"

"The guards at the nearest portal recorded him going through an hour or so before the stone was discovered missing. He didn't have authorization, but he knew a couple of them, and anyway, he was a fellow guard. They let him through."

"A portal to where?"

"To here. To New York," Claire told me urgently. "Caedmon thinks he's going to try to sell the rune, that he double-crossed Efridís. The thing's worth a fortune, and I guess it was just too much temptation."

"That was a lucky break." An invincible Æsubrand was not something I wanted to contemplate. He was already too close to that for comfort.

"Yes, but it still leaves Aiden unprotected! Naudiz is here somewhere, and I have to find it before the damn Svarestri do. It's the only way to ensure that—"

She stopped, because the temperature plummeted about fifty degrees in an instant, like we'd suddenly stepped into a deep freeze. I looked down to see a pattern of ice creeping over the threshold, curling across the wooden planks of the floor. The day's absorbed heat had kept them soft and warm against my feet, but suddenly they were hard and cold and slippery with frost.

A glance out at the yard showed a swirl of small flakes spiraling out of the black sky, gilded by the glow from the house. I got up and walked down the steps, catching one on my palm. It melted immediately in the heat from my body, leaving a small wet spot behind. I smelled it, just to be sure. Water, ice.

It was dog days in Brooklyn, and it was snowing.

A few small flakes landed on my lips, feather soft. More drifted in the open side of the porch, collecting in Claire's hair and shining, golden bright, on her lashes. "What is it?" she asked, frowning.

"Get in the house," I told her, my heart rate speeding up.

"You said it didn't matter—that the wards protect the porch as well," she said, even as she gathered up the kids.

"The wards were designed to stop magic," I reminded her, a chill spreading through me that had nothing to do with the temperature. "Not the damn weather."

Like an exclamation point to my sentence, a fist-sized hailstone slammed through the porch roof, punching through the tin like a baseball through paper. It hit the old steps right in front of me, splintering into a thousand shards that flew everywhere. Pieces as long as my finger embedded in the railing, the side of the house and my flesh.

"Dory!"

My leg buckled, a sliver the size of a penknife sticking out of my knee, blood welling up darkly around it. "Go!"

I didn't see if she obeyed, because a wash of hail-laden wind gusted across the porch the next second. It shattered every window behind us, forcing me to dive for the floor. That was just as well, since at least it gave me something to hold on to when the porch whited out the next instant, caught in the grip of a blizzard in the middle of summer.

I felt around blind for maybe a minute, until my hand grabbed something cold and hard. It took me a second to identify it as the chain to the porch swing, because it had already frozen solid. I used it to pull myself into a crouch, turned around and headed for the approximate location of the door—only to have the wind pick me up and throw me through it.

The door opened out, not in, but the force of the gale was enough to punch a Dory-shaped hole through screen, wood and glass, bringing the storm in with it. I slammed into the wall, then skidded on a wash of snow and ice half the length of the hall. I only stopped myself from sailing out the front by grabbing the banister for the stairs.

The icy wind blowing through the back door almost ripped my hands off it, but I held on and struggled to my feet, staring around desperately for any sign of Claire or the kids. Screaming for them was an exercise in futility, but I did it anyway. And couldn't even hear myself over the screech of the wind and the sound of the house coming down around my ears.

But I heard the earsplitting crash when a hailstone the size of a wrecking ball smashed through the ceiling. It tore through three stories to hit the stairs right beside me, obliterating the bottom steps and the floor beneath them. After it came a swirling mass of snow, filtering down to pile in drifts in the hall, supporting the rectangular mass slowly working its way through the back door.

And not only was it an unnatural storm—it wasn't a natural cold, either. The air smelled strange, like the updraft from the bottom of a deep ravine, dark and sunless. I could *feel* the air growing colder around me, the fog of my breath thickening like smoke, my muscles tightening, becoming unresponsive. And I'd been in here all of a minute.

I slipped and slid across the hall to the kitchen. It was a cold, empty blue box, with frost creeping along the counters and ice covering the windows. The kitchen door had held, but the panes of glass had shattered under the pressure, allowing four square snakes of snow to worm their way inside.

I grabbed a flashlight out of a drawer and stumbled back into the hall, heading up. I needed to find Claire and the kids, but I also needed weapons. I couldn't fight the weather, so we were going to have to run for it. And I didn't doubt what we'd find waiting outside.

There was only one group I knew of who could control the weather like this, who could bend it to their will and use it as a weapon. I should have known when I glimpsed the face outside, but it hadn't been human, hadn't even been flesh—just a collection of leaves shaped in a strangely recognizable way by the wind. Or, I realized now, by fey magic.

The flashlight was all but useless. I could barely see through the white curtain that fell like rain all around, hissing through the air with deadly intent. And even if I had been able to see, the stairs were almost impassable.

Pipes had burst in the wall, unable to handle the abrupt change in temperature, and sprayed cobwebs of water across the stairs. They had flash frozen, creating an obstacle course of deadly sharp spikes and fans of ice. I stared at them, half disbelieving. It was as if the effects of a five-day-long blizzard had been distilled into a few minutes. I had no idea how to fight something like this. I'd never even heard of something like this. But one thing was certain.

We were all going to freeze to death if we didn't get out.

I made it through the maze courtesy of the hailstorm, which shattered several of the bigger clumps of ice right in front of me. I pulled more shards out of my legs, cursing the damn skirt, and hauled myself through the gap. And into what felt like a war zone.

The three stories of the house were fast becoming one as hailstones punched hole after hole in the floors and ceilings. I dodged down the second-floor hallway, throwing open the doors that hadn't already burst off their hinges because of the wind. It snatched up papers and clothes and threw them about, and set the overhead light fixtures swaying. All the movement made it hard to tell, but I didn't think Claire was in any of the rooms.

There was no one on the second floor, so I headed for the third, but the stairs were almost gone. I grabbed an old clothespress that had fallen on its side and dragged it over. Tilting it against the wall, I climbed up the inner shelves like a ladder. It was getting hard to breathe, and my numb fingers and feet felt like they were encased in mittens. But I made it, hauling myself over the side of the stairwell and into a frozen wasteland.

The third floor of the house was in pieces. At least I don't have to worry about the roof anymore, I thought dully, staring up at several holes the size of cars showing black sky and swirling snow. Everything was ice—from the floor to what was left of the ceiling to the walls. Icicles dripped from the old light fixture overhead like crystals, beards of ice hung off the stair banister, and frost as deep as my hand coated everything. It was one unbroken white expanse that glittered in the beam of the flashlight.

The storm cut out as I stood there, abrupt enough to leave my ears ringing. One last gust tore through the house with a rattling sigh, and then nothing. No more hailstones, no more crashing china or tinkling glass, no more wind. Everything was totally, eerily silent.

For some reason, that did not make me feel better.

"Claire?" My voice was barely a croak, and there was no response.

The brittle ice crunched underfoot as I pushed on, needing to be sure. I headed for the bathroom because it was nearest. The tub was full, as if someone had been about to take a bath. A toy airplane was trapped half in, half out of the ice that had formed over the surface. I pushed on into my room, but it was the same story: bed and dresser frozen lumps, buried under knee-deep snow.

Something hit me and I looked up, my breath ghosting in the air, and saw dark sky. There was a huge hole in the ceiling, spanning maybe a fourth of the room. That explained the mass of white. But it wasn't snow that was running down my neck.

The unnatural snowstorm was over, but the rain must have been the real deal, because it had resumed as if nothing had ever happened. The white blanket coating my room was already starting to turn into slush. Raindrops pitted the piled drifts and pattered against my cold, stiff hair as I forged my way across to the closet.

I shoved my feet into a pair of boots, the closet door having kept most of the snow out, and grabbed as many weapons as I could strap on. The problem was that most of mine were designed to fight the residents of this world in their various forms; the fey were still largely an unknown quantity. But I had what I had.

Getting downstairs was a lot easier than going up, with multiple holes to choose from. I dropped through one to the second floor, hitting the slick surface with soles that could grip it for a change. I'd barely gotten back to my feet when there was movement to one side—a brief pale flicker—and I whirled, gun up. It was Gessa.

She put a finger to her lips and beckoned. I moved forward as quietly as possible to join her. She was standing over a large area of missing flooring, looking down. We were partway down the hall, facing the main entrance to the house from the front. It was almost never used; the door stuck and the house kept a mountain of furniture in the vestibule, which it seemed to like just where it was. We'd all given up the fight long ago and used either the kitchen or back entrance.

But someone was headed in the front door.

Or make that some*thing*.

Chapter Six

The large windows in front of the house showed a yard blurred and streaked by sheeting rain. But I'd been wrong about it being natural. I watched with perfect shock emptying my mind as the droplets just outside the overhang of the roof began to bend, to congeal, to protrude to form the image of a man's head.

The outline was sharp, etched precisely against the dark street. It was crystalline clear except for the drops leeching off the roof, which were stained with tar. They eased down the phantom face, giving it the appearance of the weathering on an old statue. They didn't do anything to make it less impressive.

Or less terrifying.

Water dripping down the face and neck thickened, slowly forming a set of powerful shoulders, muscled arms and a strong torso. The figure itself was quicksilvered with moonlight, but I could still see the yard beyond it—the pale outline of the driveway, the dark brushstrokes of the trees, the glimmer of falling rain. Behind it, the thunderheads were mounting, higher and darker, the lightning that played inside them making them more beautiful and more ominous.

I cursed softly. I hate unfamiliar magic. The known kind is bad enough, with mages inventing new ways to kill me all the time. But at least I have a halfway-decent chance of using my own store of magical mayhem to counter it. Any I've never seen before always makes my head hurt.

"What the hell is that?" I whispered.

"Manlíkan." Gessa clutched a small battle-ax, like a child's toy, in both hands. "Light Fey make."

"But what *is* it?"

Her small face scrunched up as she fought to find the words. She was a relatively new arrival, and her English was a work in progress. But since my troll vocabulary stood at roughly twelve words, half of them curses, it was going to have to do.

"Svarestri control elements. Use power." She stuck the ax under her arm and made a weird sort of motion with her hands. "Make warrior."

"Make warrior out of what?"

"Power. Elements." She did the same sort of wrapping motion, and I swallowed, hoping I was misunderstanding her. But I didn't think so.

The cascade had dripped lower, solidifying into a firm backside, muscular legs and feet that left watery prints on the hall floor as it came inside. The figure had glided through the wards as if they didn't exist. They were obviously reading it as water, and therefore considered it harmless.

"They wrap their power around an element and form a doppelgänger out of it?" I whispered.

Gessa just looked at me.

"A double? They make a double?"

She nodded. "Make warrior."

Wonderful.

Cold, halogen white headlights crept across the floor from some neighbor arriving home later than usual. The pattern of leaded glass in the front door stretched to engulf the creature, highlighting the almost transparent body. It was amazingly detailed, the lights picking out the muscles in the thing's chest, the crease at his elbow, the dip of his naval—and the pale face, utterly cold and ominously silent as it gazed around.

The light on the floor narrowed to a wedge and slid up the wall as the car passed down the street, leaving the hall in shadows and me with a problem. I'd never seen anything remotely like that thing. Worse, I didn't know how to kill it.

I decided some experimentation was in order, pulled a gun and pumped half a dozen rounds into the thing. The sound was deafening in the silent house, and the smell acrid. But that was the only way I knew I'd fired. The bullets tore through the insubstantial body like rocks through a pond, exiting the other side to embed themselves in the wall of the foyer. The creature looked up, those eerie colorless eyes tracking across the ceiling until they met mine.

So much for that idea.

"How do we kill it?" I whispered, staring into nothingness that somehow stared back, a gleam of something feral below the ice.

Gessa shrugged. "Not alive."

I'd already figured that out. It didn't smell like a person or even an animal; more like wet stone—faintly organic with the acidity of waterlogged leaves. But the hand that had turned the doorknob had been lively enough. "How do we stop it, then?"

"Cold iron," she said, holding up her tiny weapon.

Okay, snap out of it, Dory, I thought harshly. I should have thought of that. The fey had a serious aversion to iron in all forms. Unfortunately, my knives were blackened steel and my bullets were lead and silver. And I'd just seen how much good they did.

I glanced around, hoping for inspiration. The edge of the fireplace in Claire's old room was just visible through the open door. And sure enough, there was a cast-iron poker half buried under melting snow. I grabbed it and came back out, in time to see things go from bad to catastrophic.

Claire had come out of the door leading to the living room. She'd lost her glasses somewhere, and in the low light, she didn't see the transparent form of the Manlíkan standing beside the wall. The faded stripes of the wallpaper were only slightly distorted by its watery body as it slowly raised a hand.

And then Gessa jumped, screeching, right through the hole, her little ax raised. It hit the creature at the top of the head and sliced straight downward, the "body" disintegrating behind it in a wave. Claire whirled, one hand forming a huge paw that, fortunately, slashed through the air above Gessa's diminutive height.

I jumped down beside her, and barely avoided getting sideswiped myself. "Claire! It's me!"

She grabbed me—with the hand still covered in scales like battle armor. It felt like it could rip through my bones with a flick of the wrist, causing me to go very still. Until those talons clasped onto my arm and she shook me. "Tell me you have them!"

"Have who?" I asked, my stomach falling.

"The children!" she said frantically. "I lost them in the storm, and they aren't in the living room or the library or the basement—" She stopped, looking at something out the window. A single glance showed me what I'd expected—a dozen or more fey standing in the front yard, pale smudges against the night.

I'd assumed they'd have to be close to work a spell like that, but standing right out there in the open was unexpected. And not good. It spoke of an utter confidence that I really didn't like.

Claire started for them, her face livid, but I jerked her back. "They don't have them, Claire! They wouldn't still be attacking if they did!"

"They can't attack!" she snarled. "The storm didn't bring the wards down, and they can't get in. And they don't have the power, even combined, to pull that stunt twice. But if the storm chased the kids out of the house—"

She flinched and looked down at the puddle on the floor left from the Manlíkan's demise. A crystal clear hand had formed out of the rainwater and latched onto her ankle. "What is *that*?" she screeched, shaking her foot.

I drove the fire iron through the wrist, and it collapsed. For the moment. "Gessa called it a Manlíkan; I don't know—"

The puddle suddenly erupted, flowing upward this time, like a waterfall in reverse. The thing was only half formed, but one of its powerful legs reached out and kicked me hard enough to send me flying back into what remained of the stairs. A splintered railing stabbed my thigh, a bright, sharp pain that was worse when I tore it out.

It was bad—I needed to bind it up—but there was no time. Two more of the things came through the door, one making straight for me. I slashed at it with the poker, but it dodged and I barely managed to take off an arm. And when it righted itself, what grew back in place of the missing appendage was a long, icy shard as sharp as a spear that it used to stab at me.

I dodged as Gessa hacked at the first creature's legs, cutting them off whenever they tried to re-form. Claire slammed and locked the front door, before disappearing into the kitchen. She was back a moment later, a cast-iron skillet in one hand and a large lid from a stew pot in the other. She sent the latter Frisbee-style at another creature, which had just slid in under the door. It sliced cleanly through the middle of him, causing a wave to splash against the wall as he disintegrated.

The icy spear trying to skewer me slammed into the wall, punching all the way through to the living room before pulling back out and shattering on the step where I'd just been standing. It re-formed almost at once, the snow piled around providing plenty of new material, and it was wickedly fast. I parried several dozen blows, a glittering savagery that drove me slowly back up the potholed staircase. I'm better than good with a blade weapon or a reasonable facsimile, but I could barely even see the thing.

That wasn't helped by the light situation—or the lack of it. The dim glow from moonlight sifting down through the wreckage, the pale wash from the street-light out front and a golden beam from some lantern left burning in the living room weren't enough. The transparent quality of everything but the frozen arm combined with the low light to make it almost impossible to track when in motion. And it was rarely in anything else.

I hacked and slashed at it, dodging quicksilver strikes,

and managed to connect here and there—more by luck than anything else. But every time one of my blows sheared off a piece, it grew right back. And coming into direct contact, I soon found, was not a good idea.

The foot I planted in that strange chest, trying to shove the creature back down the stairs, just kept on going. My leg plunged into the icy interior up to the knee, causing a slight splash of droplets out the other side. And then the body solidified around it, trapping me and slinging me into the wall.

I hit with a bone-shattering thump that almost jarred the poker from my hand. I somehow kept a grip and slashed out with it, and I must have gotten lucky and hit the head this time, because when I managed to focus my eyes again, there was nothing there but a cascade down the steps, making rivulets through the muddy sludge. Gessa, however, wasn't so lucky.

She was directly beneath me, battling a creature three times her size, which had latched onto her fist. It flowed up and around her like a watery shroud, completely enveloping her small body. Within seconds, it had covered her face, leaving me staring at her through rippling bands of water.

She fell to her knees, obviously unable to breathe, her ax protruding from the mass but only the wooden handle touching the creature. I started back down the stairs, but the puddle in front of me began to coagulate, drops running together as if magnetized. It was half formed before I could blink, so I threw the poker, aiming for the head of the thing that had trapped Gessa.

I saw it hit, saw the creature collapse around her, saw her gasp in a desperate breath, and then I was scrambling up the stairs, my own problem right on my heels.

My foot hit a stair on the edge of a hole. It had been covered over by a thin layer of ice, which crunched and then gave way under my weight. My foot fell through, dragging my body along with it. And, thanks to the destruction wreaked by the storm, I just kept on falling.

I crashed through what remained of the floor below the stairs and on into the basement. I landed on one of the smelly piles of rags my roommates preferred to a bed, stumbled and fell against the wall—just in time to see a stream of water trickle down the puke green paint and re-form into an arm. It caught me around the throat in a solid choke hold.

I grabbed for it, trying to keep it from crushing my neck, and the substance under my hands felt nothing like flesh. The closest I could come was the slippery, staticky feel of the surface of a ward. And that was exactly what it was, I realized, as its grip constricted like a band.

The fey were using their power to construct a ward around an element, in this case water. It gave them the body they needed to attack and ensured that their power was too disguised for our wards to read it. Normally, that would have been very bad news, as wards—particularly fey ones—are damn hard to break. Unless, of course, there happens to be a powerful projective null on the premises.

Claire's job at the auction house had been quieting the often-volatile objects up for sale, ensuring that they didn't explode and take out half the prospective purchasers. It had been an easy gig for her as she was a null witch—someone born with the ability to absorb magical energy and disperse it harmlessly. With a little effort, she could bring down any ward ever made.

But not if she didn't know about them.

A wash of light-headedness assaulted me, the room spinning dangerously. I had to get out of this, had to get upstairs to tell her. But my vision was already going dark, and beating at the glasslike arm was doing no good at all.

I let go of it with one hand to fumble around on my belt, a flicker of panic sizzling through me as my throat constricted further. Knives, guns, potions—all useless against a thing like this. I had enough weapons to kill a platoon, and not a single damn thing to so much as hurt a Manlíkan—which was fair, as I'd never even heard of the things before tonight.

And I was running out of time. Multicolored spots were swimming in front of the darkness, and none of my struggles moved that damn arm one iota. I needed iron or I was dead—something, anything—and then I spied a linen-wrapped handle sticking out from under the rag pile.

I couldn't tell what it was attached to, but I pulled at it with my foot anyway. A huge medieval-looking mace slipped out onto the floor, a couple of its spikes caught on a grimy pair of socks. I slid a toe under the small space between the handle and the heavy iron ball and gave a jerk, catching it just before it turned my face into hamburger.

My strength was almost gone and my angle was lousy and I was as likely to hit myself as anything else. And I didn't care. All I could think about was air, and dragging in even a single breath. I slammed the club against the heavy arm trapping me, again and again, feeling a sharp spike of pain from a glancing blow. But then came the sound of cracking ice, and I was abruptly released, falling to my damaged knees with a thud.

Dizzy and gasping, I tried to clamber to my feet, but my useless flailing nearly cracked my head open on the edge of a nearby trunk. So I settled for crawling instead, moving away from the wall and the puddle beneath it as fast as possible over the frost-slick concrete floor. I'd made it about halfway up the stairs when something grabbed me.

My body was jerked back down so fast I didn't even hit any steps on the way. I kicked out, even as it dragged me to my feet—and slammed me back into the wall hard enough to daze me. And then again, this time with the pressure concentrated on my right wrist. I felt the stabbing pain and heard the snap as my wrist broke, and then the mace clattered away over the floor.

Both hands were pinned over my head as the creature slowly drew closer, in a flowing, serpentine movement unlike anything flesh could mimic. Pale, colorless eyes looked directly into my own. They reflected the lightning outside the cellar's high, narrow windows, flashing silver bright for an instant. But that wasn't what had my skin crawling up my body.

The face had been fairly amorphous, just vague indentations for eyes, a lump for a nose, a slash for a mouth. But the features slowly coalescing in front of me were more distinct. And more familiar.

"You're supposed to be in prison," I said, staring at a coldly beautiful face I'd hoped never to see again.

"And you are supposed to be dead." The "mouth" of Æsubrand's doppelgänger hadn't moved, but the words shimmered in the air around me. A projection of his power, much like the body. "It seems that neither of us is very good at following others' plans."

"How did you get out?"

There was no answer. Instead, both of my hands were transferred to one of his, grinding the bones of my wrist together, making me bite my lip to hold back a scream. The move seemed to make no difference in the power holding me in place. I struggled, but I doubt he even noticed; my limbs were suddenly as wooden and unresponsive as a mannequin's.

A translucent hand, watery bright, pushed up my tank top. The move bared my chest and the thin ridge of too-sensitive skin that ran from breastbone to belly button. His mark, which had never entirely faded.

A single finger traced the impression, leaving a chill, watery outline behind. It highlighted the difference between the slightly slicker, redder tones of the old burn and my unmarked skin. "Do you know what this is, dhampir? Have any of your Dark Fey friends dared to tell you?"

"A scar," I spat, remembering clearly the excruciating pain that had created it. I'd thought I was dying, that my very flesh was being burned from my bones. But he'd wanted information from me, and letting me die would have been counterproductive.

So he'd just made me wish I could.

"It's more than that. An animal that gives particularly good sport is marked by us and released, to be hunted again. It is a sign to others of my kind that you are my prey alone."

"I'm honored," I said, refusing to give in to the panic that was leeching up my spine.

"You should be." The finger moved across my chest to circle a nipple, its icy-cold peaking the tender flesh. "Give me what I want, and perhaps we will hunt again someday."

"Go to hell!"

He smiled, fingers grasping my breast, suddenly so cold they burned. "You first."

His head lowered the last few inches, and I froze at the first touch of his mouth, soft, cold and wet. A clammy tongue ran deliberately over my lower lip before nudging for entrance I was too shocked to deny him. And a frozen thickness slid past my lips.

It was inhumanly cold and impossibly long, freezing my tongue as it coiled around it in a parody of affection. I twisted my head, my gut roiling with revulsion, but the hand on my breast moved up to my jaw, jerking me back to face him. Fingers dug into my flesh as that terrible face paused, mere millimeters from mine.

"Last chance."

I stared into those strange inhuman eyes and knew he wasn't bluffing. Æsubrand had never pretended anything but contempt for humans, or for most of the fey. He hadn't been joking with the animal comment. I was no more than that to him, and he would kill me with no more conscience than he'd slay a deer.

I was suddenly profoundly grateful that I didn't know where Aiden was.

"Nothing to say?" he mocked.

"I hope Caedmon kills you slowly."

He laughed. "Do you know, I am almost sorry to have to end your life?"

But apparently not sorry enough to stop. The pressure on either side of my jaw increased, forcing my mouth open. And, immediately, that terrible protrusion was back.

It was slimy, cold and spongy, totally unlike any human flesh as it pushed into my mouth. And everywhere he touched froze. My breast where his hand had rested was hard and cold, like a mound of ice, my lips were numb and my tongue felt thick in my mouth, too heavy to talk, too heavy to scream.

I thrashed, but he pressed against me, grinding our hips together as that icy snake of a tongue coiled into me. It widened as he poured more of himself into it, distending my throat, threatening to choke me. Starbursts of bloody violet flared behind my eyes as a fury rose up in me, my body aching for motion, to *act* and to *strike*....

But I couldn't move as that frozen mass worked its way downward, like an icy stake headed for my heart. But the heart wasn't the target, I realized dully, when it suddenly liquefied. Granite wetness filled my mouth, my nose, and gushed into my lungs, until I could see nothing, hear nothing, except my own frantic heartbeat.

I felt him suddenly explode around me, the rest of his form drenching me in icy water as his hold released. I felt myself falling, felt my half-frozen body hitting the hard concrete of the floor and splashing in the icy puddle of his doppelgänger. Then nothing but darkness.

Chapter Seven

I came back to consciousness with someone whacking me on the back hard enough to expel my lungs. Or at least what was in them. I rolled to the side, ripping myself free of the ice I lay on, coughing and retching a pink-tinged flood.

It went on for a while, me trying to draw in a breath in between eruptions and only making it half the time. Then my stomach decided to get in on the act. A hand held my hair back from my face, as I gagged and retched and choked.

I finally looked up to see Claire haloed in the wash of light spilling down the cellar stairs. Her red hair was everywhere, curled untidily against her neck and stuck to her skin. Her right hand and arm were still armored with iridescent scales as if she'd simply forgotten to change it back. Her left hand gripped mine hard enough to threaten the bones.

My lips moved, but for a moment, no sound came out. It felt like there was a rubber band inside my throat, pressing. Or a hand.

"Dory!" Claire leaned over me, her curls tumbling into my face. "Dory, say something!"

I cleared my throat. "Don't slap me," I told her, worried about the talons at the end of that paw. And then I threw up some more.

She dragged me against her, holding me almost too tight for me to breathe, sobbing out things I couldn't quite understand. Gessa was there, a slash across her forehead drizzling black blood into her eyes. She smeared a line of it onto my face, grinning, before heading off upstairs.

"I take it we won?" I croaked.

"They're gone," Claire said viciously, wiping a hand across her eyes. "I think creating the storm drained a lot of their power, and when they couldn't get in—" Her arms tightened.

"Please don't squeeze," I said thickly.

She let me go, and I sagged back against the concrete for a moment, waiting to see if my stomach planned an encore. It was cold but reassuringly solid, a nice, hard surface against my back that damn well stayed that way. There was no horrible shifting and sliding into something completely—

"I guess there's a reason we're not all dead?" I asked, to cut off my own thoughts.

"Manlíkans are just wards encasing an element," Claire told me distractedly. "They were used for war games back in Faerie, like practice dummies, and—" She waved frantic hands. "Why am I even talking about this? I disrupted them."

I rolled my eyes up at her. "Not to sound ungrateful, but you couldn't have done that earlier?"

"I thought if I started attacking them, the house wards might fall, too. And then it would take minutes for them to cycle back on and the Svarestri would get in—"

"They were already in," I said, and then wished I hadn't as she burst into tears. "It's okay," I told her. "We're all okay. Aren't we?"

"I can't find the children," she told me, her voice shaking. "I've looked everywhere! "They must have taken them—"

"I don't think so." I pushed myself into a reclining position with my good wrist as Gessa trotted back downstairs. She had a blanket and a bottle of water, and I accepted both gratefully. I washed out my mouth and spit on the floor because, really, it couldn't get any worse. Then I wrapped the blanket around me and tried sitting up.

My stomach stayed more or less where it was supposed to be, but something crunched under my butt. I fished the remains of a fortune cookie out of my pocket and read the tiny scrap of paper inside: *Your guardian angel got laid off.*

No shit, I thought, and started laughing, even though it hurt.

I looked up to find Claire gaping at me, eyes huge and horrified. I sobered up, wiped my lips and levered myself to my feet. The room spun alarmingly, but she caught me around the waist. "Upstairs," I told her, grabbing the banister.

"They aren't there! I looked everywhere. This was the last place I checked because I'd already been down here. That's why I almost didn't find you in time—"

"But you did," I reminded her, as the room steadied somewhat. "And I think I might know where the kids are."

Claire hauled me to the top of the steps, pretending that I was doing most of the work. I didn't need the ego validation, but the supporting arm was nice. My throat was on fire, my legs were throbbing and I was soaking wet. But nothing else had come up, so that was something.

The living room was oddly normal-looking, maybe because it still had a roof. That was more than I could say for most of the hallway. There were holes in the old wallpaper, and a miniature waterfall down what had been the stairs and three stories of destruction overhead. It was still raining, and a light drizzle filtered down to wet our hair and to splash on the already soaked floorboards. A clump of half-melted snow followed it, smacking onto the ground at my feet.

I knelt and felt around until my fingers hit the indentation for the trapdoor. It was coated in a thin rime of ice, like the myriad pools that had collected in depressions here and there. But the heel of my hand broke through and the heavy piece of wood came free with a crack.

I pushed it up, sending a miniature flood against the wall, and looked inside. And then had to shy back when a hairy little head popped out. Huge gray eyes blinked blearily at me, before the face cracked into a lopsided grin.

"The smugglers' hole!" Claire knelt and snatched Aiden out of the depths of the small space, hugging him fiercely. He was still clutching a chess piece, which fell to the floor and scampered away down the hall as fast as its tiny legs could carry it.

"It seemed a good guess. They'd just seen it."

Claire ignored her son's protests over how hard she was squeezing. From the look of things, it might take amputation to get him away from her. "I can't believe they were in there through all that!"

"I wouldn't worry too much about their recall," I said cynically, watching Stinky trying to crawl out of the hole.

Usually, he hopped around, over and up the furniture like a miniature acrobat, but not today. One long-toed foot made it over the edge and stuck there. He stared at it in some surprise, as if unsure what this strange new thing might be. Then the toes wiggled, and he broke down in helpless giggles, falling back against the rows of bottles he hadn't yet drained.

"I don't think they're feeling any pain," I told Claire.

Her eyes roamed over the devastation before meeting mine. "For now."

"Now's good."

She stared at me a moment and then nodded, still clutching her struggling son. He scrunched up his face, looking vaguely like Stinky for a moment, but not out of fear. He wanted to chase the escapee and didn't understand what all the fuss was about.

I left the kids with Claire, and went to assess the situation.

As I'd suspected, the house was pretty much unlivable, but the wards had held, including the glamourie that hid the destruction from casual passersby. From the street, everything looked perfectly normal—or at least no more dilapidated than usual. Except for the front yard, which was already becoming a swamp as the house started to expel some of the four feet of snow it had collected.

I watched the overflow tumble into the water-slick street and drain down already busy gutters for a moment, pondering alternatives. But there really weren't any. The fey didn't seem to find human wards all that impressive, and I strongly suspected that the only reason they hadn't been able to get in was the recent upgrades Olga had done.

The house now boasted a combination of human and fey protection that would be hard to top anywhere. It might be a trash heap, but it was a damn well-guarded trash heap. We were going to have to make the best out of it, like it or not.

I went back inside. The living room and the kitchen were the only areas on the ground floor that could be considered livable. Claire was in the former, but not bedding the kids down as I'd expected.

She must have been upstairs, because she'd changed into dry clothes, a black T-shirt and jeans, and she had a small suitcase at her side. She was struggling to get Aiden into a rain poncho when I came in the door. But he wasn't having it, fat little hands batting it away as she tried to push it down over his curls.

"What are you doing?"

She looked up, guilt and resolution in about equal measures on her face. "Getting out of here before I get you killed."

"And get yourself killed instead?" I asked, grabbing the suitcase.

She grabbed it back. "I'm hard to kill!"

"So am I!"

She shook her head. "You didn't see yourself down there. You didn't—I won't be responsible for that!"

"I'm a big girl, Claire. I'm responsible for myself."

I don't think she even heard me. "This whole thing . . . None of this was meant to happen," she told me wildly. "I'd planned it all out—I was supposed to have a couple of days before everything went to hell. And then Lukka died and then—"

"Life rarely cares about our plans," I told her cynically. In fact, it had always seemed to delight in screwing up mine.

"Life can suck it!" She started for the door, dragging Aiden after her, still caught in his plastic prison.

I got my back against the door, which was stupid. Claire could move me—along with what remained of the wall—if she felt like it. But she'd seemed kind of upset at the thought of me dying, so I was trusting her not to squash me like a bug.

"So what's the plan now? Run off into a night filled with known enemies?"

Claire gave me a frantic, frustrated look, and pushed bushy red hair out of her face. All the moisture in the air had turned it back into a huge fuzz ball. "I'm not stupid, Dory. They expended a lot of power on that storm, and more making those damned things. They're exhausted. It's why I have to leave now."

She started to push past, but I didn't budge. "They seemed to be doing fine until a few minutes ago. And if those things re-form and you're gone, it'll leave the rest of us defenseless."

Claire shot me a look that said she knew exactly what I was doing, and it wasn't going to work. "They can't re-form, at least not right away. Iron only disrupts the field, costs them time while they rebuild it. I didn't do that. I drained away the power they need to make the creatures to begin with."

"So once it's gone, it's gone?"

She nodded. "At least until they rest up. And considering how much energy creating that storm must have used, that will take a while."

"Assuming Æsubrand used everyone in the attack, which we don't know," I pointed out. "He could have left a few of his people out, hoping you'd panic—"

"I'm not panicking!"

"—and run, making their job easy."

"To do that, he'd have had to assume that his initial assault would fail," she said impatiently. "And Æsubrand is far too arrogant for that."

I couldn't really argue that one, so I changed tactics. "So you run. Then what?"

"I have a lot of contacts in the auction business," she told me, her color high. "If the rune is up for sale, someone has to know about it. I have to find out who has it before it ends up in a private collection somewhere and disappears."

"Fair enough. But you can't do that with the heir to the throne of Faerie on your hip."

"The fey don't know this world—"

"But plenty of other people do! And nothing is easier than hiring a bunch of mercenaries." I should know; I was one.

She blinked, as if that had never even occurred to her. "I don't think ... I don't think they'd do that. The fey handle their own problems." But she didn't look sure.

I pressed my advantage. "Okay, setting that aside, do you know what Aiden would be worth in ransom?"

"As soon as the shops open tomorrow, I'll dress him like a human child. No one needs to know—"

I stopped her with a hand on her arm. "Look."

Aiden had freed himself from the grip of the poncho and curled into a sleeping ball on the rug. Stinky was resting his head on the princely bottom, staring at him with liquid eyes that reflected a soft golden glow. It spilled over the muted colors of the old Persian and highlighted the scuffed floorboards like lantern light. It wasn't.

"Human children don't shed light shadows," I said softly, and watched her face crumple.

She put a trembling hand to her forehead. For the first time, what must have been months of constant strain showed. She looked almost haggard. "What am I going to do? They're going to kill him, Dory. They're going to kill my little boy, and I can't stop it!"

"No, they're not." I put an arm around her, feeling awkward because I'm not a hugger. But she looked like she could really use one. "The wards held, despite everything. And that was a pretty good test. I'll talk to

Olga tomorrow, see what else can be done. We'll keep him safe, Claire. Long enough for us to find this rune of yours."

"Us?"

"Well, now I'm all interested."

She stared at me for a moment, before breaking down into half-hysterical laughter.

"You're insane," she finally told me, wiping her eyes.

I cocked an eyebrow. "You're only figuring this out now?"

I don't think I'd have won the argument, but Claire looked like she was ready to drop. We hunted around and found some blankets in the hall closet that were miraculously still dry, and used them to bed the kids down on the sofa. Stinky was snoring almost immediately, and Aiden never even woke up in the transfer. Then we went up to check out Claire's room.

It was about the same as mine, except the holes in the roof weren't directly over the bed, and the mattress pad had kept the mattress largely dry. I helped her get the mattress downstairs, which mostly consisted of shoving it through a massive hole in the ceiling. It got a little waterlogged when it hit the river the melting snow was making out of the hall, but I didn't think Claire cared.

We dragged it into the living room and threw a few blankets on it, and then she dove in. "There's plenty of room," she mumbled, as I snuffed the lamp someone had left burning.

"Thanks. I'll be right back," I told her, and shut the door behind me.

I went back up to my room to rescue my cache of weapons. I was standing in front of the closet, wondering if I should take the swords or if they'd be okay in their scabbards, when my legs started feeling a little funny. I sat down on the waterlogged mattress for a moment, suddenly gasping.

At first I thought it was blood loss. The wound in my thigh had bled heavily, staining my skin below in a red sheen that was starting to turn dark. I went to the bathroom for my first-aid kit and caught sight of my-self in the mirror. My skin was waxy pale, my eyes and lips darkened as if bruised, the skin around my mouth crusted with something white and scaly.

I wiped it off and sat on the edge of the tub to bandage my leg. The bleeding had stopped in my thigh, although the knee still dribbled a little whenever I moved. And being a joint wound, it hurt like a bitch. But I'd had worse, and with my metabolism, I'd probably be well on the way to healed by tomorrow. Yet for some reason, my hands shook as I taped my knee off, and my lungs kept dragging in more oxygen than I needed.

They'd been doing it downstairs, too, like they thought there might be another shortage soon and needed to stock up. But it was worse now, to the point of making me dizzy. It took me a moment to realize that I was close to hyperventilating. I sat there, struggling to calm down, and wondered what the hell was wrong with me.

I'd come that close or closer to death more times than I could count, with many of them more painful and a lot more messy. I'd woken up from fits covered in my own and others' blood, with broken bones still reknitting, or burned flesh still sloughing off. Then there had been the memorable incident of coming back to consciousness only to interrupt the feeding of the vultures who had mistaken me for a corpse.

Sometimes I still had flashbacks to that one, the feathers dragging over my skin, the claws digging into my flesh, the beaks tearing. Yet I'd beaten them off, retrieved my weapons and stolen one of the horses of the men who had tried to gut me to get to my next job. I was used to dealing with the aftershocks of near disaster: the taste of blood, the scent of death in the air and the quiet that followed.

But, I realized slowly, I wasn't nearly as accustomed to the disaster itself. Most of the time, I was out of my head when the mayhem happened—a fact I'd always dreaded. I had never realized before how much I'd also relied on it.

It had been terrifying but also strangely comforting

to know that death for me would simply mean failing to wake up from one of my fits someday. It meant knowing every time I heard the familiar rushing in my ears that this might be the last time, but it also meant being pretty sure that I wouldn't see the end coming. Yet I'd almost seen it tonight.

And this is how you deal with it? I thought angrily. Five hundred years and this is the best you can do? Freaking out because your damn weapons failed? Because you finally met an opponent you don't know how to kill?

I got up, furious with my body for its weakness, with myself because I hadn't anticipated this, hadn't realized after getting my ass kicked by the fey once before that it damn well might happen again. I didn't know their magic, didn't understand their weapons. A weapon to me was the reassuring weight in my hand, a sword, a club, a gun; how the hell could I fight people who had the very Earth and sky on their side?

I didn't know, but I knew one thing. If Æsubrand was alive, he could die. And I really, really wanted him to die.

Chapter Eight

I awoke to the smell of freshly brewed coffee and frying bacon, which was impossible. But since I needed to get up anyway, I rolled out of bed—and fell three feet to the floor. I hit with a thump that didn't do the crick in my neck or the knots in my back any good.

My eyes crossed, focusing on a huge pair of smelly socks. They reeked badly enough to act as a kind of smelling salts. I sat up, fully conscious, and bumped my head on the underside of a table.

In front of me was a wreck that I vaguely identified as the living room. Blankets and old quilts had been thrown everywhere, clothes and bags of personal items had been piled in a heap by the cellar door, and a trail of huge, muddy footprints led from it to the hall. They obliterated most of the rug but skirted a waterlogged mattress.

The footprints had three toes each, pretty standard for mountain trolls, so I relaxed. I assumed they belonged to the large lumps curled up in a couple of wingback chairs in front of the fireplace, snoring loud enough to bring down what remained of the rafters. I ignored them for the moment, and stood up, my back cracking like old knuckles.

The edge of a quilt trailed off the tabletop, and I recalled what I'd been doing up there. Claire had been sprawled in the middle of the mattress when I returned last night, and I hadn't had the heart to move her. I'd failed to find a dry patch of floor, so I'd piled some bedding onto the felted surface we used to play poker.

It was only about four feet around, which explained the knots, and had a two-inch lip, which explained the crick.

After some much-needed stretching, I checked myself out. The wounds in my thigh and knee had ripened to purple with green and yellow around the edges. The knee was also puffy and tender to the touch, swelling up like bread dough when I peeled off the bandage. But both wounds had closed over, and my throat no longer felt like I was being choked from the inside. My wrist still hurt like a bitch, but overall, I'd woken up in worse states.

I wandered over and took a quick peek under the first lump's blanket. A small green eye opened and regarded me unhappily. "Sorry, Sven."

He grunted and went back to sleep. I didn't check the other one, but it was probably Ymsi, his twin brother. They were a couple of Olga's boys, second cousins or something, who acted as muscle in the business. It looked like word had gotten around that we might need a little added protection.

I walked out into the hall, yawning. The stairs were basically kindling, with more missing than still in place, and the wallpaper hung in dispirited strips, a victim of the damp that had mostly receded. But the ceiling looked better than I remembered.

It was still possible to see all the way up to the attic, but I was having a hard time figuring out which opening Claire and I had used to get the mattress down. None of them looked large enough for a twin, much less her queen. Even better, no more rain appeared to be getting in.

I found Claire in the kitchen, wrestling with the ancient stove. Her hair was a limp mess around her flushed face, and her glasses were about to slide off her sweaty nose. The house has air-conditioning, but with the wards on full, it didn't work any better than the lights. It had to be ninety degrees in there.

The kids were at the table. Aiden had spread the chess set out on his half and appeared to be attempting to dry it out. He had stripped the soldiers of their armor and laid it out in a line on a paper towel, and was now struggling to get a small ogre out of its damp clothes. The ogre wasn't too happy, but without its weapons, it could do no more than shake tiny fists.

Stinky was at the other end of the table, sleeping. Or at least I thought so, until a pitiful groan erupted from the fuzzy lump. I walked over, trying to get a look at him, but he kept shielding his eyes.

"He's been sick twice since he woke up," Claire told me, looking worried. "And he won't eat anything. I gave him some aspirin, but it didn't seem to help. I was about to wake you and ask if you want me to call a healer."

I pulled his head up and peeled the woven place mat off it. It left a checkerboard pattern on his cheek, which did nothing to hide the pallor and the under-eye bruising. I watched him for a moment, then went and got a dishrag and filled it with ice.

"Sit up," I told him. I was rewarded by a slitted eye glaring at me from under a snarled mass of hair, but no horizontal movement.

"What are you doing?" Claire asked.

"He's not sick." I pulled him up again and slapped the compress over his eyes. He mewled with protest until the cold started to work. Then he groaned in appreciation and flopped his head back down.

"He's hungover?" Claire asked, looking faintly appalled.

"Considering that he drained most of a bottle of your uncle's home brew last night? I'd say it's a safe bet."

I squatted down beside his chair. "Hurts, doesn't it?" I got a faint nod. "Are you going to stay out of my stash from now on?" A more vigorous nod. And then another groan. I decided he'd been punished enough.

"Have you seen my cell phone?" I asked Claire, staring at the empty recharger in my usual morning haze. I always envied the types who could roll out of bed and be bright-eyed and sharp within seconds. It took me a good hour, and that was with the help of large amounts of caffeine.

"No. Why?"

"Since it'll be a few days before any backup can arrive from Faerie, I thought I'd call Mircea. Get some protection down here."

Claire glanced up from the stove, brow furrowing. "What kind of protection?"

"The Senate's running short-staffed these days, but they should be able to spare a few masters—"

"You mean vampires." Her voice was flat.

"It's the Senate. What else?"

Her expression tipped over into a full-fledged frown. "I thought about what you said last night, about what Aiden would bring in ransom. I think the fewer people who know he's here, the better."

"I'm a little more concerned about the people who already know he's here," I said sardonically. "The house wards should stop the riffraff."

"They won't have to if nobody knows he's here in the first place."

"I'll tell Mircea to be discreet."

"I'd prefer to let fey deal with fey."

"Olga's boys are resistant to most magic, including the fey variety," I told her, while rifling through the bread box. "And God knows they're strong enough. But there're only two of them, and they aren't exactly deep thinkers. And whatever else I can say about Æsubrand, he's not stupid."

"Neither am I. And I know better than to trust a vampire!" I couldn't blame her for being wary. Claire had been kidnapped by Vlad on his recent rampage. She had every reason to mistrust the breed.

"They're not all the same," I admitted uncomfortably. Louis-Cesare, for example, seemed determined to mess with my head, constantly challenging my preconceptions about what a vampire was and how one behaved. It was only one of many ways the guy was a pain in the ass.

"You can say that when your job is killing them?" Claire demanded.

"My job is hunting revenants—" She looked confused. "Vampires who had something go wrong with the Change."

"Wouldn't they just"—she waved a spatula—"stay dead, then?"

"Most do. But once in a while one will survive physically, but mentally . . . Let's just say he's not all there. And a revenant will attack anything—human or vampire—that gets in his way. And since he's insane, there's no reasoning with him. He has to be put down."

"And you've never killed any vampires other than these revenants?" she asked, skeptically.

"I take commissions occasionally to hunt down vamps who have violated Senate law in some way. But I don't go around killing random vampires." I wouldn't have lasted long if I had, no matter who daddy was.

"I don't see much difference," Claire said, scowling.

I thought about Mircea's expression if he knew he'd just been lumped together with Vleck and a bunch of slavering beasts with little more brains than an animal. "You probably shouldn't mention that view around any vamps you meet," I said drily.

"I'm not going to be meeting any." It sounded final.

"You ought to reconsider," I told her seriously. "It's easy to distrust something that views you as food, but right now—"

"I don't want those things near my son, okay? I'm sick of guards I can't trust!"

"They'll be master-level vampires on loan from the Senate. They're not going to do any snacking."

"I know they're not, because they're not going to be here." She saw my expression and sighed. "Think about it, Dory. What could they have done last night, other than get carved to pieces?"

"I think you might be surprised."

"Well, I don't. I've seen what a fey warrior can do."

"And I've seen a master vampire in action."

She shot me an exasperated look. "If Æsubrand could get through the wards, he'd have done it, rather than resort to creating those things."

"Which he could do again."

"He knows that I can defeat them now. It would be a waste of time."

"And the next thing he comes up with?"

"He's not going to be coming up with anything today," she said firmly.

You hope, I didn't say. Because it would have been a waste of time. Claire was as stubborn as they came when she was convinced she was right, which was frequently. It didn't help that she usually was. I just hoped this wasn't going to be the exception that proved the rule.

I gave up on the phone and started looking for a mug instead. There weren't any in the usual spots—scattered around the table, littering the counters or piled in the dishwasher someone had installed back when olive green appliances were all the rage. It didn't actually work, but sometimes people stuck things in there anyway. But not this time.

"What are you doing?" Claire asked, watching me.

"Trying to find the mugs. They've all disappeared."

She rolled her eyes and opened a cabinet, and there they were—several rows of gleaming white cups, all perfectly aligned. She'd even gotten the stains out. *Must be fey magic*, I decided, pouring my morning brew.

I took the coffee and picked my way up the stairs to my room. I found it suspiciously clear of ice, snow or even water. I kicked a heel against the old floorboards, and they seemed solid enough. There was some staining, but they were dry.

Huh.

The lights didn't work, of course, but the holes in the ceiling let in plenty of daylight, plus a couple of birds who were poking around, checking out nesting opportunities. I ignored them and went to find my toothbrush. I'd located it before I remembered: the pipes had burst. I turned the faucet anyway, just for the hell of it, and a stream of water gurgled out into the rust-stained sink. I stared at it for a moment, perplexed, then shrugged and brushed my teeth.

The shower also seemed to work, so I took full advantage, washing away the blood from the previous night and the sweat from this morning. The house was hot and, thanks to the rain, uncomfortably muggy. I was toweling off when I got sidetracked by a small square of blue.

It had popped out of the tile work at some point in the mess last night and landed on the far end of the counter that held the sink. But it was currently on the move. I watched it skate across the linoleum and pop back into place, the yellowed grout filling in around it.

I stepped cautiously out of the shower, staring at it, and something bumped my foot. I snatched it back and looked down to find several more AWOL tiles jockeying for position. They moved across the floor, one having a rough time of it because it got stuck in the fuzzy bathroom rug. But it plowed on and finally tore free, scurrying over the floor and up the wall as if magnetized.

Once I started looking for them, I noticed a few more minute signs of change: stains on the floor slowly shrinking, a gash in the wallpaper closing up like a healing wound, a couple chips in the bathroom mirror melting back into the surface like ice into water. I quickly threw on some jeans and a tank top, ran a comb through my hair and grabbed a jacket to cover my not strictly legal arsenal. Then I padded back downstairs.

"There's something very weird going on around here," I told Claire.

She glanced up long enough to roll her eyes. "What gave it away?"

"I'm serious. I think the house is repairing itself."

"I know." She pointed the spatula at the front of the fridge, where several dents were popping back out, one by one, making small pinging noises.

"How?" I demanded.

"You know how it never lets us move anything or get rid of anything?"

I nodded. We'd spent a lot of useless time when I first moved in, trying in vain to adjust the place to fit our lifestyle. But every time we threw something out, it was back in place the next day. And the house could be vindictive, with that odd sort of consciousness magical objects sometimes acquire over time. The last time Claire had tried a reno, half her clothes had ended up scattered across the front lawn.

"I think Pip spelled the place to maintain the status quo, probably so he wouldn't have to do any maintenance," she told me. "But the ley-line sink has so much power that it tends to magnify spells, so . . ."

"It got a little too enthusiastic?"

"Essentially, yes."

I glanced at the hole by the threshold that had been there since shortly after I moved in. "Not everything comes back," I pointed out.

"It's a housekeeping spell," she told me. "I don't think it was designed to recognize demon blood. But more normal types of damage it should be able to handle."

"Then why isn't it putting it back *better*?" I was taking in the same rust line along the top of the fridge door, the same warped cabinets above the stove and the same scuffed boards on the same dusty old floor.

"Because it was designed to maintain everything exactly as it was at the moment Pip laid the spell. And I don't think he cared too much about decor."

"So that stain on the ceiling in my bedroom—"

"Is always going to be there, yes. Assuming the ceiling knits back." She looked up. "I'm hopeful, but that was a lot of damage."

I stared up, thinking about all the weapons I could buy if I didn't have to put a new roof on this thing. Of course the spell also meant I could never get rid of the ugly furniture, hideous wallpaper and outdated fixtures. But it wasn't a perfect world.

"I guess we'll find out," I said, peering over her shoulder to see what smelled so damn good. I blinked in disbelief. "That's *meat.*"

She shot me an evil look. "I know. Don't start."

"Are you planning on *eating* it?" I peeked under a row of paper towel–covered plates by the stove and discovered piles of bacon, eggs and toast. Considering that her usual breakfast had been wheat flakes and almond milk, it was a bit of a shock. But a good one. I filched a piece of bacon and pulled my hand back before she could slap it.

She scowled. "No."

"This has something to do with going scaly, doesn't it?"

"It has something to do with my other half slowly driving me nuts!" Claire said, stabbing at the remaining bacon. "It keeps trying to influence me."

I thought it already had, given a few of her comments from last night. And that wasn't such a bad thing. If ever a situation called for a little more ruthlessness, having a bunch of homicidal fey after your kid was it.

"I've tried to compromise," she groused. "I tried eating fish and eggs."

"Did it help?"

She made a face. "No. It doesn't want fish. It doesn't *like* eggs. It wants big piles of meat—the rarer and the greasier, the better. It would prefer live, squirmy things that it could kill first, only it knows better than to ask for that. So it tortures me with dreams of steak and sausages and ribs grilling over a fire."

I grinned. "So you're cooking all this to what? Torture it back?"

"The kids have to eat something. And I wanted to make enough for the twins and for a snack for them later. I don't know how long I'll be."

"How long you'll be?"

"Checking on Naudiz. It's not the kind of thing anyone is going to discuss over the phone. I need to go in person."

"Actually, no," I told her, stealing another slice. It was the good kind—thick, with a honey, peppery glaze. "You need to stay here with Aiden. I have to go in person."

"You don't have my contacts," she protested.

"I have Olga."

Claire looked skeptical. "Your secretary?"

"Her late husband was pretty well known in the supernatural weapons trade. And Benny wasn't too particular about where he obtained his goods."

"And that's a plus?"

"It is if you're looking for a hot fey battle rune. I don't think that guard is likely to go through legit channels. Her people are more likely to have heard something."

"But I can't just stay here and do nothing! That's all I ever do!"

"You're not doing nothing. You're guarding your son. And frankly, you're a lot scarier than I am."

She shot me an exasperated look. "Thanks!"

"You know what I mean. I can't do what you can do, Claire. So let me do what I know how to do, okay?"

I was surprised by a greasy hug. "You're a good friend, Dory," she told me fervently. I hugged her awkwardly back, my hands full of salty, fatty goodness. I couldn't remember the last time I'd been hugged this much in a twenty-four-hour period.

She pulled back, blinking, and I pretended I didn't notice. "Do you want something before you go?" She gestured at the stove. "There's plenty."

"I thought all we had in the fridge was beer and mayo. And I wouldn't trust the mayo." I'd caught a small troll with his head in the jar a few days ago, eating it like candy.

"Olga sent enough for an army over with the twins." Claire pulled a jar out of the fridge and frowned at it.

"You haven't seen them eat yet. It was probably lunch."

"How much more should I make?" she asked, eyeing dishes on the stove.

"Beats me. I've never actually seen them get full. Anyway, I have to go, before everyone I know turns in for the day." I topped off my coffee and headed out, before she could ask why there were tongue marks in the mayonnaise.

Chapter Nine

I found my duffel bag in the car and my cell inside the duffel, so things were looking up. The Camaro itself had some obvious new dents and smelled a little mildewy, but it started, so I counted it as a victory. Ten minutes later, I parked it next to a mini-mart that looked like any other in Brooklyn from the outside.

It did on the inside, too, at least in front. Customers could prowl the deserted aisles, buy rubberlike hot dogs, get a scratch-off card and stock up on overpriced toiletries, all while being ostentatiously ignored by the staff. The locals had eventually gotten tired of the lousy service and gone elsewhere, which of course had been the point. There were rumors that the store was a front for mob activity, drug running and/or gambling.

The truth was a whole lot weirder.

The back room was accessible through a brief hallway and a speakeasy-type door. I bent down and knocked, because the eyehole was roughly in line with my navel. A tiny green eye peered back at me suspiciously. "What?"

"Open up. It's me, Dory."

"How do I know that?"

"Because you're looking at me?"

"Turn on the light."

I sighed. "It is on." There were half a dozen hundred-fifty-watt bulbs in the overhead fixture, enough that I could feel their heat slowly frying my brain. Not that it mattered. Troll eyesight is universally terrible, and no spell I've ever heard of seems to help.

There was a low-voiced conversation on the other side of the door. "You don't have to whisper. I don't speak troll," I said helpfully.

"You should learn," a familiar voice said as the door swung back.

I was still bent over, giving me a view of about a mile of shiny black leather encasing two massive thighs. A flick of the eye downward showed me a pair of high-heeled slides adding another three inches to an already towering height. Three gnarled toes peeked out the end, the usual number for a Bergtroll, or mountain troll. Although most don't have nails painted high-gloss red.

Or so I liked to believe, anyway.

A trip upward showed me a very healthy bosom encased in a bright red vest, which was mostly hidden behind a flowing brown beard. It matched the hair framing the wide face above, which had been teased to within an inch of its life and streaked with platinum highlights. Its owner regarded me quizzically.

"Why you bent over like that?" Olga demanded.

Out of shock, I didn't say. "No reason."

I stood up and she pulled back, giving me access. The tiny mountain troll who had answered the door clambered back onto his stool, pushed over to one side where he could smoke in peace. He'd also been used as a doorman by the proprietors of the establishment's former incarnation—a crowded gambling den. I guess it had gotten too crowded, because it had been replaced by a beauty parlor.

"New look?" I asked, settling myself onto an empty stool.

Olga plopped back onto a chair by a manicure station. The chair groaned, but held, and the manicurist went back to work on her thick, curved nails. "You should try," she said, eyeing my short nails and casual hairstyle without favor. "You look like boy."

I raised an eyebrow. "Most guys don't think so."

"I not see you married."

"Hell has yet to freeze over," I agreed.

She snorted. "What happened to that vampire?"

"Which one?" Lately, I had more in my life than I liked. Of course, since I liked zero, that wasn't hard.

Olga spread her giant hands, turned them upward and made grabby motions. I grinned, thinking of Louis-Cesare's expression if he ever found out that his name sounded like the troll word for "tight ass." Not that it didn't fit. On several levels.

"I haven't seen him in a while."

"You see him more often if you—" Olga looked at the manicurist. "What that word?"

"Gild the lily?" the girl asked, shooting me an appraising glance. "You'd look great with highlights."

"I look like a skunk with highlights." The curse of dark hair.

"You just haven't had them done right," she told me. "I'm a whiz at color. As soon as I'm done here, we could—"

"Maybe later," I told her. I'd just gotten the blue.

I sketched the problem out for Olga while the rest of the rhinestones were appliquéd. "We don't know that he's here to sell it, but it seems like a good guess." The war in the supernatural community had driven up the price of all defensive wards. And this was supposed to be the grandfather of them all.

She nodded and then just sat there. Unlike humans, trolls don't have a problem with long silences. They also aren't big in the idle chitchat department. Since I suck at that sort of thing myself, I found it oddly refreshing.

I flipped through a few magazines, went out front and bought a soda, came back in and perused the new stock of weapons in the back room. There was enough firepower to take out half of Brooklyn shelved alongside the peroxide and bags of hair extensions. Olga had needed a cheap place to start up her business again, and the proprietor had needed some security, so they'd worked out a partnership agreement. It was currently possible to come in for a shampoo and leave with the magical equivalent of a bazooka.

Most of the stuff I already had two of, but there was a

nice selection of iron weapons I'd never really bothered to look at before. They were heavy and lacked the grace and flexibility of steel. There was nothing elegant here: no mirror-bright ceremonial blades, no inlaid grips, no fine-tooled scabbards. They were ugly, brutish weapons for ugly, brutish warfare.

I hefted a short sword that was more like a club, and liked its weight in my hand. It was well balanced, with a dull, slightly pitted surface. No one would see this coming on a dark night. I also selected a couple knives and a mace that must have weighed fifty pounds, and took them back into the main room.

And found Olga watching me. "What you do?"

"I need weapons."

"You already have."

"Yeah, but they don't work too well on fey. And you may have heard, we had a little visit last night. By the way, thanks for the twins."

Olga inclined her head. "What you do with these weapons?"

I thought that was an odd question. "What do I usually do with them?"

"You not go after Æsubrand."

It had been more of a statement than a question, but I answered it anyway. "I didn't go after him this time. And how did you know he was here?"

"People talk."

"What else do they say?"

She shrugged. "He here to make trouble. Not know what kind. But you stay away."

"I told you, he came after me."

Small blue eyes narrowed on my face. "And you not go hunt?"

"What are you trying to tell me, Olga? That you won't sell me weapons if I'm going after Æsubrand?" She just looked at me. "Why?"

"You good fighter, for little woman. But you no match for him. He kill you." It was said with such toneless conviction that it sent a chill down my spine.

"Well, cheer up. I'm not planning on searching him

out. But in case he comes around again, I'd like something a little more lethal than highlights!"

We finally reached an agreement, and I took the mace over to the doorman to arrange delivery. No way was I carrying that around all day. But the other stuff I tucked into my duffel. They weighed the thing down a lot more than normal, but it couldn't be helped. I wasn't going to get caught flat-footed again.

I turned to find Olga levering herself to her feet. "Come."

She led me out the back door and into a small parking lot, where a specially built van was parked. She settled herself into the passenger's side while the van's struts creaked and groaned. Four hundred pounds of troll is a lot of troll, although she's considered pretty petite for her species.

The supernatural community in New York is broken into sections, much like the human city. The vamps prefer Manhattan; the mages have their East Coast base in Queens; and the Weres live mostly in rural areas upstate. Brooklyn, on the other hand, is fey territory. To be more precise, it's a Dark Fey stronghold where the creatures who populate Earth's nightmares hang out and attempt to make a living.

A sizable minority of these are trolls, the human term for a wide variety of Dark Fey with a few obvious similarities. In reality, "trolls" were made up of dozens of different species, many of which had been enemies back in Faerie. But in the unfamiliar landscape of the human world, they'd bonded to form a tight-knit community. Olga's late husband hadn't even reached her waist.

The rain had slowed everything down, and we got stuck in traffic going over the Brooklyn Bridge. "I hate Manhattan," I said, itching to get there already.

Olga nodded sympathetically. "In Faerie, Earth considered hell dimension."

"I didn't know that."

"Yes." She caught my expression. "Upper hell," she said, placatingly.

"I guess that's something."

Traffic started to move again, and we inched into the city. There was no parking near our destination, so I dropped her off and went to find a garage. By the time I got back, she'd disappeared into a dimly lit restaurant decorated with raffia-wrapped wine bottles and paint-by-number images of Italy.

It was fey run, meaning she could drop her glamourie like a coat at the door, the restaurant's camouflage ensuring that everyone looked more or less human. Most of them were, but I spotted the slightly blurred outlines of at least three Others at the bar and a couple more eating spaghetti Bolognese at a corner table.

"Lucas," Olga told the waiter, who was in a glamourie to match the decor—dark hair, perfect little mustache, slight paunch, balding. What he actually looked like—or what he actually was—was anyone's guess. I could detect glamouries unless they were very, very expensive ones. But I couldn't see through them.

That was, after all, kind of the point.

The little man took us over to a table where a distinguished white-haired gentleman of maybe seventy was enjoying some cacciatore. His wrinkles were discreet, like the subtle stripe in his four-thousand-dollar suit and the shine on his Prada loafers. He seemed human enough, as far as I could tell, but he didn't so much as blink as Olga explained what we wanted.

"You check," she finished, summoning the waiter with a regal gesture.

"My dear lady, I don't have to check," he said, blotting a daub of sauce off the end of his chin. "I can assure you, nothing like that is being offered for sale in New York."

"How can you be so sure?" I asked, as Olga basically ordered the menu.

"Because it is my business to know!"

"And your business would be?"

"I find rarities for discerning purchasers, matching specialized items with buyers able to appreciate them. I know the inventories of all the major auction houses, as well as quite a few of the small ones."

"But not all. I mean, there have to be hundreds in this country alone—"

"My dear young lady," he said severely, "no small house would handle a prize like that. Naudiz is one of a set of runes rumored to have been carved by Odin himself. It would be worth . . . Well, in essence, it is priceless. If it came up for sale, it would cause a stir around the world. It would be as if the Hope Diamond came up for auction in the world of jewelry."

I munched a bread stick and thought about it. "No, it would be as if the Hope Diamond was stolen, and then someone had to figure out a way to sell it. A minor jewel would be no problem; you could unload it anywhere. But the Hope freaking Diamond?"

"Well, one could always cut down a diamond," he said, starting on a supersized gelato. "Not that it would be necessary in the case of such a famous stone. A discreet sale to a private collector would be more likely, if the thief wasn't a total novice. But it is a poor analogy since a magical object cannot be divided in such a way."

"So how would he do it? If someone wanted to fence it?"

He quirked an eyebrow. "One doesn't 'fence' an item of that quality."

"Then what does one do, hypothetically speaking?"

He shrugged. "Arrange a private sale, as I said, or a small auction, by invitation only, for a select company. The latter would be slightly more risky, but would also probably result in a greater return."

I accepted a glass of wine from the bottle the waiter had brought Olga, and sipped at it as I thought it over. "Say he's a novice. First-time thief. He wants the maximum return, so he needs to arrange a small, private auction. Who could do that for him?"

"Any number of people. There are many unscrupulous types in our business, I am afraid. And quite a few others who could be persuaded into error by such a commission."

"But how do I narrow it down?"

"Do you know what auction houses the individual has dealt with in the past?"

"None, as far as I know."

"Does he have any contacts in this world, people who might have been able to provide him with suggestions?"

"I don't know." The Blarestri, Claire's group of Light Fey, didn't venture into our world that much, but there was no law against it. The guard could have been here, either officially or not, any number of times, and there was no way to know who he'd met.

"Hm." He thought about it while Olga dug into a party-sized platter of antipasto. She pushed it at me, and I figured what the hell? I'd finished another glass of wine and enough prosciutto to kill an average person by the time he nodded. "If you can't narrow it down on his end, the only thing you can do is to narrow it down on ours."

"Meaning?"

"There is a good deal of fraud, in the case of some unscrupulous auctioneers, and it is often buyer beware. But no one would even attempt to sell something like this without providing cast-iron proof of its legitimacy. A valuation would need to be performed, to convince the potential buyers that it was, indeed, what the auctioneer said it was."

"And who would do this valuation?"

"It would have to be an unquestionable authority, probably fey since the item is so, of proven discretion and sterling record."

"Do you know anybody like that?"

"Oh, yes." His spoon rang on the side of his glass and he sat back with a sigh. "Assuming you can find the little tick."

The heavy old slab of wood and metal, a relic of a twenties-era speakeasy, groaned as I pushed it open. "SHUT THE DOOR!" The usual chorus greeted me as I slipped inside and turned to shove the door closed behind me.

With the daylight firmly shut out, the stairwell was dim enough that I had to be careful of my footing heading down. The bouncer at the bottom, a large water troll, raised a clammy hand in greeting as I entered the large cellar. It was a lot easier to see here, and not just because of the lanterns scattered about.

Graffiti scrolled down the wall, golden lines rippling as they passed over the spaces between bricks. Some near the ceiling were written in black and stayed in place, as static as if they were drawn with paint instead of magic. But the rest flowed down the walls and onto the cracked cement floor, constantly uncurling and re-writing themselves as the odds changed.

It had odds on everything from dog racing and jai alai, to table tennis and golf. Not that the fey needed a sport to bet on. A couple of dwarves at the bar were raptly watching a pint to see which bead of condensation would hit the bar first. The bartender, who was also the owner, scowled at them, preferring bets to be made with him instead of one another. But at least the winner bought another round.

One of the few constants about the fey was their love for games of chance. They opened betting parlors before they did grocery stores, and they'd put money on anything. And despite its fairly mean decor, Fin's was one of the best places in Brooklyn to put down a bet.

"What do you mean, you don't know?" I asked, frowning at Fin. "You know everybody."

"In Brooklyn I know everybody," he corrected, hopping down from his perch on a milk crate to get me a drink. Fin was a Skogstroll, which was Norwegian for forest troll, although to my knowledge he'd never been out of Brooklyn in his life. But he still had the nose—only a foot long because he was still young—and he had to stand on a box to be able to see over the bar.

He clambered back up and slid me another longneck. "The guy you want works out of Chinatown. Manhattan's vamp territory—you know that."

"So what's a fey doing there?"

Fin shrugged. "He's Chinese?"

"He's *fey*," I repeated, pausing to drain half my drink. It was hot as hell outside, and I'd been running around all day, lugging half a ton of iron. And all I had to show for it was a pounding headache and a couple of blisters. *I would have had to take the leather coat today*, I thought, eyeing it resentfully.

"Yeah, but luduans left Faerie a long time ago, and most of them settled in China. The Chinese emperors used them in interrogations."

"I know that," I said crabbily. The human world has sodium pentothal and lie detectors; the supernatural world uses luduans—when it can find them. But this one had gotten fired from his job, wasn't at his apartment and hadn't been seen for two days at any of the places he liked to hang out.

A trio of trolls erupted with stomps and hoots from their primo place in front of the large mirror on one wall. It was currently reflecting the qualifying heats for the insane mage sport of ley-line racing. The World Championships were coming to town, and it was all anyone could think about. Including Fin, who was raking in the bets hand over fist.

I waited while he took some money off a Merrow, who of course was favoring an Irish driver. She wrapped her webbed hand around a pint and moved off, and I leaned over the bar. "I'm getting desperate, Fin. I don't have time to wait around days or weeks for this guy to show. I've checked everywhere, and it's like he just fell off the face of the earth."

Fin shrugged. "All I know is he put a couple bets down with me a week ago, but never paid up. So I sent the boys after him."

The "boys" were a couple of cave trolls, short and squat like the rest of their breed, but with the long arms and huge, shovel-like hands needed for excavating large areas of earth. Those hands were also good for slapping around welchers, so much so that Fin rarely had a problem.

"Did they find him?" I asked.

He scowled. "Not yet. They went by his job, but he wasn't there."

"He isn't going to be. The management fired him after they found out about his gambling debts. I think they were afraid he'd walk off with some of the merchandise."

Fin paused to serve another customer, with the molasses-type beer trolls prefer. I suppressed a face. You can eat that stuff with a spoon. "You're talking about that auction house he used to work for," he finally told me. "He got another job last week—at a gambling den in back of a pharmacy over there."

I got out a notebook. "What pharmacy?"

He shook his head. "Don't bother. Didn't I tell you I sent the boys?"

"No disrespect to the boys, but tell me anyway."

A spear of light interrupted the cheering going on around a big-screen TV mounted to one grimy wall, washing out the horse race it was showing. "SHUT THE DOOR!" we all yelled, and it quickly slammed closed.

"The owner had some trouble a few months back with mages coming in and cleaning up using spells to cheat," Fin told me.

"There are charms against that sort of thing."

"Yeah, but they're expensive and have to be renewed regularly, and he wasn't exactly making a killing. So he started keeping a luduan on-site so whenever somebody started a major run, he could have it question them. Make sure it really was a lucky streak."

"Sounds reasonable."

"Yeah, it worked pretty good. Until the damn thing stopped coming in. The owner said he didn't show up for work last night or the one before. And he didn't call in."

"Great." He'd either done a runner, in which case it could take weeks to track him down, or one of his other disgruntled bookies had decided to make the lesson a little more permanent. Either way, I was screwed. "I need to talk to this guy, assuming he's still alive, and I need to do it today."

I got back sympathetic eyes and nothing else. And that wasn't promising. Everybody came to Fin's, and he kept his tiny ears open. He was my first stop on most jobs that involved the fey, although today he'd been last because I'd already been in Manhattan so I'd checked there first. If Fin didn't know, nobody did—with one possible exception.

I called Mircea on my way home. "I need a favor."

"What a coincidence."

It took me second. "You need me to make that pickup."

"Yes."

I looked around and finally found the folder sticking out from under the seat, half hidden by a couple of crumpled fast-food bags and my tennis shoes. So that was where I had left them. I tossed them in back and flipped through the file.

It was another seedy nightclub owner with a smuggling habit, only this one preferred weapons to drugs. Same old, same old. "Okay," I told him. "I need a luduan. No name—apparently they don't use them—but supposedly he's the only one around." I gave him the particulars, such as they were.

"Very well. I will have inquiries made."

"I need him by tomorrow at the latest, Mircea."

"And I need the vampire alive."

"Yeah, you made that point already. I'll call when I have him." I hung up. This shouldn't take long.

Chapter Ten

Everything was going great until I cut his head off.

That sort of thing tends to shock someone into silence, but not this time. The body's arms were flailing around uselessly, the crocodile skin loafers were making scuff marks on the bathroom floor and the detached head was screaming bloody murder. Great.

I stuck a wad of paper towels in its mouth and hurried to the door. Fortunately, it seemed that the DJ's pounding beat was enough to deafen even vampire ears, because none of the black-clad "bouncers" were rushing to aid their fallen boss. Instead, the short hallway contained only a couple making out and a guy waiting for the bathroom.

"This is for employees," I told him. "There's one for customers up front."

"Yeah, but there's a line. Can't you two get a room or something?"

"Sorry."

He tried to peer through the crack in the door behind me. "I thought I heard a scream."

"I'm being mean to him."

He took in my black leather jeans, bustier and cropped jacket—chosen for ease of cleanup—and a slow grin spread over his face. "I wouldn't mind if you were mean to me."

"You know, I really think you would."

I ducked back inside to find the body's hands feeling around the floor, trying to locate its missing piece. That was a no-no, as freshly severed vampire parts could often reattach. I picked the head up by its spiky black hair and tossed it in the sink.

My knife, a ten-inch bowie, had fallen to the floor in the tussle. I took my time cleaning it, giving the vamp a moment to adjust to the new state of affairs. I'd finished and tucked the head back in my duffel bag by the time he managed to spit out the towels.

"You cut off my head!" Shock and outrage warred in his pale blue eyes.

We both regarded his remains, which were still twitching. They were undeniably headless, but also strangely lacking in gore. Vampire hearts don't pump unless the vamp is trying to appear human, so there's nothing to cause any inconvenient spurting. I had a few drops on my jacket, but they weren't too noticeable against the leather. Most of the rest had pooled beneath the body, leaving it looking oddly pristine.

I glanced back at the sink and found the head glaring at me. It looked like outrage had won. "You crazy bitch! You can't just walk into my club and—"

"The name's Dory."

"—try this shit on! Do you have any idea who I am?"

"Of course."

"Because when I—" Thin eyelashes fluttered in confusion. "What?"

I dragged the file out of my duffel. "It never ceases to amaze me how many people think I kill for fun."

"Don't you?"

"Well, not *just* for fun." I bent the file's front cover back, showing him the photo that had been paper-clipped to the inside.

His eyes crossed as they focused on the image of his own narrow face, overgrown nose and sulky expression. "This is a *hit*?"

"If it was, you'd be dead by now."

"What the hell do you call this?"

"Temporarily inconvenienced. A fifth-level master can live for up to a week without a head."

"And how do you know that's what I am?" he asked haughtily. He'd probably been telling people he was third or something. There are rare vampires who can hide their true levels, appearing stronger or weaker than they actually are. But this joker wasn't one of them.

"Because it's in the report," I told him patiently. "Not to mention that a senior master wouldn't be glaring at me while he bled out. He'd—"

The body's left leg abruptly jackknifed, dumping me on the floor and allowing it to get a hand around my throat. So I stuck a knife under the breastbone, pinning it to the stained linoleum. Instead of pulling my weapon back out and trying to stick it into me, the hands fell away to flap against the floor, like fish out of water.

He was so fifth-level.

I flipped open the folder. "Raymond Lu. Born in 1622, the result of a beachside union between a randy Dutch sailor and the slowest Indonesian woman in her village."

"It was a love match!"

"Sure." I moved back a little to keep the creeping bloodstain off my boots. "You earned a tenuous living thereafter as part of the most inept band of pirates ever to sail the seas, and only became a vamp because you robbed the wrong guy."

The head said something, but it was indecipherable because it had slipped down the side of the bowl and ended up with its nose in the drain. I fished it out and wedged it snugly beside the faucet. It thanked me by trying to take a bite out of my thumb.

"These days, you pose as a respectable Chinese businessman despite the fact that you aren't respectable, you aren't Chinese and your 'business' consists of running errands for the undead version of the Hong Kong mafia."

"It's a living."

"Not for long. You've been a very bad boy, Raymond. The Senate would like a word."

"Wait. You're working for the *Senate*?" He looked almost relieved. Since the Vampire Senate usually made vamps quake in their designer shoes, that was a little strange.

"I'm freelancing," I informed him.

"But you're a dhampir!"

"Like you said, it's a living."

"God! I thought . . . Never mind."

I unzipped the roomy main compartment of the duffel. "We're going to go see the senator in charge of fey affairs. He has some questions about that illegal portal you've been running to Faerie."

"I don't know what you're talking about."

"Sure you do. People walk in and out of here all the time, and some of them leave carrying nasty fey weapons. You cough up the location to the portal, we blow it up and everybody lives happily ever after."

"I still won't have a head!"

"There are people who can fix that—assuming you have all the requisite parts. I'll leave the body here; I'm sure your boys will take good care of it. And as long as you come through, you and it will be happily reunited in a couple of—"

A handsome young Asian guy burst through the door energetically enough to send the lock flying. He was in the black jeans, boots and muscle shirt of a bouncer, the latter untucked to hide the gun at his back. He started to say something, then stopped, gaping. His eyes flicked from the body on the floor to the head in the sink, then back to the body. His mouth dropped open.

"Don't just stand there!" Raymond spluttered. "Kill her!"

The vamp jumped at the sound of a voice coming from the gory head, but his eyes obediently made the rounds again, looking for a target. And passed over me without so much as a pause. He saw me, but assumed I was human, which put me in the same threat category as the paper towel dispenser.

I gave a little wave. "Dhampir," I added helpfully.

He blinked and finally focused on my face. He took in the delicate bone structure I inherited from my human mother, the dimples I received from the iffier side of the gene pool and my unimpressive height. "You are not!" He sounded almost offended.

"No, really."

"You don't look like a dhampir!"

"You've met one?"

"No, but ... a dhampir would be taller. And you'd have a tail." His eyes flicked downward for a second, and he looked almost disappointed at my human-looking butt.

"That's a myth," I told him gently.

He still looked skeptical, so I flashed my tiny fangs. They're vestigial in my kind, since we don't drink blood, but they got the message across. His eyes widened, and he retreated a step before he caught himself. "Dhampir!"

"Out of curiosity, what did you think had decapitated the boss?" I asked, as he went for his gun. I'd expected that, and mine was out before he'd completed the gesture. The reflexes aren't a myth, or I'd have been dead a long time ago.

He looked at my Glock. It's a .45. He'd pulled out a tiny little .22.

"Size really does matter," I observed, and he scowled.

"Oh for— Go get help!" Raymond ordered.

The vamp's eyes shifted back to his master, and some of his initial panic returned. "But sir. Lord Cheung is here!"

"What?" Raymond suddenly looked more freaked out than when I'd decapitated him. "But he's not due until midnight!"

"I believe his plane arrived early." The vamp's eyes kept flicking back and forth between the two parts of the boss, as if unsure which one he should be addressing. He finally settled on the head. "He commands your presence, sir."

"Oh, shit! Oh, shit!" Now Raymond was the one looking around wildly.

"What's your master doing here?" I demanded.

But Ray wasn't listening. "If he's here early it must mean— Oh, shit!" His body gave a sudden heave and wrenched itself off the floor, only to stumble into the side of the sink, slip on some blood and go back down.

"Must mean what?"

"That you're too late! He's going to kill me before the Senate gets the chance!"

"That's why you were cowering in the bathroom?" For once, I hadn't had to go round the perp up. He'd already been in here when I arrived. I'd thought it convenient, but I had wondered. It's not like vamps actually need to use the facilities.

He shot me a purely venomous look. "I wasn't cowering! I needed someplace quiet to think. To figure out how—" His lips abruptly snapped shut, and those pale eyes narrowed on my face.

I sighed. Why did I get the feeling that this nice, easy assignment had just gone pear-shaped? "And your master wants to kill you because . . . ?"

"There may have been a slight . . . misunderstanding . . . about some merchandise."

"You *stole* from the vampire mafia?"

"Something was *misplaced*, and it wasn't my fault!"

"Of course not."

"Look, all you need to know is that—" He stopped, staring past me at the guard. "What are you doing?"

The vamp looked at the gun he'd aimed at my head. "I'm going to kill her?"

Raymond rolled his eyes. "Oh, for the love of— Can you at least *try* to keep up?"

The vamp lowered the weapon and stood there looking awkward.

"What do I need to know?" I prompted.

"That there's not one portal," Ray said hurriedly. "There's a whole network, and I know where they are. Well, most of them. More than you're likely to find on your own—that's for sure. You get me out of this, and I talk. You leave me here and I die, and don't think you're going to find anyone else to squeal!"

Great. I should have known Mircea wouldn't give me

two easy jobs in a row. But this was going to be a real bitch. For one thing, it meant I couldn't leave the body behind as I'd planned. Ray was already decapitated; all his master had to do to be rid of him was to stake the heart. And a lumbering corpse was going to be a bit harder to hide than a head in a bag.

And for another, there was Cheung. The job had been to kidnap a fifth-level screwup, not to face a first-level master and who knew how many subordinates. The only smart thing to do was to wish Ray good luck and get the hell out.

And that was exactly what I would have done, except I didn't think Mircea was going to be too pleased if I showed up empty-handed. I needed this job and I needed his help. I was going to have to come up with something.

My knife was still protruding from the vamp's chest. I ripped it out and looked up at the bouncer. "If I provide a distraction, can you get your boss's body past Cheung's men?"

The vamp didn't reply, but Raymond's eyebrows lowered. "What do you mean, my *body*? Why can't he take all of—"

"Because I don't trust you. I'll get you out of here, but it's the same deal as before. Your family takes the body, and I get the head. If you're not playing me, the two of you get reunited. Otherwise—"

"All right! All right!" Raymond glanced at the bouncer, who was just standing there. He sighed and the fingers on his body snapped. "Hello! Answer her!"

"Sir, Lord Cheung specifically instructed me to bring you to him."

"So stall him!"

"Sir, I *can't*." And it was obvious he meant that literally. Tendons were sticking out like cords on either side of his neck, his face was red and he was sweating small drops of blood. Conflicting orders play havoc with baby vamps, and this one was a couple decades dead at best. "He said we were to bring you to him *immediately*—"

"We?"

"He instructed the family to find you as soon as he came in—"

"And as your master's master, he can command you," I finished for him. Well, shit, to borrow Ray's favorite word.

"Fight it!" Raymond ordered, like the guy wasn't already trying. The bouncer nodded, but at the same time, he stooped, picked up his boss's body and heaved it over one shoulder. More thick, sludgy blood spattered the dingy tiles. "What are you doing?" Raymond demanded shrilly.

"I'm sorry, sir." The vamp looked miserable, and his voice was trembling, but he nonetheless started for the door.

"He's not even a master," I pointed out. "He can't fight it, Ray!"

"Shit!"

That was less than helpful, so I grabbed baby vamp by the belt. He wrenched the door open anyway, so I swung him around and put my back to it, slamming it shut. At the same time, Ray's foot kicked out and clipped him on the knee; the guy slipped on blood, and they hit the floor.

As soon as they were down, Ray hit the vamp in the neck, kneed him in the groin and tore out of his hold. He scuttled into a stall and flipped the lock—why, I don't know. Its side was the usual ugly green metal with a graffiti rash, which might as well have been rice paper for all the good it did. The bouncer leapt to his feet and punched a hole through it with his fist.

I moved to assist, but never got the chance. There was some pretty violent banging for a minute, and then a tearing sound. Finally the stall door flew open, and Ray's shirtless body emerged and started bitch-slapping everything in sight.

His aim was off, probably due to the difficulty of having his eyes on the other side of the room, but he made up for it with sheer determination. A condom dispenser went flying, and a urinal got a blow that severed a pipe, sending a gush of water spearing across the room. A lucky blow pushed the baby vamp back into me, and I grabbed the opportunity and his throat.

A choke hold isn't really much use on vamps since they don't need to breathe. But he was new enough that he instinctively clutched my arms, trying in vain to break my grip. It didn't work, which seemed to startle him.

"Is there anyone who didn't hear Cheung's command?" I demanded, as he struggled and gurgled and didn't tell me shit. He finally wised up and elbowed me in the gut, and I lost patience. I shoved him away and grabbed the bowie out of my bag. When he started for me again, I pinned him to the wall with it.

He stared down at the bone handle, eyes huge and disbelieving. "It's not wood. You'll live," I told him tersely. It was more than Ray and I were going to do if we didn't get gone. I plucked the head out of the sink, wrapped it in the towels I'd brought along and dropped it in the duffel.

"What the *hell*?" Ray demanded indignantly.

"How did you think I was planning to get you out?" I asked, stripping off my jacket.

I threw it over the body's torso and stepped back to check out the effect. It looked a lot like a headless corpse with a jacket over it. I bunched up a towel and shoved it underneath, trying to approximate a head. It remained more hide-the-victim than staggering drunk, but it would have to do. I grabbed the duffel, flung an arm around the body's waist and kicked open the door.

Outside of the restroom's fluorescent glare, the club was dusk blue and dim, like the color put in public toilets to stop junkies from finding a vein. It silvered the graffiti sprayed on the raw brick walls and painted my skin cadaver white. But it helped us blend in with the sea of bodies gyrating in a pulsing mass on the old warehouse floor.

A quick glance around the room showed me shadows flowing along the walls, blocking off the side doors, and others cutting through the crowd like sharks. It was an apt image, since the smell of blood would draw them to us within seconds even through the soup of perfume, alcohol and body odor in the air. It looked like Cheung wasn't planning to make this easy.

I headed for the nearest exit as fast as Ray's stumbling feet would go, but had to stop short. Two large shadows were standing beside the doors. The first had a gun bulge under his sleek black coat; the other looked like a weapon would be an insult to his hulking masculinity. But he was probably faster than he looked. Not all giants are lumbering, at least not when they're also master vampires.

My every instinct said attack, but my instincts always say that. And right now it wouldn't be smart. On my own, two was doable, even two masters. But I wasn't on my own. And a fight would allow the rest of the family time to zero in on our location.

There was some muffled foul language from the duffel. I gave it a poke. "Settle down!"

"Let me out! I'm suffocating in here!"

"You don't have lungs."

"I'm going to puke in this thing."

"You don't have a stomach, either," I told him, steering the body over to the wall. I unzipped the bag and a big nose popped out. "Gah! What the hell have you been carrying in this thing?"

"It's my gym bag."

"It smells like something died in here!"

"If we don't get out of here soon, something might," I told him grimly. "The main exits are guarded. Tell me you've got a secret way out."

"Do you have any idea what those cost?"

Of course. I would decide to kidnap the only vamp dumb enough to skimp on the necessities. "A back door, then!"

"There's a courtyard behind the bar, but it's just a space between buildings. There's no exit that way."

"There's about to be."

We booked it back across the club, wove through the five-person-thick crowd around the bar and pushed through a door. The storeroom proved to be a claustrophobic brick rectangle, with no windows and only a narrow aisle between shelves. But a small breeze drifted through a slightly ajar back door.

I pushed it open and found myself in a narrow courtyard containing broken pallets, bags of garbage and a couple cats. Their eyes glowed at me for an instant before they scampered up a fire escape to safety. On every side, buildings rose tall and dark, hemming us in, as Ray had said. The shortest was three stories, and while I might have scaled it on my own, I couldn't do it towing a half-dead vampire.

It looked like the only way out was the one the cats had taken.

I tugged on the pull-down ladder, wondering how I was going to get Ray's well-padded ass up four flights. And then I wondered if I'd get him up at all when the structure shrieked in protest and refused to budge. Decades' worth of rust clung to my hands and sent a cloud of red flakes into the air. The ladder probably hadn't been touched since the building was erected, maybe a century ago.

It finally came down, but it wasn't wide enough for me to haul anybody up alongside me, and I doubted it would hold the weight of two adults anyway. So I sent the body up first. Its coordination was about what you'd expect for someone without a head, and it didn't help that the stairs shuddered with every step. But amazingly, they looked like they might hold.

Of course, the universe wasted no time in punishing me for that nanosecond of optimism. Halfway up the second landing, a scream of overstressed metal echoed around the courtyard and a hail of old bolts came rattling down. The fire escape tore away from the building on one side and sagged out into the air.

The body stopped, quivering in fear, and one look at Raymond's face showed why. The two parts were obviously in some sort of communication, or it wouldn't have been able to move. But the only thing being communicated at the moment was terror.

So I slapped him.

Furious blue eyes swiveled up to mine. "Wasn't be-heading me *enough*?"

"*Move*. Or you're going to be headless permanently," I hissed.

Ray's eyes swung back to his body, which had slumped over like the corpse it was, causing my jacket to begin to slide off. I moved forward to catch it, and thereby narrowly missed being skewered by a spear of metal that fell off the building. It took out the awning over the back door instead, crumpling the heavy aluminum like paper before slamming into the paving stones.

Ray gave a startled yelp, but the near miss got his body moving again. And this time, he wasn't messing around. Freedom was a few steps away, and he went for it, taking the last few flights with the fire escape collapsing under him. He leapt into the air on its final shudder and grabbed the edge of the roof next door, dangling there precariously.

I didn't wait around to find out if he made it. Rusted metal rattled down the old bricks and exploded against the paving stones, flinging shrapnel everywhere. Along with it went a crashing cacophony of sound loud enough to wake the dead—and that included the dead searching for us.

Chapter Eleven

Grabbing the duffel, I headed back across the court-yard at a run, leaping over fallen pieces while trying to dodge the ones still raining down. Something hit my right shoulder like a hammer blow, but I couldn't waste time seeing how bad it was. I charged back through the storeroom and burst through the door—just in time to see half a dozen vamps converging on it.

I ducked back inside and slammed it behind me. It was sturdy old oak—probably a relic from the club's original incarnation as a factory—but that would buy us seconds at best. Maybe they hadn't seen us, I thought hysterically, before doing a Ray and throwing the lock.

"Did you see that?" Raymond sounded vaguely awed. "Did you see what I did?"

"What's on the other side of this wall?" I asked breathlessly.

"I was like . . . like Superman or something! I almost *flew*—" He broke off as the door shuddered under a heavy blow. So much for hoping they hadn't seen us.

"*Ray!* I need to know—"

"My office is next door. Why?"

"You're going to need to redecorate." I pulled a wad of explosive putty out of one of the duffel's side compartments and worked to get the wrapping off.

"What's that?"

"Something I planned to use on the portal." It was the latest thing, specifically designed to use an energy sink's own power against it. But it ought to do a pretty good job on the wall, too. I tore off a small piece and slapped it in place.

Ray stared at it, his small eyes wide. "Are you kidding me? This is an old building. You'll bring it down on our heads!" He paused for a moment. "And that's all I got left!"

"I'm not using that much," I told him, tugging my jacket back on for protection. I retreated to the other side of the room, threw up an arm to shield my face and pulled my Glock—only to have a leg smash through the bottom half of the door and kick it out of my hand.

So I grabbed my backup Smith & Wesson and emptied a clip into the vamp, but other than shredding the guy's trousers, it didn't have much effect. His flesh absorbed the bullets like water before forcing them out again, the wounds closing almost as soon as they were formed. He was obviously a master; all I was doing was pissing him off.

As he demonstrated by shooting a basketball-sized hole in the top of the door. For once, I didn't feel like complaining about my lack of height. If I'd been a couple inches taller, Raymond wouldn't have been the only one missing a head.

And then a cascade of bullets from a machine gun came through the hole, kind of negating the height advantage. Raymond was screaming, despite the fact that I'd hit the cement floor in front of the door, flattening us out. That didn't stop the stream of bullets, but it allowed me to reach through the hole in the door, grab our attacker's leg and *pull*.

He hit the floor, and I jerked him through the opening. I'd pulled a stake out of my jacket, but I didn't need it; one of the tough old pieces of the splintered door did the job for me. Another vamp yanked him back out, using his body to snap off the remaining shards, and slid through the cleared gap as quick as if he'd been oiled.

I'd hopped back to my feet, but he used the shotgun he'd brought along to sweep my legs out from under me. He tried to bring the butt down on my head, but I jerked aside, got a foot in his sternum and shoved. He staggered into the far wall, and I dove for my Glock. My hand closed on it just as I heard the distinctive sound of a shotgun cock. I looked up to see it leveled on me, and the vamp grinning.

"Mine," he told the others, who were jockeying for position at the new porthole in the door. He noticed my little gun and his lip curled. He spread his arms wide. "Go ahead," he told me. "Give it your best shot."

So I did.

A second later I had a room full of smoke, a jacket coated with vampire bits and a three-foot fissure in the bricks. The bullet had passed through the center of the vamp's chest and hit the patch, setting off the equivalent of half a stick of dynamite. I glanced at the remaining vamps, who were gaping at my weapon. "Okay. Size doesn't *always* matter."

They didn't say anything, and nobody made any attempt to open the door. I snatched up the duffel and scrambled through the hole, ignoring the edges that tore at my flesh. And belatedly noticed white tile, bathroom stalls and a woman with a jagged line of lipstick running from her mouth to her ear.

"Oops," Raymond said.

The woman stopped staring at the hole to stare at my duffel instead. "Th-there's something sticking out of your bag."

I looked down to see a by now familiar nose poking out the side. Damn it, he'd bitten a hole through the nylon. "I don't see anything."

"It's right there!"

"One too many, huh?" I sympathized, pushing Raymond back inside.

"I don't drink."

"Well, maybe you should start!" Raymond yelled, as I burst out into the hall. "I gotta make a living here!"

There was more smoke outside, of the fake variety usually seen on Halloween boiling out of plastic skulls and jack-o'-lanterns. It allowed the laser light show to cut ominous blue flashes through the darkness and ensured that I couldn't see a damn thing. But the sense that allows me to tell when a vampire is near doesn't need sight. It's like a tidal pull in the blood, forceful and elemental. And at the moment, it was shaking me harder than the bass line throbbing under my feet.

The place was crawling with vamps, even more than before. It looked like Cheung had called in some backup. And wasn't that just all I needed?

And then the front doors blew open, allowing another dozen vampires to pour into the room. I don't think most of the patrons noticed, other than those getting jostled aside as the new arrivals cut a swath across the floor. But the power emanating off them almost knocked me down.

They were all masters. Third-level, at a guess, easily able to have courts of their own. Which made it a little ridiculous that they were after one lone dhampir. I mean, I'm good, but I'm not that good. They surged forward, and I didn't even hesitate. I turned on my heel and ran.

The pulse of the music felt like the rhythm of my heart—fast and frantic—as I fought my way over the sticky floor to the elevated DJ booth and climbed the vibrating metal frame. The lousy visibility wouldn't bother the vamps, but it was a different story for me. I needed a vantage point.

The DJ was another young Asian guy with a fall of bleached blond hair. He was also human, judging by the fact that his tank top was stained dark down the spine. "Lost my date," I yelled.

He nodded in time with the deafening music. "What's your name?"

I pretended I couldn't hear him and scanned the room. It was obvious at once that the ground floor was hopeless. The warehouse dated from the bad old days before anyone started worrying about things like natural light or ventilation for the toiling masses. It had no windows that I could see that hadn't been bricked up long ago. But there was a catwalk around half the room with the old manager's office perched in the middle. And I was betting *he'd* had light.

The DJ grabbed the back of my jacket as I started down. "Hey, hey, hey," he said into his microphone, "if anyone out there has lost a lady, she's up here keeping me company. Don't hurry to claim her, all right?"

He turned a spotlight on me, causing the eyes of half the people—and all of the vamps—in the place to swivel in my direction. I hit the switch for strobes, slammed my heavy-ass duffel into the side of the DJ's head and jumped the six feet to the floor. I landed badly enough to almost twist an ankle, and knocked over a guy with a tray of Jell-O shots. The room went black-and-white and stuttering as I slipped in the mess, righted myself and headed for the balcony.

I didn't make it.

Someone darted in from the side, snapped the strap on the duffel and took off. I changed course to follow and saw the duffel disappear into the hallway beside the bar. It was empty by the time I got there, but a door beside the ladies' was just closing. I kicked it back open and got a brief glimpse around—a desk, a chair, a sagging fan set in a water-stained ceiling—and then a furious vampire caught me by the wrists, using his body to pin me to the desk.

I tried to wrench free, but nothing happened. I tried again in disbelief, because I'm stronger than all but the senior masters. This time, he did let go, but only so he could grab my hips instead. He swung me up and slammed me backward onto the scarred wood, clearing the surface with a sweep of his arm. Papers, a laptop, glass and metal went flying, half of it shattering against the nearby wall.

I managed to wrestle a knife out of my boot, but he grabbed it before I could drive it home, flinging it away to land quivering in the side of the fake wood paneling. I got an elbow in a sensitive spot, but he pinned my wrists to the desk. He pressed his hips hard against me and swore softly, viciously, "If we get out of this alive, I will *kill* you!"

Startled out of fighting for a moment, I paused, staring at him. There wasn't much light in the room, but a few beams of pale blue leaked in from the hall. They struck highlights in the thick auburn hair, which as usual was confined by a gold slide at his nape, and turned his face into a sculpture of elegant bone, skin and shadow. It made him look more dangerous than the man I remembered, and he'd been plenty dangerous enough.

But at least I knew why I couldn't move. Tight black jeans and a matching cashmere sweater showed off six feet of solid muscle he didn't need. A first-level master, Louis-Cesare could have held me against the desk with a tendril of power he wouldn't even miss.

"You haven't been alive in four centuries," I pointed out, as he tore off my jacket. My weapons hit the floor, followed in short order by my tank top and bra. "Hey!"

"They saw what you were wearing."

"Pretty soon I'm not going to be wearing anything!"

"Exactly."

He ripped my belt out of its loops and popped the line of buttons on my jeans, all in one smooth motion. I caught his arm. "This isn't going to work. They'll scent us!"

"No, they won't."

"We have a bloody head in a bag!"

"I have hidden talents."

Not so hidden ones, too, I didn't say, as he shoved his own jeans down. It was the only disrobing he bothered to do before pushing me onto my back. The desk was cold against my bare skin, like the steel of the knife he used to cut my thong away.

I started to ask if the vamps had seen the color of my panties, too, but he swallowed the words, kissing me as his fingers worked roughly, expertly, between my thighs. He broke the kiss after a moment, to give me time to breathe, I suppose, but air wasn't what I needed. I knew he was just trying to fool Cheung's boys into believing we were having an assignation, but it had been a long, dry month and, damn it, I'd missed him. My hands fisted in his shirt, giving me leverage to pull him down and kiss him back, brutally.

He tasted sweet, with a bitter edge of hard liquor, and he smelled even better. And he wasn't wearing anything under those jeans. My hands slid down the thickly muscled back to the taut mounds below, fingernails sinking deep.

Olga had definitely been right, I thought vaguely, as a shudder went through him. He raised his head to glare. "That was completely unnecessary."

"Oh, it was necessary," I said, wishing it had been my *teeth*, but I couldn't reach that far, and then he did something with his fingers that made the breath fracture in my throat. The best I could do was a growled command: "Faster, faster, you son of a *bitch*—"

He obliged, although the desk really wasn't built for our current activity, and my head and shoulders fell off the back. Not that I was complaining. Not even when his fangs—*damn him*—sank into the tender flesh his fingers had been tormenting. My spine arched with a combination of pain and pleasure so intense that I didn't even notice when the door burst open.

Until he spun, snarling.

"Sorry," a deep voice said, and the door shut again.

He drew in air he didn't need, his lips glossy and a little swollen. I thought of how they had gotten that way and met his eyes. "If you stop now, *I* will kill you," I told him distinctly.

The threat had no apparent effect, but a shiver went through him when I suddenly grasped evidence that he hadn't been entirely playacting, either. "Dorina ..." The tone was a warning, but I was way past caring.

I tugged him a little, sending a shiver through that strong frame. "Louis-Cesare. It's good to finally have you in hand."

He winced, either at the pun or the sensation, and his right hand tightened on my thigh. His left was occupied with the duffel, which he'd snatched from under the desk as soon as the door closed. I found that pretty telling, considering that he hadn't even bothered to pull his pants up first. "You don't."

"More or less." He was a big boy. Everywhere. "Although I'm a little fuzzy on why you stole my duffel bag."

"It seemed the easiest way to get you off the floor without a fight."

I stared at him incredulously. Louis-Cesare was the dueling champion of the European Senate. He didn't walk away from fights; he relished them. I guess it's true what they say about only being able to think with one head at a time.

"Then why's your hand still on it?" I asked sweetly.

"I'm not the only one who is acting possessive." He stared down at my own hand, blue eyes gleaming. "Are you planning to do anything with that?"

"I'm debating it. Are you going to tell me what you're doing here?"

"That is not your concern."

I stared at him, half in awe, half in exasperation. Louis-Cesare had been born the son of a king, and none of the centuries that had passed since had diminished his arrogance one iota. I had his dick in my hand, and he was still acting like he was the one in control.

"Okay." I gave him an experimental stroke. It was a new interrogation technique, but I thought it had possibilities. "How about a trade? Give me back my property and I'll return yours—in good working order."

He didn't look too impressed. So I varied my technique and was rewarded with a shift of hips and a heavy weight pressing into my palm. His eyes squeezed shut for a moment, and when they opened again, they were darker. But he wasn't about to admit that I was getting to him.

Stubborn vampire. The evidence was rather . . . outstanding . . . in my favor. I picked up the pace, wondering if I should gentle him along to make this last longer or stroke him harder just to see how crazy I could make him. I felt a reaction ripple through his body and heard a hiss through tightly clenched teeth.

An answer if I'd ever gotten one.

But a second later, my wrist was caught in a grip of steel. "The vampire does not belong to you."

I shrugged. "Give me back the *Senate's* property then. And while you're at it, you could explain why everyone is suddenly so interested in a loser like Ray."

"Hey!" A protest drifted up from the duffel.

But the only answer I got from Louis-Cesare was a callused fingertip tracing a swollen lump on my cheekbone. It was a minor wound, collected who knew where, and his touch was unexpectedly gentle. But something about it made me tremble. My skin felt too sensitive suddenly, enough that I didn't know whether the barely there touch hurt or felt good. But it *felt*.

Not too long ago, I'd thought that was something I'd forgotten how to do. Lately, people kept reminding me, with Louis-Cesare's name at the top of the list. I still wasn't sure if that was a good thing or not.

His eyes dropped to my nipples, which had pebbled in the cool air. He grasped one of my breasts, firmly and without hesitation, like he had some kind of claim on it. It filled his hand, as I've never been small that way, at least. He seemed to approve, based on the squeezing that was going on. And God that felt . . . pretty amazing, actually.

He ducked his head, silky hair tickling my skin, and ran a wet and raspy tongue over the peaked tip. The small contact was shockingly arousing. Fresh sweat broke out all over my body, and my legs wrapped around his thighs, clenching when the hot, wet suction started. It made my eyes want to close, made me want to stop wasting time with questions, made me want to—

"I need him, Dorina," he murmured against my skin.

Okay, now I was sure.

I moved my thumb an inch, just brushing across the sensitive tip of him. "Don't try that shit on me," I said evenly. And the next second I was on my back on the desk again, lengthways this time, so he had room to crawl up my body.

He trapped my hands over my head, eyes burning. "And what 'shit' would that be? The kind your father sent you to stir up?"

"What are you talking about?"

A laugh huffed out of him, or more accurately a breath of air, because there was no amusement in it. "Do you think I'm stupid? You rail against him, threaten him, swear you hate him, but when he snaps his fingers, you go running!"

"Bullshit! Mircea has enough yes types around him; it's part of what's wrong with him. But I'm not one, as you damn well know."

Sapphire eyes searched my face. In the right light, they could look anything from cobalt to aquamarine; but they were always guarded. My fantasies tended to forget that.

"I can't believe a word you say," he told me roughly, although it sounded more like he was talking to himself.

"When did you decide that?" I demanded, stung. The last time I'd seen him, we'd been filthy, bloody and half dead—and would have been all the way there if we hadn't learned to trust each other.

"When I saw you here tonight—" His fingers gripped my arms, his body radiating a tangle of emotion that I couldn't even begin to unravel. "I should have known he would send you."

"Why the hell shouldn't he?" I asked, confused and angry. "I'm—"

"Then you may tell him that I will not be distracted from my duty. Regardless of what temptation he throws in my way!"

"Tell him yourself!" I said, stung. And to think I'd actually missed the bastard. "And don't talk to me about duty! You disappear for a month and then show up only to—"

My mind tripped and stuttered at the feel of him sliding languorously up and down the length of me. It was an awful tease, a deliberate distraction. And it worked, damn it. My heart rate sped up and my breath came faster and I wanted. Now.

A shiver shot through him, and he kissed me, deep and hungry. I approved of the tongue in my mouth, the heat radiating through his clothes, even the feel of his jeans against my naked legs. But that damn sweater was too much. It was as thin and soft as silk, contrasting perfectly with the hard body below.

Louis-Cesare in cashmere had a completely unfair advantage. I tugged it off over his head, but the heady rush of skin on skin was even worse. Particularly when he suddenly pulled me into his lap in one smooth move that had me straddling his hips.

He spread his own legs, pulling mine apart as well. A large hand dipped down to my ass before sweeping up to my shoulder blades, pressing me against heat and hard muscle. The other slipped between my legs, and a callused thumb began to move back and forth, tauntingly slow, like the barely swishing tail of a cat.

I managed to choke back an embarrassing whimper, but there was no way to hide full-body goose bumps. And still he just stroked. "Stop teasing," I hissed. "Or can't you find it?"

His tongue ran up my neck to my ear, hot breath on my skin, teeth teasing my lobe. He bit down just as he suddenly thrust knuckle deep—and hit the spot on the first damn try. My body bucked against him, clenching desperately, and my teeth sank into his shoulder to stifle a moan.

"I think I can find it," he told me, amused.

"But do you know what to do with it?" I gasped, after a moment.

He did.

In moments I was shivering, my muscles quivering and aching, hovering on the brittle edge ... until a final touch provided that tiny bit of extra friction, and everything came apart in a blaze of gold. My hands clenched on sweat-slicked shoulders, and I had to bite my lip to swallow the scream that bubbled up in my throat.

He grasped my hips, holding me tight as it went on and on, bright shock waves radiating outward to my skin, like my body was a live-wire that kept pulsing with pleasure. My hands fell away after a moment, too weak to hold on. He laid me back against the desk, kissing my neck under my sweat-slicked hair. My eyes slipped closed on a satisfied, groaning sigh.

"If that was hello, you need to go away more often," I told him shakily.

There was no answer. After a moment, I sat up, wanting to see those ever-changing eyes looking at me. And saw the door shutting instead.

It took me a disoriented second to realize that I was sprawled over the desk, naked and alone. Louis-Cesare was gone, and a brief glance informed me that the duffel was, too. Son of a *bitch*!

I hit the floor, wobbled embarrassingly on unsteady legs, and threw open the door. The hall was empty except for a guy sneaking a smoke. He looked vaguely familiar for some reason. He caught sight of me and almost swallowed his cigarette.

A glance down informed me that I'd forgotten a little something. I ducked back inside and slammed the door, but a quick look around showed me what I'd feared. He'd left my weapons, but that sneaky, triple-damned son of a rat bastard had taken my clothes. All of them.

The mirror on one wall informed me that my lips were swollen, that my hair was clinging to my sweaty cheeks and that there were hickeys on my breasts. Very little embarrasses me anymore, but even I preferred not to go out looking like this.

I cracked the door again. The guy hadn't budged. I looked him over for a second and suddenly it clicked. "Still want me to be mean to you?"

His eyes widened. "Yeah?"

"Well, come on then."

A minute later, I had an oversized T-shirt that worked as a dress, a belt to shove my weapons into and a too-large leather jacket to toss over it all. I slammed out into the hall, leaving the guy tied to the desk chair by his underwear. Judging by his expression, he'd just learned a valuable lesson about screwing with strange women.

It was something I intended to teach a certain master vampire, as soon as I caught his beautiful thieving ass.

Chapter Twelve

The main room of the club was still packed, but I didn't see Louis-Cesare among the partiers. It had taken me only a few minutes to get out of the back, but that was more than enough for someone who can move like the wind. And who probably had an escape route worked out in advance.

The surprise was that Cheung's men seemed to have gone as well, probably off on a wild-goose chase. The few vampires left milling about were Raymond's boys, looking lost and confused, and none even tried to keep me from leaving. Or even seemed to know that they should.

I guess they hadn't checked the bathroom yet.

Outside, the rain we'd had for a steady week had turned the street into a glossy black mirror. It reflected red splashes from the lanterns edging the club's roofline, a green electronics store sign next door and a yellow Buddha buzzing across the road. But no arrogant master vampires.

Not being a total fool, I had of course tagged him back at the club. According to the little charm, he was three streets over and moving fast. I moved faster and caught up with the charm on a corner—attached to the collar of a stray dog.

"Very funny, smart-ass," I muttered, and retraced my steps.

Scent turned out to be no more useful than sight or magic. There were too many competing scents: ginger and garlic from a guy selling chicken wings, incense floating from the open door of a shop, car exhaust and garbage. To make matters worse, the rain was still drizzling down in patches, wiping out pieces of the scentscape like someone had taken an eraser to it.

After fifteen minutes, I admitted defeat. Most dhampirs have heightened senses, and my nose is considerably keener than a human's. But no way was I following Louis-Cesare through the scent maze of Chinatown. He was well and truly gone, and it was my fault. I'd let him waltz out the goddamned door and hadn't even tried to stop him.

I leaned against a corrugated door and waited for my heart rate to slow. It didn't seem to feel like obliging. Damn it! I never fell for that sort of thing, couldn't even remember the last time I'd been so stupid.

Oh, wait. Yes, I could—the last time I'd dealt with Louis-fucking-Cesare.

I scowled. Louis-Cesare might be a prince in Europe, but this was my territory, my home turf. He was going to learn the hard way that he couldn't come in here and dick with me and not pay the price. When I finished with him, Raymond was going to look good by comparison.

Or then again, maybe not. Because old Ray was looking kind of rough by the time I located his body, huddled in a fetal position on the roof of the building next to the club. His shirt was missing, his pants were dirty and blood-streaked and he'd lost a shoe. For a minute there, I almost forgot about the missing head.

He didn't hear me approach, not surprisingly, considering his ears were probably on the other side of the city by now. But as soon as I put a hand on him, he leapt up and swung wildly. I ducked, but of course he couldn't see it and just kept on going. That was a problem, considering that he was steps away from a three-story drop.

I got a hand on his waistband, jerking him back from the edge before we found out just how much abuse a vampire body could take. He fell hard against me as I wrestled him back onto the roof. He also copped a feel.

"Cut it out, unless you don't mind losing a few more

body parts," I told him, before I remembered that he couldn't hear me.

His hands jerked away like they'd been burned, and he stopped, dead still.

I did, too, as a completely new idea occurred. "Sit down," I told Raymond, who obligingly buckled his knees and parked his tush on the edge of the roof. His legs swung free over the courtyard below like a little boy's. A little headless boy coated in gore, but still.

There are other explanations, I told myself. He could have stopped feeling me up once he'd figured out who I was; he could have sat down because he was weak from blood loss. I might be totally misreading this.

"Raise your right arm if you can hear me," I said, and the arm obligingly shot up.

Or maybe not.

I patted down my borrowed jacket, but found only change, some matches and half a pack of cigarettes. But Ray had a cell phone in his pocket, although he didn't seem inclined to give it up. "What?" I asked, slapping his hands. "It's not like you can use it."

He gave me the finger.

I ignored him and dialed a number that doesn't show up in the phone book. It took me a minute to get through because there was some sort of party going on. And because the staff hates me.

"Senator Mircea Basarab," I repeated for the fourth time, several minutes later.

"Lord Mircea cannot be disturbed," yet another supercilious voice informed me. "Might I take a message?"

"Yes. You can tell him that his daughter's on the phone. And if he doesn't take my call, I'm going to dump that corpse he wanted in the river."

There was some murmuring in the background, but no answer. Vamp #4 hadn't hung up, though. I could hear party noises: music, laughter and the muted chime of fine crystal. And then a voice that managed to be more beautiful than all three.

"Dorina, are you all right?"

It was unfair what vampires could do with intonation,

especially that one. Warmth, concern, love—it was all there in one short sentence, and it was all a lie. He was in a good mood because he thought I had Ray. He was going to be a little less amused when he discovered my part didn't talk.

"Why wouldn't I be?" I asked, my voice sounding harsh in my ears.

"This isn't one of the numbers we have on file for you."

"Yeah, well, there's been a snag."

"Do you require assistance?"

"I require answers. It seems there's a few things even I don't know about vamps."

"Such as?"

"Say there's a fifth-level master who's lost his head—"

"I assume you mean that literally," was the dry response.

"—and say that said appendage is no longer in the immediate area—"

"It's *missing*?"

"I'll be glad to give you a play-by-play later! Right now, I need to know why a headless body would continue to hear and obey commands."

"It wouldn't." The sounds of the party faded, so I assumed he'd moved somewhere more secure for this conversation. Good. He might actually plan to cough up a few facts for a change.

"Yeah, well, empirical evidence would suggest otherwise."

There was silence for a moment, while he debated it. I doubted he felt any shame about siring a monster who regularly went around killing his kind, but only because that particular emotion wasn't in his repertoire. But he nonetheless avoided telling me any facts that might make my job easier. He was probably afraid that I'd use them against him someday.

Smart man.

"A vampire's body is connected on the physical plane like a human's," he finally told me. "But we also have a metaphysical connection to our corporeal form that is not easily severed."

"So, metaphysically speaking, he still has a head?"

"Yes. Its sensory perceptions are dulled, of course, and will rapidly become more so. But for a time, our limbs can move and carry out commands even when detached from—"

"I know that." I should; I'd been attacked by enough hacked-off body parts through the years. "I need to know if the brain can send more than just signals to muscle groups. Can it transmit information—like where it is?"

"That is what I am attempting to tell you," Mircea said, sounding faintly annoyed. No vamp ever dared interrupt him like that. I was such a trial. "The metaphysical link becomes strained without the physical to reinforce it. Eventually, it will fade altogether, usually in about a week at that power level—"

"I know that, too! I just want to know if it can draw me a freaking map!"

"—with the higher brain functions being the first casualty."

Shit. "So no map."

"At that level, I am surprised he is mobile. However, he may yet be of use. The connection will be stronger the closer the severed parts are to each other. The body should therefore act somewhat like a Geiger counter, telling you by its strength and coordination how close you are to your goal."

"So, the more energetic the closer, the more sluggish the farther away?"

"Essentially. How animated is it?"

I glanced down at Ray, who had confiscated the cigarettes. He had somehow managed to light one without barbecuing himself, and now he was smoking it—through the hole in his neck. I understood the need for a nerve settler, but still . . .

"Pretty animated."

"Then the missing item remains in Manhattan. Give me your location. I will have a search team join you."

I didn't reply, because three vampires had entered

the courtyard and were looking around. They weren't Ray's—I could feel the energy they generated from here, which meant that they were masters. Even worse, at least two of them were Hounds.

The two in front were scenting the air, mouths open, looking almost comically like their nickname for a moment. But there was nothing funny about it. Hounds— vamps with an almost uncanny sense of smell—were one of the few creatures who might have a chance at tracking Louis-Cesare through the scentscape of a city.

Or of picking up the trail of Ray's other half.

Almost as though he'd heard me, the lead vamp lifted his head and sniffed, deep. A second later, bright black eyes were staring directly into my own. "Dorina?" Mircea's voice was a static tickle in my ear.

"No time."

"What is it?"

"Hounds." I snapped the phone shut and towed Ray across the roof. The other side overlooked the street, which was empty but wouldn't stay that way for long. And by the time I maneuvered a stumbling vampire down three flights of steps, they'd be on us.

It looked like we were going to find out about that abuse thing, after all.

I waited until I saw them emerge from the club and vanish into our building. They should have left someone in the street, maybe several someones. But there were only three of them, and they had to know by now what I was.

Occasionally those old legends came in handy.

"Uh, Ray? The next step's kind of steep," I said, and pushed him off the roof.

He landed on the top of an ancient tan Impala parked along the curb, shattering a window and punching a hole in the top with one leg. That was lucky because I didn't have time to break in properly. I landed hard on the sidewalk beside him, suppressed a groan when my ankle twisted, stumbled over to the car and yanked him out.

I looked up to see three furious faces glaring down at us from the roofline. They prepared to jump as Ray rolled off the top and began desperately trying to get the door on his side open. I reached in through the hole and popped the lock on mine, and was about to do the same for him when he busted out the window and slithered through the forest of shards.

Each to his own.

I wasn't exactly unskilled in the fine art of carjacking, even under pressure. But that was with proper tools. I'd brought them along, just in case, but they were in the duffel along with everything else. I mentally added another tick beside Louis-Cesare's debt as I feverishly worked to get the car started.

A bullet drilled into the seat just beside my left ear. I pulled my Glock, slammed another clip home and pressed it into Ray's shaking hands. "Try not to shoot me or the car," I told him, and crawled under the dashboard.

The vamps must have landed in a V formation around the car, because the bullets came from three directions at once. Ray returned fire wildly, and from the sound of things, he killed a bag of trash, the windshield of a car across the road and the streetlight overhead. I doubt he so much as winged the vamps, but they nonetheless backed off, waiting for him to run out of ammo. Bullets might not kill them, but no one likes getting shot. And I guess they didn't think we were going anywhere.

It was a point of view I was starting to share, as I struggled to strip wires without the proper tools and without electrocuting myself. Then Ray started kicking me. I glanced up and saw him miming needing another clip. I shook my head. "They're in the damn duffel!"

He kicked me again, just to be an ass, then began chucking things out of the hole in the roof. The car must have served as one of Chinatown's infamous tailgate stores during the day, because the back held several cases of knockoff DVDs, fake Gucci handbags and a big box of glass bongs. Ray threw it all, as well as a large portion of the backseat, but it wasn't enough. A vampire's fist smashed through the windshield and grabbed him.

The vamp tried to pull Ray through the shattered window, but I grabbed his waistband and pulled back. Ray's stylish khakis strained and then split down the middle like stripper wear, leaving each of us holding a leg and him in a pair of red satin boxers with *Feeling Lucky?* emblazoned across the crotch. "Not really," I said, and punched the vamp in the face.

He staggered back, but the two others had figured out that we were out of ammo—of all kinds—and rushed forward. One of them reached through the hole in the top and grabbed Ray, by the arm this time. That left me struggling one-handed to break the lock on the steering column—with a knife, no less—while holding on to Ray by one hairy leg.

It would have been easier if he hadn't been struggling like he was afraid he'd end up the same way as his pants. I kept getting kicked in the head, which did nothing for my concentration. And to make bad matters worse, the club doors banged open and more vamps poured out.

But instead of jumping us, they went for Cheung's men. It looked like the boss had neglected to order Ray's boys not to help him, and protecting their master is one of a vamp's foremost priorities. Not that they were any match for the much more senior vamps, but they did manage to overwhelm one by sheer numbers. Unfortunately, it wasn't the one holding Ray.

I'd finally gotten the steering wheel unlocked, but I couldn't start the damn engine and hold on to Ray at the same time. Then someone embedded a tire iron in the vamp's head, sending him staggering backward. I started the car, and when the master launched himself at the windshield again, I ran him over.

Of course, that just pissed him off. I saw one of the other vamps run for a dark blue Mercedes coupe parked down the street. And Ray's boys weren't going to be able to delay them for long without getting shredded. "Buckle up," I told Ray, and floored it.

I concentrated on putting some distance between us and the club, while he rooted around in the glove box. He threw a flashlight out the window, and did the same with a tire gauge. But a ballpoint pen he kept. I skidded around a corner onto Canal Street, and he started jabbing me in the leg with it. Hard.

"Give me that!" I tried to take it away from him, but he jerked it back and started waving it around. It took me a second to realize that he was making scribbling motions.

I got this weird idea and started looking for some paper, but there was none to be had. I did come up with an old map of the city, however, in a pocket behind the seat. I gave it to him to doodle on while I did my best to confuse our trail, hoping against hope that he'd manage to circle his missing piece's location.

He stabbed at the paper with all the coordination of a two-year-old. He finally proffered his masterpiece when we stopped at a red light. The lines were wobbly and slanting, like a right-handed person trying to communicate with the left. But they were definitely words.

I snatched it out of his fingers and held it up to the windshield. *I HATE YOU.*

"You can write?" I stared at him incredulously. So much for expecting Mircea to give away trade secrets. "Then how about telling me where you are?"

Ray took the map back and painstakingly crafted another sentence around its margins. *I DON'T KNOW!*

"What do you mean, you don't know? You've got to be able to see something! A street sign, the name of a shop, anything!"

IT'S DARK.

"What the hell do you mean, it's dark? You're a vampire! You see at night!"

NOT IN A DUFFEL BAG!

"A duffel with a hole in it," I reminded him impatiently. "Look around!"

AND SEE WHAT? I'M IN A TRUNK!

I frowned. "A car trunk? Are you moving?"

NO.

"Give me sounds, then. Smells, anything!"

THERE'S NO NOISE. AND ALL I SMELL ARE YOUR DIRTY SOCKS.

Great. There weren't too many places that would be totally silent to a vampire's ears, even a somewhat-mangled vampire. So they were in an enclosed garage, probably underground. And Manhattan only had about a thousand of those.

"Try harder!" I ground out. "We have a week here, remember? Then you and I are both—"

The car behind us laid on the horn, and Raymond and I simultaneously flipped it off. A second later, the interior of the Impala was strobed with garish light. I glanced in my mirror and confirmed that, yes, we'd just given the finger to a policeman. At least we're wearing our seat belts, I thought, and hit the gas.

The cop had gotten out of his car before I took off, giving me a few seconds while he scrambled back into his vehicle. I used it to grab the phone. "You know that assistance you mentioned? This would be a good time," I said when, miracle of miracles, Mircea actually answered himself.

"Where are you?"

"Headed south on Mott. Cop on my tail."

"The *human* police?"

"Yes!"

"And this constitutes an emergency?"

"It does if he draws attention to us," I hissed, as a dark Mercedes coupe did a 180 and swerved into the street behind the cop.

I hate being right all the time, I thought, and floored it.

"I'll arrange something," Mircea said, his voice going crisp. "Remain on the line."

The cop turned on the siren as I whipped onto Hester, and also took the turn on a dime, while no doubt radioing for backup. And in case I'd had any doubt about who was in the coupe, it stayed glued to the cop's tail. Mircea finally came back on the phone to give me a complicated set of directions that had me totally lost in less than five minutes, but didn't do the same to my pursuers.

"I'm hearing multiple sirens now," I pointed out.

"Not for long."

Mircea had barely finished speaking when a huge moving van rumbled out of an alley. I managed to squeak by on the sidewalk, sacrificing the front bumper to a fire hydrant, but the cop wasn't so lucky. He stood on the brakes, judging by the sound, but still plowed straight into the side of it. The coupe rear-ended him and their combined force pushed the truck onto the sidewalk and took out a candy store.

"If I'd known you were that efficient, I'd have asked for help before," I told Mircea.

"You don't usually require it." It was mild enough, but it sounded like a rebuke.

"I don't usually get mugged by family, either!"

"Who?" Mircea asked sharply.

"Radu's bright-eyed boy. You might have mentioned Louis-Cesare was involved."

"I was not informed." His voice suggested that someone was going to pay dearly for that little lapse.

"There's a lot of that going around," I said tightly.

"Meaning?"

"That I don't think it's coincidence that three first-level masters from three different Senates all suddenly formed an intense desire to talk to—"

"Dorina!"

"—a certain person on the same night. There's more here than you bothered to tell me." Not like that was new.

"It should have been an easy errand. You didn't need to know."

"Oh, no. No, no. That's not how I work. If I'm going to take someone's *freaking head*, I need to know why! You want blind obedience, send one of your boys." It suddenly occurred to me to wonder why he hadn't.

"You do freelance assignments for many people," Mircea said, before I could ask. "You were not as easily connected with me as one of my own stable."

"I hate when you do that," I told him.

"Do what?"

"Answer questions before I ask them. It makes it seem

like our conversations are planned out four or five steps ahead, and you're just waiting for me to catch up."

"If that were the case, they would not end in arguments much of the time."

"Most of those arguments are because of this kind of thing. Start trusting me with the truth, or use someone else."

"I will explain the situation later, if you wish it." Translation: it's bad enough that I don't want to talk about it over the phone. "Did Louis-Cesare mention what his interest was in your errand?"

"He wasn't feeling chatty. But probably the same as yours. Whatever that is."

He was silent for a moment. "I sincerely hope not," he said quietly.

It really is amazing what they can do with their voices, I thought, as gooseflesh broke out over my arms. I couldn't translate that particular tone, because I'd never heard it before. But it had sounded a lot like: I'd hate to have to kill a member of the family.

"Come again?"

"Pull over. My men will locate you and assist with the search." Translation: I'll have my loyal minions take over and find Louis-Cesare, because you might not like what I plan to do to him.

I stared at the phone for a moment. I owed Louis-Cesare a world of hurt, and I fully intended to deliver. But that wasn't the same thing as throwing him to the lions. This was personal, and until somebody bothered to give me a good reason otherwise, it was going to remain that way.

"Sorry. I didn't get that," I said.

"Dorina! Pull off and wait for—"

"I'll call you back," I told him, then chucked the phone out the window so he couldn't use it to track me.

It looked like we were on our own.

Chapter Thirteen

A quick check in the rearview mirror showed that the coupe was back on our tail, with a crumpled front bumper but no other obvious damage. It had also acquired a buddy, a black sedan. It sped past the accident, passed the coupe and was coming up fast.

Ray flapped a hand frantically at me and held up the map. *HE'S AT THE CLUB. I RECOGNIZE THE CARPET.*

"The club? But why would he go back—"

The sedan rammed us from behind, and it was a hell of a hit. We went spinning into an intersection, barely missed a motorcyclist and didn't miss a streetlight. Fortunately, the Impala was from the era when cars were built like tanks. Even more fortunately, the light toppled onto the sedan as it tried to follow us onto Leonard Street, and put a mass of white cracks in the windshield. Things were starting to look up until the coupe screeched in behind us, and our front left wheel started going soft.

I didn't know if we'd run over some glass or if the tire had just been crappy all along, but either way, we were screwed. A bullet whizzed through the air, like an exclamation point on that thought, and took out my driver's-side mirror. And Ray stuck the map in front of my face again.

It was flapping in the breeze, and there wasn't a lot of light. But even so I managed to see that he'd circled a street five or six blocks ahead. "Read the map," I told him impatiently. "That's a dead end."

He snatched it back and wrote *PORTAL* over the top in bold black letters.

"That doesn't help! If I stop, they'll shoot us before we get anywhere near it!" Not to mention that portals give me the creeps, and that's even when I knew where they went.

Ray shook a fist at me and stabbed the spot, repeatedly. If he'd had a head, he'd have been screaming it off. "I get it!" I told him, stabbing back with my finger. "But I can't stop, and cars don't go through portals!"

We were rammed again before he could respond, and the pen in his hand went flying. But he really didn't need it. I didn't know what our odds were of surviving the portal, but they had to be better than staying here.

"You better be right about this," I told him, and swerved hard to the left.

There aren't many true dead ends in Manhattan, but this one qualified. On either side were tall buildings and narrow sidewalks, and in front, only more of the same. There was a walkway for pedestrians that cut through to another street, but it didn't look wide enough for the car. And then it didn't matter, because Ray wrenched the wheel toward the plywood-covered front of a restaurant.

We hit going about forty, which doesn't sound like a lot unless you're plowing into a wall of wood. The plywood front was apparently real enough, because it splintered and flew everywhere. As did glass, brick and drywall as we hit something fairly substantial on the other side. But there must have been an active portal in there somewhere, because I felt the usual nauseating drop as it caught us.

I'd never heard of portals being approved for vehicular use, and now I knew why. There was suddenly no road anymore, no up or down, no anything but a rushing slur of color and noise and out-of-control momentum. We were tossed down its long gullet, twisted violently around and then hurled out onto a quiet, tree-shaded street. Upside down.

We hit the ground hard, smashing in what was left of

the roof and shattering the remaining windows, before flipping twice. Then something caught on the asphalt, slinging us sideways toward the curb—and the very large, very hard-looking tree just beyond it. I couldn't do anything—the engine had died, and anyway, there was no time. I braced for impact.

It didn't come. Instead, we rode a wave of sparks toward the side of the road, with various metal bits cutting deep gouges into the street. They slowed our momentum somewhat, but we still hit the curb hard enough to tip us over onto one side. We scraped along the gutter like that until the car finally came to a halt. It teetered on the edge for a long moment, while deciding whether to give up the ghost or not. Then it gave a metallic sort of whine and slowly fell back onto all four tires.

I clutched the steering wheel with nerveless hands, wondering why I wasn't in a thousand pieces, while the car bounced up and down like a boat on rough seas. I finally swallowed and glanced to the side, to see Ray clinging to the seat next to me. He was clutching it backward, with a leg wrapped around one side, and vibrating from missing head to toe.

"I told you to buckle up," I said shakily.

He'd have probably flipped me off, but that would have required moving, and he and the seat appeared to be welded into one entity. That was a problem, because we weren't out of the woods yet. If we could use the portal, so could the vamps, as soon as they figured out it was there. And that wouldn't take them long, since there weren't too many ways we could have vanished into thin air.

"Come on, Ray." I tugged at him, but he was having none of it. He was clinging to the seat like it was a lifeline, his fingers buried deep into the leather cushion. "You know we can't stay here!"

Nothing.

I tried pulling his fingers out of the seat manually, but as soon as I let go of one, plop, back in the seat it went. "It's like a roller coaster, Ray. If you don't get out, they make you go again."

That did it. He scrambled out of the wreckage, but then the portal activated, and I had to drag him back in. There was no way the car was going to start, or drive if it did. But I turned the ignition anyway, because it was even less likely that we were going to outrun a group of masters on foot.

Unbelievably, the engine caught. I gave a whoop of disbelief and pressed the gas. For a second, nothing happened. Then the mostly flat tires hit the asphalt with a flapping sound, and we slowly lurched forward. We'd gone maybe half a block when the coupe came slinging into the road out of nowhere.

It landed on one end, hitting hard enough to send it somersaulting into the air before it smashed back down, almost on top of us. Humans would have been dead, but the crash did not noticeably inconvenience the vamps. They immediately began piling out of the car, and one of them saw us. Three black blurs started down the road after us—and disappeared.

It took me a second to realize that they had been broadsided by the sedan. It had come hurtling out of the portal at maybe fifty miles an hour, smashed into them and then into the tree, and burst into flames. I just sat there for a second, feeling the heat on my face and watching car parts fly through the air, because I don't get that kind of luck.

And then lights started coming on in brownstones all along the road, which didn't look like it got a lot of traffic—especially of our dubious variety. Concerned citizens were probably dialing the cops right now, giving me yet another reason to get gone. I floored it, and we took off, going all of twenty miles an hour.

I chewed a thumbnail and wondered how much time this bought me. I suspected it wouldn't be a lot. The vamps in the pileup might be out of commission, but it didn't matter because they'd had plenty of time during the chase to call for backup. And with two flat tires, a whine in the engine and something grinding ominously under the dash, no way could we outrun them.

We needed to go to ground, but if we did, the Hounds would be on us in no time.

This is why I hate Uptown, I thought, staring around at the well-tended brownstones of the wealthy. They kept their cars in luxury, air-conditioned garages. Not to mention that they were probably all late models I couldn't have hot-wired even with the tools I didn't have. I was a Downtown kind of girl, and this was a strange land.

I clamped my teeth on what I suspected would be an hour-long string of obscenities. Not that I had an hour. *Come on, come on, think! You've lived here for years. There has to be* someone—

I got a glimpse of the nearest street sign and stood on the brakes, craning my neck to be sure. I parked the Impala in the middle of the road, tossed my jacket over Ray's stump and dragged him over the seat behind me. Come to think of it, I did know one Uptown kind of guy.

I just hoped like hell he was home.

"Home" to senior masters traveling outside of their territories could mean a lot of things. For those on Senate business, it usually meant staying at one of the Senate's many properties worldwide. But if they were traveling for pleasure—or if they were up to no good that they didn't want their fellow senators to know about—they usually sponged off a subordinate. But what if they didn't have a flunky in the area? Then they went to the vamp equivalent of a hotel. They stayed at the Club.

Vampire owned and Senate approved, with branches in most major cities, the Club provided visiting masters with luxury, convenience and, most important, security. If someone wasn't on the approved list, they didn't get in. And I was most definitely not on that list.

Fortunately, I was with someone who was.

"Raymond Lu to see Prince Radu Basarab," I told the little bald daub of a desk clerk.

He didn't answer, being too busy gaping at Ray's gory stump. My jacket had fallen off somewhere in the mad dash here, and even I had to admit that the result was kind of gruesome. The blood flow had finally stopped, though, so that was something.

"I—I—"

"Radu Basarab," I repeated slowly. "He's here, right?"

The vamp swallowed, and his hand disappeared under the counter, his shoulder jerking as he repeatedly stabbed the panic button. I glanced over my shoulder and wished whoever was in charge would hurry the hell up already. And then it was too late.

A truck rumbled down the street, its bed full of men. They were seated on benches along each side, like a bunch of soldiers on their way to a fight, which looked a little out of place in this area. It was pretty accurate, though, I realized a second later, as a streetlamp caught a familiar face.

It was one of Cheung's boys, the one I'd fought in the storeroom. He must have been a senior-level master, because that shot should have killed him. Instead, livid and puckered scars crisscrossed his face and neck, and disappeared into the collar of the new shirt he'd acquired. He'd probably taken it off a subordinate, because it was too small, showing off a large indentation where his stomach ought to be. He'd heal eventually, of course, but in the meantime, he looked a little peevish.

Scarface spied me through the leaded glass in the front door and his mouth dropped open—for a split second, until he leveled his shotgun at me. I jerked to the side, and it blew a hole through the door and across the room and would have taken out Ray's head, if he still had one. Instead, it exploded against the expensive wood paneling behind the desk.

"Never mind. I'll find him myself," I said, and dragged Ray over the counter.

We dashed down a hall and ran straight into a group of well-armed security. "Oh, my God, look what they did!" I screamed, and pointed at Ray, who obligingly slumped against the wall. The security guard shied back; then his jaw set, and he and the rest of the team streamed past, headed for the lobby.

Ray and I scurried ahead as the sound of shots, curses and breaking glass echoed down the hall. A waiter coming out of the kitchen saw Ray and dropped a tray of glasses. "Have you seen Prince Basarab?" I asked him. He just stood there, the tray clutched to his chest, and didn't say anything. So I poked him. He jumped and stared at me instead. "Radu!" I repeated.

He pointed up the stairs, and Ray and I took them two at a time. Vamps were peering out of all the doors on this floor, and none of them was 'Du, so I kept going. But at the top of the next flight of stairs, a handsome young man in a light blue dressing gown was just pulling a door shut behind him. I thought I recognized him, and sure enough, he saw me and smiled. "Dorina, isn't it?"

"That would be me." The guy was one of Radu's humans, brought along as a snack, among other things. I didn't remember his name, but it didn't matter. I doubted very much if most of the vamps did, either.

He pushed sweaty blond hair off his neck. "I thought so. Things always get so much more ... lively ... whenever you're around." He looked past my shoulder. "Radu was wondering what all the commotion was about, but I suppose you'll tell him."

"You bet."

He glanced at Ray and made a little moue of distaste. "So much for a quiet weekend," he sighed, and edged on by.

I slipped into the room he'd just left, closed the door and turned to see Louis-Cesare's maker sitting up in bed. Radu Basarab shared his brother's darkly handsome good looks, most of which were on display at the moment because he appeared to be wearing only a sheet. He snatched it up breast high, like a modest woman, and stared at me out of annoyed turquoise eyes.

"Dory. You can't be here, you know. Really you can't."

"Why not? This is a vampire club." I nudged Ray. "He's a vampire."

"He doesn't have a head."

"Okay, most of a vampire. And you said we'd get together while you were in town."

"I said I would come see you," he said crossly. "That's a very different thing! And what are you doing?"

I looked up from settling Ray into a camel-colored wingback chair. "What am I supposed to do with him? Prop him in a corner?"

Radu threw up his hands, but he stopped bitching long enough to wrap the sheet around himself and pad across to the bathroom. He emerged a moment later in a quilted orange silk robe and threw a towel at me. "For his neck. You have no idea what they charge here for incidentals. It's a disgrace."

"Why aren't you staying with Mircea, then?"

Radu made a face. "Because of those damn races—"

"Races?"

"The World Championships, Dory!"

"Of what?" I asked, spreading the towel along Ray's chair back. He didn't really need it, but arguing with Radu was a pointless occupation. His conversational style defied all logic except his own. And we were going to get interrupted in about thirty seconds anyway.

"Ley-line racing. You know, the mages' favorite sport."

"I don't keep up with it," I said, listening to the bumps, crashes and shouts coming from downstairs.

"Well, neither do I! That's the point. I planned this visit weeks ago, assuming that of course I would stay with Mircea. Only to be told that he was already hosting guests and was full up."

"What about vamp central?"

"If you mean the Senate's East Coast headquarters, I tried there, too. But it's the same story. I told them I didn't need much space, although considering all I do for them, I would have thought they could have found something suitable. But even when I offered to stay in a single room—"

"The horror." I wandered over to a rosewood chiffonier, which looked like it might have been converted into something interesting.

"—they insisted that nothing was available! Reducing me to this. I tell you, the things I do for family—"

"Family?"

The door burst open, and three security officers rushed in. Radu ignored them in favor of narrowing his eyes at the dusty bottle in my hand. "Tell me that's not the Louis XIII."

I looked down at the label on the very nice cognac I'd just poured myself. "Uh."

"Do you have any idea what they're going to charge me for that?"

"You should get them to comp you, along with the room. If I was the bad guy, I could have had you in a dozen pieces by now."

Radu's narrowed gaze turned on the lead guard, who failed to notice because he was staring at Ray, who had started smoking again. I guess that was fair because it wasn't like he could drink anything. But it didn't get any less appalling.

"Must you do that?" Radu demanded. Predictably, Ray flipped him off. Radu looked at me. "Dorina!"

"What do you want me to do? Spank him?"

"That sounds like an excellent idea," Radu declared. The guard and I both looked at him blankly. "I believe I shall have a talk with management."

The guard looked bewildered, having made the mistake of trying to follow Radu's thought processes. "Are you all right, sir?"

"Of course I'm all right, no thanks to you," Radu told him severely.

"We would have been here sooner, but there was a disturbance in the—"

"But there shouldn't be any disturbances, not at these prices. I was assured that this was a quiet and peaceful retreat. Yes, here it is." He picked up a flyer off the nightstand. "*'Quiet and peaceful haven in the heart of one of the world's most cosmopolitan cities.'* Cosmopolitan!" he snorted. "Why, I suppose that's true. The caviar is American, the vodka is British and I strongly suspect the plumbing of being Russian!"

"You don't need plumbing," I reminded him.

"I do bathe, Dory!" he snapped. "And then there's Gunther."

"And Gunther would be your—"

"Bodyguard."

"Is that what they're calling it these days?"

"We're all required to have them now, since the war. Anyone senior, that is."

"Making a virtue out of a necessity?"

"Virtue?" He examined the embroidery on his cuff. "Well, that would be a novelty."

The guard had been looking back and forth between us, and finally decided he'd had enough. "Sir, I—"

"And for what I am paying, I should have a guard permanently assigned to my room!" Radu said, rounding on him. He swept an elegant hand, indicating the cream-and-ice-blue drapes, the matching Aubusson carpet and the large sitting area with the antique marble fireplace. "Not that there's space in this closet."

Several of the guards started looking at their leader with apprehension. I didn't think there'd be too many volunteers. "Sir, I will inform the management of your, uh, concerns," the leader said, backing slowly toward the door.

"See that you do! I naturally expect some inconveniences when away from home, but they seem to believe we should all live like savages!"

The door shut on Radu's final word, and he slumped back against the pillows, fanning himself with the flyer. I tilted the bottle at him, and he nodded gratefully. "You had better hope that works, Dory, or I may be staying with you," he said as I handed him his drink.

"I wouldn't worry about it, 'Du. You're a Basarab. They're probably going to name the room after you."

"Not if I keep getting visits like this. Did you do a great deal of damage?"

"I didn't do any. The guys chasing me, however . . ."

"Yes, well. Let us hope they're blamed instead. Although that would be more likely if you weren't here when management stops by."

"Are you trying to get rid of me, 'Du?" I asked thoughtfully.

"Yes! Yes, I am! It's nothing personal, Dory, but your condition—"

"I'm a dhampir. It isn't catching."

"But it's hardly going to help the Club's reputation, is it? You're the sort of thing most of the guests stay here to avoid."

"They're not going to see me with the door closed," I pointed out, swirling the amber liquid around my glass.

"See, no. But scent—"

"I smell like a human." I knocked the drink back, faster than the quality deserved. But it was a shame to waste good cognac.

"Perhaps so," he said crossly. "But you see how it is."

"I'm beginning to." I put the delicate crystal glass down carefully on the side table, and was out the door before he could stop me.

There were only three other rooms on this floor, so my odds were pretty good. The one right across the hall was empty and obviously unrented, with a light film of dust over the antiques. The one next door to Radu's was occupied by the blond human, who was lying on the bed flipping through a magazine.

"I'm disappointed," he told me. "The last time you paid us a visit was a lot more dramatic."

"I'm not done yet."

I went to the last door, which opened before I could get my hand on the doorknob. *"Merde."*

"I suspected the family would have the whole floor," I told Louis-Cesare.

Chapter Fourteen

"How did you find me?" he demanded, exasperation in the glassy blue of his irises. They matched the fresh blue shirt he'd put on over impeccably pressed charcoal trousers. The shirt had a tone-on-tone stripe in a satiny weave that caught the light, like his perfect shining hair. Mine was everywhere, my borrowed T-shirt was wet with sweat and I smelled like cigarettes and beer. And I hadn't even gotten to drink the beer.

I scowled. "You mean after you left me naked and defenseless—"

"You are never defenseless, and I left you your weapons."

"—in a club full of vampires—"

"I made a commotion upon leaving. Lord Cheung's men followed me!"

"Oh, well. That makes it all right, then."

He frowned. "How did you find me?" he repeated.

"Because I'm just that good," I lied. "Now let me say this nicely. Give me back my fucking head!"

"We cannot do this now!" he told me, trying to push past. Like it was going to be that easy.

I caught his arm and spun him into the wall hard enough to cause a cascade of photos, small mirrors and the vase on the hall table. "Sure, we can."

He scowled and pushed off the wall. "Go home, Dory."

"Give me what I want, and I will!"

Radu appeared in the doorway. "I know this is a stupid question before I ask it, but is there any chance that we can discuss this like civilized people?"

Louis-Cesare glanced at him over his shoulder, then looked back at me, eyes narrowing.

He stepped back a pace and dangled the duffel off one long finger. "Come and get it."

I stared. "Oh, no, you didn't."

"Oh, yeah. He did. You gonna take that?" Raymond piped up from the depths of the duffel.

"You really want to do this?" I demanded. "Because I'm not going to play nice. You know that, right?" The only answer I got was a flying tackle that caught me around the knees and sent me skidding on my back over hard wood.

I grinned. Well, all right, then.

"That's what I thought," Radu sighed.

I'd landed at the top of the stairs, with my knees up and Louis-Cesare on top of me. So of course I flipped him. He went over my head but didn't fall far because security was on their way up again. He landed on a couple of guards, who grabbed him for the second it took for them to recognize him as a guest. It gave me a chance to jump back to my feet and topple over a grandfather clock.

It went chiming downward, only to be batted aside by Louis-Cesare in a blow that turned it into musical kindling. The same was true for a marble statue, a painting in a heavy gilt frame and a large potted plant. The junk in the stairwell caused a few vamps to lose their footing and slide backward, and the disorienting sphere I pulled out of my duffel and exploded in their midst had the rest staring around in bewilderment.

Except for Louis-Cesare, who in one inhumanly liquid movement topped the stairs and caught me in a tackle that sent me sliding backward again, this time on the carpet runner. It was tacked down, so it didn't move, leaving me with a massive case of rug burn. "Ow," I said distinctly.

"This wouldn't be necessary if you would—" He smelled the blood and flipped me over, yanking up the T-shirt. "*Dieu!* I never know what to do with you!"

"How about telling me the truth?"

"Would you know it if I did?" His voice was sharp enough on the edges to cut steel.

"Try it."

His hand smoothed along my back instead, soothing, calming, healing. "The truth is that your father has no stake in this anymore," he told me, his breath in my ear because he was bent over me, shielding me from the stares of the guards. "He lost. It may be a state with which he is unfamiliar, but it is nonetheless—"

"For the last time, I don't know what you're talking about!" I said, exasperated.

"Then why are you here?"

I felt like throwing his own words back at him, like telling him it was none of his damned business. But if I wanted answers, I was probably going to have to cough some up myself. And it wasn't like there was any big secret.

"I'm freelancing on the smuggling task force. You know, the one you're supposed to be helping with? And not because Mircea snapped his fingers. I happen to like the idea of the war ending early and the arms manufacturers dying poor."

"And that's all."

"Yes! That's all!"

Louis-Cesare frowned, and his hands stilled on my ass. "That is why you want the vampire? Because you suspect him of smuggling?"

"Well, it damn sure isn't for the pleasure of his company!"

"Right back at you," floated over from the duffel, which had landed by the wall.

"Why? What do you want with him?" I asked, thoroughly confused now.

"To buy back Christine!"

I blinked. Okay, that wouldn't have been my first guess. Christine was Louis-Cesare's former mistress, who had been kidnapped in order to blackmail him. A vampire who was accustomed to getting what he wanted had asked Louis-Cesare to stand in for him in a duel.

One of his subordinates had challenged him, and if he lost the duel, he wouldn't just lose his position, but his life.

That sort of substitution was allowable by vampire law, and Louis-Cesare had fought for other people in the past. But the man in question this time—Alejandro, head of the Latin American Senate—was known as a sadist who regularly did things that made even vampires blanch. The general consensus was that he wouldn't be missed, and I guess Louis-Cesare agreed, because he told him to fight his own battles. So Alejandro had—by kidnapping Christine and vowing to return her only after his enemy was dead.

Unlike most vamps, Louis-Cesare seemed to have a problem with cold-blooded murder. He'd defeated Tomas, the challenger in question, but refused to kill him because the man's only crime was trying to rid the world of a monster. So Alejandro had refused to release Christine. It was the sort of brutal politics vampire courts abound in, counting the lives that were ruined as insignificant as long as a sought-after goal was reached. I'd been burned by that sort of thing myself, and normally I'd have been sympathetic.

If it hadn't all happened a century ago.

"That's where you've been?" I demanded, squirming. He let me turn over, but didn't get up. Which would have been nice if we didn't have an audience of staring guards, and if I wasn't close to livid. "We're fighting a war and you're off— God! She's been missing for a century! What difference does a couple more years—"

"She doesn't have a couple of years!"

The leader of the guards seemed to have recovered, because he put a hand on my arm. "Sir, would you like me to—"

Louis-Cesare knocked the man's arm away. I used the moment of his distraction to get a knee in a sensitive spot and, when he flinched, roll out from under. I grabbed the bag, scrambled to my feet and fled down the hallway, in the opposite direction from the stairs. We were only two flights up, and I could do that jump easily—

Louis-Cesare grabbed the duffel's strap and jerked, but I'd expected that. I already had a knife in hand and cut the thin nylon. He staggered back a pace, and I put my foot through the window—and almost got it blown off. "Goddamn it!"

"What is it now?" Louis-Cesare demanded.

"Cheung's men. I thought they'd left."

He took a quick peek out the window, prompting another volley from the vamps camped out on the sidewalk below. He shied back and rounded on the guards. "Why haven't you cleared them out?"

"Sir!" The lead guard was beginning to show signs of stress. "The management felt that a dhampir on the premises was more of a concern than—"

"A party of mercenaries in the street, shooting out windows?"

"With all due respect, sir, they only blew out the window because they sighted *her*!" The vampire gave me a less than friendly look. I showed him some fang.

Louis-Cesare didn't look much happier. He glanced at his watch. "Radu, my apologies. But I must—"

"Yes, yes, we'll be fine. Go." Radu waved him off.

"Running away again?" I demanded.

"I don't have a choice."

"Explain it to me," I said, backing up. I put the bag between me and the wall. Ray's big nose was stabbing me in the butt, but no way was Louis-Cesare prying it out of my hands.

"Dorina—"

"It'll be faster to convince me than to fight me."

He said something in French too colloquial for me to translate, which was probably just as well. But he seemed to reach the same conclusion himself. "Alejandro swore that Christine would live only as long as Tomas was no threat to him," he told me abruptly. "For over a century, I was forced to keep him in thrall, virtually imprisoned at my estate unless he was with me personally. But a month ago, he managed to escape, and search as I might, I cannot find him."

"Mircea says he's hiding out in Faerie," Radu chimed

in from the doorway, before ducking back inside to avoid another volley of gunfire, which took out the last few knickknacks on the wall.

"Putting him beyond my reach," Louis-Cesare added, his jaw tight. "To make matters worse, Alejandro learned that Tomas was free and informed me that I had thirty days to secure him again."

"That's why you left so abruptly last month," I said. I had wondered. Our acquaintanceship hadn't been long, but it had been . . . intense. A good-bye would have been nice.

"I knew if I didn't find Tomas quickly, Christine's life was forfeit."

"And Ray knows where he is?" I asked, confused. I couldn't see where a seedy club owner fit into all this.

"No. But I can exchange him for her."

"Come again?"

Someone took that moment to lob in a grenade. Louis-Cesare caught it midair and lobbed it back, but it exploded close enough to break the rest of the glass in the window. And from the sound of things, several more besides. The remaining guards decided that maybe I wasn't the biggest threat, after all, and went running downstairs. The sound of fighting from the street escalated a moment later, along with the distant wails of sirens.

"Alejandro knew that I would have people watching his every move," Louis-Cesare told me quickly. "And he was afraid that I might be able to buy loyalty at his court. He therefore sent Christine to Elyas, of the European Senate, with whom he'd had business dealings."

"And you couldn't find her before this? You're her master."

"Not at present. Alejandro broke my hold and established his own."

All right, I should have guessed that much. Master vampires traded servants from time to time, or lost them in duels or picked them up after their master died. And one of the first things they did with any new acquisition was to establish control by replacing the vamp's master's blood with their own.

"How did you find out he had her?"

"I didn't. Last night, he contacted me and offered a trade."

It took me a minute to get it, because it was so absurd. "Elyas will trade Christine for *Raymond*?"

"In a way. He wants one of the items Raymond recently smuggled in from Faerie. Elyas was involved in a bidding war for it, and he lost."

"Let me guess. He doesn't take losing well."

"In that regard, he reminds me of your father."

"Mircea was involved in this auction?" I asked, my eyes narrowing.

"Yes, but he could not go himself. It might have appeared awkward for the head of the new task force to be seen profiting from the smuggling trade. He therefore sent a proxy." Louis-Cesare looked past me at his own father, who was peering out of the bedroom door again.

Radu's turquoise eyes were worried, and he'd shredded most of the silken tassel on his robe. "Well, I didn't know," he said crossly. "He simply said he wanted me to bid on something for him."

"You didn't think that was odd?" I demanded.

"Why should I? I've done it dozens of times before. They raise the price when they find out a senator is involved."

"Okay, so you went to the auction for Mircea, but didn't get the item."

"It wasn't my fault! I kept bidding and bidding, but the price kept going up, up, up. It just became ridiculous!"

"So Mircea lost, too." I looked at Louis-Cesare. "And you assumed he'd sent me to do what? Steal what he couldn't buy?"

"It is impossible to steal something unless you know where it is. And Raymond handled the sale."

"Son of a bitch." I hated getting played, especially by my own father. Maybe because it had happened once too often. "Mircea sent me to fetch Ray, but of course he didn't mention what he really wanted to ask him about!

I assumed it was that ring of portals we've been searching for."

"I've no doubt that it would have come up, after Lord Mircea had gained his primary objective."

"I told him he was better off," Radu put in. "He'd said to spare no expense, but we're talking about the cost of a small country! And it was just some old rune. But he's in a snit about it."

My brain came to a screeching halt. "Old rune?"

"Yes, ugly little thing."

"Did it have a name?" I asked intently.

Louis-Cesare's eyes narrowed. "You said you wanted the vampire for smuggling."

"No, that's what Mircea told me he wanted him for. I took the job to help Claire."

"Your fey friend?"

"She's here looking for a little something that was recently stolen from the Blarestri royal house."

Nobody had ever accused Louis-Cesare of being slow on the uptake. His blue eyes hardened to lapis. "No."

"Yes. It's her property!"

"And it's Christine's life!" He snatched the bag in a move even I had trouble tracking. One minute, I was holding it; the next, it was in his hands.

I grabbed it, but he didn't let go. "It may be Aiden's life if we don't get the damn thing back!"

"Aiden? Who is—"

"Claire's son! Half the fey are trying to kill him, and the rest aren't sure that isn't a good idea. The rune is his protection."

"He has an army to protect him. Christine has no one!"

I glared at him and pulled hard enough that the bag's fibers started splitting. "If you want Christine so badly, fight Elyas for her."

"The Senates have prohibited duels between masters for the duration of the war."

"Then buy her."

"Do you not think I have tried?" He let go of Ray

abruptly enough that my back hit the wall. "I offered him money, my vote on Senate matters, my sword to fight his duels! Yet the rune is the only thing he will take."

"We can get the Senate involved—"

"They will not interfere in a private matter between two senators."

"Your consul then." The senior vampire in charge of a Senate could occasionally be persuaded to help out a valuable member, and Louis-Cesare's fighting ability was a major asset.

"Dorina! Do you not think I have explored all possible options? I was told in confidence that, should I be so impolitic as to make an issue of this, they will only drag out deliberations until she is dead! They do not care about Christine. They care only about their precious alliance."

And, okay, I could see that. The Senates had recently joined forces to fight a greater enemy, and after centuries of mutual dislike and mistrust, it wasn't the sturdiest of alliances. No way were they going to rock the boat over a single vampire. But that didn't change my position any.

"And I care about a little boy who deserves the chance to grow up."

Louis-Cesare stared at me for a moment, before turning away with a cry of anguished frustration. "What do you wish me to do?" he demanded, whirling back to face me. "I am responsible for the woman whose life I ruined! I must put that right!"

"You didn't ruin it. You saved her." Louis-Cesare had made Christine a vampire to save her life. From what I'd heard, she'd been less than grateful.

A pulse jumped in his neck. "You cannot save someone if they do not wish it. She believes herself damned because of me. I cannot change what was, but I can prevent her from having to pay the price for another of my mistakes."

"Not if it takes—" I stopped. Radu was down the hall, flapping his hands frantically.

"The desk just called. Lord Cheung is on his way up!"

I licked my lips. If Louis-Cesare broke the Senate's prohibition, he'd be punished, probably severely. And he would break it rather than give in. He had a stubborn streak a mile wide and pride enough for any ten people.

"We'll share," I offered.

"How?"

"When are you meeting Elyas?"

"Now. I was leaving when you arrived."

"Then we'll go together. You promised him the information; you'll deliver. And I'll be there to hear it at the same time he does."

"That does not guarantee you anything."

"This is my city. I have contacts he can only dream of, and I have no intention of fighting fair. I'll get to it first."

He looked like he wanted to argue some more, but boots were coming up the stairs, and there was no time. "Agreed."

Gunther appeared in his doorway, a Luger in his hand and a backup at his waist. They looked a little incongruous next to the blue satin robe. "Okay, I take it back," he told me, heading toward the stairs. "You do know how to bring the drama."

"You really are a bodyguard?"

"I like to diversify."

I caught his arm. "They'll shred you!"

"I'm not planning to fight them. But demanding what they want will buy you a few seconds. I suggest you use them."

He disappeared into the stairwell, and Radu flew down the hall, dragging Ray by the arm. He pushed me back into Louis-Cesare's room while pressing something hard into my hand. "It's brand-new. I came to town partly in order to collect it. Please, please, *please* don't scratch it!"

"What about you?"

"Lord Cheung can't hurt me because of the truce, and anyway, with you two gone, he'll have no cause." Radu opened the heavy old wardrobe, shoved back the clothes and pushed me inside. I was about to ask what good he thought that was going to do when he gave another shove, and I was falling.

I slid on my back, headfirst, down something like a laundry chute, and landed on very hard concrete. And a second later, Ray arrived, his knee driving the air out of my lungs. I'd have liked a moment to lie there, wheezing, but Louis-Cesare landed—on his feet, the bastard—and helped me up in order to steal the keys.

We were in an underground garage filled with fabulousness, but there was no doubt which car was 'Du's. We were in a hurry, but I took two seconds to stare anyway. A Lamborghini Murciélago convertible deserves it. Hot damn, I thought, feeling a grin breaking out over my face. And then I was running toward my new upscale ride.

Chapter Fifteen

We were already late, but we didn't have far to go. I stared up at the familiar limestone building, with its turn-of-the-century architecture and its Central Park views. "You have got to be kidding me."

"Elyas recently purchased the penthouse," Louis-Cesare informed me, with a twist to his lips.

"Is he crazy? Out of everywhere you could have met, he invites you *here*?"

"He likes taking risks."

He also liked being a dick. He'd taken the penthouse a couple floors above the apartment Mircea had recently acquired. I strongly suspected that he'd chosen that penthouse in that building just to spite him. It was the sort of petty one-upmanship that the world's most powerful creatures regularly engaged in, as opposed to doing anything useful.

An attendant jogged over, and Louis-Cesare got out of the car. He'd driven, because there hadn't been time to wrestle him for the keys. I started to follow and then stopped, watching curiously as he walked around the hood.

And opened my door.

I stared at him blankly as he offered me a hand. It was beyond bizarre, but after a moment, I took it anyway. He helped me out and turned to the attendant, who had shied back when he saw Ray. Louis-Cesare tossed him the keys. "Do not let him drive."

"Very funny." I opened the back door and dragged Ray out. "We can't leave him here."

"You expect to take a headless vampire to a social event?"

"No, but there's an outside chance Cheung's boys tracked us, and I don't want them staking him while we're inside."

Louis-Cesare looked pained. Ray was even dirtier than I was, and his bright red briefs had gotten a tear across the butt at some point, flashing a glimpse of hairy cheek whenever he moved. An awesome trophy he was not.

We marched Ray under the portico, past the horrified-looking doorman and over to a cherrywood-paneled elevator. I leaned Ray against the wall, fished my cell phone out of the duffel and called Mircea's apartment. Mircea's old tutor and longtime butler answered. "What?" he demanded querulously.

No amount of training has ever taught Horatiu the proper way to answer a phone. Mircea doesn't give a damn, since most of the people who call him on his public line do so to grovel anyway, and he's the only one with any control over the old vamp. Not that I think he has much.

"It's Dorina," I yelled, because he can't hear worth a damn.

"Who?"

"DORINA!"

"Well, there's no need to shout."

"Is Mircea there?"

"No, no. Everyone's gone," he said impatiently. "Middle of the night, isn't it?"

"Do you expect him back soon?"

"Not for a few hours. Why?"

"No reason. I'm coming up."

Louis-Cesare quirked an eyebrow as I replaced the phone. "I need a bath," I said, before he could ask. He just looked at me. "What?"

"You are a dhampir on your way to a vampire cocktail party, and you are worried about your *toilette*?"

"No," I said defensively, as he started to smile. "And you're the one who wanted to park Ray somewhere."

"Very true." It was a genuine smile now, curving his lips, lighting his eyes, and I blinked. I hadn't seen one too often from him, and it was ridiculously attractive.

"I don't get why Elyas involved you in all this," I said as the elevator doors opened. "If he wanted to talk to Ray, he could have gone himself or sent one of his men. It's not like the guy was hard to find."

"Lord Cheung is known as a competent duelist. Elyas . . . is not. The truce will only last as long as the war, and once it is lifted, Lord Cheung will be well within his rights to demand satisfaction for his loss and for the indignity perpetrated on his servant. Elyas preferred me to have to deal with that eventuality, rather than him."

"But why didn't he just buy it?" I asked, confused. "Cheung is a businessman. If Elyas offered him enough—"

"The winner of the auction was Ming-de," Louis-Cesare said simply.

He didn't need to say anything else. Ming-de was the powerful Chinese empress, their version of a consul. It would be a rare vampire who wanted to risk breaking a promise to her, and certainly not one who resided in her territory. She could crush him like a bug, and probably would, if he crossed her.

"So no reversing the sale."

"The auction was yesterday, and Elyas spent most of the last twenty-four hours bombarding Lord Cheung with offers, pleas and threats. To no avail."

We got out at Mircea's floor, and I rang the doorbell. "If the auction was last night, why was Elyas pestering Cheung?" I asked. "Doesn't Ming-de already have it?"

"The fey who owns it refused to bring it here until a sale was agreed upon. He was due to arrive last night, after the auction, at which time the evaluation would be made. If the rune was genuine, it would be delivered tonight and payment made. That is why Lord Cheung is here, I suspect. He no doubt planned to deliver the rune to the empress personally."

"Only he can't," I realized. "He obviously doesn't

know where Ray put it, or he wouldn't be chasing us all over the city."

Louis-Cesare nodded. "The auction took place here, because most of the participants were already on hand for the races. But Lord Cheung's business kept him in Hong Kong until today. He wasn't here when the fey came through the portal, and therefore he doesn't know where the rune is. As far as we can determine, only one person knows that."

Well, no wonder Ray was a popular guy.

A tiny old vampire with a nose to rival Ray's and tufts of silver-white hair finally answered the door. Unlike most vamps on the planet, Horatiu doesn't actually hate me, maybe because he's not entirely clear on what I am. The watery blue eyes don't work right, and he hasn't been able to see his hand in front of his face in centuries. Which might explain why he didn't so much as flinch at the sight of a bloody dhampir and a headless guy on his doorstep.

"Who's that with you then?" he demanded.

"This is Raymond." I pushed him forward.

Horatiu squinted behind his glasses. "You're a strange-looking one."

Ray shot him the finger, but of course Horatiu didn't see it, so that was all right.

"And this is Louis-Cesare," I said.

"Ah, yes. The mumbler."

"I refuse to shout every word I utter," Louis-Cesare explained wryly.

"There he goes again," Horatiu sniffed. He sniffed again, and this time made a face. "You need a bath, young lady," he informed me.

"I know. So does Ray."

"Use the master's room," Horatiu ordered. "The guest ones are all taken. I'll take this . . . person . . . to mine." He ushered Ray's body off, and Louis-Cesare and I headed through the understated opulence of Mircea's digs.

He'd only acquired the apartment recently, so he wouldn't have to do anything so gauche as stay at a hotel when he was in town. As a result, it was still primarily the way it had been when he bought it, in quiet shades of camel and sand with little personal stamp over the designer blandness. The only exceptions were a few bright postmodernist paintings spotting the walls. They were new, and they gave the place an energy it had sorely lacked the last time I was here.

Louis-Cesare stopped in the living room to make another call, and I made a detour by the kitchen. I'd skipped dinner and my stomach was protesting, and no way was I getting anything to eat upstairs. At vampire parties, the snacks serve themselves.

The kitchen turned out to be bright and functional, all honey-colored wood and matching striated marble, and looked like no one had ever used it. Which, considering who lived here, may well have been the case. I pulled open the fridge and, as I suspected, the food on offer was minimal. But somebody up there loved me because there was beer. I pulled one out, drank half of it and then just stood there for a minute, soaking up the cold air.

My head hurt. Come to think of it, so did my neck, my left shoulder, the right side of my rib cage, my ankle and my right hand. In contrast, my ass felt fine, except for a slight tingle from where a certain someone's hands had rested.

And then those same hands were sliding under the T-shirt, next to my skin, and my whole body started to tingle. "I thought we were in a hurry," I said, gripping the fridge door tightly. The combination of heat behind me and cool, cool air in front was a little dizzying.

"Elyas is not expecting us for an hour."

"An hour, huh?" I could do a lot with an hour.

Apparently, Louis-Cesare could, too, although it wasn't quite what I'd expected. He pulled me away from the fridge, bent me over the marble-topped island and dug his fingers into the tense muscles of my back. I groaned.

He started at the base of my spine, teasing out the knots as skillfully as if he'd done it a dozen times before. My body recognized the coarseness of familiar calluses, and a heavy warmth spread through me. He paused to tug the T-shirt off over my head, and I didn't resist.

When he reached my shoulders, which had been tight long before tonight, he leaned more of his weight into it, spreading his palms flat and moving them in slow circles along the lines of the muscle. When they were roughly the consistency of jelly, he moved on to my neck. I leaned into the strokes involuntarily, head rolling back as he kneaded away at the tension knotted around the base of my skull.

By the time he finished, the pain was gone, although it was possible that I'd fallen madly, irreversibly in love with Louis-Cesare's hands. I might have said something to the effect, because he chuckled and brushed his lips over the back of my neck, meltingly warm. "Get dressed."

"Thinking about it." I wasn't actually sure I could move.

He let his fingers, soft and featherlight, comb through the short ends of my hair. "Get dressed before I call Elyas and tell him we will see him tomorrow."

Sounded like a plan to me.

"And before I take that pose as an invitation."

I turned my head and found him right there, his breath on my face, and his lashes almost brushing my cheek. There was no conscious decision. I put a hand behind his neck, and pulled up to meet him, my lips finding his as easily, as naturally, as if we did it every day. He tasted spicy and musky and mouthwateringly sweet, like butterscotch candy right before it melts on the tongue.

A bone-deep shudder tore through him, and he gripped the back of my neck and returned the kiss, deep and hungry. His skin was hot to the touch; his mouth even hotter, wet and suddenly iron-edged with blood. The tenderness was gone, but I didn't miss it. This was better; this was perfect, sensation spiraling out of control into blatant need.

My hands spidered up to tangle in the thick mass of his hair, and my leg wrapped around him. His hand clenched on my ass, pulling me against him, and he was already half hard behind the thin material of his trousers. One of us groaned—I wasn't sure which—and his lips moved to my ear.

"Please get dressed," he said hoarsely.

It took a second to register, and then I jerked away, snatching up the T-shirt.

"Make up your damn mind!" I told him, pulling it on. "One minute you strip me; the next you tell me to get dressed. One minute your tongue is down my throat, and the next you're glowering at me. Do you even know what you want?"

"There are things we want, and things we may have," he said tightly. "Sanity lies in knowing the difference."

"Okay, you want to translate that for me?" I waited, but he didn't say anything else, and his posture was as closed and uninviting as a statue.

Or like a guy who's just remembered his mistress is waiting upstairs.

Screw this, I thought bitterly. It was exactly like last time, only then I hadn't stepped back. I'd let him take my face in his hands, let myself lean into his touch, just enough to fall and keep on falling. Only to have him leave, without a word, to chase after his mistress.

It was the same woman he was going to redeem tonight. And then this would be over and he would be gone, and I couldn't *wait*. I snagged my abandoned bottle and the duffel bag off the floor and headed for the bedroom without another word, frustration lingering like a sour taste in my mouth.

It's the beer, I told myself firmly.

Mircea's bedroom was the same gray expanse of boredom I remembered. Like the rest of the apartment, it was ultramodern, sleek and minimalist, like something transplanted from one of the glass-and-steel high-rises. It didn't fit well in this old-world charmer any more than the blinding white bathroom did.

Some things just weren't meant to go together, I thought viciously, and stepped into the shower. I turned it on high, refusing to think about anything except the pounding water and the enveloping steam. It didn't work. That shouldn't have surprised me. It hadn't worked any better all month.

He was a vampire. I was a dhampir, born to detect the monster within the pretty package. And until now, I'd had a flawless record. But breeding, training, and experience all failed me in his case. When I looked at Louis-Cesare, I didn't see a monster.

Part of the problem was his unique talent for appearing human. I'd never met another vampire who got all the little things right so effortlessly, who breathed as though he really needed to, whose heart rate went up when I came in the room, who flushed in passion. If it hadn't been for the frisson that went up my spine whenever we met, he might have fooled even me.

But it wasn't the appearance that had me so confused. A lot of vamps looked pretty damn human, but they didn't act it. From the newly changed babies to the age-old consuls, every damn one of them evidenced the same focused self-interest, cold-blooded practicality and utter ruthlessness.

Everyone except for Louis-bloody-Cesare.

He didn't live by the vamp code; he had his own. It was classist and had a heavy overtone of noblesse oblige, and it frequently made me want to smack him, but it was a code nonetheless. He didn't always act in ways that would benefit himself, the mess with Alejandro being a prime example.

Every other vamp I knew would have either sacrificed Christine, if Tomas was considered too much of a threat, or have killed him and taken her back. Some of them would have made Alejandro pay for the insult later, but none would have so much as considered any other options. They probably wouldn't have even seen any.

Vampires were emancipated when they reached the level of their master, and sometimes before, because the more powerful they became the harder it was to control them. Eventually, the problems in keeping them outweighed the benefits. I could just see Mircea's face if someone suggested that he divert a huge amount of his personal power for more than a century to hold a vampire in thrall who could be of absolutely no use to him. Yet Louis-Cesare had done exactly that.

First-level masters varied in power, and obviously, Louis-Cesare had been stronger than Tomas. But even so, the cost must have been enormous, a constant, ongoing drain with no end in sight. And for what? The benefit of a vampire he didn't even know? It was the sort of behavior that made my brain hurt because it challenged everything I knew about the self-serving breed.

Not that it mattered. Whatever he looked like, whatever he acted like, Louis-Cesare *was* a vampire. I needed to remember that.

I also needed to figure out what the hell I was going to wear. I didn't intend to try to compete—vampire parties are all about outshining, outdazzling and outdoing everybody else, and my wardrobe wouldn't have been up to the challenge even if I'd had access to it. But I also wasn't wearing a smelly old T-shirt that wasn't even mine.

Fortunately, Mircea is a shade over six feet tall, while I am barely five two. That makes his shirts on the order of dresses for me, easily hitting midthigh or lower, and it wasn't like he couldn't spare one. He was the biggest clotheshorse I'd ever met; if he hadn't had a steady stream of mistresses through the years, I'd wonder about him.

I'd settled on a big shirt and maybe a cummerbund for a belt by the time I stepped out of the shower—and saw a piece of black silk hanging from the hook behind the door. It was a dress, sort of. It was mostly straps on top, cleverly designed to reveal more than they covered, yet managing to stay on the right side of slutty. The skirt was more problematic, long and black and slit high enough that my lack of underwear was going to be a problem.

"There's some panties and things on the counter," Ray said, from inside the duffel.

I'd parked it on the floor beside the door. I picked it up and peered into the hole in the side. "Are you spying on me?"

"Hell, yeah. Get me out of here."

"Why? So you can get a better view?"

"So we can talk while you get dressed."

"I'm not getting dressed," I told him, threw a towel around myself and went out into the bedroom. It was dark and empty, except for the wash of light from the bath, so I passed through to the living room. Louis-Cesare was on the couch with the lights off, staring out over the view of Central Park.

I held up the dress. "What is this?"

He looked up, his eyes dark in the dim light. "I had it sent over."

"It's one o'clock in the morning!"

"Concierge," he said simply, like he'd picked up the phone and ordered a pizza.

"There are *shoes*." I'd tripped over a pair of black satin heels on the way out of the bathroom.

"You wished to dress for the occasion—"

"I said I wanted a bath."

"—and I thought to oblige you. And myself. I have never seen you in a gown."

I crossed my arms and glared at him. "How did you know my size?"

He just looked at me. And yeah, okay, I could probably guess his pretty accurately, too, if it came down to it. Not that it *mattered*.

"I'm not wearing this."

He regarded me in silence for a moment. "Do you wish to fight with me, Dorina?"

"Yes!" At the moment, that was exactly what I wanted.

"If it will help." I blinked. He'd spoken in the toneless kind of voice new vamps used when they hadn't yet learned to operate dead vocal cords. Except Louis-Cesare never made slips like that.

A passing car lit up his face for an instant, and the strained blankness of his expression jolted me with an unpleasant shock. He looked like a vamp for the first time: the face beautiful, but pale and cold, like it was carved out of marble; the chest immobile, unbreathing; the eyes fixed and unblinking. I felt a chill run down my spine.

The man I knew was haughty, impatient, demanding, passionate. Not this blank. Not this *thing*.

"What the hell is wrong with you?" I demanded.

"Nothing." Toneless, flat, dead.

Yeah, that was convincing.

Chapter Sixteen

I walked over, the dress trailing on the floor behind me. I sat on the edge of the coffee table across from him because I was still dripping. "Try again," I told him.

He didn't say anything.

"I'd have thought you'd be pleased," I pointed out. "You're getting Christine back."

"I am relieved," he said, after a moment. "Elyas is a sadist, delighting in the pain of others. I did not like to think of her there."

"You think he hurt her?"

"No. He assures me that she has not been harmed."

"And you believe him?"

"Yes. He enjoys the fear of his victims more than their pain, and Christine . . . As she once said to me, after one has lost their soul, what else is there to fear?"

"She hasn't lost her soul," I said impatiently. "Hell, Mircea is more devout than I am." I didn't mind going to mass so much, but confession was damned annoying. Even the supernatural confessors the Vatican kept on call always got a little . . . distraught . . . when I showed up. And, really, there weren't enough Hail Marys in the world.

"But she believes she has," Louis-Cesare said simply. "Her family was very devout. It was thought for a time that she would become a *religieuse*."

I raised my eyebrows. "How does someone get from prospective nun to vampire mistress?"

"Christine was one of those rare individuals born

with magical ability without coming from a magical family. She was never given any training, and therefore did not know about her gift until it began to manifest as she came of age."

"That must have been a shock."

"She mistook it for a miracle. She was a novitiate at the time, and people began to flock to the abbey to see her levitate the Host or to light candles with merely a touch. She believed she was the vessel of God's grace, for she could find no other reason why she should be able to do such things. But magical power is like any other kind: it requires training to work safely—training she did not possess."

"I have a feeling this isn't going anywhere good."

"No. One evening, she was startled while attempting to light the bank of candles before the altar, and the spell went awry. Within minutes, the chapel was in flames, the roof beams collapsed and many of the nuns died. The abbess survived, badly burned and newly convinced that they had taken a devil amongst themselves. Christine was whipped by the abbess and forced to run for her life with only the clothes on her back. Some of my vampires found her several days later, half dead from dehydration and unhealed burns, stumbling down the road near my estate."

"And they recognized what she was." It wouldn't have been difficult. A vampire of any age could tell blindfolded the differences among human, were, mage and fey by smell alone.

"Yes. They brought her to me, and I nursed her back to health. During her recovery, we became . . . close. But I was not a mage. I could not give her the training she needed. Once she was well again, I thought to help her by putting her in touch with others of her kind. I contacted a mage on her behalf—a man I had known for years and had every reason to believe was scrupulous." His fingers tightened on his glass, the first sign of emotion I'd seen.

"I'm going to guess he wasn't," I said, prodding him when he went silent.

"In the time since I had had dealings with him, he had amassed a great number of debts. He was desperate to find a way to clear them, and I gave him one. I brought her to his doorstep in my own carriage."

"He sold her." I knew this part of the story, at least. Radu had told me how Christine had become a target for the less salubrious part of the supernatural world. Dark mages lust after power. And a strong, untrained witch with no magical family to protect her? It just didn't get any better than that.

"By the time I realized my mistake, it was too late. I found her, but she was too close to death for any doctor to save her."

"So you brought her over." I was surprised it had worked. It often doesn't when the subject is that far gone. But then, Horatiu had been on his deathbed when Mircea Changed him.

Of course, how successful that transformation had been was debatable.

"Again, I thought to help. And again, I made a bad matter infinitely worse."

"You saved her life," I pointed out.

"Yes, but Christine was not concerned for her life. She was concerned for her soul. Something she believes is now lost, wholly and irretrievably."

"I don't see why. She'd been a witch before. How is that any less 'damned' than a vampire?"

His lips twisted. "Magic, in her mind, was something that she *did*, requiring a conscious effort on her part, and was therefore something she could stop doing."

"That's stupid. Magical humans are *not* the same as—"

"But she did not see it like that. Her parents, her siblings—they were human. There must have been some magical blood in the family line, yes, but it does not seem to have manifested in anyone else. She therefore believed that her new abilities were the devil's way of tempting her, and they could be overcome by prayer and good works. But vampirism?" He smiled grimly. "That was not something she did; it was something she *was*, and it could not be undone once the transformation was complete."

It made a kind of sense, if you had a late-medieval mind-set. "And yet she chose to remain the mistress of the man who had damned her?"

His gaze shifted to the window, not that there was much to see. There also wasn't a lot of traffic this late, and with no more passing headlights, I couldn't see his expression that well. Assuming he had one. "The bond between a new Child and her master is very strong," he finally said.

"But many of them aren't lovers!"

"She wished it. My actions had deprived her of the love of her family, the solace of her religion and the comfort of a world she understood. I had destroyed her old life. It was my responsibility to provide her with a new one."

"And now?"

He didn't say anything, which was as good as an answer.

"She's what?" I demanded. "A few hundred years old? I think she's her own responsibility."

"You know it does not work that way."

"What I know is that vampires can be emancipated."

"When they reach a certain power level, yes. But Christine has never advanced beyond what she was when she first awoke. I do not know what she might have been, but her loathing for our kind has made it impossible for her to mature. She has remained a child."

"Children grow up."

His eyes closed. "Human children do. But sometimes, with us . . . they simply remain."

"Then maybe they need to be pushed a little more! Vampires aren't human, but they're part of the natural world. And that world thrives on change."

"But that is how we differ, is it not?" he asked, opening his eyes. They glittered with some emotion I couldn't even begin to define, contrasting sharply with the dead look of his face. "Vampires do not grow old. We do not die. We are as unchanging as the mountains."

"The mountains change, Louis-Cesare," I said harshly, getting up. "It just takes them longer. And vampires die all the time. Trust me on that."

I went back to the bathroom.

Ray had hooked his long nose over the side of the duffel so he could stare at me as I stomped back in. I threw a towel over him and proceeded to dry my hair. "Get this thing off!" he bitched.

"It's not like you're going to suffocate!" I snapped.

"Yeah, but we gotta talk."

I ignored him in favor of running my fingers over the soft material of the dress. It had gotten crushed in my hands, so I spread it out on the counter, careful to keep it out of any wet spots. The silk was so fine and lightweight, I bet it felt like wearing nothing. *And why the hell shouldn't I find out?* I thought angrily. The bastard owed me an outfit.

"Are you listening to me?" Ray demanded.

"Talk about what?"

"About Elyas."

"You're going to be talking to him in a minute," I said, examining a pair of ebony lace-topped thigh-highs. There was a matching thong, too, but no bra because there'd never been one invented to work with that dress.

"That's just it," Ray whispered, his eyes on the closed bathroom door. "No, I'm not. As soon as you turn me over, he's going to kill me."

"Why would he want to do that? He needs you to tell him where the rune is."

"He already knows where it is. He stole it after he killed Jókell."

"Who?"

"The fey!"

"What fey?"

"The fey who brought the rune. And don't say, 'What rune?' "

Now I was the one glancing at the door. It was closed, and I'd slammed the one to the living room coming back in, but two doors and the width of a substantial suite didn't mean much with vampire hearing. Ray started to say something else, but I shushed him, wrapped another towel around myself and hauled him out the window.

An elaborate wrought-iron fire escape overlooked a small alley between buildings. The wind had picked up enough to ruffle the tops of a couple ornamental trees below, and some traffic still flowed along Fifth Avenue. It should be enough to mask a low-voiced conversation.

I hoped.

I shut the window behind me and unzipped the top of the duffel. Anxious blue eyes swiveled up to me. "You want to start making some sense here, Ray?"

"It's like this. Jókell was Blarestri—that's one of the three main houses of the Light Fey."

"I know what it is."

"Yeah, well, not a lot of people do. Anyway, he was in what I guess you'd call their military, and he regularly pulled a shift guarding one of the main portals into our world."

"Let me guess. He sometimes let a little something slip through."

"A lot of somethings. We had a good thing going. He found people on his end who had stuff they'd rather not pay the duty on, and I took care of selling it on this side. Anyway, about a week ago, he calls and tells me he's got a lead on something special. He told me to arrange a private sale, even told me who to contact—and that was some list! It made me nervous, because I don't usually handle the big stuff, and these were not people I wanted to piss off. But the boss said to go ahead with it."

"And something went wrong."

"Everything! For starters, he wouldn't bring me the rune until we'd already made the sale. I told him it didn't work like that, but he said it did this time or no deal. I don't like selling something I don't got on hand, but the boss said to do it. And it went okay. He got the reserve he'd wanted and then some, and after the auction, I sent him a message and he said he'd be here in a couple hours."

"But he didn't show?"

"No, he came through the portal on schedule, but that's the last thing that went right!"

"And this portal would be where?"

"At the club. It's upstairs, in the manager's old office—"

"At the— Are you crazy? You distribute from there! Everybody knows that!"

"Which is why it was perfect." The little shit grinned at me. "You idiots were running around, checking my apartment—oh, yeah, I knew about that—and my warehouse and that tea shop I own, but nobody ever thought to look in the most obvious spot."

"Because it's stupid!"

"Stupid like a fox," he said, and then frowned. "No, wait—"

"What. Happened?"

"Oh, yeah. Well, I'd called in a luduan to authenticate the piece before payment was made, and he was late. And I get nervous around those things."

"Luduans?"

"Fey." He made a face. "They don't move enough or they move weird; I don't know. Anyway, they give me the creeps. And so I tell Jókell to make himself comfortable, and I go down to get some refreshment, and I don't hurry back, you know? I chat with some of the guys at the bar and remind Ken—that's the DJ—that some of us like something besides techno occasionally—"

"Ray!"

"Right, right. So, after about fifteen minutes, I go back up with the tray. I push open the door, and I don't see him, but I don't panic because I figure even the fey have to use the john once in a while, right? And then something grabs my ankle, and I look down and it's this bloody hand. And that's when I found him, squashed between the desk and the wall. Or what was left of him."

"And Elyas was there?"

"No, but I could smell him, so he must have just left."

"And how do you know what Elyas smells like?"

"Maybe because he'd been down to the club that afternoon," Ray said sarcastically. "He was trying to bribe me to give him the rune before the sale, and getting really pushy about it. I finally told him I didn't have it, that it wouldn't be delivered until after the sale, so he might as well go away."

"You *told* him?"

"Well, I didn't expect him to come down and murder the guy, did I?" Ray asked huffily. "Anyway, the fey are supposed to be hard to kill. And I guess maybe they are if you use magic. But this one had been gutted. He died a couple minutes later."

"And the rune was missing." I didn't bother to make it a question.

"Damn straight. He had this gold thing around his neck when he arrived, fist-sized, with like a sunburst pattern. Kinda gaudy, but it looked expensive. But he said it was nothing, just a carrier for the rune. He showed it to me, and the rune fit inside in this little space. But when I went back up, it was gone."

"The rune or the necklace?"

"Both."

"Then that thing you said you 'misplaced'—"

"Was the rune, yeah. I called Elyas as soon as I calmed down and told him that he either returned the damn thing or I'd finger him for killing a fey. And you know what they're like about revenge."

On a personal level. "But he refused?"

"No. I mean, he was pretty nasty about it, but he finally agreed. But it was almost morning by then, and I didn't want him coming over when my boys were all asleep. So I told him to send it over tonight. But he didn't show, and I couldn't get him on the damn phone, and the boss was due in a couple hours! And I was freaking out, you know? The boss was flying in special to take the rune to Ming-de tonight, and I didn't have it! I knew he'd kill me."

"That sounds about right," I agreed. That was the way the vampire hierarchy worked, even in the more legitimate families. Cause your master to lose face, and you were likely to lose yours, along with a lot of other body parts.

"Elyas never intended to show," Ray said, getting worked up again. "He just wants me dead and conned that French guy into doing his dirty work!"

"Louis-Cesare. And you could have mentioned some of this earlier!" I pointed out.

"Yeah, I can't imagine why I'd have trouble trusting the freak who decapitated me!"

"So what changed?"

"What changed is you told Louis-Cesare you want the rune. Well, you're not going to get it from Elyas. He's not going to give it up, and if it does its thing and makes him invincible, you can't kill him. The only chance you got is to blackmail him. I can tell everyone what I saw if he don't cough it up."

"But you'd have to be alive for me to do that," I said, seeing where this was going.

"Which I won't be, once he gets his hands on me."

I stared blankly at the trees. The leaves shook, the tops swaying in the freshening wind. The sky above was a troubled gray, dark clouds mounting, heralding another thunderstorm. It perfectly matched my mood.

On the one hand, if Ray was telling the truth and Elyas really had killed the fey, it opened up some interesting possibilities. He might be invulnerable, but his family and property weren't. The fey could ruin him, making blackmail far from an empty threat. With a little luck, it might be possible to get the rune and Christine.

On the other hand, I had to convince Louis-Cesare to ignore Elyas's offer and that wasn't going to be easy. Christine was within his grasp; all he had to do was turn Ray in, and it was a sure thing. Blackmail, on the other hand, included risk: Ray might be lying and Elyas might dig in his heels, counting on the word of a Senate member to beat out that of a nightclub owner.

No. Louis-Cesare wasn't going to take a chance like that. Not when he could walk upstairs and end this right now.

Get away, keep Ray alive and willing to talk. That was the plan. I glanced down at the deserted alley. The fire escape made getting out of here easy, except for one small problem. The rest of Ray was in a guest room somewhere, and I didn't even know which one.

"If you're lying to me to save your skin, I'll find out," I told him, dragging us back through the window. "And I'll be ten times worse to you than Elyas."

"Yeah. Like I could make this shit—"

Ray cut off midsentence because someone rapped on the bathroom door. I paused half in, half out of the window. "Dorina, it has been half an hour," Louis-Cesare said. "Are you ready?"

Chapter Seventeen

Ray and I stared at each other. "Almost," I said quickly. "Let me just . . . uh . . ."

I slithered the rest of the way through, set the duffel on the counter and started pawing through it. I had things in there that could kill a person fifty different ways, but my less lethal alternatives were few and far between. I'd been going into a vampire club, and not a lot works on them.

And that's especially true for first-level masters. I rejected magical cuffs—he'd be out of them in five seconds—a stun spray—he probably wouldn't even feel it—and a disorienting sphere, which I already knew was a waste of resources. I finally had to admit that I had nothing that could trap Louis-Cesare long enough to do any good.

"Dorina?"

"Coming!"

I started pulling on the dress, or trying to. But that top would have defeated a puzzle master. "Where are you?" I mouthed at Ray, who was watching me anxiously.

"You mean my body?" he mouthed back.

"Of course! Where is it?"

"In the tub."

"What?"

"That old guy left me and never came back."

Typical. Horatiu had probably forgotten he was there. "Get out the front door, fast."

Small eyes popped. "By *myself*?"

"Yes! Go to the car."

"What?"

"To. The. Car. I'll stall him."

I ran a comb through my hair, which was still wet, forming a sleek cap around my head. I tried again to sort out the straps, but it was hopeless. They were a twisted mess that made no logical sense.

"Dorina. Is there a problem?"

I threw open the door. "I can't get the straps right," I said.

Louis-Cesare stood there, his hand raised for another knock. His face was wearing that expression men get when a woman takes three times longer to get ready than she'd promised. It didn't last long. Okay, I thought, watching blue eyes dilate black. Maybe the dress looked better than I thought.

"A little help?" I prompted.

He hesitated for a moment, but he finally stepped behind me. He made a few minor adjustments, the calluses on his fingertips catching slightly on the soft material. Miraculously, the dress fell into place, every shining strap lying perfectly flat against my skin.

I twisted in front of the mirror. I decided that it wasn't too bad. It was sleek and simple, and it let the cut do the work instead of requiring embellishments. And it fit perfectly, except for being maybe an inch or two too long. But the plain black satin heels should take care of that.

A hand smoothed down my side in a totally unnecessary movement. It lingered in the indentation where waist flared into hip, burning through the thin silk, sending a jolt to the pit of my stomach. "Elyas is waiting." His voice was rough.

"Let him wait." I sat down on the bench at the foot of the bed and pulled on the thigh highs. They were gossamer soft, like spiderwebs in my hands. Utterly impractical, they'd probably run within minutes. But they felt like a dream.

I pointed my toe and pulled one on. It felt utterly decadent, a silky, sensual glide all the way up to the wide band of lace around the top. I pulled on the other and then pushed the skirt out of the way to admire my pretty new hosiery.

It was rare to find pure silk hose these days, but that was what they felt like—light as a feather with a pearlescent quality that caught the light. It subtly drew attention in all the right places, making my legs look unusually long and better-shaped than they actually were. I flexed a leg, enjoying the feel of the silky stuff sliding against my skin.

I looked up to find Louis-Cesare watching me. I couldn't complain about lack of expression now. He looked like a starving man faced with a banquet he couldn't have. It made me furious all over again.

He looked away. "The dress suits you."

"You have good taste," I said acerbically. In some things.

I picked up the delicate black satin strappy things pretending to be shoes. Trust a man, I thought darkly. They had to be six inches, with heels so high and so thin, they looked like they would snap at the slightest pressure. I slipped them on and then just stared. Whoever designed them had to be a sadist. They were a broken ankle waiting to happen.

"You did this on purpose," I accused.

"I can have something else sent, if you prefer," he told me, challenge sparkling in those blue eyes.

My own narrowed. "These will be fine."

I slowly stood up, feeling like I was wearing a pair of stilts. It had been years—decades, really—since I'd owned a pair of stilettos, and I suddenly recalled why. My left ankle buckled, and I corrected myself, glaring down at it. If I could run along the edge of a rooftop and never miss a step, I could walk in these damn shoes.

And I did. For about two steps. Then I wobbled, stumbled and ended up on my butt on the bed.

One of the shoes had gone flying. Louis-Cesare retrieved it and knelt in front of me, his eyes amused. "There is an art to it."

"How would you know?"

"I used to wear them."

"I beg your pardon?"

"At the French court. They were all the rage—among both sexes—for a time."

I tried to imagine Louis-Cesare, all six foot plus of hard muscle, in a pair of high heels. And, despite everything, I laughed. "Care to show me how it's done?"

"I do not think those are my size," he said, grasping my calf in one large hand. I went a little dry-mouthed.

His fingers were warm on my arch for a moment, as he slid the shoe back in place. He looked up, his eyes suddenly serious. "I suppose it is useless for me to request that you remain here while I attend to this."

I just looked at him.

"It will be difficult for me to protect you without breaking the truce."

It was moments like these when I wondered if he truly understood what a dhampir *was*. "I don't need protection."

"Against some of those who will be there tonight?" His jaw tightened. "Yes, you do."

"I'll be on my best behavior," I promised, with a straight face.

He smiled slightly. "Why am I not reassured?"

He pulled me to my feet and drew my hand through his arm in one smooth, natural movement, with no signs of flinching. I didn't know a single other vampire, including family, who didn't tense up slightly when I came within arm's reach. Yet, from day one, he'd never minded getting close, had in fact used every possible excuse to do so.

Strange behavior for someone pining away for his mistress.

But then, maybe I'd just been available, an easy conquest, a creature he didn't have to worry about offending because our natural relationship was antagonistic anyway. I really didn't know what he felt, if anything. I just knew what I did.

"Then maybe we should take out a little insurance," I said, and sank to my knees.

He looked confused, until my fingers went to the button of his trousers. I saw it register, felt when he stilled completely, not even breathing. And then he caught my hands.

"What are you doing?"

"What does it look like?"

"Why?" It was in a low, urgent tone I'd never heard him use.

"Because it helps to take the edge off." He looked like he didn't understand my answer. "I'm dhampir," I reminded him. "We have these fits, remember? Rage-induced blackouts where we kill everything in sight?"

"That is all it takes to control your fits?" He looked incredulous.

"I didn't say it controlled them. I said it took the edge off, much the way good-quality weed does. If someone provokes me enough, I'll still go under. But not as easily. Now let go, or are you the only one who gets to touch?"

Apparently so, because he pulled me back to my feet, keeping my hands trapped between us. His were strong, with the warmth of familiar calluses. I felt my breath speed up as I remembered what those hands could do.

Something of my thoughts must have shown on my face, because he flushed slightly. "I was told that you had found a cure."

"It's genetic. There is no cure."

"Lord Mircea said—"

"You asked him about me?"

"He mentioned it in passing."

I narrowed my eyes but let it go. "I've found something that cuts down on the frequency of the attacks, and controls some of the symptoms. But there are problems."

"What kind of problems?"

I sighed. For a Frenchman, he was the hardest damn man to seduce I'd ever seen. "It brings out dormant magical abilities in humans."

It was Louis-Cesare's turn to narrow his eyes. "You

are speaking of fey wine? Do not tell me you are still taking that concoction."

"Okay, I won't tell you."

"It is dangerous!"

"So am I, without it!"

"And that is worth risking your life? You do not know—"

"I haven't had a full-on attack in weeks. And the last time I did, I was conscious." His expression said he still didn't get it. "I was *conscious*, Louis-Cesare!" I repeated, struggling to find words to explain just what that meant.

But there weren't any. He'd never had to worry about blacking out for days, only to wake up in some unknown location, covered in blood and surrounded by corpses. He would never understand the constant nagging fear that next time it wouldn't be an enemy I killed. That next time I would wake up to find my hands buried in the throat of a friend.

Something must have shown on my face, because his gaze softened. "I thought your friend was looking for a cure."

"She was. She is. But so far, no luck."

"There are other physicians. Have you sought out their help?"

"I don't need them. I have something that works."

"Thus far. You have no idea what the long-term effects might be."

"Whatever they are, it's a damn good trade!"

He set his jaw, that old stubborn look coming over his face. "There must be an alternative."

"There is." I deliberately slid my hands up his chest.

"Dorina—"

"Don't. Don't say anything." I didn't want to talk anymore. I didn't want to think. I wanted to drive him as crazy as he had me, wanted to see him lose control, wanted him to *feel something* when I damn well left.

I cupped his face in my hands and kissed him. His body was a tight wall of muscle, as yielding as rock. But his lips were warm and soft as they met mine, asking nothing, forbidding nothing, surrendering to my need as I had known, deep down, that he would.

He tasted like smoky whiskey and Louis-Cesare, an elusive sweetness that had haunted me in odd moments for weeks. I pulled him even closer, and my leg wrapped around him, hunger mounting as I deepened the kiss. I felt a surge of pure satisfaction as his arms went around me, one hand settling on my nape, the other cupping my jaw, the thumb stroking with a terrible gentleness.

It was so easy to lose myself in this, in the searching caress of his tongue, in the silken press of his lips. Running my hands over the broad planes of his back, I traced light fingertips over the knobs of his spine, felt the smooth roll and flex of hard muscle under the soft material of his shirt. So warm . . .

And so dangerous. A dhampir inside his defenses, at his neck, close enough to kiss or to kill. He had to feel it. *I* felt it, the usual tingling sensation of a vampire's presence screaming a warning along my nerves.

Yet his only movement was to draw me nearer, his hands sliding down my sides to grasp my hips. It left us close, so close, as I never was with any of them, never could be, because being this near meant violence, meant fear, meant death for one of us. It always had and it always would, and there was no goddamned other way it could be. And yet he was still there, hard and hot and *so close*. . . .

So close, the scent of her, wild and comforting at once, enveloped him. He needed to stop this; he needed to leave. If he immersed himself in that scent, grew to depend on it, need it, it would starve him when it was gone.

He was already too hungry as it was.

Shut *up*, I thought savagely. I didn't want one of Louis-Cesare's random memories intruding, especially not of some other woman. Not here, not now. This was *mine*.

I deliberately slipped, falling backward onto the bed and dragging him down on top of me. "Dorina—"

"You're breathing heavy."

"Vampires don't breathe."

I pressed up against him, and his breath caught in his throat. "Guess you're right," I said, and flipped him.

The high slit made it easy to straddle him. So I did, before running my hands down to the waist of his trousers again, and tugging his shirt loose. I liked the way his hands clenched on my arms as I unfastened his belt, the delightful tensing as my fingers slipped just inside his trousers.

He did nothing to help me, his own hands curved around my waist, softly stroking my skin through the silk. But he didn't stop me, either. My hands smoothed around his hips, my fingers finding the dimples at the base of his spine.

They were a frivolous feature on such a body, like that overabundant fall of hair that he took such pains to keep in check, or the absurdly long lashes on that strong-boned face. It was as if his body had somehow known that the man was going to be a pile of contradictions, and had woven them into him, skin and bone and flesh. I stroked the small indentations lightly, feeling the muscles tighten underneath my tender exploration, before moving on.

A sweep of sinfully rich lashes against moon pale skin. A coy look, a flash of white teeth, as she slowly backed down his body. He needed to end this. But she was touching *him, and it felt so good, just this, even this. More was going to kill him, and he wanted it, fiercely.*

Louis-Cesare stared as if mesmerized as I slowly bent lower, close enough that he could feel my warm breath on him, yet he still didn't move, didn't try to stop me. I decided that was as much of an invitation as I was likely to get. The dark tailored slacks were skin-warm under my lips as I bent forward, mouthing the soft material and the hardness just beneath.

He wasn't wearing anything under those trousers, and the wool was so fine that it felt like silk, more an enticement than a barrier. I outlined him with my tongue for a moment, watching with a kind of fascination as the trousers tightened impressively. It was an addictive kind of power, knowing I was doing this to him, shaping his body the way I wanted. I gave the tiniest of bites, and he made a sharp, startled sound and jumped against my lips.

"Dorina." He sounded a little strangled.

"Don't rush me," I admonished. "You had your turn."

He breathed in sharply. "I was trying to relax you!"

"Oh, is that what you were doing?" I asked, amused.

"Yes!"

"All right." I let him have the lie. "Now shut up and let me return the favor."

I wanted to torment him some more, but he was so teasingly *close*. My throat ached with wanting him; my tongue craved the intimacy of flesh. I slowly pulled down the zipper and peeled back the smooth material, freeing him. The sound he made as the cool air hit him was almost unbearably sensual. But not as much as the sight of him, thick and long and straight and perfect.

He was near enough for his scent to fill my senses, a deep, rich musk that made me lean in, suddenly hungry. Pure silk slid against my cheek. I sighed across him, watching him leap helplessly.

The seconds dripped like honey as she leaned closer, her thumbs settling against his hip bones, and he had all the time in the world to move away. But he didn't. He was too busy watching her eyes go dreamy and half-closed, the usual smirk fading and becoming something softer, something just for him.

I ran my tongue over my lips, and he immediately went from tense to rigid. I glanced up and saw that his eyes had turned the color of polished silver, and I hadn't even touched him yet. I decided it was time to rectify that. One hand slowly caressed his hip, while the other dragged across warm skin to wrap around him.

A faint flush darkened his cheeks, his breath caught and his pulse went from quick to frantic. I could feel it under my hand, a rapid staccato beat that seemed to follow my slowly gliding fingers. Like the blush of his skin, rose and gold, ebbing and flowing as I willed it.

I knew what he wanted, what his body craved, and I deliberately didn't give it to him. I teased him instead with light butterfly touches, too gentle, too slow, until his thighs were granite and his hands were fisting at his sides. He was beautiful like this. The Senate's greatest warrior, helpless in my hands.

Ray was safely away by now, but I didn't care. I wanted to see Louis-Cesare lose control for once, wanted to watch the tension in those proud features drain away, wanted to remember this. *Dangerous game*, a disconnected voice murmured in the back of my mind, but I pushed it aside. He jumped again, and this time, I caught him with my mouth.

A long, shuddering breath rushed past tight lips, and his head fell back.

One of my hands curved around his taut backside, the other circled warm satin, as the smooth solidity of him slid against my tongue. He was firm and slightly resistant, warm, with faint traces of salt and Louis-Cesare. Delicious.

My tongue slowly circled the tip, caressing him softly, letting him squirm. I flicked the sweet spot once, twice with the end of my tongue, then ran it up the side. My hand wandered backward, tracing a featherlight path to the velvet globes contracted high against his body. I teased and tormented, stroked and fondled, while my tongue swirled languidly around him.

Flashes of intense sensation seared up his spine and coiled in his belly, regular as clockwork and then deliberately arrhythmic as she modified her stroke to torture him anew. He shivered at the slight, purposeful rake of teeth, the edge of danger driving his need higher. Dieu, *a man could die from this, die and not care. . . .*

His thoughts leaked through in pieces, and I wasn't worried about them being memories, not anymore. They were too in tune with the expressions flitting across that changeable face. We'd shared something like this before, some emotional connection I didn't understand, almost like the mind-speak of the vampires. Only I'd never been able to do that with anyone else.

Normally it would have intrigued me, but right now I wasn't too concerned.

I swallowed, abruptly taking him deep, my lips stretched tight around the width of him. His hips jerked up reflexively, trying not to thrust, trying to stay in control when he so clearly wasn't. I hummed deliberately, wanting to see how crazy I could drive him, and I was rewarded with a groan that sent my own pulse racing.

Pulling back, I let him go with maddening slowness, allowing him to feel the drag of my tongue along his whole length. I paused for a long moment, with just the tip of him under my lips, reveling in the feel of the tremors that rippled under my hands. I let the anticipation build, caressing him softly with just the tip of my tongue.

"Dorina, *please*—" It sounded strangely like a prayer.

I let him squirm for a few moments longer. It felt so damn good to hear him begging in whispers and moans when I was the one getting what I wanted. And then, with no warning, I suddenly slid all the way back down.

The sound he made that time was really quite satisfying.

My head bobbed a few times, until I found a dreamy sort of rhythm, drinking in the soft sounds he made. And everything seemed to affect him. The soft brush of my hair against his thigh brought on a shudder, the feel of my teeth, scraping oh so carefully along his length, made him groan, the sight of me completely embracing him turned his eyes wild.

And then I wasn't able to think anymore, my own need spiraling up to envelop me. I heard when he finally broke, when he cried out my name, when he gripped the bed frame hard enough to crack it. But it was distant.

I looked up to find his eyes closed, his head thrown back, his face more vulnerable than I'd ever seen it. I stared for a long moment, wanting to memorize that expression. For once, it wasn't something gleaned from a tumbled mass of memories, a stolen glimpse into some-

one else's pleasure. It was something we'd made together, something new and uniquely *mine*.

A moment later I was down the fire escape with Ray
and running flat out for the car, my heart thundering in
my ears.

Chapter Eighteen

I didn't intend to end up drunk in a seedy dive. It was pretty cliché, after all, but there are times when the only response to life's little jokes is to get hammered. And if this wasn't the greatest joke ever, I didn't know what was.

There's a bar downtown that's so well-known to the regulars that it doesn't need a sign. Just as well, since it's named after the owner and there was no way that many syllables would fit. I left Ray's body in the back of the car, because if Cheung found it here, good luck to him. The garage was guarded by a couple of demons who really loved thieves—preferably seared with a shot of tequila.

I took the duffel in with me. After everything I'd been through to get it, there was no way it was leaving my sight. Possibly ever.

I grabbed my usual booth in the back, under a suspended TV that flickered blue light across the tabletop. It was showing one of the telenovelas the bartender loved. He wandered over after a minute and put down my usual, beer. "Nice dress."

"The reserve, Leo," I told him, scowling. There was nothing on the regular menu that was going to give me the burn I needed.

The shaggy eyebrows went up, but he didn't say anything, just took the bottle away and shambled into the back.

Claire was going to be worried. It was going on sixteen hours since I'd left the house, and I needed to call her. I also needed to get the ball rolling with Elyas, or at least make the attempt. But I didn't want to do either. I didn't want to think at all. I wanted to keep drinking until I was so staggeringly smashed that I couldn't remember how stupid I'd been.

But I wasn't sure Leo had that much in stock.

He returned and sat a small blue bottle on the table in front of me. I drank the contents straight, keeping pace for three shots with the cigarettes a guy at the bar was chain-smoking, until I started to feel the burn. Then I slowed down and stared at the TV without seeing it.

It was just the novelty of it, I told myself. A vampire who didn't act like I might go for his throat at any minute was a new experience, much less one who talked to me like a person, who held me like I might be fragile and who bought me silly, soft clothing, like he wanted to know how it felt against my skin. . . .

I decided the whole not-thinking thing had been the best plan, after all.

Another inch gone and the glass hit the table, tipped and rolled off the edge. Leo slid into the opposite seat. "Want to talk about it?"

"No. Want to get wasted." I started to retrieve my errant glass, but succeeded only in hitting my forehead on the very hard tabletop.

"I think you're already there," he told me, and pushed my hair out of my eyes. His face was craggy and scarred, but his mouth was soft, the eyes assessing my condition without judgment. "If you were anyone else, I'd say it was man trouble."

"He's not a man." Not anymore.

Leo raised those caterpillar eyebrows. "Some Weres can be very nice."

"Not Were, either." I took a drink straight from the bottle and wondered why I hadn't gone home to get shit-faced. Oh, yeah. I hadn't wanted to drive that far.

"You're dating a demon?" He leaned forward. "What kind? And don't tell me it's one of those damn incubi. They get all the pretty girls."

Leo was only the first part of a half-hour-long name,

but it fit. His type of demon has vaguely leonine features, and he always wore his sandy blond hair long. Like all bartenders, he could be damn talkative, although usually he had more tact than this.

"Just drop it, Leo."

"I knew it. It is an incubus. Useless damn things—"

I slammed down the bottle. "It's not a demon, okay? And can I please get drunk in peace?"

"Not a—Oh, no." He looked shocked. "You're not dating a fey. You can't trust those bastards, Dory. Ask anybody."

"Just because they overcharge you for your supply—"

"It's price-gouging," he said resentfully. "They know nobody but fey can make the stuff, so they set the price as whatever they want and we damn well have to pay! You don't want to have dealings with them."

"Funny thing—they say the same about demons. And he's not fey."

Leo wrinkled his massive forehead. "Not human, Were, demon or fey? What's left?"

"Hey, once you go vamp, you never go back," Ray said from the depths of the duffel.

Leo jumped. "What the—"

Something buzzed against my hip. It was my phone, wedged up against me inside the duffel bag. I almost didn't answer it, but it was Mircea, and I was going to have to talk to him sooner or later. Considering how that usually went when I was sober, I decided to try it drunk for once.

"You're dating a *vampire*?" Leo asked, looking shocked.

"No, just boinking," Ray told him.

"I'm not—That's not even a word," I told him, and hit TALK.

"Dorina?" Mircea wasn't putting so much effort into the dulcet tones this time, I noticed.

"Yeah?"

"Where are you?"

"Downtown. Leolintricallus—something or other. It goes on for a while."

"We get an additional syllable for every century we live," Leo said, frowning. "Although I never thought I'd live long enough to see this. What the heaven were you thinking?"

"I wasn't."

"That's clear enough!"

Great. The only thing worse than falling for a vamp would be having Leo tell everyone I'd fallen for a vamp. "Look, Leo, it's not what you—"

"Dorina!" Mircea's voice snapped.

"You sound annoyed."

"It would not be without cause!"

"What now?" I asked wearily.

"Point number one," he said grimly.

"Wait. There are points?"

"You do not tell me you are being chased by Hounds, and that you will call me back and then fail to do so! You have not answered your telephone for the majority of the evening!"

"I didn't have it for the majority of the—"

"Point number two: you have free access to my properties, but I would very much appreciate it if in future my bedrooms were off-limits!"

"Woah. You did the boinking in your dad's bedroom?" Leo looked vaguely impressed.

"Stop eavesdropping!"

"Are you kidding me? Your life is way better than anything on the soaps lately."

"Dorina." It sounded like Mircea might be grinding his teeth.

"Is there a point number three?" I asked. "Because you're interfering with my drinking here."

"Yes. If it will not inconvenience you too greatly, I should like to speak to Louis-Cesare."

"Sorry. You missed him."

"And yet Horatiu tells me he recently left tracking you."

"Tracking?" I asked, getting a sinking feeling.

I jerked open the duffel, and there it was, buzzing softly. I stared at it for a moment in disbelief. He'd tagged me. The son of a bitch had tagged me with my own damn charm.

"I'm going to have to call you back," I said grimly, clicked the phone shut and jumped up—only to find myself staring into a pair of burning blue eyes.

"Uh-oh," Ray muttered.

Louis-Cesare didn't say anything, unless you count breathing heavily.

"Look, this isn't what you think," I said, getting a solid grip on the duffel. "I wanted to get Ray away so we could talk—"

"There is nothing to say. You will return the vampire to me. Immediately." His tone might have been that of a king talking to a peasant. It made me quietly furious.

"I'm not one of your servants," I snapped. "You can't give me orders. And if you'd listen for a minute, you'd learn why you don't want to take Ray to Elyas."

"I know precisely what I want to do."

"Okay, then while you're up there, you might want to ask him what he was doing at the club just before the fey was found murdered," I said sarcastically. "And why Ray thinks he already has the rune, and intends to keep it *and* Christine. You might want to ask why he's been playing you!"

There was silence for a moment. "An excellent idea," Louis-Cesare said softly. And disappeared.

I stood there for a second, staring stupidly at empty space. I'd seen vamps move quickly before, but that was just ridiculous. And then I snatched up the duffel and headed out the door.

"What are you doing?" Ray demanded as I dashed across the garage floor, stabbing at the key fob repeatedly with my thumb.

"Going back."

"Are you crazy?"

"Not at the moment." I slid into the seat, threw him on the passenger side and started the engine, all in one motion. Louis-Cesare was on foot; if I didn't hit any traffic, maybe there was a chance—

"You could have fooled me!" Ray said as we tore out

of the garage on burning rubber. "When two first-level masters are determined to rip into each other, the only sane place to be is somewhere else!"

Normally, I'd have agreed. But there was no way Louis-Cesare could win a confrontation. If Elyas had the rune, he was toast, and if he didn't and Louis-Cesare killed him, it would break the ban set by the Senate. And their punishments tended to be draconian even when there wasn't a war on.

Five minutes later the car fishtailed to a stop in front of the mansion, and I leapt out. I grabbed the duffel, which contained most of my weapons, and headed for the front door. "What about the rest of me?" Ray shrieked.

"Stay in the car!"

"What if the master shows up?"

I threw him the keys. "Outrun him!" My last sight rounding the first bend in the stairs was his hairy butt, bent over searching for where the keys might have landed.

I took the stairs three at a time, hoping it would be good enough. It wasn't. I'd barely hit the foyer when I felt it—a swell of power coursing through the apartment, flickering though every vamp in the place who had ever tasted Elyas's blood.

Marlowe had been right: the death of a vampire hits his children hard, and at no time is that more true than the death of a first-level master. Heads whipped around; confusion and fear gripped the younger ones, one of whom screamed and collapsed from the shock. But there were enough masters around to regroup— fast.

Doors and windows slammed shut on all sides, including the ones behind me. I barely noticed. I stepped over a collapsed doorman and ran up a staircase in the direction of that swell of power.

A long corridor branched out from the stairs in either direction. A door was open at one end, and I went that way. It turned out to be a large study with a fireplace, a couple of maroon leather chairs, a cherrywood desk and a dead man.

The head was down, cradled in his arms, almost as if he was sleeping. Blond curls spilled over a green velvet jacket that matched the drapes and the marble desk accessories. If it wasn't for the knife protruding out of his back and the cloying scent of blood, I might never have known anything was wrong.

Then again, the vamp standing over him, clutching another blade sheened in blood, might have given me a clue.

For a moment, I just stared. I'd expected a confrontation, maybe even a duel, since master vamps weren't that great at following other people's rules. I hadn't expected cold-blooded murder.

Then I snapped out of it and kicked the door shut behind me. "You *killed* him?"

"Non." Louis-Cesare looked up at me, his eyes dark with shock.

"Then what the *hell*—"

"I came here to demand Christine. I found him like this."

Ray snorted from inside the duffel. " 'He was like this when I got here'? *That's* your alibi?"

"I do not need an alibi!" Louis-Cesare told him stiffly. "I did nothing!"

"And you're holding a knife because ... ?" I asked.

"The knife was on the floor, and the blood dripping from his wound was rapidly covering it. I picked it up to get it out of the way, and as I did so, he died."

I stared at him in disbelief. If that was his story, he was completely screwed. And then running footsteps were coming down the hall, and I realized it didn't matter. He could have the best damn story in the history of the world, but no vampire was going to take time to listen when his master had just been killed.

We needed to get out of here and worry about damage control later. There was a single window in the room, or there had been. The force of Elyas's passing had blown it out, letting in a breeze that stirred the heavy drapes. I used my elbow to knock out the remaining glass, then stared downward. A five-story plunge onto concrete, which was not doable for me. But Louis-Cesare ought to be able to manage it.

"Feel like giving me a—" I began, turning. Only to see him disappear through a door to the left.

"Where the hell is he going?" Ray demanded.

I just shook my head and ran after him. Beyond the door was some kind of sitting room, with a big window and a lot of soft, comfortable-looking armchairs. There was no one there, but a door on the other side of the room was open. I went through and found Louis-Cesare about to put his foot through a locked door.

"What are you doing?" I demanded, as the sound of fists pounding on the study door came from behind us.

"Searching for Christine." He kicked in the door and disappeared inside.

"*Now?* They're going to kill you if they find you here!"

"And they will kill her in three days if I do not."

"You don't know that she's here! Elyas could have her anywhere."

He didn't even slow down. He disappeared into what looked like a bathroom, while I stared back and forth between it and the office. Damn it! I turned around and ran back.

The door was shuddering under the blows from outside, but it must have been warded, because it hadn't already caved in. I didn't know how long it might last, but I needed a look at the body. God only knew what kind of condition it would be in by the time any of the Senate's people got here, and a dhampir witness was better than none at all.

The big leather chair was on wheels, so it was easy enough to move it out from the desk a couple inches, to give me a view of the body from underneath. The only light in the room was a thin ribbon under the door, the residue of a few low-burning sconces in the hall, and a little grayish city light from outside. At first I didn't see anything other than the unnatural tilt of his head and the wet, clotted gape of his slit throat. Then I took a pencil and pulled at the open collar of his dress shirt and there it was: a glint of gold.

"I don't get it," Ray said. "He had the rune—I know it. So why's he dead?"

I tugged at the chain and the heaviness already told me Ray was right, even before the necklace appeared. Ray had been correct about the size, but not the gaudiness. It was large, maybe four inches across, but beautifully made. The striations of gold radiating out from the center caught the light in a starburst that lit up the floor with a pattern of rainbows.

"Jókell's?" I asked, holding it up.

"Yeah. That's it," Ray told me, over a cracking sound.

A glance at the door showed me that someone had tried to put a foot through it. They hadn't quite made it, but part of the wood had bowed inward, with splintering around the indentation. Only the ward was keeping the fibers in place at this point, and it was failing. We were out of time.

I pulled the carrier off Elyas's head and shoved it in the duffel. I spared a second to check the knife sticking out of his back, to make sure I knew what had happened. Then I ran for it, hearing the door explode into pieces behind me.

A couple vamps had been smart enough to go around the long way. I guess the waiting room door must have been warded, too, because they met me in the bathroom. One was a medium-grade master—level five, at a guess—who tried to put a fist through my head. I dodged, and he hit the mirror instead, spraying glass everywhere and giving me a second to shove an incendiary stick down his pants.

It went off with a hissing flare and he fell back into the bathtub, screeching and fumbling for the faucet. The baby vamp with him just stood there for a second, before quickly putting his hands up. I rolled my eyes, pushed him out of the way and ran out the door.

It exited into the hall, where a crowd of people now wreathed the ruined study door. And, of course, one of them saw me. There was one of those startled moments when everyone just looked at one another, and then came a collective surge down the hallway. Louis-Cesare reached out of a small bedroom, jerked me inside and slammed the door.

Yeah, like that was going to help.

Someone put a foot through the door a second later, and when they drew back, I threw a disorienting sphere out the opening. It was designed to make vamps forget why they were fighting, but either I'd gotten a dud, or these vamps were especially motivated. Because an arm reached through, grabbed mine and slammed me into the door headfirst.

I twisted the wrist enough to get myself free and turned, still seeing stars. And then I saw Louis-Cesare gathering a woman into his arms. "We must get you out of here," he told her gently.

There was no light, but a spill of moonlight through an open window highlighted high cheekbones, sensual lips and sleek dark hair pulled back into a smooth chignon. She looked like a fashion model, if they'd had them in the nineteenth century, which was when her high-necked white lawn nightgown appeared to have been made. And she smelled like apples—crisp, fresh and succulent.

Oh, yeah. He'd really been suffering, I thought viciously.

And then the arm grabbed me again.

I stuck a knife through it as the woman turned her face up to his. She smiled. "Louis-Cesare."

The French window led onto a small balcony. He carried her out and looked over the edge. "It is a long drop," he told her in French. "Land on your feet in a crouching position."

She shook her head, grasping him around the neck. "It is too far for me."

"It is not too far," he said patiently. "You must try."

She shook her head more violently, starting to panic as she looked down. "No! No, I cannot. Please do not make me—"

"Oh, for God's sake!" Ray said. "What? Are you afraid she'll bruise?"

Louis-Cesare looked at me. "I'm with Ray on this one," I told him, as someone kicked in the door.

It fell onto the bedpost, which blocked it somewhat, but several vamps slithered around the sides anyway. Louis-Cesare put Christine down to face them, and she ran into an adjacent room. I followed her and found her hugging the back wall of a small dressing room.

"Please, please do not let him force me!" she begged.

My first thought was that Louis-Cesare had been right—her power signature was so low, she could have been a newborn. If I hadn't been paying attention, I might have mistaken her for a human. My second thought was that for someone who wasn't afraid of anything, she seemed pretty damned timid to me.

My third was how lovely that head would look on a pike, but I shook it off and grabbed her wrist.

"Okay," I promised. "It's okay. Louis-Cesare won't make you do anything you don't want to do."

"You promise?" With tears trembling in her dark eyes and her color high, she was truly stunning.

"I promise," I told her, pulling her back toward the door.

She followed me through meekly enough, flinching when Louis-Cesare broke off a bedpost with a crack. He wedged it against the door, which he'd somehow forced back into place. "We must go!"

"Couldn't agree more," I said, and shoved Christine off the balcony.

Louis-Cesare ran to the edge, looking over. "What did you do?" he asked me, in disbelief.

"What needed to be done." I pulled out a gun and emptied it into the swarm of vampires behind us. And then his arm was around my waist, and we were falling.

We landed on something hard, but more yielding than concrete, and then we were moving into Central Park in a squeal of tires. We were in the Lamborghini, with Christine in the front, clutching the seat. And Ray driving.

"You can't drive!" I told him, trying to get my limbs sorted out as we barreled diagonally across the street, heading straight for the curb.

"No shit!" We jumped it, and the resulting jolt almost threw me out of the car. I grabbed the back of Christine's seat as we slammed back down on a footpath and careened toward a fountain. And then somebody started shooting at us.

The only good thing was that by midnight, even most of the bums had gone home to sleep it off. That was lucky for them, because Ray was the worst damn driver I'd ever seen. And that was after I jerked his head out of the duffel and parked it on the dashboard.

"Gah! That makes it worse!" he told me, as I tried to get the eyes facing forward.

"How can it possibly be worse?"

"Because I got double vision now! Get it off! Get it off!"

He batted at his own head and succeeded in sending it tumbling into Christine's lap. She immediately went into hysterics and slapped it away. The head fell out of the car; Ray hit the brakes and we came to a screeching halt.

"What are you doing?" I screeched, as he hopped out. "There are people firing at us!"

"Tough!" came from somewhere under the car.

Louis-Cesare had pulled a gun from the duffel and was returning fire, and either he was a good shot or he got lucky, because the left front tire of our pursuers' car suddenly blew out. The explosion of rubber caused their car to swerve violently, sideswiping a tree and disappearing over an embankment.

I used the brief reprieve to roll under the chassis to help find Ray's missing piece, but the car was built too low to the ground to provide me much access. I was feeling around with my arm when a line of bullets strafed the side door, causing me to hit the dirt. A quick glance showed three vamps' heads poking up over the embankment, a streetlight gleaming on the muzzles of the guns they had pointed at us.

And then the car took off, leaving me hanging out in the open.

Fortunately, Ray had decided to move it only a few yards, apparently having the same trouble retrieving his missing part that I was. It jerked to a stop, scraping along the side of a rock wall, and stymieing Christine's attempt to climb out over the side. She turned around the other way, scrambling into the backseat just as I slid back behind the protection of the bumper.

Louis-Cesare was holding on to her with one hand and trying to return fire with the other, which wasn't working out too great, judging by the number of bullets that peppered the ground around me—half of them his.

"Would you cut it out already?" I snarled. "If I'm going to get shot, I'd like it to be by the bad guys."

He glared at me over the head of a hysterical Christine, who had him in a sobbing neck lock. "And if you will hurry up, we can get out of here before they manage to fix their vehicle!"

"Why didn't I think of that?"

More bullets slammed into the back side of Radu's baby as I peered under the car. But I could see the whites of two small, angry eyes glaring at me from near the right back wheel. I swept out a leg and hit the side of the head, and it rolled out from under the car—just in time to get drilled through the forehead with a bullet.

"What? What was that?" Ray demanded, his eyes crossing, as I snatched him up by the short and spikies.

"Nothing," I said, and dove over the backseat, and we were off.

The vamps abandoned their car and took off after us on foot, which was a smart move considering the number of obstacles in our path. They were gaining and Ray was cursing and Christine was sobbing. "Please, please let me out!"

"If I let you out, they will shoot you!" Louis-Cesare told her in French.

"They won't!" She shook her head hard enough that a spill of ebony hair flowed down over her shoulders. "I know them; I can talk to them!"

"I don't think they're in a talking mood," I said as Louis-Cesare thrust her at me. I thrust her back.

"You cannot drive a stick shift," he reminded me.

"I also can't return fire and hold on to your girl-friend at the same time," I snapped, scrambling over the seat.

"Relax—we'll lose them," Ray told me as I tried to take the wheel. "I got a portal right up ahead."

"We can't go through another portal!" I said as we bounced across grassy hills, apparently not missing a rock or a root on the way.

"I'm not looking forward to it, either, but you got a better suggestion?"

"Any suggestion would be better!" I said, dropping his spare part in his lap and trying to ease in behind him. "If we go through a portal, we'll explode."

"We didn't explode last time."

"I didn't have my duffel last time!"

"What difference does that make?" Ray demanded, his cheek smushed against the steering wheel.

"The putty's in there."

"What putty?"

"The putty I was going to use to blow up the portal at your office," I panted, finally realizing that he had the damn seat belt on. A bullet parted my hair as I worked frantically to get it undone.

"So don't shoot at it and we'll be—"

"It doesn't need to be shot!" I told him as the seat belt slithered free. "If it comes into contact with a portal's energy, it detonates automatically. And that much would not only kill us, but take out a full city block!"

Ray paled. "Then you might want to turn here," he said as a familiar flash split the air right ahead.

I swerved hard to the right, sending his hairy butt tumbling into the passenger seat. We plowed through a park bench, skidded into a road and were back on asphalt, if not out of trouble.

I leaned over the seat. "Where to?" I yelled.

Louis-Cesare shot me a pained look. "Vampire hearing!"

"Human adrenaline!" I shouted back, just as loud. "Where?"

He swallowed and faced the inevitable. "We have to report this."

I nodded and shifted gears. For the first time in my life, I was actually relieved to be headed to vamp central.

Chapter Nineteen

It was an hour later and Elyas was still dead. We were back at the mansion, and things were starting to get a little creepy. Not so much because of the dead body, but because of the ones that remained alive. So to speak.

Exhibit number one was in the hall outside the study. The vamp must have been young enough not to have much power of his own, because without his master's to aid him, he was little more than an automaton. He had a broom in one hand and a dust pan in the other, and he'd been sweeping the same patch of already-gleaming floor over and over for the last ten minutes.

I had this crazy vision of him standing there, sweeping and sweeping, until he dried up entirely and began to crumble. Until he became dust himself. *If his arms go last, he could sweep himself up....*

"How long does it take to find a freaking bullet?" The crabby voice jolted me out of an exhausted haze.

Ray was exhibit number two in the creepy undead department. He, Christine and I were in the sitting room next to the study, waiting until the big shots decided we were needed. I'd taken the opportunity to dig the bullet out of Ray's skull before the wound healed over. But so far, I wasn't having much luck.

"I'm working on it," I told him. I had him in my lap, catty-cornered on a towel. But if he strained, he could manage to glare up at me. He'd been straining a lot.

"Well, work faster. I'm getting a migraine here."

"It's not my fault. The knife blade's too wide. I can't get it far enough in."

"Then use something else!"

"I don't *have* anything else," I said, yanking it out of his skull. Christine suddenly jumped up and fled the room. "What's wrong with her?"

Ray gave an eye roll. "Who cares? I got an emergency here. You don't find that damn thing, and I'm gonna have to go to a bokor. And I hate those things."

He was referring to the legal sort of necromancer. They worked for the vamps instead of against them, smoothing out damage to vampire flesh the way a cook would knead bread dough. "What's wrong with going to a bokor?"

"They're nothing but hacks. And don't believe those ads they run, either."

"What ads?"

"You know, in the backs of all the papers."

"Guess I must have missed them."

"The ones that promise to make things bigger."

"What things?"

"You know. *Things.* The one I tried charged me a fortune, and all he did was make it lumpy."

"Oh." I'd seen Mr. Lumpy; Ray should have sued.

Christine came back a minute later with a sewing basket over her arm and proffered a knitting needle. "Will this help?"

"Couldn't hurt." Our fingers brushed as she passed it over, and she jerked back like she'd been burned. "I'm not going to bite you," I told her impatiently.

"I'm sorry." Her eyelashes fluttered, and one hand went to her hair, nervously. She seemed horrified to learn that it was still down, and quickly pinned it back into a chignon. The hairstyle left the bones of her face bare, but they could take it. "I . . . I have never before met a dhampir."

"Lucky you," Ray muttered.

"How do you know what I am?" I demanded.

"Louis-Cesare informed me."

"Really. What else did he say?"

"Ow! Watch it!" Ray groused. I looked down to see that I'd jabbed him in the eye.

"He did not say anything else," Christine said, sitting back down. She'd changed out of the bloody nightdress as soon as we returned, with a squeamishness that seemed a little odd in a vampire. The new ensemble was a deep rose gown with scads of antique handmade lace around the low neckline. It complemented the glossy dark hair, delicate features and big brown eyes.

I went back to work, but I could feel those eyes on me, like a weight.

I sighed. I'd known this was coming. She could probably smell Louis-Cesare all over me and vice versa. And while it wasn't a servant's place, even a favored one, to criticize her master, I was fair game.

I looked up, waiting for it, but she didn't say anything. She just sat there, her gaze steady on mine. And weirdly enough, there was no challenge in it. If anything, it held a kind of childish wonder.

"Take a picture; it'll last longer," Ray told her.

She blinked. "I'm sorry," she told me again. "I did not mean to stare. But I must admit that I find you fascinating."

What I found fascinating was that the needle just kept going in. Half of it had disappeared inside Ray's skull, and it hadn't hit anything yet. Well, nothing hard anyway. I tried wiggling it around, but it made his eyes cross so I stopped.

"Any particular reason why?" I asked Christine.

"You kill vampires."

"Only the bad kind," I told her, to prevent another freak-out.

"They're all bad."

I would have thought she was kidding, but that beautiful face was perfectly serious. "*You're* a vampire."

"Yes."

"So you're evil?"

"Yes."

"Well, that's a novel approach." She tilted her head to one side in a question. "Most vamps I've met are like anybody else," I explained. "They find ways to justify what they want to do so it leaves them the hero of the story."

A small frown appeared between those lovely eyes. "But that would be useless. Denying what we are does not change it. Evil is evil, regardless of the face it wears."

This conversation was getting a little surreal. And that was from someone used to talking to Radu. "So you're a self-professed evil vampire?" A nod. "And I kill evil vamps." Another nod. "Should I just kill you then?"

"Oh, not yet," she told me earnestly. "I have done little to redeem myself."

"Elevator don't go all the way to the top, does it?" Ray muttered. And then his eyes lowered to half-mast, and he started to grin, lazily. "Oh, yeah, baby. Right there. That's the spot. Hit that a—"

I hastily pushed the needle a little farther in, and he shut up.

"I thought you believed that vampires lost their souls," I reminded her. "How do you get redemption after that?"

"It is not easy," she told me seriously. "For years I could not understand why God would allow this to happen to me. I felt betrayed, lost, unclear what path I should take. I hated my master for making me like this, for giving me these terrible cravings—"

"But you got over that." I didn't bother to hide the sarcasm, but Christine didn't look like she'd noticed.

"Yes. He did not mean to hurt me, merely to change me into what he was. And he does not see himself as a monster, did you know?" she asked, apparently amazed.

I stared at her. "If it hadn't been for that 'monster,' you'd have been dead a long time ago!"

She sat forward, nodding eagerly. "Yes, yes, precisely. That is what I finally realized, too. Louis-Cesare was doing God's work, although he did not know it. I was meant to live this life, to have this chance. You understand, don't you?"

"Well, I'm glad you worked through all that pesky guilt," I told her. And then the point of the needle popped out the back of Ray's head on a little gout of blood.

Christine and I stared at it for a moment. "Is it . . . supposed to do that?" she asked.

"Do what?" Ray rolled those eyes up at me. "Did you get the bullet out?"

"Um."

"Dorina!" Mircea's less than pleased voice cut through my dilemma. He'd been in a pissy mood since we showed up on his doorstep with a headless naked guy, a terrified hostage and a bunch of vampires claiming that Louis-Cesare was a murderer.

Go figure.

I tucked Ray's head under my arm and wandered next door, where Mircea, Marlowe and some older vamp I didn't know were bracketing the dead man. Louis-Cesare sat on a sofa off to the side, with his head in his hands, looking about like I felt. I doubted it was good old-fashioned fatigue on his part—more like the depth of the shit he was in had finally impressed itself on his mind.

Good, I thought evilly.

Mircea had gone casual today, in a midnight blue suit with a slash of pearl gray for a tie. He had the suit coat off and the shirtsleeves rolled up. He had examined the dead man and hadn't wanted to ruin the Armani, I guessed. "We are ready for your evidence," he informed me.

"There's no time for this," Marlowe said, running a hand through his already-messy curls. He was dressed in his favorite deep burgundy, although it was rumpled enough to make me wonder if he'd had to dress quickly.

"We must make time," Mircea said sharply. "I need something, Kit. I cannot stand before the Senate and defend him successfully with what we have."

Marlowe shook his head violently enough to send the curls dancing. "The only evidence she can give will hurt our case, not help it. She took the only thing he had to trade for Christine. And the current ban on duels meant there was no other way to save his servant's life but to kill the man who held her captive."

"Louis-Cesare does not stab people in the back," I pointed out.

"Which is why it would have been an intelligent method to use," Marlowe snapped. His tone said that he'd have vastly preferred to blame me for this, and how dared I have been with other people when it had happened?

"I had an appointment—" Louis-Cesare began.

"An appointment to give him the price he'd demanded for Christine's return—a price you could no longer meet," Marlowe said.

"I used the front door and was ushered in by one of his servants! Even had I lost all conception of honor and decided to murder the man in cold blood, I should hardly have chosen to do so under those circumstances."

"If you were thinking clearly, perhaps not. But you admit yourself that you were enraged." Marlowe was good at playing devil's advocate, but even I knew he wouldn't be the only one saying these things soon. This was bad.

"Tell me again what happened," Mircea said. Between the screams and the accusations and the gun pointing, we hadn't had time to discuss the evening's events in detail at vamp central.

"After speaking with Dorina, I came up to confront Elyas about his duplicity," Louis-Cesare said tersely. "I was ushered into the waiting area." He nodded at the small room with the comfy chairs. "I waited. But after a time I became impatient and—"

"How long a time?"

"A minute, perhaps two. I was in no mood to indulge Elyas's power games. In the end, I went through without an escort and found him as you see."

"Then explain why he died while you were standing over him, holding the knife used to sever his arteries!" Marlowe demanded.

"I cannot. I smelled the blood when I opened the door, but I did not know that it was his. I only discovered what had been done when I bent over the body. The knife was on the floor, and I picked it up to get it out of the way of the spreading stain. As I stood up again, he died. I felt it when it rippled through the house, and a moment later, his family was there, along with half or more of his guests."

"Yes! Dozens of witnesses and a story a child wouldn't believe." Marlowe threw up his hands. "If you are going to lie to the Senate, at least make it plausible."

"I am not lying." It was the king-to-peasant tone again, and it didn't look like Marlowe liked it any better than I had.

"The wooden knife was in the *heart*, Louis-Cesare," Marlowe said, pointing at the gory thing that now resided on the desk. It wasn't the usual plain-Jane stake, but a hand-carved specimen with a long, slender blade and a distinctive finial. I even thought I caught a glimpse of some metal—steel or silver—at the tip.

Elyas had been stabbed with the Cadillac of stakes.

Nothing but the best for a senator.

"As soon as the wood penetrated the muscle, he died." Marlowe continued. "There is no delayed reaction; you know this!"

"There are two ways into the study, as you can plainly see," Louis-Cesare said icily. "Someone must have entered from the hall, killed him, and left while I was waiting. The study is soundproofed—I would have heard nothing!"

"And this mysterious murderer did this in what?" Marlowe demanded incredulously. "The thirty-second window of opportunity he'd have had?"

"It is possible," Mircea commented. "Elyas was playing host for most of the evening. He doubtless retired to the study to meet with Louis-Cesare only shortly before he was killed. It may well have been the first chance a murderer would have had to get him alone."

"It was also the first chance Louis-Cesare had."

"The master retired to the study not ten minutes before his death," the old vamp put in, although no one had asked him. He was dressed like a butler, and he looked vaguely like one, too, with bushy salt-and-pepper hair, muttonchop sideburns and a mustache that said he was overcompensating for something. He was likely the senior vamp in Elyas's household.

I moved around the desk while Marlowe and Louis-Cesare glared at each other. "What is it?" Mircea asked, as I leaned over the body.

"Don't touch that!" Marlowe ordered, seeing what I was doing.

"I hadn't planned on it." The wooden knife in Elyas's heart hadn't been disturbed, and the telltale sign was still on the bottom of the blade, on the portion that had stayed outside the flesh—a small ring of pale, almost translucent gray.

"Dorina?" Mircea glanced from the hilt to my face, eyes suddenly sharp. He knew I was about to hand him something. And damn it, he was right.

I stood back up. "Elyas could have been killed at any time during that ten minutes," I told them.

"He could not!" Marlowe barked. "We know when he died. The reaction was felt by everyone in the apartment—including you."

I sighed. This was going to cost me a fortune. "There's a way to delay the reaction."

His eyes immediately narrowed on my face. "How?"

"You asked me a question yesterday, about how I get out of clubs and homes after killing a master, without his servants immediately zeroing in on me."

"And?" His eyes had gone a bright, glittering black.

"I behead the master first, because—I don't care who you are—that's going to be a shock to the system."

"Damn straight," Ray commented.

Marlowe never even glanced at him. "And then?"

He was like a goddamned dog with a bone, I thought resentfully. "Then I tie his hands behind his back and jam the stake into his heart—a special one I previously coated in a thin layer of wax."

His eyes widened.

"I don't see why that would make a difference in the time of death," Muttonchops said.

"The body's heat melts the wax," I said, spelling it out for him. "But not right away. I have anywhere from thirty seconds to a couple of minutes to get away before any of the actual wood touches the heart."

"And you can control the amount of time by the thickness of the wax," Marlowe said, blinking. "It's so bloody simple. Why didn't I think of that?"

"Maybe you don't kill as many vamps as I do," I said sourly. "The point is, anyone could have offed Elyas. Set him up like I described. Then hurry out into the hall, and either leave the apartment entirely or—"

"Or rejoin the other guests as if nothing had happened."

"And remain to see the body being found to make certain that nothing went amiss," Mircea added. He looked at Muttonchops. "I would appreciate a list of all your guests tonight. Invited and otherwise."

The vamp did affronted dignity well. "You cannot believe one of them to be responsible! I assure you, everyone here was of the finest—"

"Of course," Mircea murmured soothingly. "I would expect no less of an illustrious house. However, it is the usual protocol, and I will be asked for it."

The vamp nodded stiffly but made no move to leave. He concentrated for a moment, probably trying to summon a flunky, but they all appeared to be out of order. He gave a disgusted sound and walked to the door to bark an order to a human servant instead.

Mircea thanked him and turned back to the body, still looking grim. "That's how it was done," I told him. "I promise you."

"*I* do not doubt your word, Dorina," he said, with emphasis.

"You don't think the Senate will believe me?"

"Well, I don't believe you," Muttonchops said. "It's preposterous. I've never heard of such a thing. A first-level master would merely break the bonds and remove the knife."

"Not with his head just cut off and a stake through his heart," I said drily.

He gave me a purely venomous look. "I could do it. And I'm second-level."

"Want to try?"

"Dorina." Mircea gave me the look that said, "You're not helping."

"Believe me, I've done this enough to know," I told him. "It works. Maybe if the vamp in question had more time, he could figure a way out of it. But he has only seconds. They may struggle a bit, sure, but they are mostly paralyzed, and the majority don't even realize the danger. They think I missed the heart and left them for dead, and that one of their servants will find them shortly. And they're gone before they realize their mistake."

Muttonchops turned to Mircea. "Even if you accept this creature's evidence, the fact remains that no one else had reason to kill the master!"

"Like hell," Ray said. I thumped him hard, and he shut up. But Mircea shot me a look.

"You can point out to the Senate that Louis-Cesare had the rest of the week," I told him. "If he planned to kill Elyas, he'd have done it later, after he had exhausted all other possibilities. There'd be no reason to do it tonight, especially in so public a way."

"It's the best we're going to get," Marlowe said, looking at Mircea. "Will it be enough?"

Mircea closed his eyes. He didn't look optimistic. "The Senate is meeting in an hour in an emergency session. We will soon know."

A couple of large vamps approached with a stretcher, but Marlowe waved them off. "The Senate may ask to see the body in situ."

"But dawn approaches," Muttonchops said, sounding scandalized.

Since it was only about one a.m., the guy was exaggerating. But then, he was upset. And he didn't know how long the Senate bigwigs intended to leave his master exposed.

That sort of thing was a major taboo in the vamp world. Once a vamp's power leaves him, his protection against the sun goes with it. Any stray beams after that will fry what is left to a crisp in a matter of seconds. The last service a vampire performs for his or her master is ensuring that the body is hidden away so that the sun can never touch it.

Marlowe's expression said he couldn't give a shit, but Mircea moved in with soothing, reasonable arguments, his voice taking on the cadence that said power was being exerted, but subtly. Muttonchops's frown smoothed out, and within moments he was nodding, as if leaving his master's gory body slumped at the desk was the best idea he'd heard in a while.

Marlowe met my eyes, and I could tell he was thinking the same thing: too bad that kind of thing wouldn't work on the Senate.

Chapter Twenty

Muttonchops left a moment later to arrange for extra blackout curtains. As soon as the door closed behind him, I got up and put the necklace on the desk. There was no way a dhampir was going to be allowed to address the Senate, which didn't even recognize me as a person. But Mircea was going in there, and he needed more than a speck of wax.

"Plenty of other people had a reason to kill Elyas," I said simply.

Mircea clicked on the lamp and bent over the desk to get a good look. Then sharp, dark eyes turned up to me. "Where did you get this?"

"Off Elyas's neck."

Marlowe started to squawk something, but Mircea held up a hand. "Tell me," he said quietly. Louis-Cesare moved to the door, making sure that we had a moment of relative privacy.

"Elyas tried to buy the rune before the auction, but was told he'd have to bid for it like everyone else. When Ming-de won, he was furious—"

"A great many people were," Marlowe said resentfully. "The auction was obviously rigged."

"Yeah, only Elyas wasn't going to take that lying down. He went to the club, killed the fey and took it—"

"Raymond saw him?" Mircea asked sharply.

"No, he smelled him. You can ask him if you want details, but there aren't many. Basically, the fey showed up, Ray left him alone for a few minutes, he returned and the guy was dead. Elyas's scent was in the air, and the necklace was missing."

"How lovely," Christine said breathily, her face alight. She'd come in so quietly that even the vamps hadn't heard her. I saw Marlowe start.

She didn't notice, being too busy gazing raptly at the carrier. The cold electric light sparked a fountain of prisms off the intricate surface, bathing her face with rainbows as she leaned closer, seemingly mesmerized. And before anyone could stop her, she'd picked it up.

"Drop it!" Marlowe barked.

She looked up, eyes wide and startled. And the carrier slipped from her fingers, hitting the desk and sending dancing beams across the dead man as it rolled toward the edge. She stared at it. "*Je regrette!* I did not mean—"

"You foolish girl!" Marlowe looked like he wanted to shake her. Christine transferred her gaze to him, looking part-mortified, part-confused.

"No harm donc," Mircea told her, and caught the heavy disk with a handkerchief.

"No harm done?" Marlowe demanded. "You'll never get anything off it now!"

The supernatural community didn't usually check fingerprints, because there are plenty of things that don't leave any. But a good clairvoyant might be able to get something off the thing, if not too many people had touched it in the meantime. It was why I'd been careful not to handle it.

"That remains to be seen," Mircea said mildly.

Christine backed into the wall, looking like she wished she could melt into it. She seemed on the verge of tears again. Louis-Cesare came over and led her to a chair. "*Ça ne fait rien.*"

Marlowe looked disgusted. "Oh, no. Not important at all. Just one less piece of evidence that might have exonerated you!"

"This held Naudiz?" Mircea asked me, wrapping it securely in the square of linen. "You are sure?"

"Originally. Ray saw it when the fey first arrived, but

it was empty when I took it off Elyas's neck. There's a space in back where the rune should be, but there's nothing there now."

He frowned. "But . . . did Elyas steal an empty carrier, or did he succeed in stealing the rune and was killed for it tonight?"

"If he'd had the rune, he wouldn't be dead," I pointed out.

"Not necessarily. I have seen other runes from the same set. If this one functioned similarly, then it had to be cast in order to function. Wearing it alone, particularly when not touching the skin, might not have been enough."

"If he was fighting for his life, I think he'd have cast it!"

"But was he?" Mircea nodded at the body. "He did not die in a fighting pose and there are no wounds on the body other than the ones that killed him. It appears that he was caught off guard."

Marlowe nodded. "If he knew his attacker or did not expect to be assaulted when surrounded by his family—"

"They never do," I muttered.

"—he might well have chosen not to use the stone. It is a talisman with a set amount of power at its disposal. Exhausting it for no purpose would be foolish."

"Unlike wearing it around his neck while somebody killed him," I said sarcastically. Louis-Cesare had said that Elyas liked to take risks. It looked like he'd taken one too many.

"Whether the rune was stolen last night or tonight, it gives us something to offer the Senate," Mircea said. "Anyone at that auction is a suspect—"

"And at least one who wasn't," I added reluctantly. I didn't know how the hell I was supposed to tell them about Æsubrand without landing Claire in the middle of this. But they had to know. The ice-cold prince of the fey was probably the prime suspect.

Mircea had been putting the carrier in his suit pocket, but he paused at my tone. "Dorina?"

I got a reprieve because Muttonchops took that moment to return with the list of party guests, and everyone crowded around the desk. "Was anyone on this list at the auction?" I asked Ray.

"It doesn't have to have been someone who was invited," Marlowe pointed out.

Muttonchops shook his head. "On the contrary. We had someone on the door. No one who was not on that list would have been allowed in. Other than Louis-Cesare, of course, who was expected."

"What level?" Marlowe asked.

"What?"

"What level of master was acting as doorkeeper?"

"We do not typically use a master for such a menial task," he was told.

"Menial? Is that how you consider your frontline defenses?"

The small amount of cheek showing between Muttonchops's mustache and sideburns reddened. "This is a home, not a fortress!"

Marlowe looked pointedly at the dead man. "So I see."

"It could have been anyone at the auction," Mircea said calmly. "None of them would have had difficulty fogging the mind of even a low-level master."

"That goes for a lot of other people," I pointed out.

He shook his head. "I do not think any of the participants would have been eager to discuss the auction. Some of their families doubtless knew, but they were under their direct control. It would have been foolish to tell anyone else and increase the competition."

And the chance that the fey will hear about it and hack your head off, I thought silently.

"Any one of them could have determined to do as Elyas did," Mircea mused, "and have gone to the nightclub in search of the fey, either to make a bargain with him or to kill him."

"Only when they arrived, they found that someone had beaten them to it," I said. "And they either smelled

Elyas on the air or actually saw him leaving. But why not attack him last night? Why wait?"

"Perhaps because the idea of killing a Senate member was more daunting than merely disposing of a fey guard," Louis-Cesare said.

Marlowe shot him a cynical look. "Or perhaps because he had been invited here tonight and thought the party would be a good cover. If the culprit was on the guest list, he didn't have to fog any minds to get in!"

Ray still hadn't said anything, so I poked him. "Who was at the auction?"

He licked his lips, looking between Mircea and Marlowe. "I—I won't have to testify, will I?"

"Yes," Mircea told him, holding up the list so he could see it.

"But . . . but . . . in front of the *Senate*?" Ray's voice dropped to a whisper. He looked terrified.

"I can tell them only hearsay. You were there," Mircea pointed out.

"Yes, but . . ."

"And testifying might help your case."

"My case?"

"The smuggling case against you."

Ray looked like he'd almost forgotten that trivial detail.

"He also has master problems," I put in.

Mircea's lips twisted. "We will see what can be done. Assuming his memory improves."

"Ming-de, Elyas, Radu, Geminus, and Peter Lutkin," Ray said quickly.

"Cosmopolitan group," I commented. "Ming-de from the Chinese court, Elyas from the European Senate, Radu bidding for Mircea, and Geminus—"

"Also North American Senate," Mircea said, somewhat grimly.

"Oh, yeah. The prick." He was one of the older senators, rivaling the consul in age, but not in power—or in anything else except ego. He also believed he was God's gift to women and didn't know how to take no for an answer. He'd grabbed my ass within thirty seconds of meeting me, and had not taken the resulting knife through the wrist well.

"I don't know any vampires named Lutkin," Marlowe said thoughtfully.

"He's a mage." Everyone looked at Ray. "Their money spends, too," he said defensively.

"Lutkin was here tonight," Louis-Cesare pointed out, tapping a name near the bottom of the list. "And Geminus. But none of the others."

Marlowe's expression brightened. "We can blame it on the mage. The others are too prominent or too unreachable in any case."

"And if he did not do it?"

Marlowe looked at him like he didn't understand the question.

"There were no silent bidders?" I asked Ray. "Nobody bidding by phone?"

"No. Seller insisted on a binding spell. And that don't work unless someone's physically there."

"He was worried about fraud?" I asked incredulously. "With that group?"

"He was worried *period*. The guy was freaking paranoid."

"He probably knew who was chasing him. He didn't want to risk anyone using a glamourie and impersonating one of the bidders."

"That's what I figured."

I frowned. "So he knew he was being hunted, knew he was in serious jeopardy, yet he still let his guard down enough for someone to . . ."

There was a sudden silence around the desk. I looked up to find everyone staring at me, a ring of bright, narrowed eyes. "Hunted by whom?" Mircea asked quietly.

There was no point in postponing it. "Æsubrand."

Louis-Cesare's head jerked, like he'd been stung. *"Comment?"*

"And you know this how?" Marlowe asked, his expression darkening.

"He dropped by the house last night."

"Dropped by?" Mircea asked sharply.

"In a manner of speaking."

Marlowe glared at me. "Our spies have reported no such escape."

"Then maybe you should get new ones."

"I don't need new ones. You clearly mistook another fey for him."

"Doubt it," I said drily.

"You are sure?" Mircea pressed. "You saw him clearly?"

"He was about an inch from my face while he was trying to kill me," I said sarcastically. "So, yeah, I'm pretty sure."

"He tried to—" Mircea broke off, his jaw tightening.

"Why did you say nothing of this?" That was Louis-Cesare.

I shrugged. "It didn't come up."

"It did not come up?"

"What happened?" Mircea demanded.

"I already told you: he tried to kill me; he failed. The point is that he's here and he has a definite interest in the rune. His mother was the one who stole it in the first—"

"Stole it from whom?"

That was Marlowe, and if I hadn't been so tired, I'd have really rubbed it in. The guy thought he knew everything. "The Blarestri royal house."

"The *what*?" Marlowe was the only guy I knew who could bellow in an undertone.

I glanced at him impatiently. "Well, where the hell did you think they got it, Marlowe? Or didn't you and Daddy bother to ask?"

He flushed. "You're telling me that the rune up for sale was a royal fey relic?"

"Yeah. And they want it back."

"And how do you come to know this?"

"I'm acting for the family."

"Another fact you failed to mention before now," Mircea said pointedly.

I smiled. "Like you failed to mention what you really wanted with Ray?"

"That is hardly the same thing."

"It is exactly the same thing! You sent me after him under false pretenses."

"There were no false pretenses."

"You let me believe he was a smuggler."

"Which he is."

"And which had nothing to do with why you wanted him. If we're going to keep working together, you have to—"

"You do not work with Lord Mircea," Marlowe informed me. "You work *for* him. It is not your place to question his commands."

"Is that how you think, too?" I asked Mircea.

Before he could answer, the door opened, and several vamps walked in like they owned the place. Which one of them did, I realized, as Muttonchops's head jerked up. "Master!"

He obviously wasn't talking to Elyas, so that cry could mean only one thing. Elyas's servants hadn't been the only ones to feel his passing. His master had done so, too.

"Anthony," Mircea said, straightening, as Muttonchops almost fell over himself trying to get around the table. "I thought we were meeting in an hour."

"Yes, I received your message," the dark-haired vamp said carelessly. He wasn't tall, maybe five nine, and his features were handsome but not outstanding. His nose looked like it had been broken at some point, and his skin was a little weather-beaten. It meant he wasn't exerting power to alter his appearance, which was strange, considering how much he had to spare. It felt like it seared my skin, even from this far away.

"Anthony?" I asked Louis-Cesare, who was looking a little ill suddenly.

"My consul."

Oh. That Anthony.

The vamp circled the desk, taking his time, getting a look at the body. "Oh, don't mind me," he said, looking up with a smile. "Continue with what you were doing."

"We've already examined the body," Mircea told him. "You are, of course, welcome to do so yourself—"

"How kind of you," Anthony murmured.

"But we will be reporting the findings shortly."

"Really? To whom?"

"To the Senate."

"And which Senate would that be, Mircea?" Anthony asked, whiskey eyes gleaming as they looked up from examining the gory throat.

I felt Marlowe tense beside me, but Mircea showed no outward change. "This happened on North American soil."

"But Elyas belonged to the European Senate." He smiled. "As does Louis-Cesare."

"That is under discussion," Mircea said sharply, which was news to me.

"Yes. But you have not stolen him away from me yet." The smile didn't slip, but the tension in the room suddenly ratcheted up about a hundred notches. "Therefore he will be judged by his peers—not his family."

"And defended by whom?" Mircea demanded.

"Whomever he likes." Anthony waved over his companion—a young vamp with long, dark hair spilling over the shoulders of a tailored gray suit. "As Elyas's master, Jérôme will, of course, be prosecuting."

Not so young, then, I thought, staring at the vamp. I wouldn't have guessed. Big eyes that matched his suit almost exactly in color, pretty, almost feminine features, delicate white hands—and a power signature no greater than that of the vamp I'd nailed to the bathroom wall at Ray's. It was hardly even discernible next to the inferno of Anthony's, like a single candle next to a bonfire.

But if he was prosecuting, he had to be a Senate member. So the signature was a lie. He had to be one of those rare vamps who could hide his true strength. If I hadn't known better, I'd have mistaken him for a baby, something that would have gotten me killed very fast—if I was lucky.

"And you?" Mircea demanded.

"Oh, didn't I say?" Anthony's smile broadened slightly, showing some fang. "I'm the judge."

Nobody moved; nobody blinked. But the air was starting to feel a little thick in my lungs. I suddenly really, really wanted to be somewhere else.

Luckily, Anthony agreed.

"And now, if you wouldn't mind, we would appreciate the same recourse to the body you have enjoyed."

No one had anything to say to that, so we retired to the adjacent sitting room. Or at least I tried to, before I was waylaid by an angry vampire and jerked into the hall. Christine had followed us out, and started to say something, then saw Louis-Cesare's face and shied back.

"I—I thought I would go pack," she said quickly, in French.

Louis-Cesare glanced at her, and his expression softened. "Yes, yes, please." It was gentle enough, but she all but fled down the corridor. Too bad I couldn't go, too, but I appeared to be trapped between his body and the wall.

"What bug crawled up your ass?" I demanded.

"If you mean, why I am upset? I should think that would be obvious!"

It took me a second, but I got it. "Oh, come on. You're not still pissed about—you did the same damn thing to me!"

He had the utter gall to look offended. "I did nothing of the sort—"

I stared at him. "And just how do you figure that? You stripped me butt naked, diddled me over a desk and stole my duffel bag. *And* my clothes!"

Somebody made a choking sound. I glanced up to find the door to the study open, and the old vamp looking scandalized. "Diddled?" Anthony asked, apparently delighted. Mircea closed his eyes.

Louis-Cesare made some indeterminate French sound and dragged me farther down the hall. A bedroom was empty, so he shoved me inside, which was a complete waste of effort. If it wasn't soundproofed—and I doubted Elyas had wasted an expensive spell on a guest room—the others could hear us perfectly well.

But Louis-Cesare didn't look much like he cared.

"I was speaking of Æsubrand. You knew you were in danger, yet you said nothing."

"Why should I have? It was none of your business."

"If someone is attempting to murder you, it is most certainly my business."

"Why?" He didn't say anything, which pissed me off. I was tired and starving, and I must have bumped my hurt wrist somewhere, because it throbbed in time to every heartbeat. I was in no mood for games.

"Why is it your business, Louis-Cesare?"

"You know damn well why!"

"No, I don't know. I don't know a goddamned thing. Maybe you should try spelling it out for once."

"And perhaps both of you should try learning some discretion," Marlowe hissed. He came in and slammed the door behind him. It wouldn't help with privacy; I think he was just pissed off.

"We would like some time alone," Louis-Cesare snapped.

"It seems to me you've had too much of that already." Marlowe stared back and forth between the two of us. "I don't know what's going on here—and I *really* do not wish to know. But now is not the time to hand Anthony more ammunition."

Louis-Cesare didn't even look at him. "What did he do to you?" he demanded.

"Maybe I should get it on a T-shirt," I said, crossing my arms. "None of your—"

"You have been favoring your left hand all night. Is that why?" Trust a swordsman to notice.

When I didn't say anything, he pulled me to him and began running his hands over me—as if he hadn't done enough of that already.

I was about to knock his hand away when Marlowe did it for me. Louis-Cesare's usually sunny blue eyes suddenly went chrome—cold, flat and dangerous. "Have a care, Kit."

"I am not the one who needs to take care. Have you gone mad? She is *dhampir*!" Marlowe said it in the same tone someone in medieval Europe might have used for leper, which was fair, since that was pretty much the way he'd meant it.

I don't know what would have happened next, because both men were crackling with energy, and neither was the type to back down. But then Mircea walked through the door. "Your consul wishes a word," he told Louis-Cesare mildly.

Louis-Cesare cursed under his breath and started to say something, but Mircea held up a hand. "This is bad enough as it is. Provoking the man for no reason would be foolish, do you not think?"

Apparently he did think, because he went, after shooting me a look that said this wasn't over. He'd barely gotten out the door when Marlowe rounded on me. "What in the *hell* game are you—"

"Kit. I think we have given Anthony enough amusement tonight, don't you?" Mircea asked.

"More than! Do you know what this will—"

"Yes. We'll discuss it in a moment."

Marlowe sent me a final glare and left. I'd have been right behind him, but Mircea was between me and the exit, and he showed no sign of moving.

"Don't you think it's time we talked?" he asked with a smile.

Chapter Twenty-one

"What about?" I asked warily.

Mircea leaned against the door, casual, elegant, like he had all night. Fortunately, I knew that wasn't true. Unfortunately, diving out the window wasn't a real possibility at this level. Maybe the roof . . .

"I do not want to play word games with you, Dorina. Tell me what happened last night."

"I've told you—"

"Nothing. Other than the bald fact that a very dangerous creature attempted for the second time to kill you. What you have not told me is why."

"He tried to kill me before—"

"Because you were in his way. Are you again?"

Nobody ever won a verbal sparring match with Mircea by taking the defensive, so I ignored that. "Are you going to tell me why you wanted the rune so badly that you practically threatened Louis-Cesare's life tonight?"

"I did nothing of the kind. And you didn't answer my question."

"Not in so many words, maybe. But the intention was conveyed. And you didn't answer mine."

"When you start being honest with me, perhaps I will."

I just stared at him, too shocked to speak for a moment. Because of all the people to chastise me for a lack of honesty or trust, Mircea's name should have been last on the list. In fact, it shouldn't have been on the damn list at all.

His brother Vlad had killed a lot of people in his short reign of terror, one of whom had happened to be my mother. Mircea had wiped that little fact from my adolescent head, afraid I'd go after my crazy uncle and get killed. Or so he said. I had no independent way of verifying that since wiped memories are gone for good.

"I don't think you're really one to talk. Do you?" I finally asked softly.

"I have never kept anything from you that was not necessary."

"In your opinion! Did it never occur to you that I might not agree? That I might have wanted those memories, however unpleasant?"

Mircea hesitated, taking a half second to adjust to the conversational leap. Not that it was much of one. Our history of deception had started almost as soon as our relationship had. "They would have done you little good had you died because of them."

"That was my decision!"

"You were too young to make that decision. It was my duty to make it for you."

"A duty you've kept up ever since." I rubbed my eyes, suddenly weary in more ways than one. I was tired of it—of the constant games and the verbal matches, of wanting to trust him but never knowing whether I could, or how far. I'd spent years avoiding a relationship with him for exactly those reasons, and I should have known better than to think that anything was ever going to change.

I'd told them all I could about Æsubrand's attack. There was nothing more I could do here. "This is a waste of time," I said, and headed for the hall door.

Mircea didn't budge, but his fingers bit into my arms. "Running away again, Dorina?"

I stared up at him, angry and tired and hurt. "I don't run from my problems!"

"Unless they include me. In which case you never do anything else."

"What else is there to do?" I demanded angrily. "Nothing changes, Mircea. We go on this same merry-go-round, over and over, until I'm dizzy. You manipulate me, lie to me—"

"I have never lied to you."

"Just twist things around to say what you want them to say, instead of the truth."

His jaw tightened. "Sometimes, the truth can be dangerous. If I had allowed you to retain your memories about Vlad, you would be dead. Merely another of his victims."

"And what's the excuse now? Because I'm sure you have one, and I'm sure it will sound perfectly plausible. And I'm equally sure it will be bullshit!"

"And do you not do the same to me?" he asked, a spark of amber lighting the deep brown of his eyes. That wasn't a good sign, but I was too pissed to care. "You almost died last night, practically under my nose, and you said *nothing*?"

"There were extenuating circumstances."

"There always are with us, it seems."

I started to shoot back a reply, but stopped. He looked tired suddenly, hollowed out and drained, in a way that was terribly familiar. It could be another game; it probably *was* another game. But it stopped me anyway.

"If you don't start to trust me, this is never going to work," I told him simply.

"And what is 'this'?" he asked carefully.

"Whatever the hell it is we're doing here. You wanted me to work with you, or so you said. And now Marlowe seems to think you meant *for* you, and I think he may be right. Because all I do is the same menial crap you could send any of your boys to do just as easily, and you never tell me a damn thing. It's been a month, and we've yet to work *with* each other even once!"

I expected another excuse, a platitude, an elegant brush-off. Mircea was the master at that sort of thing, and so smooth that half the time, the people who had been put off didn't even realize it. With vampires it was always smarter to pay attention to what they did rather than what they said, especially this one.

But he surprised me. Without a word, he turned and opened the door, indicating with a gesture for me to pre-cede him. I walked out, and then he led the way back to the soundproofed sitting room, where Marlowe was pacing. His head jerked up as we came in the door, and his expression darkened when he saw me.

"This is a very bad idea," he said, low and intense.

"And not telling her would be a worse one." Mircea went to the tall windows and drew the full-length drapes. Just in case someone had scaled the side of the building in order to lip-read, I presumed.

"I don't see how."

"You do not have a daughter, Kit."

"I do not—" Marlowe broke off, a look of disbelief spreading over his face. "That's your reason? You would risk—"

"Nothing. I think Dorina has proven that she knows how to keep a secret." Mircea pulled one of the chairs out from beside a small round table and then just stood there, waiting for me.

I cautiously moved forward, wondering if this was some kind of a test. Until recently, Mircea and I had spoken maybe once a decade, and those conversations always ended the same: I got louder and louder, and he got colder and colder, and eventually, I stormed out. That was how the world worked; that was the natural order of things. This . . . was not. And it worried me.

My hesitation seemed to anger him. "I wish to talk to you, Dorina! Please stop looking as if you suspect me of arranging an ambush."

An ambush might be easier, I thought, as I slid onto the smooth leather. I knew how to handle those. I wasn't so sure about whatever this was.

"Talk about what?" I asked cautiously. I had a lot of questions, but I knew better than to think I would get any answers. Mircea never came entirely clean with any-one. All vampires were cagey, secretive, guarded. But in his case, it was more than a personal preference; it was his job.

He was the Senate's chief diplomat, which meant a lot more than just pressing the flesh at parties. He did his fair share of that, but it was also his responsibility to find the weaknesses in people, to figure out what made them tick, to know what pressure points would yield results. That was why he and Marlowe had practically been Siamese twins since the war. Marlowe gathered info; Mircea exploited it. They were both very good at what they did.

But in Mircea's case, it had had a side effect. He'd done the job so long now, lived with the lies and half-truths and hidden agendas, that it had bled over into the rest of his life. Sometimes, I really didn't know if he knew the truth anymore.

"What did you ask for?" He sat down opposite me and crossed his legs, effortlessly elegant, as if we did this every day. Just a casual little father-daughter chat. Uh-huh.

"I'm listening."

"This cannot leave this room," he told me. "Not a word, not to anyone, not anywhere, no matter how secure you may think the location to be."

I'd have made a smart remark about melodrama, but one look at his face was enough. He was serious. "Okay."

"I assume you are familiar with the World Championships?"

I nodded.

"The Senate is sponsoring them this year, partly to improve our new alliance with the mages, but mainly as a cover."

"Cover for what?"

"A meeting of delegates from many Senates to discuss the war. If our enemies knew where we were strategizing, they would target it. But everyone goes to the races, which in turn sparks an endless stream of balls and parties—and numerous possibilities for meetings that do not look like meetings."

"Following you so far."

"But it is not merely the war that is being discussed. As you are doubtless aware, our Senate recently lost four members, and a fifth is incapacitated for the foreseeable future. Even in a time of peace, this would be intolerable, as it puts a heavy burden on those of us who are left. But with the added burden of the war . . . it is impossible."

"I can see that." The Senate members all had portfolios, like the members of a president's cabinet. Having so many missing must have placed a big responsibility on those that remained.

"The Senate is using the cover of the races to permit high-ranking masters who do not yet have a Senate seat, but who are strong enough to contend for one, to meet. A test will be held, and new senators will be selected from among the winners."

"I don't see what this has to do with the rune."

"Do you not? The test will be of combat, as is traditional."

A lightbulb came on. "So whoever has the rune will be automatically among the winners."

"Yes."

"That's too simplistic," Marlowe said, sitting up. It looked like he'd decided to join the conversation, after all. I guess since Mircea was already spilling the beans, there was no reason to keep quiet. "It would have been little use in battle—its designated function—were its energy easily depleted."

"You think it could be used again," I said, seeing where this was going.

"And again and again!" He flopped back against the seat, his expression dour.

"Giving whoever controls it the possibility of also controlling the outcome of the entire contest," Mircea said more calmly.

"But Ming-de is already the head of a Senate," I said, getting a very bad feeling suddenly. "She has no reason to join yours."

"She doesn't want to join it," Marlowe said savagely. "She wants to control it."

"That is, perhaps, overstating things somewhat," Mircea said soothingly. But it didn't look like his voice tricks worked on Marlowe, either.

"The hell it is." He sat up, talking with his hands in that very un-English way of his. "At most, there is perhaps one open Senate seat a century, among all the Senates around the world," he told me. "Whenever one does come open, competing Senates always try to get one of their people—someone loyal to them, that is—in it, to give them eyes and ears into what their rivals are doing."

I nodded. I'd never really thought about it—high politics weren't my usual purview—but it made sense. Vampires invented paranoid; of course they'd want to keep an eye on the competition.

"And yet now, suddenly, there are five. Five seats open, all at once, on the same Senate! It gives an unprecedented opportunity for her to re-form our Senate from the ground up, undermining our sovereignty, and turning our consul into little more than her puppet!"

"So Ming-de wanted the rune to help make certain that her candidates won their fights, and therefore limit your selection of new senators to people loyal to her," I deciphered.

"Yes."

"But even say she somehow managed to fill all five seats, that still won't give her a majority."

"But it will give her a powerful faction," Mircea told me, before Marlowe could go on another rant. "And the ability to sway others or to bog us down in constant gridlock should we ignore her 'requests.' "

"And the other names Ray gave us? Are they trying to do the same thing?"

"I do not know about the mage's involvement. But Geminus is on our Senate, in a rival faction to my own. The ability to place his people in the empty seats would give him the upper hand."

"That's why you asked me if I'd seen Louis-Cesare," I said, a few pieces suddenly fitting together. "You want him to fill one of your empty seats."

"With the emphasis on 'was,'" Marlowe said sourly. "He promised to switch Senates a month ago, then promptly ran off chasing Christine. The challenges drew close, and we had heard nothing, not a word. And then, when he finally did surface, it was to become implicated in something like this."

"Will this disqualify him?"

"Killing another senator? Oh, no," Marlowe said, waving a hand. "They'll give him a bloody medal, won't they?"

"He didn't do it, Marlowe."

"A fact that matters not at all, considering that the judge in the case is the very consul he's planning to desert."

"Anthony knows?"

Mircea sighed. "Louis-Cesare insisted on telling him. He did not feel it would be honorable to do otherwise."

"I can't do anything with the man," Marlowe said in disgust. "I truly can't."

"Louis-Cesare will not be found guilty," Mircea told me. "Anthony will use this to force him to remain on the European Senate. They have no desire to lose their champion."

"Which doesn't help us, Mircea!" Marlowe exclaimed.

Much as I hated to admit it, I could kind of see Marlowe's point. The vamp world worked because it had a defined hierarchy; everybody knew his or her place and stayed in it. They didn't have a choice, because there was always someone above them in rank and power to ensure that they did so. Except for the consuls, who were pretty much a law unto themselves. The only ones policing them, if it could be called that, were the other consuls.

Of course, that made the other consuls their only real rivals, too. This was getting really scary, really quickly. But at least it explained why everyone was going quietly out of their minds over that stupid rune.

"So that's why you were angry with Louis-Cesare earlier tonight. You thought he'd deserted you to . . . what? Run his own game?"

Mircea shrugged. "It seemed unlikely. He had not been invited to the auction; I could not conceive of how he had learned of the stone's existence. And it would have been out of character for him. But then—"

"That kind of power corrupts quickly," Marlowe finished for him.

"Indeed."

"And that's why you asked Radu to bid on Naudiz—you wanted it to build a Senate to your liking."

"Not just to our liking," Mircea said. "To our necessity. We cannot afford constant power politics, bickering and infighting during a war. We have to be united—something that will not happen if candidates under obligation elsewhere win the right to a seat on our Senate."

"You didn't know about the stone until a few days ago. What were you planning to do before?"

"Kit and I have been working to ensure a favorable outcome, hand-selecting candidates who are not only of a like mind politically, but who have no outside ties and have a good chance in their matches. It has been a difficult search, but we believe we have found our champions."

"Yet no one can stand against an invincible opponent!" Marlowe reminded him. "I don't care how good they are; if anyone at that damned auction has the rune, it'll skew everything. Ming-de isn't the only one who can play power games."

"But if we find the rune, we find the killer," I realized. "Setting Louis-Cesare free to challenge for one of your empty seats."

"A fact that would make me feel a good deal better if the matches did not begin tomorrow night," Marlowe said.

"It's also a short suspect list," I pointed out. "I think we can eliminate Ming-de. She won the auction; she would have had no reason to steal her own property."

"Unless she knew the rune's provenance," Marlowe argued. "She may have doubted her abilities to keep it from being reclaimed by the fey, even should she pay for it. But if it was supposedly stolen before it reached her hands . . ." He shrugged.

"You're a sneaky son of a bitch."

He smiled. "Thank you."

"Ming-de is not what anyone would call naive," Mircea said sardonically. "It appears that we cannot rule anyone out at present. Other than Radu, who was there on my behalf."

"But we have to add back in Cheung," I said. "He wasn't here for the auction, but he could have murdered Elyas. He was chasing Louis-Cesare and me half the night, trying to recover Ray. After he lost us, he could have returned to the club and questioned some of Ray's servants. And if any of them mentioned Elyas, he had plenty of time to come here."

"Five then," Mircea said. "Ming-de, Geminus, Lord Cheung, the mage Lutkin and Æsubrand."

"I need about six hours sleep; then I'll start on the list," I told him.

"No," Mircea said flatly. "I told you all of this to avoid your involvement, not to solicit it. You needed to know how high the stakes were; now that you do, you must understand that—"

"I understand that you need all the help you can get!"

"You have a number of useful talents, none of which will work on anyone on that list!" he told me, suddenly angry. Or maybe he'd been so all along and just hadn't shown it. Mircea was one person whose emotions I'd never been able to read with any accuracy. "You will not get in to see them, and if by some chance you did, they wouldn't tell you anything."

"The vampires, maybe. But I can talk to the mage—"

"I am not concerned about the mage. If he wants the stone for personal protection, all well and good. In that case, it will not interfere with the outcome of the competition. But you will stay away from the rest, the fey prince in particular."

"Why does everyone assume I plan to go after Æsubrand? I'm insane, not stupid."

"I have never assumed you to be either. But you wish to help your friend."

"I don't recall mentioning any friends." And if Louis-Cesare had, I was going to skin him.

Those dark eyes met mine. "I am not stupid, either, Dorina. When the stone is recovered, assuming it is, it will be returned to its owners. I have no wish to make an enemy of the fey. In the meantime, you are to stay out of this. Once you are no longer in competition with him for the rune, Æsubrand will have no reason to trouble you."

There was no safe reply to that, so I didn't make one.

"I'll get people on it," Marlowe said. "But it isn't going to be easy. Not with that group. Our best bet may be to wait and see whose candidates start cleaning up at the challenges. Although what we're supposed to do about it then, I don't know. Prying it loose from any one of them, with the possible exception of the mage, will not be easy."

Funny thing, that's exactly what I'd been thinking about Marlowe.

Chapter Twenty-two

Anthony made his rather flamboyant departure a moment later, surrounded by a passel of genuflecting flunkies. "Not coming?" he asked, peering in the door at Mircea.

"I will be along presently."

"Oh, good. We'd hate to have to start without you." He strode away, cheerfully chatting with Jérôme, and I suddenly realized that he was wearing a toga. His personality was so big that it had eclipsed everything else. I simply hadn't noticed.

I did notice that Louis-Cesare didn't even look in at me as he passed, however. It looked like some of Marlowe's comments had gotten through, after all. Slumming with a dhampir was okay as long as nobody knew, but now it was clearly time for damage control.

I don't know why it surprised me. No vampire had a dhampir lover. A few had tried to seduce me over the years, for the thrill or the bragging rights or just because they liked living dangerously. But anything more than a one-night stand? No.

And that wasn't going to change. Best-case scenario, it would be social and political suicide. Worst-case, someone influential might start to wonder about said vampire's sanity. And there was only one solution for insane vampires. I should know; I was the one called in to dish it out.

But it did surprise me. It also hurt, and that was unacceptable. I was tired and I was drunk off my ass and

I was in danger of getting maudlin. It was clearly time to go.

I started to get up, when a cool hand slid onto my undamaged wrist. "Could you give us a moment, Kit?" Mircea asked.

Marlowe didn't even bother to argue. I had the feeling he wasn't exactly looking forward to facing the Senate. He went out the door, and Christine came back in. She was lugging two large suitcases and had a third under her arm.

"Christine. Dorina and I need to have a short conversation. Perhaps you could wait in the office?" Mircea asked politely.

Christine looked up, saw him and blinked. Then she smiled, the way women always smiled at Mircea. "Of course."

"We're not done?" I asked warily. This was already more than we'd talked in . . . well, ever. At least in one sitting.

Mircea selected a small cigarette—Turkish, by the smell—and proffered me the case. "Not quite."

"Nasty habit," I said, declining. I only smoke weed.

"There are worse ones."

"Meaning?"

He put the case away and sat back in the chair, lighting up with an easy, unhurried motion.

For a long moment, he didn't say anything, which wasn't good. Mircea never has to gather his thoughts. Mircea has entirely too many thoughts. That's his problem.

Well, one of them.

"I've never spoken to you much about your mother, have I?" he finally asked.

For a minute, I just sat there, frozen. Of all the things I'd expected him to come out with, that would have probably been dead last. I'd given up asking about her years ago, because the result was always the same: a few dead, dry facts that told me nothing more than I already knew, uttered with cold indifference. She'd been a peasant girl; they'd had a brief affair; he'd left when he discovered that he'd joined the life-challenged segment of the population, which, coincidentally, was about the same time she found out she was pregnant. The end.

Then, a month ago, he'd dropped the bombshell that she hadn't died in a plague as I'd always assumed. His crazy brother Vlad had killed her by slow torture. And then Mircea had made Vlad a vampire so that he could torture him in return—for five hundred years.

Nobody ever said the family didn't know how to hold a grudge.

It hadn't been a fun conversation, and I wasn't eager to repeat it. But I knew so damn little of her, thanks partly to him and the memory wipe. Not that I would have had direct recall anyway; we'd been separated when I was too young for that. But I'd gathered bits and pieces, from what little others recalled, later on. Almost none of which remained now.

Trust Mircea to pinpoint a person's weak spots with surgical precision. He knew that one sentence would hold me, knew I wouldn't jump up and leave, no matter what he wanted to discuss. Not if there was any chance of learning more.

"What about her?" I asked harshly.

"She was a beautiful woman," he told me calmly. "You look a great deal like her."

"You're keeping the Senate waiting to tell me that?"

"She came to us when she was seventeen," he said, ignoring me. Mircea would get to the point when he damn well felt like it. "Her father had been a wood carver, but he died early, and her mother had a hard time of it thereafter. She eventually found employment in our kitchens, and when Helena was old enough, she joined her there."

"And you saw her and took her." It wasn't hard to imagine. Servant women were pretty much easy prey back then, particularly one with no close male relatives to defend her. And most would have thought themselves lucky to attract the attention of the family's handsome, generous elder son.

"It was not quite as simple as that. When I first noticed her, I admit I did try to steal a kiss."

"And?"

He blew out a thin stream of smoke, which drifted slowly skyward. "And she slapped me. Hard."

I blinked. "You could have had her beaten for that. Or worse."

Romanian women of the time had had few rights over the males of the species. A woman could not join her husband at the dining table, but had to stay behind his chair, waiting to serve him. She ate what was left—which in peasant homes wasn't much—when he was finished. She walked behind him when they went out, and if she went alone and a male walked in front of her in the street, she had to wait to continue on until he passed. Even if she was wealthy and he was a beggar.

Women's lib hadn't been big in old Romania.

Mircea had been tapping his ashes into a crystal tray, but at my comment he stopped and looked up, his face blanking. "Sometimes, Dorina, I wonder what it is you think of me."

I didn't answer that, since half the time I didn't know myself.

And the other half would only get us in another argument.

After a moment, he continued. "She informed me that she was not there to be a gentleman's amusement, but to save money toward a respectable marriage. And that she did not intend to lose her virginity price over me."

I'd almost forgotten the old custom of rewarding virgins the Monday after the marriage for their chastity. They received jewels, clothes, and sometimes money, which they were allowed to keep even if the marriage ended in divorce. It had been a lot more effective than the modern virginity pacts for ensuring abstinence.

Well, that and fearsome Romanian fathers.

"And what did you say to that?"

He shrugged. "I was young and foolish, and had yet to realize that my vaunted success with women was due at least as much to my name and position as to my person. I informed her that I would gladly reimburse her for any losses she might incur."

"I take it she agreed."

He arched an expressive brow. "No. She slapped me again."

"And you found that attractive?"

"Oddly, yes. Most of the women I had encountered were docile to the point of boredom. It was a chore to get them to so much as look at me when we were speaking. I had been intimate with women whom I do not believe could have described my face in any detail had their lives depended on it. That was especially true of noblewomen, who were taught from childhood that good breeding meant utter passivity."

"So she was a challenge."

"She was *alive*, Dorina, in a way none of the other women, and damn few of the men, I knew were. She fascinated me. She infuriated me. . . . Eventually, she enchanted me."

"I guess she got over the slapping part."

"Never entirely." He smiled again. A soft, odd expression on a face that so seldom wore any at all.

I stared at him. I had never considered that he might have felt anything for her; I had always just assumed that she'd been one in a long line of conquests, easily made and easily forgotten. And maybe she had been. Maybe I just wanted to believe that his expression meant something else. Wanted to think that at least one of their kind was capable of something like real affection.

God, I must be drunker than I thought.

"After we finally began a relationship," he said, "I bought her a house in her village and visited her there rather than keeping her in the castle."

"Because you were ashamed to have a servant girl for a mistress."

"No, Dorina!" He regarded me through a cloud of smoke, his countenance impatient. "I was never ashamed of your mother. I was fearful for her. And my fears were eventually realized."

"You couldn't have known Vlad was going to do what he did." I blamed Mircea for a lot of things, but not that.

"No. But I knew she would be a target, should anyone realize that she was important to me. Some would have used her to attempt to influence me; others would have harmed her to hurt me. It was a cutthroat time, and one's family was never safe. I would not let circumstances proscribe my life to the extent of choosing my lover for me, but I was careful. I was cautious. I was *discreet*."

"Ah. Light dawns."

"Louis-Cesare must occupy one of those empty Senate seats," Mircea said, dropping the analogy. "I need someone I can trust, and I need his vote to help sway others during the war. Anything likely to prevent that is unacceptable."

"I thought you'd already decided to scrap that plan."

"The incident with Elyas is unfortunate, but I am owed a number of favors by members of the European Senate, and the consul is owed more."

"You think you can convince them to let him compete?"

"It is possible. It helps that he has refused to join any faction, preferring to vote his conscience on matters as they arise. That has made him a dangerous loose cannon for years, and left many of the power brokers on his Senate tearing their hair out on a regular basis. I think some might prefer to see him gone. Unfortunately those same people would just as soon see him destroyed. And if he cannot have him, Anthony will do his best to ensure that no one does, lest his abilities be used against him one day."

"And this has what to do with me?" I asked, pretty sure I already knew.

"A liaison with a dhampir could destroy Louis-Cesare's credibility at the worst possible time," Mircea told me bluntly.

"In case you missed it, Louis-Cesare has a mistress," I reminded him.

"No, I did not miss it. I also did not miss how he looked at you, or that outburst."

"Or the fact that he left without a word?"

"As well he might, after that! This could ruin him, Dorina. It has already damaged our case considerably."

"Anthony didn't hear that much—"

"He heard enough to ensure that I cannot introduce your evidence about the way in which Elyas was killed!"

I frowned. "But Louis-Cesare wouldn't have killed him that way! He couldn't have, even if he wanted to. He didn't know how until I—" I broke off, feeling a little queasy suddenly.

"Exactly," Mircea said grimly. "If I introduce our strongest defense, Anthony will make the case that Louis-Cesare received instruction in creative vampire-killing from his dhampir lover. His political opponents would jump at the chance to smear the character of one who has been, until now, unimpeachable. And even his friends on the Senate might begin to waver. If he could do that, some will think, he is capable of anything."

"Including murdering a fellow senator."

"Exactly so." Mircea sat back, the end of his cigarette drawing patterns in the air around him. "Louis-Cesare is powerful, which makes him a good weapon, but also a dangerous enemy. He and Elyas had a long-standing animosity that stretched back more than a century. But he had never before moved against him. Now, some will believe, he has done so, and those with whom he has had other disputes may start to wonder if they are next."

"Senators must have been killed before," I protested.

"In coups, yes. In carefully planned political blood-fests for understandable objectives. But they are not assassinated for personal reasons while sitting in their own homes! This is something that has rarely been seen before, and it allows Anthony to paint a picture of a dangerous loose cannon run amok. And if the Senate vote goes against Louis-Cesare, as judge, Anthony can impose whatever sentence he wishes."

"You said he won't kill him."

"He won't—if Louis-Cesare is willing to knuckle under and bind himself to Anthony in perpetuity."

"Giving him a powerful first-level master at his beck and call without any power expenditure on his part whatsoever," I finished. It would be the Tomas situation all over again, only I didn't see Louis-Cesare agreeing to what was essentially slavery. And if he didn't . . .

"I hate politics," I said fervently.

"At the moment, I am not in love with them, either," Mircea said cynically. "But the situation is what it is, and we must deal with it."

"How?" It sounded to me like Anthony had a lock on this.

"I can still bring up the rune, and show the Senate the empty carrier. That, at least, is a motive they can understand for someone else to have killed Elyas. Louis-Cesare, whatever he may lack in political acumen, needs no such crutch in a duel."

"And if Anthony mentions me?"

Mircea regarded me soberly. "Louis-Cesare tricked you. He wanted the vampire Raymond, but did not wish to fight a family member. He therefore let you believe that he cared for you, in order to steal it away."

"That will cover my outburst," I agreed. And might even be the truth. "What about his?"

"That is why you need to stay away from him! Louis-Cesare is a warrior, first and foremost. And like most such men, he is blunt, straightforward and uncompromising. He has developed a tenderness for you; that much is clear. How far it extends, I do not know. But he will not succeed in hiding it; he will not so much as understand the reason he should do so!"

No, I didn't suppose so. I could see him standing in front of the Senate, arrogantly informing them that his personal life was none of their concern. It would read like some torrid affair with a creature many of them viewed as only slightly better than Satan. Not too helpful.

"You begin to see," Mircea murmured.

"Maybe. But what about Anthony and Jérôme? They already heard him be ... indiscreet."

"Fortunately they are also the ones who have the most reason to interpret anything badly. I will point out that you and Louis-Cesare battled Æsubrand together recently, and that he was concerned that the creature might be among us once again. He wanted your information, nothing more."

"You know, sometimes you're a little scary," I told him frankly. "I was there, and that still sounds strangely believable."

"Let us hope the Senate thinks so. But no matter what persuasive skills you believe me to possess, you must see that I cannot continue to come up with plausible explanations for other such incidents. This must—"

Someone tapped on the door, and a second later Marlowe's curly head poked in. The timing made me narrow my eyes suspiciously, but the look on his face was not slyly knowing, but maddened and frustrated. "Unless you want to let Louis-Cesare handle his own defense, we have to *go*, Mircea!"

"That I do not want," Mircea said, getting up. "Dorina—"

I stood up, too. "It was business," I told him. "He stole from me; I returned the favor. That's all."

Mircea didn't look as pleased by that sentiment as I'd have liked. "This isn't—" He stopped, and again seemed to be trying to marshal his thoughts. I didn't know why he was bothering; I'd already agreed to what he wanted. Not that it was much. Louis-Cesare had Christine back; I wasn't likely to be seeing much more of him anyway.

"I want you to be happy, Dorina," he said suddenly— and strangely. I searched his face, wondering what this new game was, what the hell he wanted from me now. Like always, it was the perfect, beautiful mask, and told me nothing.

His hand rose hesitantly toward my face, and I unconsciously flinched. Mircea had never hurt me, but a lifetime of fighting and killing his kind provides a person with certain instincts. A flash of some emotion crossed his eyes, but it was gone before I could name it, and his hand dropped again.

And something lanced through me, brief and sharp, like a needle's bite.

Sunlight streamed in a small, glassless window, painting a watercolor wash over a wooden table. A woman stood beside it, her arms moving in a circular motion, kneading a pile of dough with an unbroken rhythm. Every few moments she looked out the window, over a crenellated ridge of mountains, their sheer faces lined with snow and backlit by the sun.

It was a rising sun, I concluded as I watched it swell, gleaming and red as it broke free of the landscape and drifted into the liquid blue sky. The cottage stood on the edge of the small village, near a road that ran through the trees. But the road was empty, the dust undisturbed except for a slight wind.

The air that flowed in from the mountains outside was crisp, ruffling her hair as she worked to braid the dough into a long ribbon and then form it into a loaf. She set it aside and started the process over again, while the wind died and the flour hung in the air like mist. It clung to her dark lashes and brows, to the soft down of hair on her arms, and gloved her hands in a dusting of gold.

Two arms went around her from behind, pulling her back against a warm, familiar body. "Stop that," she admonished, her voice liquid with laughter. "No baking, no bread for your morning meal."

"But I am hungry now," he said, smiling as he lifted her gilded hand to his lips, tracing the calluses there with his tongue.

Her hand came up, smearing flour against his cheek, gritty and warm from the motion of her hands. "Husband," she breathed against his neck. "My Mircea." And the love and loss that welled up inside him was so sweet and so painful, it was literally staggering.

"Mircea!" Marlowe's voice was starting to sound a little panic-stricken. "They are beginning now!"

The memory shattered and broke with his voice, and I stumbled back into the seat. I bent low, hands on my knees, and gulped air, my eyes stinging with tears. Loneliness, vast, echoing and cold, opened up around me, but it was the resignation that made a hole in me, that hollowed me out. And I wasn't even sure if it was my emotion or his.

Oh, Mircea, I thought. *Oh, my God*.

A hand slipped onto my shoulder, pale and cool. I looked up at him, blank disbelief in my mind. I don't know what was on my face, but he frowned and squatted down beside the chair. "Dorina, what—"

"You *married* her?"

He stopped, his face registering blank shock. He said nothing, but he didn't deny it. And that was just—

"I have to go," I told him, jumping up and stumbling away, my hand somehow finding the doorknob to the office. I pulled it open and slipped through, and put my back against the door. Thankfully he didn't try follow me.

I stood there, staring into space, seeing nothing. Other than the face of a woman I'd never known, a peasant girl with no family, no money, nothing—except a prince for a husband.

It felt like the room lurched sideways. It wasn't so much a physical movement as a sheering of the mind as my brain tried to wrap itself around an impossible idea. I'd assumed he never spoke of her out of indifference. But he'd been his father's firstborn, heir to a disputed throne. He was the last person on earth who could afford to take chances with his choice of wife. And yet he'd married a girl who could do nothing to help him politically, who could seal no treaties, gain him no armies, never be anything other than a liability.

Because he had loved her.

Chapter Twenty-three

"Can we get out of here already?" someone said crossly.

I looked up, feeling more than a little dazed, to see my duffel sitting on the desk. Not-a-butler must have been busy, because the area had been cleared of dead vampire parts. Except for one.

Ray was still on the desk, perched beside the duffel like a grotesque paperweight. For a moment, I ignored him. The past was tugging at me, a thousand questions suddenly shuffling through my very rattled brain.

It could be a lie, a fabrication to achieve some hidden objective. Mircea was certainly capable of mental manipulation, as I knew better than anyone. He'd used it on me before, even admitted to it. Why should I believe this to be any different?

But that had been erasing memories, not planting them. And while some vamps could create illusions almost as well as a mage could, tricking the mind into thinking all kinds of things, I'd never heard of Mircea having that ability. Not that vampires were in the habit of revealing all their secrets. He probably had all sorts of skills I didn't know about. But if he could do that, why hadn't he years ago? Why leave me with blank spaces in my memory he had to know I'd be curious about, when he could have merely spackled over them?

I'd been the victim of illusions a time or two before, and some could be damn real. But that hadn't been real; it had been perfect, down to the tiniest details: the smell of the yeast, the buzzing of insects outside the window, the grittiness of the stone-ground flour. If it was an illusion, it was the best damned one I'd ever seen.

All of a sudden, nothing made sense anymore. If I was being played, I couldn't see how, and that made it dangerous. And if I wasn't ...

But I had to be. People don't change. Not that much, not that fast. And that was even more true for vamps. They were what they were, and letting myself believe anything else just because I wanted it so damn badly was a fool's errand.

I'd spent a lifetime fighting vampires; I knew them, understood them as well as anyone could who wasn't one of them. They were selfish, self-centered, power obsessed, false. They'd say anything, do anything, to get what they wanted, and Mircea was no exception to that rule. If anything, he pretty much epitomized the vamp ideal: a cold, calculating head of a powerful house who destroyed his enemies, rewarded his allies and never let something as useless as sentiment get in his way.

Of course, he hadn't been a vamp then. That scene had taken place in broad daylight, with the sun filtering in the window like a haze. It would have been like standing in a rain of fire for a baby vamp. He should have incinerated immediately, yet he hadn't even flinched. So he'd been human. It was the Mircea I'd never known—the man he had been before the curse took effect, before it warped him, changed him.

But those emotions hadn't been part of the memory, had they? That had been a happy time, a stolen morning away from responsibilities. No reason for pain, for loss. Not when he had no way of knowing what was coming. And by the time he did know, he was vampire. But they didn't, *couldn't* feel that kind of—

"Hello? Anybody home?" Ray's strident tones cut through the endless loop in my head. For once, I was almost grateful.

"I thought you were supposed to be a witness?" I said, pushing off the door. "Why are you still here?"

"They said they didn't need me, after all. Something about having plenty of other stuff to talk about."

"I bet."

"So can we go? This place is giving me the creeps."

"It is unsettling," someone said from beside the hall door.

I looked over to see Christine sitting on a mountain of luggage. She'd been so quiet, I hadn't even noticed her. "They left you, too, huh?" I asked, dropping Ray in the duffel. What the hell? He didn't take up much room.

"They said my testimony would not be helpful," she told me. "I did not see anything, and I am close to Louis-Cesare. I believe they think that I would lie for him."

"So all that packing for nothing."

"Oh, no. Not for nothing," she said as I dug around beside Ray's gory self. As always, the keys had migrated to the farthest reaches of the bag. "I have been informed that the family doesn't want me here. They have . . . What is the term? Knocked me out."

"Kicked you out," I corrected. "So where to now?"

"I do not know. Where are we going?"

I hadn't found the keys, but at that, I looked up. "Come again?"

"Louis-Cesare said that I should stay with you."

"Oh, boy," Ray muttered.

"He said what?" I asked, very carefully.

"I am sure he will come for me, when this trial is over. Do you live far?"

"You can't come with me," I explained, my fist finally closing on the damn keys.

She frowned slightly, a small dent forming between those beautiful eyes. "But I must. Louis-Cesare said—"

"I don't care what Louis-Cesare said. And neither should you. You're three hundred years old, for God's sake. Go out. Live a little."

I grabbed the duffel and started for the door, but a delicate hand shot out, snaring my wrist in a motion too fast to see. It was the only indication I'd seen so far of what she really was. Well, that and the tensile strength of that grip.

But her face was lost, panic-stricken, and innocently distressed. "But . . . but I cannot fail him! Not on his first command in . . . I cannot!"

"You probably misunderstood," I said, striving for patience.

"No, no! I know what he said! And dawn approaches, and I have nowhere else to go, and they will throw me out on the street!"

God, she was crying again.

"Louis-Cesare probably wanted me to drop you off at his place." Not that the bastard had bothered to ask. Or to mention it.

"H-his place?"

"He's staying at the Club. Come on; I'll give you a lift."

"Oh, thank you!" Christine looked so relieved, I felt a little guilty suddenly. What would it be like to live for a century being told every single thing to do and not to do? It had to erode a person's self-confidence, after a while. And it wasn't Christine's fault that her master was a complete—

"What are you doing?" I demanded. Christine had jumped up and started to gather up some of that mountain of luggage. She looked at me blankly. "That's not all going to fit in the car."

She gazed at her cheerfully mismatched cases. "But . . . but what should I do?"

"Pick the stuff you need for today and Elyas's people can send the rest on."

"But they won't. They've been horrid! What if they throw it out? What if they never . . ." Her lower lip began quivering.

"Oh, shit," Ray said. "Squash it in! Squash it in!"

We squashed it in. After three trips, a lot of cursing, and no help at all from the family, we somehow got me, Ray, Ray's body, Christine and her worldly possessions all inside the car. Fortunately, the Club wasn't far, and they had porters.

Or make that *had.*

Fifteen minutes later I sat staring at the burned-out hulk of what had once been a luxury hotel, wondering why the universe hated me. I couldn't see much, because there were still some emergency vehicles scattered around, although it appeared that most had trundled off. But the acrid, waterlogged smell in the air would have been enough.

"What is it?" Ray demanded.

"A curse," I muttered. "It's the only possible explanation."

"The master burned it down, didn't he?" he asked. "He likes burning stuff."

Now he told me.

"I'm going to have to take you to a hotel," I told Christine.

Her eyes got wide. "A *human* hotel?" she asked, like I'd suggested throwing her in a snake pit.

"There's some very nice ones in—"

"No!" she whispered, looking horrified.

"Plenty of vampires stay at human hotels," I said, which was true for those who couldn't afford the Club's staggering rates.

"The sun—I can't—I'll die! *I'll die!*" She grabbed me by the shoulder in a grip that threatened to crush bone. I pried her fingers off, and she just sat there, huddled in the passenger seat, looking devastated. And I began to worry about whether it was such a great idea, after all.

Vamps did use human hotels when up against it. But it was dangerous. Few hotel curtains were constructed to properly block all those dangerous daylight rays. And even sleeping in the bathroom, as uncomfortable as that was, might not be enough. All it would take was one careless maid ignoring a do-not-disturb sign, and Christine would be toast.

I could take her to vamp central and toss her out on the curb, and technically, that was exactly what I ought to do. But Louis-Cesare was there facing trial for murder, and he didn't need another headache right now. And

Radu had said there were no vampire-friendly rooms to be had in town, thanks to the damn races.

"I'll be very quiet," she whispered, as if she somehow knew I was weakening. "You'll never know I'm there."

"It's not me we have to worry about," I said, thinking of a certain half dragon with a serious vampire phobia.

I really hoped she wasn't hungry.

Chapter Twenty-four

Forty-five minutes later, I pulled into my street. I was exhausted and cramped, and a bag or something had shifted when I had to stop for a red light suddenly, and it had been poking me in the back ever since. I wanted a drink or three and bed and I wanted them now.

Only that wasn't looking too likely.

"Crap," I said with feeling, almost standing on the brakes.

"What? What's wrong now?" Ray demanded. His body was squashed in back between half a dozen suitcases, two garment bags, a trunk and five hatboxes, with the duffel on his lap.

"We have a welcoming committee."

We were maybe a third of a block from the house, so I couldn't see them very well. But someone was there, all right. *Make that a lot of someones*, I thought, as more shadows broke away from the house and drifted into the street, trying to get a look at us.

Ray's body held his head up so it could see, and the tiny eyes almost bugged out. "*Shit*. It's the master."

"Cheung?" I'd almost forgotten about him. Too bad the reverse didn't appear to be true.

"What are you waiting for?" Ray asked, starting to sound a little frantic. "Go, go, go!"

"I can't go," I snapped. "Your master has a dozen guys across the driveway."

"I didn't mean go *in*," Ray said, like I might be slow. "I meant, get us out of here."

"I can't do that, either."

"Why the hell not?"

"The wards have held so far, but there's at least a couple hours to dawn."

"Which is a good argument for not getting trapped in there!"

"There are already people trapped in there. And Cheung has to know that. His Hounds can smell them from here."

"Life sucks," Ray said callously.

"It's going to suck more for you if he takes hostages."

"You'd give me up?"

"In a nanosecond," I said, switching gears.

"I thought we'd developed a bond here!"

I didn't even bother to respond to that. "Get ready to run," I told him, just as one of Cheung's men got close enough to recognize me. And then decision time was over.

A dozen black streaks started our way, and I floored it, aiming for the driveway and the line of vamps stretched across it. I didn't really think I'd make it through; playing red rover with a line of masters is not a good bet. But I didn't need to get through. I just needed to get close enough to the wards to make it inside before they caught me.

A couple of the nearest vamps grabbed the passenger door, ripping it half off its hinges. Christine screamed, which didn't help, and her heavy trunk tumbled out on top of them, which did. But the rest of Cheung's boys figured out where I was going and surged that way, to bolster their buddies in the drive. So I swerved at the last minute and cut across the lawn, throwing up grass and mud in my wake, and fishtailed to a stop just inside the wards.

The two vamps who had grabbed hold of the passenger door hit the invisible shield around the house head-on as we passed safely through. They were still sliming their way down it, like juicy bugs on a windshield, when several more ran forward and grabbed the left bumper of the car. It had remained just outside the wards, providing them with a convenient handle to use to drag us backward.

I hit the gas, but after days of rain and an unexpected blizzard, the front lawn had turned into a mud field. I had zero traction. I did get the satisfaction of seeing Cheung's men completely drenched in mud, but they were going to have the last laugh if they succeeded in dragging us back out.

Christine was scrabbling at her seat belt, trying to get it undone. I tossed the duffel onto the front steps and started helping her, while keeping my foot glued to the gas pedal. I was hoping the car would dig itself far enough into the muck to buy us a few seconds, but no dice. The vamps managed to get the whole rear end out just as the seat belt finally gave way

There was no time to exit gracefully. I grabbed Christine with one hand and Ray with the other, and dragged them over the hood. We jumped free even as the car was being yanked out from under us, and landed—of course—face-first in the sea of mud. But it was a sea of mud inside the wards, and that was all that mattered.

I got to my feet, dripping in muck. The beautiful dress was ruined, and I hadn't even gotten to wear it anywhere. And somewhere along the line, I'd lost one of the shoes.

I was royally pissed, and that was before I saw the guy coming to talk to me in my mud-slimed finery. He was wearing a suit that would have made Mircea jealous. The fine black wool fit him like a dream, the burnt orange silk tie adding just the right amount of spice. It also matched the orange-and-black tiger tat leaping from his neck to his right cheek.

And the dressing gown of the very bedraggled figure he was leading by one arm.

"Radu!" I blinked. "What the hell?"

"Yes, yes, thank you! My point exactly," he said, obviously livid.

"You said you'd be okay."

"I would have been, if not for this madman!" he said, struggling uselessly against his captor's hold. No introductions were made, but then, I didn't really need any. Radu, despite appearances, is a second-level master. Pissing him off is a very bad idea—unless you happened to be a first-level.

"Mircea will kill you for this," I said conversationally, as Cheung's polished shoe tips stopped just outside the wards.

"Had he not interfered in my business, there would have been no need to inconvenience his brother." The voice was a low, pleasant tenor without a trace of an accent. It didn't match the looks, which were anything but bland: bronze skin, high cheekbones, dark, almond-shaped eyes and a hawklike nose with a proud tilt.

"Inconvenience? Is that what they call kidnapping these days?"

"You kidnapped my servant first," he pointed out. "Return my property and I will return yours."

"That sounds familiar," I said, checking 'Du out.

His dressing gown was ripped along one seam, his hair—usually so sleek and shiny—was everywhere and he had somehow acquired a smear of mud on his nose. He looked pathetic and miserable. I smiled at him sympathetically. He smiled back.

"Ray's the Senate's property now," I told Cheung. "If you want him back, you'll have to petition them."

"What?" Radu's expression faded.

Cheung's forehead acquired a slight wrinkle. "Perhaps you did not understand me."

"I understood perfectly." A drip of mud oozed down my temple, and I took a second to wipe it off.

"Then release my servant."

"Or what?" I demanded. "I'm fair game. Ray's fair game. But you can't hurt 'Du, and you know it. It would break the truce, and even if it didn't, Mircea *would* kill you. Slowly."

"What are you talking about?" Radu demanded, his embroidered satin bed slippers slowly sinking into the lawn. "We've already been out here half the night! Give the man what he wants, Dory!"

"No can do," I said while flipping through the keychain for the front-door key I never used. "But don't worry, 'Du. I'll inform Mircea about this, next time I see him."

"Next time you—" He broke off, staring at something over my shoulder. I turned to see Christine floundering around in the mud. Her delicate little slippers didn't appear to have much traction, and every time she got up, she fell down again.

"Is that . . . *Christine*?" he asked, looking appalled.

She slowly got to her feet, hands spread out on either side of her, like a toddler learning to walk. "Lord Radu," she said tremulously, before her foot slipped and she fell backward into a puddle. The resulting splash rained muck down on me and 'Du.

"Well, that explains it," he muttered.

"You think I am bluffing," Cheung said evenly.

I sighed. "You're either bluffing, or you're an idiot, and that's not your reputation," I said, finally locating the house key. "Hurt 'Du, and you'll die for it. Let him go, and Mircea may let you off with some groveling. I don't know."

"I see I need to prove my sincerity." Cheung didn't move, but two of his boys ran up with sledgehammers—and started taking apart the Lamborghini.

Radu just stood there, mute in horror, as a beautiful piece of Italian engineering was quickly reduced to scrap. It didn't take long. I opened the front door, hauled Ray's mud-covered self inside and then went back for the duffel and Christine.

"This does not move you?" Cheung demanded, as one of his boys sent the steering wheel flying off into the night. Radu made a small whimpering sound.

"It's 'Du's car," I told him, before shutting the door in his face.

The house might be repairing itself, but it wasn't getting there in any hurry. There were still holes in the floor, the walls and the ceiling, giving a three-story atrium effect to the front hall. Moonlight cascaded down through the now much more open floor plan, flooding the old boards in a pale light that was strangely otherworldly.

It provided enough illumination to allow me to thread my way through the stacks of worm-eaten furniture in the vestibule. I didn't topple a single piece over, even while dragging Ray. That was lucky, because something else otherworldly was in the hallway, flitting through the far end of the corridor, near the back door. I stopped dead.

Everything else looked normal. The house was dark, quiet, still. But that wasn't surprising. Claire had to have given up on me a while ago and gone to bed. And while my roommates tended to be active at night, they weren't exactly homebodies. It wasn't unusual for me to come home to a mostly quiet house.

But not to one that smelled like a deep cave, dank and chill, with that curious sharp underbite that my brain had filed under "Oh, shit."

Svarestri, although I couldn't see them. Not that that meant a damn. I suddenly wondered if there was anyone left alive for Cheung to attack.

"Hey, can we—"

I clapped a hand over Ray's big mouth and grabbed my new iron sword out of the duffel. It felt good in my hand—a cold, solid weight with some serious heft behind it. I just hoped the fey hadn't come up with another way of fighting without actually being there. If they'd hurt Claire or the kids, I wanted something that could bleed.

Christine caught my arm. She didn't say anything, but her face spoke volumes. "Stay here," I told her softly. Normally, a three-hundred-year-old vamp would be an asset in a case like this, but I didn't think she was going to frighten the fey by crying at them.

The dress was already ruined, so I wove a knife through the silk at the small of my back and tied another to my thigh with one of the stockings. I stuffed the duffel under a table in the foyer and left the rest of Ray on guard over it. Then I moved carefully into the hall, keeping close to the tattered walls.

The house must have prioritized wallpaper pretty low, because pieces of it still fluttered everywhere, brushing my cheeks as I slipped past. It was like being in a forest of slowly moving tree branches, heavy with moss. The dried paste on the back felt like scaly fingers brushing over my skin, and the constant movement gave my eyes too much to watch.

Not that they were doing so hot. Light cascaded down three stories, through the ruined roof. But it was dim antique silver—a combination of moonlight and the vague radiance from the street. The city had recently installed new, energy-efficient streetlights that saved money by not actually illuminating anything.

The situation wasn't helped when a thin, cold rain began to fall. It sent odd, rippling shadows down the windows and across the squares of gray they cast on the floor. I felt my heart rate speed up, my skin prickling. The damned Svarestri were giving me a complex about the weather.

The white backing on the wallpaper glowed under the moonlight, waving across my vision like long silver blond hair. Everywhere I looked, I thought I saw fey for a split second. But I hadn't. Because there was no mistaking when I finally did glimpse one. Something black twisted down through me at the sight, from head to feet, colder than the night air at the bottom of a ravine.

It was only a brief flicker in my peripheral vision, vague and indistinct. My shadow ghosted along at my heels as I slowly moved forward, but the fey cast none. Around him there was only a quivering nothing, like negative space.

Some kind of camouflage, I guessed, and it worked pretty well. I couldn't seem to see him at all if I looked directly at him. He only showed up in the corner of my eye in glimpses, wavering in and out of the rain shadows and the strands of gently waving wallpaper.

The fey was joined by another and then another, the air around them practically sparkling with the ghostly light around their bodies. Until it flickered and went out, dimming down to the nothingness of the first. And whether it was a spell or that almost weightless gait they all seemed to have, my ears couldn't pick up a thing. Not a footfall, not a single breath, nothing. Silence filled the old house like cold water, broken only by the soft sound of the rain.

A fourth intruder joined the growing crowd. And unless the fey were as ghostly as they appeared and could walk through walls, I knew how they were getting in. He'd come from the pantry, through the door that led out into the hall. They'd entered through the portal.

Pip had the big boy in the basement, but he'd littered other portals throughout the house for security and convenience. They didn't go anywhere exotic; that one just let out into the backyard, by Claire's old compost heap. We'd mostly been using it to take out the garbage.

But it looked like the fey had found a better use for it.

There were no wards guarding it because it didn't exist when not in use. At least, that was the theory. Somehow, they had figured out it was there and had tinkered with the spell enough to get it to open from that end, giving them free access to the heart of the house.

What I couldn't figure out was why the damned internal wards weren't working. Pip hadn't been content with just exterior wards. He'd added a bunch of nasty interior ones as well, which I'd seen in action on one memorable occasion. And Olga and I had recently placed another layer over the top of that.

With four fey in the hall and who knew how many coming, there should have been a hell of a fight going on. Yet the wards hadn't so much as twinged. *Damned useless things*, I thought viciously. Spend all that money and time, and what did we get? Not so much as a warning siren when the bad guys showed up. If I lived long enough, I was going to tell Olga exactly what I thought of—

I was grabbed from behind and yanked backward into the kitchen. We hadn't even stopped moving when I slammed an elbow back into my attacker's gut, and came down on his foot with my heel. And had to stifle my own curse. I'd forgotten I was barefoot, and that had *hurt*.

But he let go and I spun, bringing the short sword up in a stabbing motion—and hit wallpaper. Whoever it was had moved like quicksilver, dodging the blade before darting back in to grab me and shove me against the refrigerator. He pinned me there with his lean, hot weight, grabbing my arms, trapping me.

So I brought up a knee, hard, and heard another grunt, just as I recognized a familiar scent. Fey didn't smell like butterscotch and whisky—at least, none I'd ever met. I looked up into a pair of furious blue eyes. *Louis-Cesare.*

"How the hell did you get in?" I whispered.

"Through the door," he said quietly, his voice a little strained.

I moved my knee. "Sorry." And then what he'd said registered. "What do you mean, *through the door*? The wards are set to exclude all but family."

"I *am* family, Dorina."

Oh, yeah.

I didn't ask him why he was here instead of where he was supposed to be because right then I didn't care. "They're after Aiden," I told him. "We need to get them before they go upstairs."

He didn't ask me what I meant. I guess he'd gotten a look in the hall, or maybe that keen nose had scented something off, too. "I counted eight of them. And there may be more," he told me grimly.

"Eight?" Wonderful. Not that it made a difference. "It doesn't matter how many there are. We've got to stop them."

I started for the hall again, or tried to, but that iron grip didn't budge. "We will not stop eight fey warriors by brawn alone," he told me harshly. "A little planning may be the difference between success and failure."

"So might delay!"

I wrenched away, but he moved to block the door to the hall, and trying to budge him would have been like going through a brick wall. Harder, actually: I'd been through a wall, but I'd never managed to dislodge Louis-Cesare when he was in a mood. I spun on my heel and flung open the kitchen door instead, intending to circle around back and hopefully take the fey by surprise.

And then I just stood there, staring.

I'd been hearing a weird noise coming from outside, but hadn't had time to focus on it. It had sounded like someone bouncing on a trampoline, which was a little odd at three a.m. But the reality wasn't that far off.

"What is it?" Louis-Cesare came up behind me.

I thought it was sort of self-explanatory. He was just in time to see another group of Cheung's boys throw themselves at the wards. A few of them must have had some serious power, because they actually managed to dent the surface a few inches, distorting their faces horribly as they pressed up against the invisible skin.

And then the wards corrected, throwing more power at the point of contact, and they went staggering backward. Or flying, depending on how far in they'd made it. The reaction seemed to be in direct proportion to the threat.

I could have told them that they were wasting their time. The house wards weren't run off a talisman that could be exhausted if enough force was applied. They were powered by a ley-line sink, which had unlimited energy. Cheung's boys could batter themselves bloody, but they'd never get through that way.

"Idiots," I said with feeling. "It would serve them right if they did get in. I'd like to see how they'd deal with—"

I stopped, staring at all the power expending itself uselessly against the wards.

When it could be in here helping us.

I watched the mud-splattered attackers for a moment and wondered if I was going crazy. No way could the two of us handle a couple dozen senior-level masters. But then, weaker ones wouldn't be any use against Æsubrand's thugs. And when Cheung's boys stormed the house, there was a good chance the fey were going to assume they were coming to our aid, and vice versa. If they tore into one another, it might buy me time to find Claire and the boys.

Of course, if they didn't, I was screwed. But I was screwed anyway, and between the devil and the deep blue sea, the devil starts to look pretty good. At least he can be bargained with. The sea will just kill you.

I felt a hand suddenly tighten around my bicep. I looked up, and saw the same idea dawning in Louis-Cesare's eyes.

"Can you do it?" he whispered.

"Yes. But Cheung will run as soon as he sees the fey." If he had any sense.

"He won't run," Louis-Cesare said, with a slight smile.

I followed his line of sight out into the yard, where I saw Cheung's head jerk up. He stared at the house, a scowl spreading over his features. "What did you do?" I demanded.

"I suggested to him that he might have his servant, if he was not too much of a coward to come in and take him."

"You called a first-level master a coward?"

"Among other things."

"And they say I'm crazy."

I mentally felt around for the bright web of power flowing about the house. There should have been a corresponding interior web as well, but it was conspicuously absent. Someone had taken down the internal wards, cutting the link between them and their power source, the ley-line sink. But they'd left the external ones intact, either because they'd wanted to fool me into thinking everything was fine or—more likely—because they just hadn't cared.

It took only a second to wrap the filaments of the external wards around my mental hand and give a hard *tug*. Within seconds, the long skeins of energy had unraveled to nothing, leaving the old house bare and defenseless. "I hope this works," I said with feeling. "Or we just went from bad to—"

I didn't get a chance to finish, because I was suddenly slung over a shoulder, carted to the pantry and shoved headfirst down the portal. It happened so fast that for a second, I didn't understand what was going on. Until it spit me out the other side.

Right at Æsubrand's feet.

"—tragic," I finished blankly.

Chapter Twenty-five

I think Æsubrand was almost as surprised to see me as I was to see him, but he recovered fast. His boot came down in the middle of compost and wet leaves, right where I'd been lying. I wasn't there anymore, because I'd flung myself backward into the now two-way portal.

I crashed to the hard floor of the pantry and rolled into Louis-Cesare's legs. And then the lunatic picked me up and started trying to stuff me back inside. *"What the hell are you doing?"*

"Attempting to get you to safety."

"That's a damn strange way of doing it!" I panted, bracing my hands and feet on the shelves on either side of the gaping maw, like a cat trying to avoid a bath.

"I will get the others out. You have my word," he said, trying to prize me off. But every time he removed one limb, I curled the others through the metal supports of the shelves, holding on for dear life.

I was sucking in breath to explain, when he jerked me back, ripping the whole shelving unit off the wall. It came away, concrete screws and all, but I held on like my fingers were welded to the metal. He cursed in exasperation. "Why will you not *let go*?"

"Because Æsubrand's out there, you complete lunatic!" And then it wasn't true, because he was suddenly *in* the house and crashing into me.

I don't think he'd expected to find someone physically blocking the portal, because he hadn't come through with a drawn weapon. But that was the only good thing. The portal flung him into me, I lost my grip on the shelves and we tumbled to the ground. And then he was suddenly gone. It took me a moment to realize that Louis-Cesare had picked him up and flung him back through.

"I can't believe you just did that," I said, half-appalled, half-impressed, as he turned toward the door. I pushed the shelving off me and grabbed him. "Stay here. Hold off Æsubrand."

"Where are you going?"

"To get my duffel."

"Now?"

"Yes, now! Ray's in there! If Cheung gets him before we do, he'll have no reason to stick around."

"I will go," Louis-Cesare said as the sound of crossed swords and gunfire came from the hall.

He left before I got the chance to tell him that I'd really prefer to face Cheung and his men than the ice-cold prince of the fey. But then the portal started to activate again. I panicked just slightly at the thought of facing Æsubrand with nothing but a short sword for a weapon. So I started throwing everything I could reach down the portal's wide gullet.

Heavy bags of beans and rice—Olga always bought in bulk—were swallowed up, along with bottles of condiments, large-sized cans of soup and vegetables, and a broken TV that someone had stuck on a shelf. I'd hoped that, if the portal was open and active on one end, someone couldn't use it to come through on the other. It seemed to make logical sense, but I forgot—magic is rarely logical. As was demonstrated when a bloody leg poked through the portal almost in my face.

No, not blood, I realized, ketchup. I hacked at it with my sword. Okay, *now* it was blood. And then the fey it belonged to emerged and grabbed me around the throat.

It wasn't Æsubrand, but he was damned strong anyway. I slashed at his arm with the sword, and he pulled back, saying something in their language that sounded fairly obscene. I took the few seconds that bought me to shove the shelf over the mouth of the portal.

That didn't help as much as I'd have liked. It was just ordinary metal shelving with an open back, through which he started slashing at me with his own sword. It was a lot longer than mine and glowed faintly, giving him plenty of light to murder by. Only I wasn't going to make it easy on him.

The open-sided shelf worked two ways, so I used that, grabbing a mop—we had a mop?—and using it to poke the fey back into the open maw of the portal. It sort of worked—his bottom half disappeared into the swirl of color on the wall—but he grabbed onto the shelf with one hand, preventing the rest of him from getting sucked inside. He made a pass with his sword with the other, and I was suddenly left holding nothing but a mop head.

I danced back out of reach as that sword took a swipe at my chest. But that gave him the chance to bat the whole unit out of the way. And then Louis-Cesare was back with the duffel. He held off the fey with a sword he'd found somewhere—it glowed slightly, so I assumed he'd taken it off one of our other attackers—while I rooted through the bag.

"Hey! That's my eye!" Ray groused, and then my hand was closing over the explosive putty.

I grabbed it and ripped off a sizable wad. "Move!" I told Louis-Cesare, who spun out into the hall as I threw the piece overhand, like a baseball. I dove for the kitchen as the explosive did what it was designed to do and collapsed the portal—with the fey still partially inside.

That was one visual image I could do without, which was just as well, because I didn't see it. The pantry exploded behind me in a hail of shelving and flying cans as the portal destructed, and I slid to a stop beneath the heavy old table. I tipped it over, grabbed my guns out of the duffel and slammed home extra clips—my last—as a couple of fey rushed in from the hall.

I sprayed them with bullets from both guns. The first one got some kind of shield up in time, but not the second, who jittered back against the wall before sliding down it on a smear of red. Looked like they could bleed, after all, I thought, as the first one jumped me.

I was out of bullets, and his weapon was longer than mine, but then it didn't matter because a glowing sword ripped through his guts. I looked up, expecting to see Louis-Cesare, and saw the vamp I'd nicknamed Scarface instead.

The name was less appropriate now than it had been at the Club, where his face had resembled Frankenstein's. The livid, puckered lines were much less noticeable now, just barely darker than the rest of his complexion. But his black eyes were no less fierce.

He'd picked up the sword of the fallen fey, I guessed, as he stared at it admiringly. "Carves through shields like butter," he said, those eyes meeting mine. "Let's see what it does to you."

"Let's not," I told him, right before my knife caught him in the throat.

It would have been a sufficient discouragement to a younger vamp, but Scarface just pulled it out, ignoring the wash of blood that drenched us both. "Bad idea," he snarled. "I was going to make it quick."

He wrenched the sword out of the fey as I scrambled back, underneath the knife rack on the wall. Stainless wouldn't do much to the fey, but it worked fine on vamps. I'd grabbed the cleaver in one hand and a serrated bread knife in the other before I noticed—Scarface wasn't pursuing me.

He was watching the fallen fey.

"What's wrong with him?" he demanded.

I didn't answer because I didn't know. The fey usually healed as fast as a vamp, but this one was floundering around like a fish out of water, yet not really getting anywhere. He tried to stand, and immediately went back to one knee. And then fell onto his stomach.

Scarface kicked him over with his foot, and I sucked in a breath. There should have been a small puncture wound, or possibly nothing at all by now. Instead, half his chest was eaten away. It was livid red underneath, with white edges of ribs peeking out. But the boundaries of the rapidly expanding wound looked almost like paper when on fire—gold and brown and then nothing at all as the skin and flesh burned to cinders.

Scarface held up the sword. The naked blade shone in the dim light like fox fire, white with a pale blue luminescence at the edges. "They must have enchanted it."

No shit, I thought blankly, as the fey started screaming and clawing at the floorboards, hard enough to leave fingernail tracks in the wood. I got to my feet slowly, keeping an eye on the sword in Scarface's hand. But he didn't raise it. He seemed as mesmerized as I was with what was happening to his opponent.

Within seconds, the strange fire had burned through the fey's ribs to the white column of his spine. He suddenly stopped moving, frozen in place like the baby vamp I'd stabbed at the club. But unlike the young vamp, I didn't think he was going to be all right.

His eyes stared into mine, and the hate drained away, replaced by a desperate sort of pleading. And I could do nothing. Except watch as the fire crept up his torso to the rapidly fluttering heart.

I'd never seen a weapon that could do something like that, that could overwhelm the body's shields and its natural healing ability so quickly and so completely. But the fey never stood a chance. His heart went up like a flame a second later, a sudden bright flare, and it was over. In less than a minute, the body had been completely consumed. All that was left was a scorched black shape on the floor, like a crime scene cutout.

"What the hell kind of trap did you lay for us?" Scarface snarled, staring from the blistered boards to me. His voice was as belligerent as always, but he looked more than a little freaked out. The sword hung limply by his side, like he was almost afraid to touch it.

I would have been, if I were him; vamps burned easily enough as it was.

"No trap," I said, my mouth a little dry. "Or did you not notice that he was trying to kill me?"

"Why? You steal from him, too?"

"I didn't steal from anyone. I'm working for the family who own the rune. They want it back."

"Finders keepers."

"Yeah, only you haven't found it yet."

"Give me a minute." he growled, and then his head jerked up. And he leapt—but not at me. It took me a second to realize that he had raced back into the hallway, and I didn't think it was out of fear of my little knives.

I dropped the bread knife, which had been a lousy choice anyway, grabbed my iron version off the floor where Scarface had tossed it and shoved the bloody thing back into the straps at the small of my back. Then I scooped up the duffel and tucked it under my arm. That left me a hand for my sword and one for the cleaver, and that was as good as things were going to get.

The rain was coming down harder now, drumming on the windows and the ceiling overhead. But not enough to muffle the ring of steel on steel. I ran to the hall door and saw two things: Cheung and Scarface, halfway up the stairs, fighting three fey back to back. And Louis-Cesare battling Æsubrand in the middle of the vestibule.

All around there were blackened marks on the boards of the floor, the stairs and, in one case, in a man-shaped smudge on the wall. Shapes I strongly suspected were the remains of Cheung's men. I glanced up, and through the ruined ceiling spied other battles going on above our heads, but there looked to be more fey than vamps.

And then I wasn't thinking anymore, because my eyes had caught sight of the glowing sword in Æsubrand's hand. My heart lurched sickeningly and an icy fist tightened in my gut. And then I was throwing everything in my bag at anything that moved, but especially at him.

I had a small fortune in legal and not so legal weapons, and I used them all. A couple of disorienting spheres did nothing—I was going to stop buying the damn useless things—but a disruptor had more luck. It packs the punch of a few dozen human grenades, and I timed it perfectly—it hit the floor at his feet and exploded almost at the same time, too fast for even a fey's reflexes to knock it away.

But when the dust cleared, I saw a chasm where the floor had been, new holes in the roof and half the remaining stairs gone. Cheung and Scarface had one less opponent, who was now a smear all over the wall behind the stairs. But Æsubrand was still standing.

It hadn't gotten through his shields.

"The little creature spits and hisses," he said, mockingly. "Come, dhampir. Is that the best you can do?"

"Get back!" I told Louis-Cesare, who in a fit of complete insanity was about to jump the chasm. He saw what was in my hand, and his eyes widened, before he changed direction and jumped for the door of the living room instead. Scarface cursed, grabbed Cheung around the waist and dove for the second story. And I threw the nastiest weapon I had.

I didn't see the dislocator hit, because I'd leapt back into the kitchen the second it left my hand. I didn't hear it, either, because those things don't explode in the conventional sense. But I felt the deadly current ripple past. I crouched behind the heavy table, huddled over the duffel bag and stared at nothing.

"What the fuck was that?" Ray whispered below me.

Oh, shit. Ray. "Tell me you were behind something," I said, belatedly realizing I hadn't thought to check.

"Fuck yeah, I was fucking behind something," he whispered viciously, as the vibrations slowly subsided. "My ass is outside with the sane people!"

I breathed a sigh of relief. Dislocators do exactly what their name implies. And it wouldn't help Ray to get him back together if the pieces were all jumbled up.

After a minute, I edged around the blackened mark on the floor, the edges of which were still sizzling, and crept across the kitchen. Everything was quiet, peaceful. I stuck my head out the door, cautiously looking around. I didn't see anything.

That was a disappointment, as I'd been hoping for an arm growing out of a wall, or maybe a torso where the banister used to be. As long as it was Æsubrand's, I wasn't picky. But there was nothing.

He must have had time to get out the back door, I thought furiously. I shouldn't have hesitated, waiting for Cheung, but as much as I had no reason to like the guy, dislocating half his organs seemed a bit much. But now that complete bastard was probably half a block away—

And someone grabbed me from behind.

"Stop doing that!" I said as I was yanked back against a hard chest. "You're going to scare me to death."

And then Louis-Cesare walked out of the living room—on the opposite side of the hall.

"That would at least be a novel way to die," Æsubrand said, casually breaking my wrist. The sword fell to the ground with a clatter.

I sucked in a breath and fought not to scream, while my brain gibbered somewhere in the background that that was impossible, that no shields held against a dislocator, that that was why the damn things were so illegal that it was a life sentence just to possess one. I'd always been willing to take the risk, on the logic that life in jail was better than no life at all. And dislocators were the option of last resort when nothing else worked.

And now we were screwed, we were screwed, we were so very screwed, my brain helpfully informed me. Because I didn't have anything worse. I didn't even *know* of anything worse.

"Release her," Louis-Cesare said, prompting a laugh out of my captor. I could feel it vibrate through me as he jerked me hard against him.

"And if I do not?" he asked, sounding amused.

I looked down at the slim hand holding me so easily. He was only using one; the other was still wrapped around that damned sword. I watched its pale glow leech over the boards and wondered if it was going to hurt much.

The fey hadn't looked like he'd enjoyed it, as I recalled.

"I will kill you," Louis-Cesare said simply.

Æsubrand sighed. "It was an intellectual challenge to breach the wards. But now that it is done, I find myself growing bored." That hand came up around my throat again, smearing mud and someone else's blood. "Give me what I want or die," he said calmly.

"I knew you were a villain," Louis-Cesare said calmly. "I did not know that you were also a coward."

Unlike Cheung, Æsubrand ignored him, instead tightening his grip on me. Louis-Cesare made a small movement and the hand around my throat cut off my air entirely. He stopped.

I was running scenarios through my mind, and the only one sticking was the time. I could hear the clock in the kitchen ticking so slowly that I was sure something must have been wrong with it. How many minutes were left until the wards cycled back on? Two, three?

Because I didn't think I had that many.

And then Æsubrand jerked and spun, throwing me against the wall and slicing through the air behind us with the sword. It should have taken off his assailant's head, but the guy who'd just nailed him in the temple with my lost stiletto didn't have one. And then the knife at my back was out and stabbing up.

Æsubrand turned at the last second, or I'd have had him; as it was, the cold iron carved a bloody furrow across his chest. It looked like those shields didn't hold so well against one thing, I thought, as two fey dropped to the ground from overhead.

They landed almost on top of Louis-Cesare, and several others poured out of the remains of the pantry. They were trying to overwhelm him with numbers, but Scarface gave a yell from overhead and dive-bombed them, a sword in each hand and a huge grin on his face. I didn't see any more, because I was trying to avoid getting the same treatment as the fey in the kitchen.

It wasn't easy. Æsubrand didn't even flinch, either at the blood pouring down his temple or at the gash in his torso. He also didn't slow down, and he moved even faster in person than his doppelgänger had, a blur of silver against the dark hallway.

I'd dropped as soon as the heart blow missed, grabbed my fallen sword and rolled to the side. But I hadn't had time to get back to my feet before that glowing blade stabbed down, hard enough to stick into the floorboards. He wrenched it out, and a split second later, it was flashing down again, and again, and again, as I rolled around the vestibule, dodging the staccato-like stabs, barely staying ahead of the blade and only getting my own sword up once.

That resulted in getting it sliced in two, as I was going to be any minute now, and then Æsubrand stumbled, cursing, the first sign of pain I'd seen. Of course, that was understandable, considering that a vampire head had latched onto his ankle like a rabid pit bull.

The rest of Ray was in the vestibule, hiding behind some furniture, which he started lobbing at us. A side table hit Æsubrand in the chest, and a lamp struck him in the shoulder, and then Ray's head was sent flying to land with a wet-sounding thump well down the hallway. Whereupon his body went into a frenzy, tossing everything and anything it could get its hands on. And it wasn't bothering to aim anymore.

Or maybe it was and it just couldn't see that well— I didn't know—but in short order I was pelted by a wooden chair, a vase, the matching side table, and I barely ducked in time to avoid a large mirror. Æsubrand had been headed for me, but had had to jerk back to avoid the mirror, giving me a second to strike. And a second was all I needed.

I lunged, the broken sword that remained in my hand up and aiming for his torso. That close, I never miss— unless I'm using my left hand and wearing a dress with a trailing hem. My foot caught on the fabric, I tripped and slammed face-first into the wall. *This is why I wear jeans*, I thought furiously, as I spun, and plunged the sword blindly into warm, yielding flesh.

There was no chance to see what, exactly, I'd hit, because the next second I was thrown back a half dozen yards into the vestibule. I hit Ray and we went down in a tangle of thrashing limbs. I jumped back to my feet again, sword in hand—only to find that the battle was over.

Suddenly the only fey in the hall were four bodies left sprawled on the muddy boards. I scrambled toward the nearest, tripped over the dress again, cursed and staggered the rest of the way to its side.

I rolled the limp, blood-soaked figure over. The face was unrecognizable, but the torso was relatively clear of wounds—no jagged stab line and minimal blood.

The next one was the same, and the next, and the next. I stood up and kicked the wall, so furious I could barely see. I'd had him. Goddamn it, I'd *had him*.

Until I'd missed.

Chapter Twenty-six

The skirt of the dress was hanging half off and threatening to trip me with every step. I tore it the rest of the way loose and threw it on the floor. I was never wearing another goddamned skirt as long as I lived. Which probably wouldn't be too long now that I'd let my best chance to rid myself of that unbelievable bastard slip through my—

Somebody whistled and I looked up, suddenly realizing that I had an audience.

And a hallway full of vampires.

The whistler was Scarface, who was leaning on the banister overhead, grinning at me. He was swinging a head by the hair, but it wasn't Ray's. The long, flowing silver-blond locks were gory, and the head itself was trailing veins and ligaments out of the neck, which hadn't been severed cleanly as a sword stroke would have done. It took me a second to realize that it had been literally ripped off a fey's shoulders.

Good, I thought viciously. And smiled back.

He patted it fondly. "Next time Convocation comes around, I'm gonna wear this on my belt."

I wasn't sure if he was talking to me or his boss. Cheung was standing in the middle of the hall, just below the railing. His suit coat was off and his natty orange tie was askew, but otherwise he looked about the same. Except for the gun in one hand and the sword in the other. And his expression, which went better with the arms than the Armani.

I did a head count and realized that we were seriously outnumbered. In all, it looked like eight of his vampires had survived. Except for Scarface, they were crowding the small hallway, backing up the boss. And unlike their buddy, they weren't smiling.

To make matters worse, it was past time for the wards to have kicked back in, if they were planning on doing it. The fey must have really screwed them up, probably so no one could raise them during the fight. It was a good strategy, but it meant just one thing for us.

If Cheung decided to attack, we were toast.

He glanced at me and Louis-Cesare stepped between us. Cheung regarded him impatiently, his face more fierce and hawklike than ever. "I have lost seven men tonight," he said brusquely. "I think that is enough."

Louis-Cesare nodded abruptly, but he didn't drop the sword. Cheung made a disgusted sound and handed his own to one of his boys. He put a hand in his pocket and Louis-Cesare tensed. But he just took out a handkerchief to wipe some blood off his cheek. If it had been human, he'd have absorbed it, but the fey kind gives vamps no nourishment. And from what I've heard, it tastes foul.

"I don't have the rune," I told him, while I had the chance.

"I know you do not," he told me, pretty calmly under the circumstances. "I saw your face when the fey threatened you. If you had had the stone, you would have used it. Or, if you did not know how, you would have given it to him."

Louis-Cesare frowned. "Are you accusing Dorina of cowardice?"

"No. I would have done the same. The stone is valuable, but I would not die for it. And now I would like an explanation for why my men did so!"

Louis-Cesare and I exchanged a glance. I didn't see any reason to correct Cheung about why the fey were here. Besides, I was fairly sure that finding Naudiz figured on Æsubrand's list somewhere.

Just not at the top.

"Jókell—that's the fey who contacted you—stole it from the Svarestri," I told him.

Cheung's scowl deepened and his tiger tat looked up, its emerald eyes gleaming. "He assured me that it was a family heirloom!"

"Maybe next time you should ask which family. The rune belongs to the Blarestri royal house. The Svarestri stole it with his help, and then he double-crossed them."

Cheung's face lost some of its color. "You are saying that there are two fey royal houses involved in this?"

"And at least three Senates. The rune's the hottest item in town, only nobody knows where it is. And we can't ask Jókell because he's dead."

"Yes. We found the body but not the stone. It had been taken."

"By Elyas, of the European Senate," Louis-Cesare informed him.

"Elyas." Cheung's hand clenched on the handkerchief. "He will pay for the losses he has caused me this night."

"That is doubtful."

Cheung bristled. "You believe that lightweight to be my equal? I would have challenged him years ago if I thought he would fight his own battles!"

"I believe only that it is difficult to revenge oneself on a corpse."

Cheung looked confused.

"Elyas is dead," I said bluntly. "Someone killed him tonight and took the stone, and no, we don't know who."

"You are one of the chief suspects," Louis-Cesare added helpfully.

Cheung stared at him for a moment. "I beg your pardon."

"Not anymore," I objected. "He was here waiting for me while Elyas was being killed. And so were his men."

"That is not an alibi," Louis-Cesare argued. "He

could have followed us to Elyas's, murdered him and been here in time to intercept you on your return."

"If he knew Elyas had the stone. But he didn't. He wasn't even in New York when Jókell was killed."

"Perhaps, perhaps not. We have only his word for it that he arrived in New York when he said he did. But let us assume that he was telling the truth. He could nonetheless have surmised that Elyas was the thief. He had been plagued by telephone calls from the man all day; Elyas told me so himself. When the rune turned up missing, it would not have been difficult to infer that Cheung might be responsible."

Cheung's face had been getting progressively redder as Louis-Cesare talked. "You are accusing me?"

"You had an excellent motive," Louis-Cesare said, as calmly as if he weren't outnumbered eight to one. "Probably the best of anyone. The other interested parties merely want the stone. You *need* it, to avoid the wrath of your mistress."

"But he was here all night," I insisted, "from shortly after we escaped him at the Club."

"And how do you know this? The man would say anything." Louis-Cesare waved a hand, fortunately not the one with the sword in it. "He is clearly desperate."

"He doesn't look desperate." Cheung looked somewhere between confused and pissed.

"Of course he is desperate. He is facing execution!"

"Execution?" Cheung said sharply, his eyes darting back and forth between the two of us.

"It is a death penalty to break the Senate's truce. It is also death to murder another senator outside of a duel. And Elyas was slaughtered like an animal," Louis-Cesare informed him. Cheung lost the rest of his color very quickly.

"But he *was* here," I insisted. "We have a witness."

"One of his men?" Louis-Cesare sneered. "They would say anything for him."

"No. One of ours. He kidnapped Radu to find out who I was and to try to get me to talk. He's around here somewhere. . . ."

"You kidnapped my Sire?" Louis-Cesare demanded, rounding on Cheung, who was starting to look a little beleaguered.

"He has not been harmed."

"That is irrelevant. Kidnapping him alone was a violent act and a clear violation of the truce!"

"She kidnapped my servant," Cheung said, pointing at me.

"She is not vampire. The truce does not affect her."

"She was sent by a vampire!"

"She was sent by the Senate, who I am sure will be receiving a formal complaint from Lord Radu very shortly." He looked pointedly at me.

"Yes," I said, hoping I knew where he was going with this. "And I might have mentioned that you were here, when I called to let them know I have Raymond."

"They already have men on the way," Louis-Cesare added confidently. "Can you not feel them approach?"

I thought that was a risky strategy, but it seemed to work. Cheung began to look a little nervous. Of course, that wasn't necessarily good for us; he might decide to kill the witnesses and blame it on the fey.

"I didn't mention the kidnapping," I said quickly. "I thought there was a chance Radu might want to forget the whole thing."

"Why would he choose to do that?" Louis-Cesare demanded. "At the very least, he could have the man formally chastised."

I didn't know what the Senate's idea of "chastisement" entailed, but judging from Cheung's expression, it wasn't anything good. "Well, technically, no harm was done," I pointed out. "And we are on the same side in the war...."

Cheung grabbed at the thought. "Yes, we are allies," he reminded Louis-Cesare.

"You have a strange way of showing loyalty!"

"It was a ... misunderstanding. I had been robbed. I merely requested Lord Radu to accompany me to this house to retrieve my property."

"And is that what he will say before the Senate?"

Every time Louis-Cesare said "Senate," Cheung flinched slightly. "There is no reason for them to learn of this."

"Radu may feel otherwise. I do not like to speak ill of my Sire, but he can be somewhat . . . vindictive."

"You could talk to him," Cheung pointed out.

"Why would I do that?"

"We fought for you!"

"Not knowingly," Louis-Cesare said.

"But the result was the same. You would not have carried the field without us. And therefore the debt is the same. And your family has a reputation for honoring your debts."

"As does yours."

Cheung's eyes narrowed. "What do you want?"

"Protection for this house for the next few days, until I can make other arrangements."

I started to say something, then stopped. There were worse things than having Claire pissed off at me about vampire security. Assuming I could even figure out where she was.

"Agreed. And it is to be made clear to the Blarestri that I had no knowledge of their connection to the stone when I arranged to handle the sale."

"Okay, but we get Ray," I countered. "I promised to bring him in."

Cheung rolled his eyes. "I have no further use for him. I wish I had never heard of him or that accursed stone!" He looked at Louis-Cesare. "We have an agreement, then?"

Louis-Cesare nodded. "I will do what I can with Lord Radu. But it would perhaps be best if you were not here when we have that discussion. Your presence might . . . inflame him further."

Cheung didn't go so far as to say "thank you," but he nodded. He pulled a sheath off the fallen fey and handed it to a servant, who carefully enclosed the unusual sword. Then Cheung and half his boys slipped silently out the back door.

The rest lingered behind, looking awkward. "Would

you . . . happen to have some tea?" one of them asked me, after a moment.

"Uh, yeah. I think so." Claire had mentioned seeing some. "I'm not sure I know how to make it, though."

"If you show me to your kitchen, I can manage."

I pointed. "It's through there. What's left of it." He nodded and the guys filed out, except for Scarface, who continued to watch us from above.

I let out a breath I didn't know I'd been holding, and sagged against the wall. Damn. That could have gone . . . well, a whole lot worse.

Louis-Cesare looked at me and smiled. "Lord Cheung is an honorable man."

Lord Cheung had been in deep shit and just dug himself out, I didn't say. Because pissing off Scarface wasn't my idea of a good time. Not when I felt like I might fall over any minute.

And not when I still had a mess to deal with. I pushed myself off the wall.

"Where are your friends?" Louis-Cesare asked me, as if he'd been reading my mind.

"I don't know." I looked at the missing stairs. A few planks still clung to the walls here and there, and the top three steps remained in place. But that wouldn't have helped me much, even if I hadn't had one hand out of commission. "Maybe upstairs."

"I will check." He caught hold of the jagged edge of the floor above and pulled himself up. Scarface waited, arms crossed, eyes slitted, until he stood up, and then the two faced off. I held my breath; it looked like there might be trouble, after all.

Then Scarface grinned. "I never had the chance to watch you fight before." He pursed his lips. "Not bad."

I didn't know what he was talking about, having been a little too busy not dying to pay attention to anyone's technique. Louis-Cesare looked bemused as well, whether at the compliment or in surprise at who was giving it. But he nodded briefly.

Scarface started patting himself down, but his trophy got in the way. So he tied it to what remained of the banister by the hair while he searched around in his pockets. I couldn't figure out what he was doing, and by the look on his face, neither could Louis-Cesare.

Eventually, Scarface located a pen and, after a moment, ripped down a hanging shred of wallpaper. He presented them to Louis-Cesare with a strange look on his face, half-hopeful, half-embarrassed. "You know, in case I don't catch up with you at the Challenge."

Oh, my God, I thought blankly.

Louis-Cesare gave me a fierce look, and I bit my lip while he hastily scribbled his name. I doubt it was very legible due to the nature of the paper, but Scarface seemed pleased. He folded it carefully and put it in his back pocket.

"You're challenging?" I asked, as Scarface reclaimed his trophy.

"Damn right, I'm challenging. You're looking at a future senator." And the scary thing was, he wouldn't be the strangest one I knew.

He eyed the remains of the fey. "You wouldn't happen to know anybody who could get this shrunk by tonight, would you?"

"I think it takes a while. You have to remove the skull and then boil it . . ." I trailed off, because Louis-Cesare was looking at me funny.

"Damn." Scarface cocked his head. "Then again, I could take it like this. Think I'll intimidate an opponent?"

"You scare the hell out of me," I told him truthfully.

That seemed to have been the right answer. Scarface laughed, clapped Louis-Cesare on the shoulder and somersaulted off the balcony, his grisly trophy bouncing against his thigh. I waited until he'd passed through the front door and went to retrieve my own.

Ray had ended up wedged in a corner by the back door. He had a muddy boot print across his face and one of his fangs had broken off. But other than that, he seemed okay.

"We got a bond now?" he demanded.

"Getting there."

I tucked his head under my arm and went hunting for the rest of him. I was trying to haul his body out of a heap of broken furniture when Louis-Cesare came back. "They are not there," he told me. "The rooms are disturbed, as if they were awakened abruptly, but there is no one anywhere above us."

My breath came out in a sigh of relief. There was a huge hole in the floor, another in the wall where the pantry had been, and then there were the missing stairs. No way had anyone slept through that. If he'd found anything, it wouldn't have been good news.

"I also cannot sense them," he said, listening.

Neither could I, now that I concentrated. There were no shuffling footsteps, no telltale heartbeats, no frightened breathing. Just the ancient fridge dumping some ice cubes, the soft sounds of tea being brewed and the pounding of the rain.

"Perhaps they returned to Faerie," Louis-Cesare said.

"Maybe." But that didn't sound right. Claire had been pretty adamant about not returning without that damned stone, and anyway, she'd have just been stepping right back into the mess she'd fled.

Of course, between Æsubrand and a palace full of assassins, I knew which one I'd choose.

There was probably another explanation, but I couldn't think of it just then. I was feeling a little dizzy now that the adrenaline had bled away, and the lack of a meal in something like fourteen hours had given me the shakes. And Ray was caught on something, and one-handed I couldn't seem to—

Louis-Cesare tugged him out and set him on his feet, and accidentally bumped my injured wrist. I sucked in a breath through my teeth. "What is it?"

"My wrist."

"You never told me what was wrong with it," he said, cradling it in one large hand.

"Æsubrand," I said simply. "He broke it last night, too."

Louis-Cesare paused, but he didn't say anything.

And after a moment, I felt warmth slide through the damaged tissue, wrapping the bones in a web of power that, whether it helped the healing process or not, felt damned good. I could still feel the throb in the injury with every heartbeat, but it was distant, manageable. I'd get it bound up in a few minutes, but for right now, this would work.

"Thanks."

He didn't reply, just pulled me against him. His hand was in my hair, his heartbeat under my ear, and it was oddly soothing. What was even more so was the fact that he was still in one piece. I wasn't sure how, but I'd take it.

There were about a hundred things I needed to do right then, but for a moment, I just stood there. My wrist was throbbing, my legs felt weak as water and a massive headache was building behind my right eye. But he was warm and his shirt was soft and he smelled so damn good. I felt my whole body relax.

He didn't say anything, but his arms tightened. And despite strict orders to the contrary, my eyes slipped closed. All at once, I just wanted to curl up and—

"Well, this is cozy," Ray said, from under my arm.

Louis-Cesare pulled back with a sigh just as the door banged open and Christine stumbled in. Her pink silk gown was liberally streaked with mud, and the priceless lace was a soggy mess. She was dragging a couple of mud-covered suitcases and muttering something under her breath. She didn't even appear to notice us, just dropped the suitcases near a body, turned and went out again.

Louis-Cesare looked after her, his face blank. "What is Christine doing here?"

"She said you told her to go with me."

"She said—" He stopped, his jaw tightening. "I believe she misunderstood."

"If you aren't here for her, why are you here?"

"Because of Æsubrand," he said, like that should in any way be obvious.

"How did you know he was going to attack?"

"He attacked last night, but did not achieve his objective. Why should he not return?"

"You skipped out *on your murder trial* on the chance he might show up?" I asked incredulously.

He frowned. Apparently, that hadn't been the response he'd expected. "It appears fortunate that I did."

"You're supposed to be facing the Senate right now! What are you planning to tell them?"

"Nothing. There is no point. Whatever I say, the outcome has already been decided."

"Mircea doesn't seem to think so."

"Mircea doesn't know Anthony as well as I do."

"Meaning what?" I demanded, as someone started stabbing at the doorbell. I stared at it a little desperately. "*Now* what?"

"The Senate's men, in all probability."

"You were bluffing."

"Not about that. I assume it is why Æsubrand left so precipitously. His spies must have warned him that reinforcements were on the way."

He started for the door, and I grabbed his shirt. "You called them?" I asked, hoping that the sinking in my gut was wrong.

"No."

"Then why are they here?"

"To take me into custody, I should suspect."

Chapter Twenty-seven

He pulled away, and after a stunned second, I followed Louis-Cesare through the ruined vestibule. The wind had picked up, billowing out the antique lace curtains and letting in the rain. And a lot of flashing lights. They strobed the small room in disco colors of red and blue, sending a flickering rectangle of light across the walls and making the shadows of the furniture jump.

We had visitors, but not the Senate. At least, not yet.

Across the muddy tire tracks, car parts and half a ton of couture that littered the lawn, I could see a dozen neighbors lining the street in their nightclothes. They were staring at the mess and the wreck of a house beyond it with the sort of keen-eyed horror people usually reserve for traffic accidents. And across the street, a third police car had just pulled up.

I should have expected it. The wards had dropped and the glamourie had gone with them. And half a dozen vampires ripping a Lamborghini apart wasn't exactly quiet. We'd probably woken up half the neighborhood.

"Christine!" Louis-Cesare called urgently. She'd been squelching around in ankle-deep mud, trying to rescue the rest of her wardrobe, but she looked up at her master's voice. "Assemble a small bag, if you please. We are leaving."

She stared at him in confusion, her arms full of muddy couture. "But ... but my clothes ..."

"I shall buy you new ones. *Vite, s'il te plaît.*"

Her lips tightened, and for a moment, I thought Louis-Cesare was going to have a rebellion on his hands. Night was fading, and Christine's good humor was going with it. But after a moment, she threw down the clothes and stomped past us, still muttering.

Louis-Cesare started across the street, where Radu was talking to a couple of cops. But I knotted a fist in the fabric of his shirt and pulled him back. It didn't sound like we had a lot of time, and I wanted some answers. "What did you mean about Anthony?"

He gave me an aggravated look, which I caught in glimpses. The cops' lights were strobing his face along with the front of the battered old house. But he stayed put. "How much do you know about the European Senate?"

"Not a lot, why?"

"Because to understand Anthony, you have to understand how he rules."

"Then explain it to me."

"There is not time to go into specifics—"

"Then go with generalities! Just tell me."

"Unlike other consuls, who have to work with their Senates, Anthony dictates to his," Louis-Cesare said quickly. "He can do so because the senators know that they cannot lose their seats as long as they accede to his wishes. Any challengers for their positions are automatically referred to me."

I stared at him, sure I'd heard wrong. "You're saying you take *all* challenges?"

"Yes."

"But every time you step into a ring, you can lose. I don't care how good you are! It only takes one slip—"

"And then Anthony would have to find himself a new champion," he agreed. "But that has not happened yet, and my reputation has grown to the point that there are few now who make the attempt."

"Like Cheung."

"Yes. The rumor is that he is good—very good. But he chose not to challenge, although he could easily have defeated Elyas and possibly three or four others on the Senate. But he knew he would not be facing them; and he chose not to face me."

"But ... why take that kind of risk for Anthony? You're clearly not that fond of the guy, or you wouldn't be trying to leave."

"You do not understand what the Senate was like when—" He stopped, staring across the street.

Radu appeared to be having trouble with one of the cops. The man must have had some mage blood somewhere, or else he was just exceptionally strong-minded. Either way, he wasn't buying what Radu was trying to sell.

The others were nodding in time to 'Du's somewhat-strident tones, but not him. His hand was on his gun, and he was shaking his head and backing toward his police car. Any minute now, he was going to—

He made a run for it, and 'Du started after him. Normally, it would have been no contest, but rain, mud and satin slippers don't mix well. 'Du took off in one direction, his shoes went in the other and his face hit asphalt, hard.

"Don't even think about it," I told Louis-Cesare. He sighed and pushed damp hair out of his eyes. He'd lost the slide he usually used to keep it confined, and it was straggling around his face.

"When I joined the European Senate, it was in constant chaos," he told me. "The numerous factions and the amount of infighting had almost frozen its ability to do anything, leading to disorder in its lands and rebelliousness by its subordinates. Some of the oldest senators were also some of the most intransigent and difficult to dislodge. And together, they were formidable enough to challenge Anthony's authority."

"But then he found you."

"And thereby discovered a way out of the quagmire. The older senators were challenged, and one by one replaced by those more willing to work with his agenda. For a time, it led to a stronger, more unified Senate and better governance."

"And now?"

"Anthony has had too much power for too long. He has become accustomed to having the Senate agree to any and all of his policies. Including those that are short-sighted or detrimental."

"He's become a tyrant, in other words."

"Let us say that some of his actions have begun to worry me," Louis-Cesare said drily. "And then I came here two months ago, to assist your consul in a duel, and saw a very different type of Senate. The senators were loud and unruly, and the consul had to flatter and cajole and threaten to get anywhere with them. Factionalism was rife and tempers were quick, and some measures had been stuck in debate for decades with very little movement. It was chaos."

"Made you rethink your conclusion?"

"No. It made me realize how ... sterile ... our Senate had become. There is no debate anymore, no discussion, no need for compromise. All anyone wishes to know is what Anthony wants to do. And then I met you and—"

He was interrupted by a shout. It looked like the fall had broken Radu's concentration—and his mental hold on the cops. Three of them were staring around like sleepwalkers waking up in an unfamiliar location. But a couple others had already shrugged it off. One of them had 'Du by the arm, while his colleague went for a CB.

"And?" I demanded.

"And by the time the date came for my return, I found that I did not wish to go."

Rainwater was running down his face and spiking his lashes. His shirt was past soaked, and his hair was flattened against his head. For the first time, I noticed that his nose was a little big, and that there was a wash of freckles, so pale as to usually go unobserved, over those high cheekbones. But there was no guile in those blue eyes, just hope, uncertainty and maybe a little bit of fear.

His hands came up to frame my face, and he pushed my dripping bangs out of my eyes. "Dorina, there is something I—"

A shout broke out. Radu had thrown off the first cop's hold and jumped the one with the CB, who had pulled a gun on him. So of course 'Du took the gun away and clocked him upside the head with it. Only to be tackled by the other semilucid cop. He disappeared behind the open door of the cop car in a flutter of orange silk. Louis-Cesare sighed.

"Wait," I said, holding on as he tried to move away. "You still haven't told me why you don't think you can win against Anthony."

He looked at me calmly. "Because unless I am very much mistaken, he killed Elyas."

That surprised me enough that I let go of his shirt, and he strode off to rescue Radu. I started to follow, before realizing that I was wearing a thong, a sagging stocking and a few straps. And that half the neighborhood was staring at me.

And then an ambulance screeched to a halt, and a couple EMTs jumped out and ran up the drive. "We got a report of a car wreck," one of them told me. "Were there any—"

"Holy shit!" the other one said, staring at me. Or to be more precise, at the severed head under my arm.

I decided the neighbors could bite me, and ran after Louis-Cesare. "Anthony wasn't at the auction," I reminded him, as he prized one of the cops off 'Du.

"Yes, but it is possible that Elyas's death had nothing to do with the rune."

"How do you figure that?"

"If Anthony loses me, he loses his stranglehold on the Senate. There would be at least five senators challenged almost immediately. Anthony has been able to promote his allies for hundreds of years, without concern for their fighting abilities, because he knew they should never need to utilize them."

"And now he's got a Senate full of people who can't defend their seats."

He nodded. "Those five would be defeated, no doubt by challengers who would be far less dependent on his goodwill. And possibly more."

"That's one of those Halloween things, right?" one of the EMTs asked. They'd followed me down from the house, and now one of them tentatively poked Ray in the cheek.

Ray's eyes flew open. "Poke me again, and I'll chew your finger off," he said nastily. The guy scrambled back with a little scream.

I sighed. I couldn't do mind control, at least not on the level needed here. They were going to have to get in line.

"But why kill Elyas?" I asked. "If Anthony was going to kill someone, he'd hardly make it a member of his own Senate!"

"Elyas was one of the five."

"So better to lose one guy who would probably be defeated in a challenge anyway than his champion?" Louis-Cesare nodded.

From a strictly profit-and-loss standpoint, it made sense. If Louis-Cesare was convicted of the murder, Anthony could enslave him and never have to worry about his defection again. But if he just let him leave, Elyas was dead meat anyway as soon as he was challenged.

"But why Elyas?" I still wanted this to be about the rune. Otherwise, my task of finding it had just gotten a lot harder. There was a limited pool of suspects at the apartment, but anyone could have shown up at the club. Not to mention that, if Louis-Cesare was right, he was screwed. How did a person win a court case when the judge had set him up?

"He needed someone with whom I had a grievance, and he knew that Elyas had Christine. No senator would take on such a favor for another consul without first alerting his own. Such a thing could easily cause a rift within his own Senate."

One of the EMTs was trying to make a call. I reached in the side of the truck, yanked out the CB cord and handed it to him. "Okay, but why tonight?"

"Anthony likely has spies within Elyas's household, who could have informed him that I was expected."

"But you were late. If Anthony set things up for your

original appointment time, Elyas would have been dead before you arrived."

"Yes, but he could have waited, concealed somewhere, and acted when he saw me arrive."

I frowned. "But you said that you were only in the waiting room a couple of minutes at most."

"About that, yes."

"So in less than two minutes, Anthony kills Elyas, sets you up and has time to steal the rune he didn't even know existed?"

Louis-Cesare shot me a frustrated look. "Why are you arguing so strongly against this?"

"Because it's a worst-case scenario! Why are you so set on it?"

"Because I scented him when I first entered the room."

"You scented Anthony?"

"Yes. It was vague, merely a trace. But that was most likely due to the window. It was open. The scent would not have lingered long."

"Why didn't you mention this?"

"I have no proof, Dorina! And there is nothing your father or Kit can do against a consul. I do not wish them to make an enemy needlessly on my behalf."

"But . . . if it can't be proven, how do you—"

"I did not say it cannot be proven, merely that they cannot do so. There is a chance—" His head jerked up.

"What now?"

"The Senate's men. Where is Christine?"

"In the house, I guess."

He licked his lips. "Dorina, it will be much easier to elude them if I do not have her with me. I know it is much to ask—"

"She can stay here," I said, wondering about my sanity. "I'll explain to Claire, assuming I ever find her again. But that's not—"

"Promise me you will look after her, that you will not leave her alone. There is only another hour or so until sunrise, and she will sleep all day. I will arrange for her security by tomorrow night."

"Why does she need—"

"Promise me."

"Yes, fine. But you haven't said what you plan to—" I blinked and realized I was talking to air. Louis-Cesare was gone.

Two large black vans screeched around the corner and skidded to a halt at the curb. They hadn't even stopped moving when something like twenty guards piled out. I watched them with a strange sort of detachment. The night had reached the point where it would be difficult to get any worse.

Then a familiar curly head emerged from the front of the lead van.

Okay. It was worse.

"It's that woman," 'Du informed me. "She's been back less than a day, and look at us. We'll probably all be dead by tomorrow."

"You're already dead."

"There's no reason to be facetious, Dory," he snapped, as a grim-faced Marlowe stopped in front of me.

"I knew it," he hissed.

"Knew what?" I asked wearily.

"Knew you would be involved in this. Where is he?"

"By now?" I shrugged.

"Sir, should we—" one of the vamps began, then quickly shut up.

The rotating lights painted Marlowe's hair with color and glinted in his narrowed brown eyes. "You're hiding him."

I waved the hand not holding Ray. "Yeah. Because this is where you come when you want to be inconspicuous."

"You deny that he was here?"

"You can scent him. You know damned well he was here."

"Yes, instead of standing trial to save his life!"

"He seems to think a trial isn't going to get him anywhere."

"And this is?"

"If he finds the killer."

"In twenty-four hours," Marlowe told me harshly,

"Louis-Cesare will be declared a fugitive, and the Senate will rule against him. Flight is as good as an admission of guilt. If you want to help him, you will tell me where he is."

"He's a first-level master. He's wherever the hell he wants to be."

Marlowe glanced up at the huge guard looming behind him. "Search the house."

He looked at me, like he was waiting for a reaction. I just stood there and dripped at him. For once, there were no big dark secrets to find. The only ones I'd had, I'd already chucked at the fey.

"He'll trash it, just to be vindictive," Radu said darkly, as Marlowe gave up and stomped off.

I shrugged and started after him. "Too late."

Chapter Twenty-eight

Marlowe glanced at me suspiciously as we passed through the front door, but I wasn't interested in checking up on him. I assumed that he'd bug the place, and that I would remove them as soon as he left. I just wanted something dry to wear.

I headed for the stairs before I remembered—we no longer had any. So I swerved into the living room for a blanket instead. I found one that didn't smell too much like troll, wrapped it sarong-style around me and started back for the hall. And stopped.

My eyes had focused on a tiny movement near the door. I bent down and found myself looking at a lone warrior, all of two inches high. It was one of Olga's chess pieces.

That in itself wasn't unusual; they ended up scattered about everywhere. But they didn't usually carry small torches that they waved around wildly. And, once it had gotten my attention, the tiny thing started off across the forest of clothes and bedding.

It finally paused at the top of the stairs going down to the basement. It looked up at me, the minuscule faceplate gleaming in the torchlight. When I stayed where I was, it started waving again impatiently, and pointing down into the blackness.

For a minute, I just stood there, swaying a little on my feet and wondering how paranoid a person had to be before she decided the toys were out to get her. But in the end, I shrugged my shoulders and just went with it. I picked the little thing up and carried it down the stairs.

At the bottom, another small warrior was doing something near the rusted hulk of Pip's still. There was no light in the basement, and the tiny torch cast wavering shadows on the walls that confused me further. But when I got closer, it became obvious that he was pushing around small sticks and bits of moss, arranging them in some sort of pattern.

The first small warrior started poking me in the side of the hand with his sword, so I put him down. He made his way across the peeling paint of the floor and touched his torch to the end of the nearest pile of kindling. Fire ran across the old concrete, forming jagged letters for a brief instant before the tiny fuel was exhausted: *OPEN*.

I stared at them and then at the wavering imprint they'd left on my retinas. The message was clear enough: it had been left in front of the wall where Pip's conduit to Faerie manifested. But if Claire was on the other side, she could open it for herself. And if she wasn't . . .

But Æsubrand would never leave a message like that. And the only time he'd been in the cellar, he'd been too busy trying to kill me to rig something up. At least, I fervently hoped so.

I reached out, wondering if I was about to make a huge mistake, and pressed the small talisman that powered the link between the ley-line sink and the portal. I jumped back, but not fast enough. A swirl of light and color appeared on the wall, flooding the ugly old basement with a rich golden light. And something huge tumbled out of nowhere and smacked me to the ground.

My skull hit the floor hard enough to have me seeing stars. But it was difficult to concentrate on that while the life was getting squeezed out of me. The massive weight shifted slightly, and while I was still crushed, I could breathe.

And that was worse.

My lungs had room to fully inflate, but they were cowering in my chest in fear. I'd once been buried under a pile of decomposing corpses, with jellylike flesh and gangrenous limbs, and it hadn't reeked like that. I retched, but my stomach had nothing left to bring up. *Lucky I never got that sandwich*, I thought, as someone started slapping troll flesh.

"Get off her! *Move*, Ysmi! Dorina, are you all right?"

I didn't answer. I wasn't sure I could talk, and anyway, I was afraid to open my mouth and let in more of that hideous stench. But I looked up.

A thick, cracked, yellow toenail stared me in the face. It was attached to a foot with knobs and warts and skin as hard as a rock, all held together by some sort of greenish yellowish fungus and a lot of dirt. My last conscious thought was to decide that, all things considered, having a troll foot in my face was the worst thing that had happened to me all day.

I awoke an indeterminate amount of time later to find myself in my own bed with rain lashing the window and a note fluttering on the door. A glance down showed that someone, probably Claire, had stuffed me into a T-shirt and wrapped my wrist. But judging by my general filthiness, she'd stopped short of an actual bath.

I drew one in the tub for myself with a lot of bubbles, a rare luxury, and got in, taking the note in with me. It was a two-pager. Claire hadn't been able to leave me one for so long, she was making up for lost time.

> *Who is this Marlowe guy anyway? He's an ass. Threw him out. Threatened to have Ysmi sit on him if he returned.*

I grinned. I'd really needed the sleep, but damn . . . I was sorry to have missed that.

> *How did no vampires turn into a houseful of them? You have weird friends. That Christine freaks me out. Put her in the large closet in the first-floor guest room because there are no windows. Okay?*

I was sure Christine appreciated being bedded down in the closet. On the other hand, the only other rooms without a view were the pantry, which we no longer had, and part of the basement, which was full of trolls. On the whole, I thought she'd gotten the better deal.

Why are there two severed heads rolling around the house? Cats tried to eat one. Mostly prevented.

I wondered what "mostly" entailed. Decided I didn't want to know.

Headless guy is in hallway broom closet with head that I think is his. Hosed body off in backyard; it was filthy. Head cussed a lot. But not as much as Radu when he found out you didn't include a new car in your deal with this Cheung person. He said to call him.

Oops. I knew we'd forgotten something. I made a mental note to avoid 'Du for the near future. Maybe for the distant future, too. I wondered if there was any way to claim a Lamborghini on my expense account with Mircea. Probably not.

FYI, Olga cut a new portal. Well, not new. It's a new destination on the old one. Two colors now: green goes to Faerie, blue goes to beauty shop. But she'd started it only today and we had no way back unless opened from this end. Sorry. Next time we'll send somebody small through first.
Knock on my door when you get up.

That last line sounded ominous, but it wasn't like I could avoid Claire, too. I sloshed my way out of the bath and checked out my bruise collection. I hadn't added as many as I'd expected, all things considered. I threw on a T-shirt and a pair of soft gray sweatpants and padded down to Claire's room, trying to dry my hair with one hand.

I couldn't have been out long, because it was still dark outside. Claire was up, or at least there was a strip of light under her door. I knocked and she opened up, her long red hair done up in fabric rollers. It looked like she'd put her time at the beauty shop to good use.

"We didn't know you were home, or we'd have waited for you," she told me earnestly before I could say anything. "But when we heard the commotion from the wards—"

"You mean they actually did something?" I'd begun to wonder.

"For about a minute. Until the damn Svarestri deactivated them!"

She moved aside and I came in. She'd moved a twin bed in here, and Aiden and Stinky were bedded down in snoring heaps. Or, at least, Stinky was snoring, sprawled out at the head of the bed like a drunken sailor, hairy limbs akimbo. Aiden was curled up at his side like a cherub. A thumb-sucking one, I was glad to note. Stinky had never done that. If he couldn't eat it, he wasn't interested.

"The Svarestri had to have altered the wards from the inside," I said, sitting on her bed. Wards could be overwhelmed from outside, but they could be taken down only when someone had access to their source of power. "How did they manage to reverse the portals?"

Claire sat on the vanity chair, propped her foot up on the quilt and continued what she'd been doing, which was to paint her toenails. "I've been thinking about that. Manlíkans are usually used for scouts into Dark Fey lands and as training dummies on the practice field. Not as warriors. I don't think Æsubrand intended to use them to fight us, but rather to find him a way into the house. I should have wondered what the rest of those things were up to while a handful kept us busy."

"Wouldn't it have been simpler to have them take down the wards?"

She shook her head. "Wards ignore Manlíkans. As far as they're concerned, they don't exist. But a portal is a different kind of magic, and the Svarestri somehow knew there was one in the pantry—"

"Æsubrand saw it the last time he was here," I said, recalling how Louis-Cesare and I had once escaped him using that very portal.

"I had wondered; they aren't that easy to detect unless you're right on top of one. Anyway, they managed to reverse it, but by that time they were exhausted from the storm and the struggle with us—"

"So they waited to break in until tonight, when we were asleep," I finished for her. It made sense.

"Yes. Attacking women and children in their beds—that's what Æsubrand calls honor!"

Personally, I thought it was what Æsubrand called smart. I didn't like his tactics, but from a purely military standpoint, it had been a flawless plan. And if Cheung hadn't shown up, it might well have worked.

I said as much, only to have Claire frown savagely. "Caedmon should have killed him when he had the chance!"

I blinked. It was pretty much where my thoughts had been going, but it was a little disconcerting to hear it from her. The woman I knew had planted marigolds in the garden to keep the bugs off the plants because she didn't like swatting them. She wouldn't talk to me for a week once after seeing me beat a rat to death with a broom handle. She'd been a tofu-eating, fur-hating, plastic-shoe-wearing pacifist, but it looked like things had changed.

She flushed, but she didn't drop her eyes. "It's true. You know it is!"

"No arguments here. What I don't get is why Æsubrand waited so long to attack. His odds would have been better had he struck sooner, before I got home with reinforcements . . . so to speak."

Claire looked up from putting a piece of cotton between her final two toes. "Yes, about them . . ."

"I know you didn't want vampires in the house," I said, marshaling my arguments.

"I'm warming up to the idea," she said, surprising me.

"It looks like we need all the help we can get. I'm just not sure about these specific vampires. That Cheung guy was parked outside the house for hours, waiting for you to get home. And he didn't look friendly. I tried calling you half a dozen times to warn you—"

"I didn't have my phone on me most of the night."

Claire raised an eyebrow, but didn't ask. "I assumed you must have seen him and that's why you hadn't come back. I left you a message and we went to bed once it became obvious he couldn't get through the wards. But now all of a sudden you trust him to guard us?"

"I don't trust *him*," I told her, stretching out on the bed. "I trust the system. It's pretty harsh on masters who get out of line. And Cheung gave his word."

"And that means something?"

"If given to you or me? No. But he gave it to a Senate member, and that's a very different thing."

"You mean he'd face some kind of punishment if he broke it?"

"And then some. Before the Senates, there was almost constant war between vamp houses, with constantly shifting alliances and backstabbing and betrayal. Think Italy in the Middle Ages, with every little city-state grasping at its neighbors, wanting to expand its lands at their expense. It was pretty much unrelieved bloodshed, and decimated whole houses. Once the Senates got organized, the rules they laid down were made harsh on purpose, to make even the richest prize not worth the price."

"So Cheung can be relied on to help?"

"For the next several days, yes. And by that time, Heidar should be here." I sat up, a giant yawn splitting my face. I needed to go to bed before I fell asleep right here. But I needed something else first. "Speaking of help, do you still want to do something to assist the investigation?"

She brightened. "Yes, although I have to say, things haven't been as boring around here as I'd expected."

"We're a lively bunch."

She snorted. "What do you need?"

"I need you to write me a note."

*   *   *

*Rain. It had started on the way, but he'd bowed his head
and pressed on, his horse's hooves churning up the mud.
It had slowed him down; there wouldn't be much time until morning. Until others arrived to wonder and stare, to
lament and question, and to obliterate what little evidence
might remain.*

*The rider dismounted, the sound of his spurs the only
noise in the unnaturally still night. The moon was up,
bulging half-full with watery light, turning the world into
stark silvers and blacks. To the left, an old apple grove
fractured the dark sky with darker traceries of branches.
They were bare, the season now over, the few remaining
leaves plucked by the cold wind and rattling against the
bark. The ones that had drifted over crackled under his
feet, dead like everything else here.*

*He tied his horse to one of the trees, keeping it well
out of harm's way, and moved forward. The coming
dawn tugged at his consciousness, but it was impossible
to move quickly. It would feel irreverent, like laughing in
a graveyard.*

*To the right was the chapel, still partially protected by
a slate roof. He paused at the door, or where it would have
been. It had burned down to the hinges; his foot uncov-
ered the old iron pieces in the sifting of leaves and sodden
ash on the cold stone floor. The roof had gone, too, having been built of wood, as had the altar. But the crucifix
remained, in a way. Its silver had dripped down the walls,
painting the old stones with a smear of beauty.*

*He moved into a dark corridor. It had once been
brightly lit by sconces that were now only glinting suggestions in the gloom of the passage, leaping into reality
when the beams of his lantern swept over them. He found
the first one there, a huddled, unrecognizable shape in the
dark.*

*He knelt beside it. Dim, filtered light poured through
a narrow window, bringing with it a wisp of cool air and
the faint sound of rain. The body was charred, unrecognizable. But the cross around the neck had been trapped
underneath, and suffered only scorching. It was small and*

plain, and made out of some metal sturdier than gold. Not the one, then.

The passage ended at what must have been the refectory. The missing roof ensured that a thin mist coated everything, but he could still just make out the rectangular shapes of the long tables where sparse meals had been served. There were bodies here, too. But the one he sought was not among them.

Down another dark passage and through two more rooms, he finally found the small room called Misericord. It was where punishments were doled out to those who had violated the strict rule. But no punishment devised by man had done this.

The body was stretched out on the floor, the dead eyes staring up at the ceiling. Unlike the others, it had not been burnt. There were no signs of scorching in the room at all, and even the roof here had survived. Perhaps that was why it was so well preserved—the rain had not touched it; the wind had not disturbed it.

It didn't help. The face was unrecognizable, desiccated and withered. The eyes were white, the once-dark hair brittle and drained of color, the mouth opened in a silent scream. The hand was a half-closed claw, as if it had been clutched around something.

He tugged gently at the bones, barely held together by skin. The small movement caused the body to settle with a dry whisper, the broken wrist making a soft popping as it tore through the tissue-thin skin of the arm. The small sound seemed to echo in his head, and a bone-dead chill settled through him.

He pulled harder, forcing the hand to give up its secret. And then he merely squatted against the shelter of a burned-out wall, palm open, a glittering cross of solid gold held loosely in his fingers. He traced the cabochon stones that decorated the piece, polished and cool under his touch, and felt a coiling tightness reeling out from his gut to his spine. Blood sang in his ears, pain stabbed through him like a million keen blades, and the bitterness of guilt settled back into its usual place under his ribs, where he always carried it.

And now, where he always would.

*   *   *

I rolled over, kicking the covers with a low grumble of irritation. The old sheets were damp and inclined to stick to my skin. My bedroom was hot and, thanks to the weather, uncomfortably muggy. I peeled off the T-shirt, exchanged it for a fresh one and pushed up the window.

I'd been hoping for a breeze, but ended up getting slapped in the face by a gust of rain instead. Of course. I perched on the ledge anyway, not caring if I got wet as long as I cooled down.

The storm ruffled my damp hair and fanned my flushed cheeks. It felt wonderful. I could hear someone's wind chimes, a faint, distant glissando riding the breeze. I leaned my head back against the smooth wood of the frame and watched lightning lick the sky.

A magical accident on our recent assignment had resulted in my sharing Louis-Cesare's memories—all of them. And since he was almost four hundred years old, that was a lot to absorb. Most of it had been a blur at the time, a lifetime of impressions pouring into my head all at once. It had been too much, too fast, too overwhelming for anyone to take in. But ever since, I kept getting flashbacks to pieces of his past.

They might have eventually settled, slipping off to lurk in my subconscious somewhere with the rest of the monsters, if it hadn't been for the wine. As it was, I was treated to an almost nightly parade of images, some so fragmented as to make no sense, but others as real as if I'd lived them myself. This had been one of the latter.

I could still smell the acrid stench of the fire, taste papery ash on my tongue, feel his bright flare of pain as if it had been my own. He hadn't believed ... something ... hadn't expected ... Damn it! It was already fading.

A patter of rain hit my dangling leg, but I sat there for a long time staring at the dark yard. Tasting bitterness, fruit gone to rot, lost hopes, ruined dreams. And didn't know what any of it meant. It was like seeing a movie and not knowing the ending. Or the beginning. Or who most of the damn characters were.

And knowing that I probably never would.

I know what I want, he'd said. And that was obviously Christine. Because despite what he maintained, there was no earthly reason why he had to stay with her if he didn't choose to. Yes, he'd screwed some things up, but he'd also gone through hell to find her again, even to the point of letting himself be drained by those same mages in payment for her freedom. He didn't owe her a damn thing.

So he wanted her. And he was right. Because despite what the stories say, love or infatuation or whatever the hell we'd had doesn't really triumph over all. Not when two people came from backgrounds as different as ours. And not when they are genetically designed to kill each other.

It had been a bad idea from the beginning, and it was just as well that one of us had realized it before it went any further than it had. Game over, book closed, the end. Except for these damn memories that wouldn't leave me alone.

The rain was getting worse and I was close to soaked. Not to mention my floor, my bedside table and my bag of nasty tricks. I pulled the duffel out from under the bed, took everything out and set it in a row on the dresser to dry. That sort of stuff was expensive, and it came out of my budget.

The second damp T-shirt went into the clothes hamper, and I tugged on another one before falling back into my hot, rumpled bed. I viciously plumped my pillow, looking for a cool spot. I had a job to do tomorrow; I didn't have time for this. I concentrated on the intermittent sound of the rain and willed myself back to sleep.

Chapter Twenty-nine

Nine hours later I was still hot. And with less than six hours' sleep under my belt, I was even crankier. Of course, my current predicament wasn't helping.

A gust of air almost knocked me to the ground, and a horn blasted my eardrums at point-blank range. I spun to see my own reflection staring back at me from a shiny chrome fender. My eyes were startled, which was understandable, considering that the fender was hovering almost six feet off the ground.

It was attached to a dusty white pickup, which was rocking slowly back and forth in the air, like a boat in the swells. The irate driver leaned out of the window to glare at me. "Get off the road!"

"I'm not in the road." I pointed up. "It's that way."

A good ten feet above us, a line of levitating cars was gleefully ignoring the laws of gravity. Their shadows rippled across the landscape, intermittently blocking the sun and causing me to flicker in and out of the shade. My eyes were having a hard time adjusting to the constantly changing light, but even so it was clear that this joker was well below the designated traffic lane.

I pointed this out, but all I got for my trouble was another loud blast from the horn.

So of course I flipped him off.

He said something rude, threw the truck into reverse, then shot past close enough to force me to duck. He swerved around another vehicle, rolled sideways to fit between a couple of buses and vanished into the glare of a blistering August sun. The resulting boom was loud enough to vibrate the ground.

Asshole.

I hadn't had time to draw a breath before the air around me coalesced and seemed to draw inward, contracting like a collapsing star. I leapt to the side as a white-hot flash sizzled across my eyes and an earsplitting bang ruptured the air. And another vehicle popped into existence in a burst of car-shaped sparks.

A kid in the backseat had his face glued to the window. He regarded me somberly for a moment before deliberately sticking out his tongue. His father hit the gas, revving the engine and grinding the gears, and the car shot up from the ground like the bird it wasn't.

I understood the principle: it was easier to enchant an inert object than something with a constantly changing energy field like that of the human body. That was why levitation spells always called for some kind of platform. Brooms had been used in the bad old days because they were convenient and didn't raise any eyebrows if spotted lying around the house. The modern equivalent was the car, which was undoubtedly easier on the backside.

But the reality still made my brain hurt.

Thundering cracks from new arrivals shook the air on every side, mixing with the roar of engines, the thrum of music and a lot of alcohol-fueled laughter. I looked from my objective—the mansion on the next hill, where a certain mage was about to give an interview—to the crazy vehicle-strewn air separating us.

Well, shit.

I'd assumed that getting to Lutkin might be difficult. He was the current World Champion, and right now that made him the center of attention. But I'd thought the main problem would be getting past security, not getting to the guy at all.

Between me and the house was more than the floating traffic jam. The cars had been elevated to keep them out of the way of the sea of gleaming white vendors' tents that spilled down the hill. They were jam-packed with scalpers hawking tickets, vendors peddling grease-

laden food and people, tons of people. They were clogging every available inch of space, buying souvenirs,
standing in line for freebies or placing bets. I'd never
make it in time.

"Want a ride?" somebody yelled. I looked up to see
a sky blue convertible hovering maybe six feet above
my head.

One look at the car, and I decided that walking didn't
sound so bad, after all. "Thanks, but I'm just going to the
house."

The blonde who had issued the invitation hung precariously over the passenger-side door to grin at me. "It's
too dangerous!" She gestured with a longneck, flinging
a wide arc of beer into the air. "Half the people around
here shouldn't even be driving."

She said this with no irony whatsoever, despite the
fact that her car's black cloth top kept rising and low-
ering like some kind of strange bird trying to achieve
flight. The driver, a young ginger-haired guy, took a stab
at making it stop, and turned the wipers on instead.

"I'm good," I assured her.

She shook her head tipsily. "You're gonna get run
over," she insisted, opening the door and almost falling
out. She stopped when the seat belt caught her, looking
perplexed. "Is it still 'run over' if you're, like, hit from
above?"

"I'd rather not find out," I said, moving so that I
wasn't directly beneath the car. Magic was magic, but
my brain was having a hard time accepting the sight of
huge hunks of metal just hanging in the air like that. I
kept expecting one to drop on my head, snuffing me out
like a mosquito under a thumb.

"Then get up here!" She turned to her companion.
"Ronnie—take us down." Ronnie nervously studied the
gears, then did something that made the car shoot up
another dozen feet. "No, no, *down*!" she yelled, as they
came within a hairbreadth of hitting a legitimate race
car with an official number on the side.

Ronnie panicked and veered sharply to the right,
missing the race car but clipping a VW Bug that had

stalled out in the middle of the air. Its hood was jacked up, and its owner's butt was hanging over the side. Or, at least, it was until the impact caused the Bug to go spinning in one direction and flung the owner in the other. He was headed for the ground headfirst, but the race car driver snatched him out of midair to the wild appreciation of the onlookers.

For his part, the rescued man seemed less than thrilled. I could hear him shouting as the blonde's convertible slowly drifted back down to my level. "Uh-oh," she said as the race car driver started shaking his head and pointing at us.

Ronnie glanced at me. "Get in if you're getting!"

I'd have refused, considering his grasp on the fundamentals of the road—or in this case, the air. But traffic was piling up around the accident, pushing more and more people outside the safe zone. And I was beginning to doubt that most of them even knew how to drive on land.

I grasped hold of the side of the car, waited for the top to lower again and hauled myself into the backseat. Ronnie floored it before I was even seated, sending me into the arms of a dishwater blond guy in a blue tank top. "Hey." He grinned, as I tried to sort myself out without elbowing him anywhere sensitive.

"Toni and Dave," the blond girl told me, hanging over the front seat. I assumed Toni was the young brunette who was currently giving me the evil eye. I crawled off her boyfriend, and she rewarded me with a sweating Bud from the cooler beside her feet. Enough empties rattled around the floorboards to explain Ronnie's lack of coordination.

Since I didn't have to drive, I drank up. The air was pungent with exhaust and heavy with humidity, and I felt like I was breathing through a damp towel. Ten minutes under the blazing sun had left my black T-shirt sticking to me unpleasantly and had me wishing I'd worn shorts and sandals instead of jeans and boots.

"I'm Lilly," the blonde informed me, completing the introductions. "It's short for Lilith, but nobody calls me that."

I nodded. I'd rarely seen anyone who looked less like a Lilith. She was wearing a pink-and-white-checked blouse over a white tube top and shorts. Her bouncy blond curls—the ones that hadn't escaped to stick to her sweaty face and neck—were trapped by a couple of Hello Kitty ponytail holders. They matched her glittery lip gloss and Pepto-Bismol nails. If the real Lilith still existed on some other plane, she was undoubtedly plotting a hideous revenge.

"Dory," I said, saluting her with what remained of my beer. I lost it a second later as a couple of kids on Boogie Boards zoomed by like they had rockets attached to their backsides, whirling over and around the car in figure eights. One grabbed my beer and they took off, whooping like savages.

"Okay, that's it," the blonde said. "I've had enough of those little bastards. Catch them!"

I thought that was unlikely, as the kids seemed to have a lot more control over their small supports than Ronnie did of his big one. But he followed orders anyway, veering around the quarreling drivers and hitting the gas, heading straight for a large oak. The boys were swooping around, laughing at the Bug, which was sticking out of the top of the tree.

A tow truck driver had also stopped by the accident, and was attempting to attach a cable with a hook on it to the Bug's cantilevered backside. But we whipped past at exactly the wrong moment, and he snared us instead. "Oh, shiiiit!" Lilly screamed, as we were slung around the tree, dragging the tow truck along for the ride.

"Hit the brake!" I yelled, as we were flung through the air like thrown bolas, the tow truck on the other side of the cord providing the counterweight.

It was the sort of situation that might have flummoxed the most experienced of drivers, which Ronnie clearly wasn't. He panicked and started grabbing at everything. In quick succession, he popped the trunk, got the top to stay down and turned on the radio. He did absolutely nothing to stop us from heading straight for the middle of the traffic lane.

A mellow reggae beat spilled out of the radio as I scrambled over Toni to try to free the hook, but it had been caught in the metal frame of the convertible's top, and with the hood down, I couldn't even see it. And then it didn't matter anyway, because the tow truck guy stomped on his brakes, hurling us around him in a furious orbit. The top tore off the convertible with a screech of agonized metal as we went spinning back in the other direction.

"Don't worry," the radio lilted as we headed straight at the race car. "Be happy."

The driver didn't look too happy, but he ducked just in time as we screamed by overhead. He immediately popped back up, and he looked pissed. So did the tow truck guy, who was heading our way trailing the flapping remnants of the convertible's top behind him. Ronnie managed to find the brake, and we spun like a top, with no traction to stop us, for several revolutions. Then he hit the gas and the car shot ahead.

We retraced our own greasy plume of exhaust straight between our two pursuers, the acrid smoke making everyone cough and my eyes water. The tow truck guy had his window rolled down, so maybe he was having the same problems and didn't realize we'd turned. Or possibly his reflexes just weren't that good. He kept going forward, toward where we no longer were, but the race car spun on a dime and came after us.

Lilly spied the tow truck and abandoned panic for righteous indignation. "Hey, that guy has my top!"

"Not anymore," Toni said as the remains flew off the cord like a giant bat, landing over the race car's windshield.

The now-blind driver slammed on the brakes, causing the car behind him to accordion into his trunk before getting creamed by a third. Meanwhile, the tow truck's empty hook had snared the top of a tent, which tore loose from its anchors, leaving a bunch of locals to swill their beer in direct sunlight. They did not appreciate this, as they demonstrated by swarming after the tent as it was dragged through traffic, until they reached the cord. Six or seven big guys grabbed it and started towing the truck back to Earth.

"Wow," Toni said as the three of us hung over the trunk.

"I'm so screwed," Ronnie moaned, watching the carnage in his mirror.

"Did you see where my top landed?" Lilly asked, scanning the ground while the three-car pileup wafted above the traffic lanes to sort things out, taking the fluttering remains of her car's accessory with them.

"Twenty on the drunk guys," Dave offered, as several more joined the tug-of-war. But then the tow truck guy stomped on the gas and tore away, taking a few of the more stubborn types along for the ride.

One unwilling hitchhiker landed on top of another tent, collapsing part of it, while two more were dragged through the crowd at an autograph signing. Several fights broke out over that, as people lost their places in line, but I didn't get to see how they turned out because Ronnie had exercised the better part of valor and got us out of there. A moment later, we merged with a line of vehicles inching toward the ticket booth hovering above the front gates.

The house was quite a sight, glimmering in the sun at the top of the hill like a marble wedding cake. Despite being in upper New York State, it looked like something straight out of ancient Rome, with columns and porticoes and a huge balcony. Most of the hosts were gathered there in plush comfort, sipping at tall, frosty glasses as if dehydration was a possibility, and watching the controlled chaos below.

I wondered what the consul thought about the wreck the mages were making of her formerly manicured lawn. It was only the third day of the event, which was scheduled to last a week. But the grounds were already strewn with trash and crisscrossed with tires tracks from vehicles that had the sense to stay where God, or at least the automotive industry, had intended.

I assumed the offending vehicles belonged to the vendors, because the fans' cars were being directed off to the side, where a colorful explosion of several thousand floated like giant, oddly shaped clouds over the landscape. They were arranged in three tiers—like a parking garage without the garage—with the highest maybe thirty feet up. There were no stairs.

The obvious message was that, if you couldn't manage a basic levitation spell, you shouldn't be here. It was typical; mages acted as if they controlled the supernatural world and the rest of us just lived in it. But considering who was sponsoring this year's event, it was pretty tacky.

We headed for the closest group, which was forming next to an ornamental pond. Beer bottles, soda cans and snack wrappers tangled in the surrounding rosebushes and bobbed beside a fountain designed by Bernini. Nearby, a massive set of weathered bleachers faced the house. It was packed with people watching the empty space over the large circular driveway with rapt attention.

Every few minutes, another line of assorted craft—mostly cars, but with the odd motorcycle, airplane or even boat thrown in—would levitate out of the mass in a cordoned-off area beside the house. They would line up even with the balcony and stay there for a moment, letting the frenzy wash over them. Some of the drivers would wave or stand up to further incite the already-rabid fans. When the flag-waving, banner-fluttering, screaming hysteria had reached a peak, the consul would rise from her seat in the center of the balcony and drop a scrap of silk. An earsplitting crack later, and the whole lineup would disappear.

The hordes in the stands would be given a few moments to rest their vocal cords and buy more beer. Then the whole process started over again. I found it monotonous, but no one else seemed to agree with me. It was that time of year again, and the whole supernatural world had gone insane. There was a war on, but nobody cared. Not during race week.

"That's gonna be you tomorrow," Dave said, his eyes on the swimming-pool-sized mirror that was floating over the house.

Ronnie twisted around to watch the mirror change. "Not likely."

It had been reflecting an image of blue skies, green fields and weathered bleachers filled with waving fans. But then it rippled and switched to a scene of leaping purple flames. Weaving in and out of the fiery mass were the same racers who had just disappeared, now looking impossibly tiny next to the inferno around them.

"Oh, man, don't tell me he bailed on you *again*," Dave groaned.

"It's for the Championship," Ronnie said, his lips tight.

"But you're the best!" Lilly said indignantly.

"Not when there's ten million dollars on the line," Ronnie told her, but his eyes looked hurt.

Lilly passed me another beer from a cooler at her feet. "Ronnie's father is Lucas Pennington," she said proudly, as if I should know who that was.

Maybe I should have, but the yearly madness of the World Championships had never been more than a flicker on my mental map. They were a mage thing, and other than doing the occasional job for a magic worker in a jam, I don't associate with them much. They tend to be more than a little strange, like their favorite sport.

The supernatural world doesn't have NASCAR. It doesn't have football, soccer or tennis. Instead, it has the insanity known as ley-line racing.

Mages figured out long ago that, with strong enough shields, they could surf along the surface of the lines, riding their energy from one point to the next. And since ley lines stitch the world together outside of real space, this meant traversing huge distances in very short periods. Assuming you survived, that is.

Every year it was the same story. Out of the two hundred or so entrants who qualified for the Big Kahuna of the racing world, maybe twenty percent would actually finish. Out of the eighty percent who were left, most would eventually limp back to the starting line, having fabricated an elaborate tale of how nature/their vehicle/the gods had conspired against them. But there were a good five to ten percent every year who were claimed by the lines.

There would be editorials in all the papers the day afterward, loudly denouncing the barbarity of it all, and some officials would make properly distressed faces. But nothing ever changed. It was just part of the race.

I must not have done a great job at looking neutral, because Ronnie flushed. "There's more to racing than driving, you know," he told me.

"Actually, I don't know."

"You don't follow the races?" Lilly looked stunned and vaguely freaked out, like I'd just admitted to eating live snakes.

"Sorry."

It was finally our turn at the floating ticket booth, where the kids forked over an eye-popping amount for three-day passes. "You shouldn't need a pass," the blonde told Ronnie indignantly, as we moved toward the levitating parking lot. "You should be in the pits!"

"I suck in the pits," Ronnie admitted. He glanced at me. "I was lollipop man last time around and I got distracted and lowered our sign too soon."

"That doesn't seem so bad."

"And Dad left without a back rear tire!"

"Well, it's not like he needed it."

"Oh, he needed it," Ronnie said, looking miserable. "The race is mostly in the lines, but they don't all intersect, you know? Sometimes you have to travel a mile or more to get from one to another. . . ."

"Ouch," I sympathized. He nodded glumly.

"But that wasn't what you trained for!" Lilly said loyally.

"What did you train for?" I asked. Because it sure wasn't driving.

"I'm a spellbinder."

Lilly nodded enthusiastically. "He's the best!"

"I'm not sure I know what that is," I said, only to have four incredulous sets of eyes turned on me.

"You really don't follow the races," Lilly said, like she hadn't believed it before.

"What *do* you know about racing?" Ronnie asked, curious. He looked fascinated, like a scientist confronted by a strange new species: *dontgiveadamnus* from the phylum *couldntcareless*.

I shrugged. "You have to be a mage, you have to pony up a big-ass fee and you have to be insane." In fact, insanity wasn't a requirement, but it may as well have been. Because nobody in their right minds would have signed up for what was essentially a death trap.

Lilly was frowning at me, and okay, maybe that hadn't been too tactful. But Ronnie just grinned. "Are you *sure* you don't follow the races?"

"I think I saw part of one in a bar once," I admitted.

"There are typically four people to a team," he told me. "The driver, who leads the team; the navigator, who helps him find the best route; the shield master, who maintains the shield; and the spellbinder, who protects the team from, er, anything they need protecting from—"

"He means the competition," Toni said lazily.

"—and gets them through the obstacles," Ronnie finished. He looked at me, expectant, and I bit.

"What obstacles?"

"There's no actual course, so the only way to make sure everybody really circles the Earth is to have them make pit stops along the way," he explained.

"With obstacles at each stop," I guessed.

He nodded enthusiastically. The races were obviously his passion. His thin face lit up when he talked about them, and his pale blue eyes shone. "They can be anything. You just never know because they change every year. Physical barriers, magical ones, even mazes—"

"And your comp-e-ti-tion," Toni singsonged, obviously half-wasted.

"The competitors are always gunning for the biggest names," Lilly agreed. "And there's no monitoring outside the pit stops because there's no set route, so it's a free-for-all! The spellbinders have to fight off the attacks of other teams, as well as get their team through the obstacles. It's the most important job in the race!"

"Sounds like fun," I lied, eyeing the crush of cars still

ahead of us. Most of the vehicles were bunched up in a midair traffic jam, waiting for one of the harassed parking attendants to slot them into place. I decided I could walk and get there faster. "You can let me off here," I told Ronnie. "I can—"

I didn't finish, because he suddenly floored it. The car shot out of the queue with either panache or reckless abandon, depending on whether he'd meant to slip through the narrow space between two rows of already parked cars. The movement threw me back against the seat beside Toni.

"There's no rush," I said, holding out the vain hope of arriving in one piece.

"Like hell there's not!" Lilly spat, pointing with her beer bottle. "They're following us!"

I twisted my neck around to see our old friend the race car driver. He'd cleared the ticket booth and was in hot pursuit, the angry Bug owner in the seat beside him. "It wasn't my fault!" Ronnie insisted, as the car dipped alarmingly.

I turned back around to see him staring past me at the pursuit, while ahead of us, the grandstand full of people loomed large. "The stands!" I yelled, pointing.

"What?"

"The. Stands!" I twisted his head back around, and he froze, staring at our collective doom.

"Oh, for—" Lilly reached over and stomped on the brakes, halting us close enough to the back of the bleachers that I could have reached out and touched the sun-faded wood. Luckily, the several thousand people assembled to watch the qualifying heats were facing the other way, except for a redheaded little boy peeking out through the slats.

He had a pink cotton candy grin and a massive treat clutched in one tiny fist. Which he smushed all over Lilly's hair. She screeched and forgot about the car, which floated up and out, wafting above the crowd like a steel balloon. That was apparently not allowed, because almost immediately an irritated-looking mage in a uniform rose from the sidelines and started for us.

"Damn," Toni said, looking a little nervous.

I was finding it hard to feel much trepidation, personally. And although I could see the wisdom of not putting the patrols in something as bulky as a car when they'd be zooming around over people's heads, the choice of substitute seemed a little unfortunate. "They couldn't have issued you guys motorcycles, at least?" I asked the mage on the Segway.

He scowled and ignored me. "Levitation isn't allowed above the stands," he told Ronnie.

Ronnie didn't respond. He was too busy staring over his shoulder at the irate duo in the race car. They'd paused behind the bleachers, bobbing just above where the multicolored pennants began, in order to shout obscenities at us.

"You're going to have to move your vehicle," the patrol tried again, this time addressing Lilly.

It was another wasted effort. "My hair!" she screeched, red-faced and outraged. "I paid a fortune for this color! Arrest that kid!"

The mage didn't reply, because a beer bottle exploded against the side of the car in a rain of green glass. "What the—" The rent-a-cop looked around, trying to figure out where it had come from, while the people below us shouted in outrage.

I doubted that much of the glass had connected, because a kid had parked his Boogie Board on that side of us as a sun shield. It floated above the crowd, deflecting most of the green hail into the aisle. But that didn't seem to matter to anyone. We were maybe twelve feet above the stands, so the spectators couldn't reach us, but that didn't mean someone couldn't fire up a spell. As least, I assumed that was what rocked the car hard enough to almost tip us out.

"All right, that's enough!" The cop dropped to issue a warning to whoever the joker was below, and I caught another bottle that had been about to bean me.

I whipped it back at its thrower—a young guy standing at the top of the bleachers. He and a group of friends had been talking to the driver of the Bug, who was still pointing in our direction and yelling. And then they froze, gawking at something behind me with their mouths still open.

I spun around to see almost the entire crowd staring at the huge mirror. In between showing the races, it had been reflecting interviews with noted drivers, car sponsors and paid ads. Only it was hard to imagine what that particular image could be selling.

But one thing was certain: the man seated in the large armchair wasn't going to be giving any more interviews.

Chapter Thirty

The man sat facing the camera, legs crossed, slumped slightly to one side in a large wingback armchair. A cigarette burned in an ashtray by his elbow, which was odd, since he looked to have been dead for at least a century. His skin was brown and withered, like old leather; his hair was stark white; and his lips had shriveled up and drawn back from his teeth, giving him a sort of ghastly smile.

"And now a word with returning champion, Peter Lutkin!" an announcer burbled obliviously.

Lilly screamed.

She wasn't the only one, and a moment later, the carefully controlled chaos wasn't so controlled anymore. Some people were still sitting in shock, staring at the gruesome image of the dead man. But others were surging to their feet, demanding explanations, calling for their kids, gathering up belongings. The cheerful, raucous mood of a second before was completely gone.

That was particularly true after a couple of stunned drivers collided near the sidelines. One of them must have dropped some oil or gas on something inflammable, because a nearby tent went up in flames. If anyone had forgotten we were at war, the pillar of black smoke billowing skyward was a damn good reminder. The already panicked crowd broke and ran.

I jumped over the side of the car, ignoring—like everyone else—the magically enhanced voice telling us to remain calm and in position. The Boogie Board broke my fall, and the momentum of my landing pushed it off on a long glide toward the bottom of the stands. I was congratulating myself on finding a fast way off the bleachers when a sudden updraft flipped the board, leaving me dangling upside down as I careened over the driveway.

My sweat-slick fingers lost their grip about the same time that a truck flew by underneath. I dropped to the bed, then used it as a platform to launch myself at the bumper of a passing patrol car that was screaming toward the house. I rode it past a couple of wide-eyed guards and straight into the private courtyard.

Of course, I didn't get any farther. Unlike Elyas, the consul didn't believe in taking chances with her front line of defense. The guard who snatched me out of the air was at least a second-level master, and I strongly suspected his buddy of being a first. I wasn't going anywhere.

Until providence intervened in the form of panicked humanity. The expensive race cars were suddenly not the only vehicles on the track, as people who couldn't get out the main gates started cutting corners. Half a dozen plowed through the air overhead and swerved around the house, heading for the road and the ley line running through it.

One rusted El Camino clipped the plaster as it tore past the side of the house, sending a cloud of particles into the air and exposing the raw brickwork below. The vamp holding me swore. I could practically hear his thoughts. If a sideswipe could do that, what would a head-on collision do? Particularly if the car had a full gas tank.

I suddenly became a lot less interesting. As far as he was concerned, I was merely a frightened human. He thrust me and a set of magical cuffs into the arms of a young servant who was hovering under the impressive Roman-style portico, out of the sun. Then he and his buddy took off after the floating battering rams.

The young vamp had soft brown hair that brushed his shoulders, soft blue eyes and soft pink lips that didn't completely hide glistening fangs. They were out because he was hungry. At his level, he should have been in a safe room somewhere, dreaming of plump pink wrists. But it looked like it was all hands on deck for the races, and at his power level, that meant a heavy drain on his resources.

He clearly thought a snack was in order. He smiled gently as he reached for me. "Don't worry; this won't hurt."

I smiled back. "Actually, I'm pretty sure it will."

A moment later, the stunned vamp's arms were cuffed around one of the support pillars, and I was through the front door. There were no wards, as I'd half expected; I suppose with all the people coming and going from the races, it would have been impossible to keep them up. But it seemed odd that the consul, who wasn't known for taking chances, would forgo such an elementary—

It hit me suddenly, like a punch to the gut, sending me staggering into a wall. Not a ward or a weapon, but a massive sense of *presence*. I'd been around vampires all my life, but not hundreds, not senior-level masters, not all together under one roof. My vampire sense almost blew my head off.

Of course she didn't need wards, I thought, clutching the wall for support. Who the hell was going to walk into *that*? Only I had, and damned if I was going to turn tail and run because of a feeling, no matter how uncomfortable.

But if I wasn't going to run, I had to *move*. The baby vamp must have called for help by now, and I was standing in the main damn hallway. Horatiu couldn't have missed me, much less the kind of guards the consul kept on hand. And there was no Mircea around to tell anyone that this was one dhampir they shouldn't kill.

Just breathing was hard enough; actually going anywhere sounded absurd. The very air felt thick and heavy in my lungs, like a couple extra atmospheres were suddenly pressing down from above. My breathing was ragged and my feet felt like they weighed at least a ton each. Merely staying upright was a struggle.

Just get to the next room, I told myself sternly. *It's a*

*couple of yards, that's all. Then you can face-plant onto
the nice marble floor.*

I don't know how I got there; I have no memory of
moving at all. But suddenly, I was staggering into what
looked like an armory, with long curtain-draped windows along one side and glass cases full of weapons lining the other. And face-planting was definitely out.

A couple of male servants were sitting at a table,
polishing some of the implements. If those were for
tonight's challenge, it didn't look like anyone was fool-
ing around. There wasn't a practice sword in the bunch.
Since I didn't want any of them used on me, I staggered
on through without stopping.

I made it through the door on the other side, but had
no idea where the hell I was going. And there hadn't
been too many clues in the projected image as to which
room in the football-field-sized house might contain the
dead man. All I could recall about his surroundings was
the edge of a fireplace and a bit of rug, which could have
come from anywhere.

But the half dozen scurrying servants I encountered
in a narrow hallway were headed toward the left wing.
They didn't look panicked—good servants never looked
panicked—but they weren't wasting any time, either.
Neither did I, dogging their heels the whole way into a
largish sitting room at the end of the corridor.

It was a symphony in yellow: from the silk drapes to
the brocaded upholstery to the shade of the dead man's
skin. Bingo. I slipped inside the door, barely getting a
glance from most of the few dozen people present. But
one curly head jerked up abruptly.

"How the hell did you get in here?" Marlowe demanded. He had the harassed look of a vampire up during the day who'd been up all night, too. He was also
still wearing the same suit from the previous evening,
which had started out rumpled and was now approaching embarrassing.

"Through the front door." For once, I wasn't trying to
be flippant. I just didn't have the energy left to explain.

Marlowe, of course, scowled. "Mircea needs to take

his own advice, and practice some discretion. Bringing you here is not wise!"

"What happened to Lutkin?" I asked, forgetting to mention that Mircea hadn't brought me anywhere.

"What does it look like?" He motioned for the servants who had blocked my path to step aside. He was probably hoping for some tasty tidbits like last time, only I was fresh out. Since my ass would be out the door a second after he realized that, I didn't waste any time examining the dead man.

I'd certainly seen more gruesome deaths. There was no blood to contrast nicely with the bright yellow decor. In fact, the body was bone dry, with not only the blood but every other fluid sucked out of it. Even his eyes had shriveled up and were lolling on his cheekbones, barely held in place by the desiccated cords.

It still looked strangely like he was staring at me. I quickly searched for something else to look at, and found it in the fingertip bruises ringing his neck. Shit.

"No fey made those, no matter how powerful," Marlowe said as I bent for a closer look. And damn it, he was right. Those were the telltale signs of a vampire pulling blood through the skin and not caring whether he left a mark.

"It looks like a revenant got to him," I said. They were never satiated, and sometimes got carried away. But why go to all the trouble to break in here with an ocean of prey just outside?

"One of those mindless animals would never have gotten past the guards, or the man's shields," Marlowe said, echoing my thoughts.

"But at least this clears Louis-Cesare," I pointed out.

"And how did you determine that?"

I frowned. "You said it yourself—no revenant did this. So Lutkin was obviously killed for the rune. He must have murdered Elyas for it, and now someone returned the favor and took it."

Marlowe's scowl didn't budge. "If he had the rune, why didn't he use it? He's a powerful mage from a prominent family. Unlike Elyas, we cannot suppose he did not know how!"

"Maybe he didn't get a chance," I said slowly. "Look at him."

Lutkin's hands looked more like claws now, the knobby bones and ligaments standing out starkly against the shrunken skin. But that didn't affect their position. One was dangling off the side of the chair, a glass of wine still wedged between the lifeless fingers. The other was curled harmlessly in his lap. Even more telling, his feet were still crossed at the ankles; he hadn't even had time to stand up.

"That doesn't help our case," Marlowe said irritably. "The only creature who could drain someone this quickly is a first- or possibly a strong second-level master. Like Louis-Cesare."

"And like half the people in the house right now! The collective energy almost knocked me down when I came in the door. Are all the challengers staying here?"

"About a third, give or take. The rest are scattered around the city."

"And most if not all of them are on the premises, right?"

That was a good bet, considering that it was broad daylight out. A first-level master could withstand that easily enough, but the power drain would be immense. And no one was going to risk that kind of loss right before facing combat—not when the stakes were this high.

Marlowe stared at the corpse, looking angry and frustrated. "On the premises, but with no motive! They weren't at the auction and had no way to know that the mage might be important."

"Who else could have gotten in here?"

Marlowe made a disgusted sound. "You mean other than Lutkin and the dozen other mages who insisted on giving their interviews out of the boiling sun? That would merely leave the challengers and their servants, all of whom were on the guest list. And the press and their support staff, who are doubtless about to descend on us like the vultures they—"

"What about Geminus and Ming-de?" I interrupted. Because none of the people he named were supposed to know about the rune, either. "They could do something like this without breaking a sweat."

"Geminus has an apartment in the city, but Ming-de brought half her court. We couldn't accommodate them all and she elected to take a house for the duration."

"Either of them could have snuck in here," I pointed out. "Geminus probably knows the place like the back of his hand and Ming-de is strong enough to fog the mind of even a first-level master."

"As is Louis-Cesare."

"And he killed Lutkin for what? The hell of it? He had no motive, Marlowe!"

"I am sure that will be Mircea's argument. Lutkin was at the auction. He was at Elyas's cocktail party. Now he's dead. Either he killed Elyas for the rune and has now been killed for it himself, or someone assumed he had it and he died for nothing. Either way, Louis-Cesare is innocent."

"Sounds logical to me."

"Really?" Marlowe asked sourly. "Then how about this? Louis-Cesare murdered Elyas over Christine. He was caught in the act and is currently in fear for his life. He panicked and ran before he could stand trial, and has now killed a scapegoat to bolster his case."

"That's ridiculous! He's on the run and yet he comes here, of all places? Why not attack the man in his own home if he wanted him dead?"

"Lutkin is a powerful, wealthy mage. His home is doubtless riddled with protection spells that Louis-Cesare would have no way of knowing. But he is quite familiar with the consul's home and could easily evade security."

"Without being seen?" I demanded. "Coming or going?"

Marlowe arched an eyebrow. "It seems you do not know Louis-Cesare as well as I had thought."

I didn't get a chance to ask what that meant, because a gaggle of reporters took that moment to storm the room. There was a metric ton on hand to cover the races, and it looked like every single one of them was trying to crowd into the limited space. I realized why a second later, when the consul's spokesman entered the room, looking harassed.

He looked a lot more so when he saw the corpse. The elegant Mircea Basarab stopped in the middle of the room, ignoring the clicking cameras, the lights and the horde of hovering reporters. And said a very bad word.

"Lord Mircea, what can you tell us about the unusual state of the body? "

"Is there a reason proper security measures weren't in place to prevent—"

"How do you feel this will affect the current state of Senate/Circle relations?"

"Can you comment on the rumors circulating about you and the new—"

"Clear the room!" Mircea snapped, and a dozen vamps fell over themselves to obey. I was a little surprised. The vamp press would print what the consul told it to, but the mages were under no such restraints. Mircea was usually more careful around them. But then, putting a positive spin on this might just be beyond even his abilities.

"This is insufferable!" he said, glaring at the corpse, as if it was his own fault he was dead. "There is no way we can cover this up. Elyas was ours, but the Circle is already demanding an explanation for Lutkin's death. I have just been informed that they have a delegation on the—" He stopped, finally catching sight of me. "What are you doing here?"

"You didn't bring her?" Marlowe asked, his face reddening.

"I didn't even know she was here!"

Marlowe rounded on me. "You told me—"

"That I came in through the front door. Which I did."

"You came—how?"

"I walked."

Marlowe's face flushed, and okay, maybe that last little quip hadn't been so smart. I started to explain when Mircea cut me off. "You promised to stay out of this, Dorina."

Actually, I didn't remember promising anything of the kind, but I didn't think now was a good time to correct him. "You said you didn't care if Lutkin had the stone or not. But Claire does. She wants the stone no matter who has it. I came here hoping to ask him some questions, and found him like this."

"You did not 'find him.' Not in the middle of a vampire stronghold! You cannot be here! Do you not understand—"

"I understand that the list is shrinking. Lutkin is dead, and Æsubrand couldn't have killed him. Not like that. And Cheung is also in the clear, at least for Elyas's death. He was at my place last night—"

"Along with others. Why did you not tell me you were hosting royalty?"

"It slipped my mind?"

Mircea didn't look like he thought that was funny, and the next moment, I felt a couple of large shapes move up behind me. "You're throwing me out?"

"You promised to stay out of this," Mircea said grimly, as someone grabbed my arm. "And so you shall."

"I can help you, Mircea!"

"Yes, you can!" he said savagely. "You can help me by—" He cut off, and the color drained from both vamp's faces. It was almost comical, it happened so fast. And then something hit me that wasn't funny at all.

I had never really understood the old "ton of bricks" analogy, but I did now. It felt exactly like that, like some massive weight had just descended on me, crushing me. I didn't even try to stay on my feet; I went to my knees, and prayed I wouldn't be on my face next.

But the pressure wasn't the worst of it. "A pretty little monster. I had forgotten about this one, Mircea," a female voice said.

And with those words, a hundred voices slipped

into the spaces between my thoughts, skittering like bugs into the dark corners. I could feel them, writhing inside my skull—spiders, snakes, every small, dark thing prying into every small, dark space inside me. If I hadn't already been on my knees, that would have done it.

"She was just leaving," Mircea said tightly.

"Oh, do let her stay," the counsul said, bending down to me. "It appears she knows all our secrets, in any case."

"She knows nothing that is not known to the meanest of our servants."

Lustrous black hair slipped over a bare shoulder, and a few strands clung to the sweat on my face. Until a slim bronze hand wiped them away, gently. Her skin was papery, almost scaly, and finely abrasive. I could almost feel my own skin crawling up my face, trying to get away from that inhuman touch.

"She is not a servant, Mircea." A single finger tipped my chin up, so that I was looking into a bronze face, beautiful and cold. "Yet she may prove helpful."

I stared into dark, kohl-rimmed eyes, and felt a coiling tightness reeling out from my gut to my spine. I tasted blood in my mouth, felt it sing in my ears, as my dhampir sense reached new heights. It was screaming— but not a warning. This time, it was a siren song, a pure driving need, breathtaking in its simplicity. For one brief moment, I had no other wish, no other purpose, no other reason for existing, than to sink my teeth into that slim throat.

And that didn't make sense. I'd met her once before, and I hadn't had this reaction, hadn't even come close. I didn't know why, but the consul was trying to bring on one of my fits. And she was doing a damn good job of it. I wanted to kill her so badly, I could taste it.

She laughed, a sound like the scrabbling of claws against glass. "Yes, I think she will do very well."

"Do? For what purpose?" Mircea asked.

The consul's lovely face turned up to his. "To help us locate our problem Frenchman, of course."

Chapter Thirty-one

The pressure released so abruptly that I fell. But I was already rolling as soon as I hit the floor, my hand reaching into my coat for a stake, my feet coming under me—and then I was picked up around the waist and crushed back against an unyielding body.

I didn't know whose arms held me, didn't care. I *wanted* her, like I'd never wanted another kill in my life. I wanted to feel that smooth flesh ripping under my hands, wanted to taste her blood, wanted to—

"Dorina! Do not—"

"Silence."

Mircea shut up, but the arms around my middle tightened. I could feel his power, soothing, calming, but it couldn't reach me, wasn't enough, not against the red tide pulling at me. The dhampir strength that comes only in my fits was rising. With that amount of strength, all poured into one hard, swift lunge, I could have her. I. Could. Have. Her.

And as soon as I did, I was dead. The thought cut through the writhing echoes, going straight to my core. I didn't know if it was my thought or Mircea's, but it was true, either way. She'd kill me, and if she didn't, the guards would. I could feel them, hovering nearby. Ten, twelve—I couldn't tell but enough. More than enough.

But it was so hard to care.

"I'm right here." The words, low, sibilant, taunting, ripped through my brain, seething like fire ants, tearing like shrapnel. Squeezing one eye shut, I flattened a hand against my ear, but it did no good. The words were *inside my head*.

"She is stronger than I expected. Or perhaps you are helping her, Mircea."

"No, Lady."

"Release her, then. Let us see what manner of control she really has." The arms around me didn't budge. "You would defy me on this?"

"With . . . regret, Lady."

And suddenly, the snakes were back, and this time, they'd brought friends. It felt like my body had been invaded by a sea of tiny spiders. I could feel them seething underneath my skin, in my head, every movement of their hair-fine legs displacing some of my flesh. The tiny erosions were multiplied by thousands, millions, until my skin was cracked and running and my flesh was flaking off the bone.

Someone squeezed my shoulder, and spiders scurried outward from the touch, crawling up through cracks in my flesh to scuttle across my skin. I considered screaming, but my lungs were teeming with them, too, sloughing away like the rest of me, and drawing the necessary breath would only split me open like a rotten fruit. So the spiders seethed and I didn't scream.

"Enough!"

The single word sliced through the black haze in front of my vision, leaving me gasping on the floor, where I'd somehow ended up. The consul laughed again, but this time, it didn't resonate. It was just a laugh. Like the carpet I was drooling onto was just carpet.

I clawed in a breath and coughed it out again, and didn't even try to get up. I just lay there, blinking away moisture. *Sweat*, I told myself firmly, as my heart beat a staccato rhythm in my chest.

Someone knelt in front of me. "Are you all right?"

I made some small sound. It was supposed to be a laugh, but even I had to admit, it sounded more like a whimper. *Pathetic*, some part of my mind said.

I told that part to suck it.

"This is why you will never be a consul, Mircea," he

was told as he gathered me up. "No matter how strong you become, you are not ruthless enough."

"I can be ruthless, Lady."

"But not with everyone."

The room swam a little about me, and my skin felt clammy and cold. But Mircea's arms were a warm, steadying presence around me. "No. Not with everyone."

"Unlike Anthony." Her voice suddenly switched to a more businesslike tone. "Louis-Cesare must be found. Once Anthony learns he is lost, our case will be as well."

"He will be found."

"In time? We must produce him tonight, after the challenges."

"We are doing what we can. You know the difficulty."

"I also know the solution. He has shown an interest in this one. He went to her aid last night."

"He went to collect his mistress—"

"Do not take me for a fool, Mircea." The voice cracked like a whip. "I do not care that Louis-Cesare indulges his perversions, only that he fights for me while he does it. We cannot find him; therefore he must find us. If he has a bond with this creature, her pain will bring him faster than any other lure we have."

"They do not have a bond. Therefore such a tactic would gain you nothing and be a waste of a resource," Mircea said. His voice was calm, but the hand on my arm pressed hard enough to hurt. "Remember Tomas."

There was no reply to that, but the room suddenly became noticeably chillier.

My eyes managed to focus on the consul, who was standing a few yards away. There were plenty of seats around, but she was probably afraid to crush her little pets. I watched the swarm of tiny snakes she wore in lieu of clothes writhe across her form from neck to feet, a glimmering, gleaming mass in constant motion. The first time I'd ever seen that trick, I'd thought it pretty cool.

I wasn't feeling so much like that now.

"Top pocket," I gasped, a little desperately. I really, really didn't want to feel those things writhing inside me again. I thought once more and I might just go crazy permanently.

Three sets of eyes focused on me, but it was Mircea's hand that slipped inside my jacket. Dark eyes ran swiftly over the short letter Claire had given me. His face did not change, but the body holding me relaxed slightly.

"I am afraid we shall have to find another method, Lady," he said, handing the letter over.

Marlowe took it from him. "What is it?"

"A letter from a Blarestri royal princess, appointing Dorina her envoy to act for her in all matters concerning the stone. Any action taken against her representative will be considered to have been taken against the princess herself."

The consul's expression did not change, but her snakes writhed a little faster. "Find him!" she snapped, and strode from the room. She didn't use the door; the fireplace was apparently an illusion, too, because she passed right through it. I was starting to wonder if anything in this house of horrors was real.

Except the bodies.

"What was the point of that?" Mircea demanded, as soon as she'd left.

"The consul is becoming ... concerned ... that the problem with Louis-Cesare may backfire on her," Marlowe said carefully.

"Explain."

"Should she lose him to Anthony, it will be a defeat on her own soil in front of her colleagues. Such a loss could damage the prestige she needs to lead in the war. And if she wins ..." He took a deep breath he didn't need. "She knows we need to be strong at this juncture, but she fears that some of us may be becoming too much so."

Mircea had been wiping my face with his pocket handkerchief, but at that, he looked up. "She is suspicious of my loyalty?"

"Ambition has blinded better men."

"And more foolish ones. I have no plans to challenge her authority."

"Perhaps not now. But with the Pythia under your control—"

"She is under the Senate's control." He paused. "More or less."

"She is under *your* control, Mircea," Marlowe insisted. "Her loyalty is to *you*. She is suspicious of the consul—"

"With reason. That stunt with Tomas was ill-conceived. I warned her as much at the time."

"You suggested using him!"

"Using, not abusing, Kit. I never suggested butchering the man! That backfired, as anyone who knows Cassie's temperament should have expected."

"But we do not know it. You do. And you were strong enough before. Now, you have control of the Pythia as well as Louis-Cesare's loyalty through his attachment to Dorina—"

"And how did she find out about that? What did you tell her, Kit?"

"Only what she asked. She'd already heard as much from Anthony. He thinks it's the best joke this century."

"Anthony is not you! You could have denied it."

"I could have betrayed my duty, you mean, in order to save this—"

"Careful."

"Mircea, what the hell is wrong with you? I'm beginning to think that damned *geis* addled your brain!"

"Or cleared it."

I lay utterly still, content to let them believe I was more or less out of it. Which wasn't far from the truth. Between the general oppressiveness of the house and the consul's idea of a good time, I was a little under the weather. The room kept shimmying like a belly dancer every time I opened my eyes, so I mostly didn't.

I didn't understand a lot of the conversation, but the basic idea came across. Mircea was growing powerful enough that the consul was starting to worry about him. And given the way she handled problems, I didn't think that was too healthy.

Apparently, Mircea didn't, either. "She truly thinks I would move against her?"

"She wonders if one with so much power will be content to serve for the rest of his life," Marlowe said.

"I am content to *live*, Kit. Perhaps it is something you have forgotten how to do."

"You are making no sense." Marlowe sounded confused and resentful. "You do realize that?"

"Then tell your Lady this. The love of power destroyed my family once; I do not wish to see history repeat itself. I will serve her loyally until such a time as she moves against those I consider mine."

"You want me to give an ultimatum to the *consul*?"

"No. Merely to request a concession. For an old and trusted ally."

"There are those who would serve her without such concessions."

"Yes. Sycophants are always easy to find. They are also easily swayed by the next power who promises them more. How many offers have I turned down to stay with her?" Mircea asked, suddenly angry. "Why this? Why now?"

"It's Anthony," Marlowe admitted, "at least in part. He has been whispering in her ear since he arrived, warning her that Louis-Cesare would add too much to your personal power base."

"She must surely see why!"

"Of course, but his words reinforced her own concerns. This was . . . a test."

"An unnecessary one."

"Was it?" Marlowe's dark eyes were serious. "You chose family over the needs of the Senate. Over *her*."

"This would not have helped either, as I believe I made clear."

"And now another member of your family has gone rogue. He must be brought in, Mircea. She cannot allow such a direct challenge to her authority to stand."

"I am not hiding the man in my closet, Kit! I know no more of his whereabouts than you do."

"And if you did?"

Mircea met his eyes steadily. "I abandoned a member of my family once, long ago. I swore then never to repeat the error."

"Then I trust you are prepared for the consequences!" Marlowe snapped, and stormed out. The reporters tried to squeeze through the open door, but a nudge of power slammed it in their faces. I heard someone yelp.

"You can almost see the consul's hand up Marlowe's ass," I said, blinking my eyes open. The room trembled a little at the corners, but it was better than it had been a minute ago. I decided that was good enough, and sat up.

"It may seem that way," Mircea said, rising and crossing to the small bar in the corner. "In reality, it is more that they think alike and always have done."

"You know he's going off to report to her right now."

"I doubt that will be necessary," Mircea said wryly. "There are few rooms, if any, in this house that I would consider truly private."

I assumed that was a warning, although I didn't have any deep, dark secrets to spill. And if I did, I sure as hell wouldn't be talking about them here. "He's right, though. Risking yourself for me wasn't smart."

Mircea poured something that I really hoped was whiskey into a couple of glasses. "When one serves such a mistress, occasionally it is useful to make a show of force," he said, handing me one. "Otherwise, she may forget which among her servants are courtiers and which are ciphers."

"You took a hell of a risk for a reminder."

Mircea joined me with his own drink. The sofa was right across from the dead guy; it almost looked like the three of us were having a quiet drink together. Very quiet, on his part.

"It would not have been, under normal circumstances," he said. "She would not expect me to turn over a high-ranking family member to be slaughtered for a crime he did not commit."

"It sounded to me like that's exactly what she expects."

"She is frightened. And when someone holds that

much power, their fear can be dangerous. That is why I want you out of this, Dorina. There are creatures involved in this from whom I cannot protect you."

I bit my lip on the knee-jerk retort that I didn't need protection. Normally, it was true. But there weren't too many things on Earth who could go up against the consul when she was in a mood. Not and live, anyway.

Which made me wonder why Mircea had done it.

I almost asked, but something stopped me. Probably the same thing that kept me from asking him about the vision I'd seen, about the mother I couldn't remember. I wanted to know, and I didn't. As long as I didn't bring it up, didn't mention it, that brief glimpse of her remained real and vivid in my memory, something I'd never had before. But if I caught him in a lie, if I found out that this was nothing more than another ploy to get me to do what he wanted, I'd lose it. I'd lose her.

Just like, if I probed too deeply into this new attitude of Mircea's, I might find that it masked the same old schemes. Was this sudden concern because Louis-Cesare had shown some interest in me? Was it merely what Marlowe had said—a way to bind a powerful ally more closely? If so, I'd have thought that Mircea would be more encouraging of a relationship, instead of all but warning me off. Unless he thought that's what I would think, in which case—

Damn it. I realized that I wanted it to be real, all of it, wanted him to have cared about her, wanted him to care about me. And I was so very afraid that he didn't. It was easier not to ask, to let the possibility last a little longer, even if it meant not learning anything else.

God, I could be such a coward sometimes.

"You think the consul is afraid of you?" I asked instead.

"Perhaps, in part. It is a balancing act with which every sovereign has to deal; the more powerful a courtier, the more useful, but also the more dangerous. No one can sustain herself in authority by relying solely on yes men, but gather too many powerful, ambitious courtiers around . . ."

"And one day, one of them will replace you."

It was strange, but I had never really thought about just how much power Mircea had. All senators seemed impossibly godlike, up there in the clouds somewhere, making decisions for us poor mortals. And compared to the vamp on the street, they were. But in fact, senators varied a lot in personal power and in the alliances each house was able to call on in an emergency.

And Mircea had always been very good at making alliances.

"I am not that one," he said firmly. "Occasionally she needs to hear that."

"And the other part?"

"The current situation has us all on edge. I cannot recall another time when so much has been in flux all at once. Anthony's court, possibly about to face numerous challenges; Alejandro's, weakened by years of misrule and neglect, about to topple; and our own Senate, devastated by the war, about to be rebuilt."

"It might be rebuilt better." I could certainly see room for improvement.

"Perhaps. But one thing is sure: it will be different. Loyalties will be tested. Age-old alliances will have to woo new members or they will not survive. And change is not something our people face with equanimity."

"Hence the freak-out."

"Yes." There was a knock on the door, and a servant discreetly looked in. "The Circle is here," Mircea said, rising. He looked at me, and his face went completely blank. "I meant to send this to you today," he said, taking something out of his coat. "I cannot give you back your memories, Dorina. I can but give you mine."

I didn't understand that cryptic phrase, and had no time to ask him about it before the Circle's people burst into the room and deluged him.

I found myself out in the hall, after getting elbowed out of the room by hungry journalists. It looked like the Circle had brought some of their own, along with medics—too late—and a couple old guys in suits.

I looked down at the small book Mircea had pressed

into my palm. It had a leather cover that looked new, but what it was protecting wasn't. There were a few dozen pages inside of good, thick paper that had aged to a deep gold color. I stared at them, uncomprehending, for a long moment.

Images covered the pages on both sides. Some were hasty sketches, done with a firm hand in dark ink, a few quick strokes picking out delicate features. Others were fully realized miniature paintings, the paper beneath them mottled with age, but the colors still as vibrant as the jewels that had once been crushed into their pigments. The subject of each was the same: a young dark-haired woman.

At first, I thought the images were of me, but I'd never worn those clothes, never posed for those sketches. And then I found one of her in front of a window, with her sleeves rolled up and her arms coated in flour, and my mind reeled. My fingers brushed the surface of the soapy old paper, tracing the raised edges of the ink in disbelief. These hadn't been hastily thrown together in a few hours, as a prop to some devious scheme. It must have taken months, years, to do them all. . . .

Suddenly, I couldn't make anything else out. Everything was a bright, smeared blur, like trying to see something when it was held right up against my face. Then I looked back at Mircea and everything came into focus again.

He was staring at me over the heads of the milling mages, silently. He should have been rearranging those handsome features into a concerned mask to placate the Circle. But there was still no expression on his face, no emotion in those dark eyes.

Maybe he didn't know how to do this, either, I thought blankly.

And then a phalanx of scowling war mages arrived, jostling me farther down the hall.

The leather coat–clad crew got one look at Lutkin and started fingering their weapons. Eyes darted around suspiciously, as if they expected something to jump out at them from the wall. Mircea was going to have fun trying to keep the peace, and that was on top of having to come up with some kind of defense for Louis-Cesare.

The rules of the vamp world weren't as arbitrary as some people thought. Masters had life-or-death power over their own families, but screw with somebody else's and there was hell to pay. And for better or worse, Louis-Cesare was attached to the powerful, dysfunctional, vindictive-as-hell Basarab line.

Even Anthony couldn't order him to be enslaved or killed if there was reasonable doubt of his guilt; Mircea would see to that. But eloquence would get him only so far. He needed something to work with, and it was my job to get him that something whether he wanted me to or not. I just wasn't sure how.

I carefully tucked the small book away, dodging more new arrivals. Nobody was smiling, and everyone seemed to feel that I was in the way. I was trying to figure out the shortest route to the front entrance when Marlowe sidled up and shoved a slip of paper into my hand.

"Don't make me regret this," he hissed.

I glanced down. Two addresses were scribbled over it in a bold hand. One was nearby, and looked like a house number, and one was an address in Manhattan. There were no names, but I didn't really need any.

"You have got to be shitting me."

"Mircea's Achilles' heel is his family," Marlowe told me quietly. "Louis-Cesare must be found by tonight, with or without proof of his innocence, or I fear your father may put his own position in jeopardy attempting to save him. And the consul *will not back him.* Do you understand?"

"I understand that you want me to drag Louis-Cesare back here to be butchered. He's not going to take Anthony's deal, Marlowe."

"I know that! But if he is here we can stall while we work to find evidence to clear him. The trial could drag on for days. But if he is absent again, they'll declare him an outlaw and issue a death warrant. Tonight."

"Why trust me with this?"

"I have to operate within certain guidelines, at least

where people at this level are concerned. You do not. And there is no time to finesse anything. We must shake something loose. Now."

There was nothing I could safely say in the consul's territory, so I didn't say anything. I hit the door and got to shaking.

Chapter Thirty-two

Outside, heat shimmered off the drive and the sea of white plastic tents. I wished I'd brought a pair of sunglasses, but no such luck. So I bought one from a vendor who was happy to get the business now that half his customers had run off.

Or, at least, they were trying to. There was a backlog of cars still attempting to exit the grounds, clogging air and roadside alike. I decided to leave the Camaro where it was and head off to my first appointment on foot.

Slinking along behind me, carefully muffled up against the glaring sun, were two very unhappy vampires. I assumed they were Marlowe's, since they made no attempt to attack me, but I didn't know for sure. They wouldn't introduce themselves or so much as deign to notice my existence. But when I moved, so did they.

Two miles and about a ton of sweat later, I found myself staring up at a rambling mansion that rivaled the consul's in size, although not in elegance. But then, it was just a rental. I showed Claire's note at the door, and was left to cool my heels for half an hour in the vast wood-paneled foyer.

Of course, there was no air-conditioning. I was certain the home came equipped, but vamps don't need it. They usually only turn it on when they have humans around they want to impress, and apparently, I didn't qualify.

Finally, I was shown into a sitting room. Or, at least, that was what I assume it had been before it had been draped with red silk and lined with braziers. The braziers were lit and it was hot as hell, but that wasn't why I staggered and almost fell. The power in the room was like a punch to the gut. It felt something like walking through the consul's front door, only most of it was radiating off the tiny, little woman on the big, ugly throne.

When I was born, the average height for a guy had been five foot four, so I'd been considered pretty tall for a woman. Then times had changed, diets had improved and I'd ended up shopping in the petite section. But one look at Ming-de, and I decided maybe to hold off on the complaints for a while. If she'd been shopping at the local mall, she'd have had to go to the kiddie store.

Not that she appeared to have that problem. Her bright yellow silk robes were embroidered within an inch of their lives with a glittering menagerie of fantastic beasts. She wore a headdress with pearls as big as cherries and a lot of gold tassels that shimmered whenever she moved. And her little feet, maybe all of three inches long, were encased in lotus shoes so crusted with embroidery that the fabric couldn't even be seen.

The tiny useless feet were tenderly propped on a tufted stool, with a large guard kneeling on either side. Why, I don't know. It wasn't like she needed the help.

I finally scraped myself off the floor and staggered to the bottom of the set of stairs leading up to the dais on which the monster throne squatted. It had gilt mythical beasts writhing all over it or, hell, I don't know. They might have been solid gold. It didn't look like Ming-de was hard up. It was backed by a couple of tall, similarly decorated screens so that the whole end of the room was an explosion of gold.

I stood there in my sweaty T-shirt, feeling a little inadequate.

And then she poked a head on a stick out at me, and I cheered up. Mine was bigger.

The tiny shrunken head had been Ming-de's English translator for a few hundred years, since she would be damned if she was going to learn the barbarian tongue herself. Rumor was that she'd cut it off some English sea captain back in the day, although after the shrinkage and subsequent wear, it was a little hard to tell. It looked dusty.

"Please tell her serene highness that I come as a representative of a princess of the fey," I instructed, glad to have found a way to communicate.

"She knows that," the tiny head informed me grouchily. It was about the size of a crab apple, and appeared to have a personality to match. "You sent in a note, didn't you?"

"Tell her I'm here to inquire about a missing item of fey property."

"She knows that, too. She said to inform you that she purchased it in good faith and with the understanding that it was the property of the fey selling it. She would return it to the princess, but as she never received it, it's a moot point. Have a nice day."

"Please tell her serene highness that the princess appreciates her cooperation. She is trying to avoid a possibly ugly encounter when her family arrives tomorrow. Were she to receive the stone back before then, the whole thing could be forgotten. Otherwise . . ."

"Otherwise what?"

"It will be out of the princess's hands. Her family will take over the hunt for the stone. And they may wonder how someone as astute as the empress could be taken in by such a fraud. They may also wonder why she has yet to retaliate against anyone for the duplicity."

"She hadn't paid for it," Crabby said, frowning. "It disappeared before it could be authenticated, and the transfer of funds was never made. She lost nothing."

"She lost a valuable object that she had every reason to assume was rightfully hers. She lost face in front of the other bidders, most of whom now know that the stone is missing. She also lost the advantage it would have given her at tonight's challenge."

"You are accusing the empress of cheating?" The little thing looked outraged. He had yet to communicate a damn thing to the empress, whose beautiful face was as serene as ever. But her long fingernail guards were going *clack, clack, clack* on the arms of her throne.

I was starting to think that "translator" might not be quite the right word.

"I am merely pointing out what the fey might think," I said, eyeing him suspiciously. "If the stone is returned to her before the challenge tonight, everything can be forgotten."

"And now you accuse her of what? Stealing her own property?"

"It was not her property; it was fey property. And your lady is wise. Perhaps she had discovered this and realized that the only way she could retain the stone was to—"

I didn't get any further, but I did discover what the two guards were for. A few seconds later, my butt hit the dirt in front of the elegant circular driveway. Frick and Frack were waiting just outside the gate, huddled in the inadequate shade of a small maple. They weren't bothering to conceal themselves anymore, I guess because I'd already spotted them. They took in my disheveled appearance and grinned.

I grinned back and glanced up at the blazing sun. "I guess we better get started. It's a three-mile hike back to the car."

The double doors to the Manhattan triplex were opened by a beautiful young man with silky blond hair, big blue eyes and a pulse. I hadn't expected a phalanx of guards—this was a private residence, not vamp central—but a human doorman was almost a novelty. "You're late," he admonished gently, stepping to the side.

Since I hadn't bothered to call ahead, I thought that a little strange. "Sorry."

He let me in, but not my shadows. I'd left them in the lobby, assuming Geminus wouldn't want to talk in front of Marlowe's men. The last rays of the setting sun streamed in the floor-to-ceiling windows as we crossed the large foyer.

It made the one at the Senate's New York office look like a poor relation. A crystal chandelier sparkled from a twenty-foot-high ceiling, lighting up a sweep of carrera-clad stairs edged by an elaborate wrought-iron railing. A shining path of marble led off to the left, where I could see a glimpse of a double-height ballroom through another set of doors.

"Main salon," the doorman said, indicated the ballroom with a sweep of his hand.

I passed through, expecting an ambush but not getting one. The room was huge, with tall windows looking out over the twighlit cityscape. The decor reminded me a lot of vamp central, all old woods, gilt-edged moldings and, in this case, a black, white and gold color scheme. It was the sort of room that called for grand masters in heavy gilt frames on every wall, yet despite there being plenty of space, there wasn't a painting in sight.

But then, there was a reason for that.

A vamp stood by the fireplace, his cap of auburn hair shining under the lights. He didn't look up as we approached; his focus was on the young woman writhing face-first against the wall. Her dress was long, red and pooled around her high heels. She hadn't been wearing anything under it, and her bare skin gleamed in the low light.

Her hair was down, except for a few sweaty strands clinging to her cheeks. It cascaded almost the full length of her back, until the vamp brushed it carelessly aside. It flowed over her shoulders like a fall of russet silk, revealing a scarlet ribbon laced up her back. The ribbon was threaded through a set of corset piercings that framed her spine, eight tiny golden loops biting deeply into her skin and glinting palely.

The vamp stood behind her, toying with the piercings. He ran a finger up and down the tiny loops, just hard enough for them to tug at her skin, to bite a little bit harder than usual, to pull a groan from her lips. His back was to me, so I couldn't see much of him, just dark auburn curls tickling his neck and the back of a tuxedo. He'd taken the coat off and draped it over a nearby chair, leaving him in white dress shirt and perfectly fitted black slacks.

At first I thought I'd caught him in the middle of dinner. Vampires could feed by touch, pulling blood molecules through the skin, or through the air in the case of a master. And the woman was definitely being fed upon, if her reaction was anything to go by. She hugged the wall, panting, as he slowly began drawing the ribbon from its little loops.

She had it pulled tight, and it slithered out easily, over skin already so sensitized that every tiny tug made her tremble. His finger drew a line down her spine, causing a quick, indrawn breath and a helpless shudder. It might have been pleasure or pain now, because he'd stopped being careful. His touches were raising bruises as he let the blood pool under the skin, not bothering to absorb it all.

And then something happened that shook my belief that I knew pretty much everything about vampires. The masses of small bruises on the woman's back suddenly began to change, to coalesce, to flow together into new shapes. Where there had been only ugliness before, a mar on her beauty, a crenellated ridge of mountains appeared.

His hand did a second pass, and the remaining bruises became an intricate latticework of gnarled branches, brown and black, framing the hills. And I finally figured out what he was doing. He was healing some sections of the damage in a few days, others a week, still others two, in order to have the bruises change to the hue he liked.

It gave a whole new meaning to the term "living color."

"Nice," I said. The overall effect was surprisingly attractive, if you ignored how it had been created. And if you didn't care that, once the euphoria of the feeding process wore off, the woman was going to be in excruciating pain.

"She is a good subject," he agreed.

A glance around showed that he wasn't the only "artist" in the room. The weak struggles of other canvases ringed the walls, bare bodies splayed against exposed brick. Many of them were manacled in place to keep them upright, although most hung limp in their chains, passed out from blood loss. I assumed it was no worse

352

than that. Death would cause the blood in the body to pool in the extremities, ruining the artists' hard work.

Most appeared to be young women. I guess I knew why I'd had it so easy getting in.

Livid lines cascaded over one pale buttock and down her thigh, a riotous abstract design that mimicked brush-strokes. He was signing his work. "Geminus," I said, watching the lines etch themselves across her skin.

"At your service." He finally looked up, and it was still a shock, after all this time, to see how handsome the monsters could be. This one had bright hazel eyes, riotous brown curls and a cherubic face, which brightened in recognition. My feet suddenly slid across the polished floor and my arms flew up, pinning themselves to the wall.

Geminus pulled off my jacket and let it fall to the floor, then smoothed a hand down the length of my back to my ass. Before I realized what was happening, he had casually unzipped my jeans and tugged them down past my hips. I struggled, but I doubt he even noticed, and I certainly didn't get anywhere.

That doesn't happen to me often. My strength is better than average and I have a natural resistance to vampire powers. But then, most of the vamps I meet aren't two thousand years old, either.

He cupped one cheek, running a thoughtful thumb over the skin just above the line of my thong. "I wonder, is it true what they say about dhampirs?"

He pressed down, hard enough to leave a thumb-shaped imprint behind. I didn't need to see it to know what was happening: I don't heal as fast as a vamp, but I'm no slouch, either.

"Interesting." He circled me, his face thoughtful. "I can't use vampires for my work," he told me. "They heal too quickly—even the new ones. There is no time to exhibit a piece before it is gone, erased by the body as if it never existed."

"What a pity."

"It is, really. They can take so much more damage than humans."

"You seem to have done enough," I said, watching

the woman. She'd fainted near the end of his "paint-ing," and now hung limp in her invisible shackles, a thin strand of drool falling from her lips. Her chest rose and fell shallowly, but her skin was dead white—except for the colorful bruising. That she would wear for a while.

"Humans are marvelous canvases," he agreed. "But they have their limitations. Beyond the need to take such care, they also heal so slowly that my creations are static. I may as well be drawing on the wall."

"Why don't you? It doesn't bleed."

"But you offer some intriguing possibilities. You heal fast, but not too fast. I can see a landscape. It would change with the seasons over the course of an evening as you slowly healed. The centerpiece at a party, perhaps." He looked around at the gathering crowd, people drift-ing over from other entertainments in twos and threes. "Like this one."

"Too bad I'm all booked up."

He tugged my T-shirt off over my head. "We'll have to see if we can clear your schedule," he told me gently.

"You're not worried about reprisals?"

He looked at me innocently as he unhooked my bra. "You came here uninvited and fully armed. And you are dhampir."

"I came here to talk," I said sharply.

"But I had no way of knowing that." He pulled the scrap of cotton away from my body and tossed it care-lessly aside. It landed on the floor with the crumpled shirt, like rags I wouldn't need anymore. "And I had to defend myself."

"I'm warning you. Let me go, Geminus."

Instead, he suddenly pressed against me, a line of heat down my back, and without warning grasped my breasts. It was a firm grip, but not rough, designed for humiliation rather than pain. It was a domineering stance: his clothed groin against my bare ass, the slow glide of his hands over my motionless body, his fingers plucking at my nipples, compelling them to hardness. He was saying without words that he could do whatever he liked with me, that I was no match for him, just a canvas to be molded to his will.

He rested his chin on my shoulder while his hand continued to lazily stroke my breast. "For someone so powerless, you have a big mouth."

"And for someone attacking a representative of a fey princess, you have a lot of nerve."

My voice didn't shake, but I was becoming seriously disturbed, not least because his men were watching. They had crowded close on all sides, clearly relishing the newest diversion their boss had designed. Their thoughts skittered across my skin like grasping hands, making me cringe with just the echoes of what they planned to do to me. I'd been too angry to be afraid before, but some of those images had my heart hammering in my chest hard enough to hurt.

"I don't know any princesses," Geminus told me, sounding amused. "But next time she's in town, do tell her to stop by."

The crowd seemed to think that was funny. I wasn't feeling so amused. I'd assumed my chances with Ming-de were pretty low. She was powerful enough that even the fey were going to think twice about challenging her, particularly when there was no evidence that she'd done anything more than place a bid. But I'd had higher hopes for Geminus.

He was a senator, not a consul, with far less personal power to draw on. And his own Senate wasn't likely to protect him over a power play gone wrong. I'd thought that there was at least a decent chance that he'd panic at the thought of facing the fey and cough up the rune.

Only he didn't appear to be panicking.

"You may not know her, but you know something about a piece of her property," I said. "You were at the auction—" An unseen hand suddenly clasped me around the throat, restricting my air. Not enough to truly choke me, but a definite warning.

I hadn't planned to mention Naudiz, hadn't even wanted to bring up the fey, especially not in front of an audience. But I wasn't going to stand there and be drained—or whatever else he had planned. Let him explain what the fey wanted with him.

After a moment, the pressure eased a bit. "What princess did you say?"

"Read the note. Left-hand-side pocket of my jacket."

He picked it up off the floor and felt around the pocket. He took enough time to read the note two or three times, before he finally moved away. The power holding me broke at the same moment, so abruptly that I went to one knee.

"And what does this princess want with me?"

"To do you a favor." I got my back against the wall before I even pulled up the jeans.

"I like favors from pretty women," he told me easily. "Come."

I jerked the T-shirt back on, not bothering with underwear, grabbed my jacket and followed him through a door on the far side of the room. We passed down a long corridor, which gave me a moment to get my breathing under control and remind myself that I wasn't allowed to kill him. Yet.

We eventually stopped at an office. Or, at least, I guess it was supposed to serve that function. It was so stuffed with weaponry that it was a little difficult to tell. I shoved an antique shield off a chair and sat down, as Geminus got behind the desk.

"What is this princess going to do for me?"

"Her name is Claire, and she's half-human," I told him shortly. "She grew up here and only recently claimed her heritage when she agreed to marry a Blarestri prince. But she's never really gotten used to the way the fey do certain things. She's a vegetarian pacifist, for instance; she hates unnecessary violence."

"I'm fascinated."

"You should be. Anyone else would have just turned you over to her family for punishment."

"I don't recall angering any fey. Not of the royal kind, at any rate."

"They tend not to like it much when you steal from them."

"Then I am fortunate, for I have stolen nothing."

"You were seen at the club, right before the fey ended up dead and the rune went missing."

It was a lie, but I thought it was worth a shot. But he didn't take the bait. "Was I?"

"And you're certainly strong enough to take out a fey warrior."

"You flatter me."

I glanced up at the wooden sword mounted over the fireplace. It was old and crumbling, barely held together by some stained twine, but carefully preserved behind a glass case. Two thousand years ago, Geminus had gotten his start as a gladiator, one of the few ways for poor young men of the time to rise to fame and fortune. He was rumored to have been fearless, despite a seer prophesying that he would die on the arena sands. He hadn't, instead winning the sword and his freedom after successfully defeating numerous opponents.

By all accounts, he'd been doing the same thing ever since.

"I don't think so," I said simply.

He laughed. "Strong enough but not stupid enough. No relic is worth that kind of trouble."

"Not even if it gets you control of the Senate?"

"But I do not wish to control the Senate," he told me easily. "Let them bicker and squabble and plot and plan. My interests lie elsewhere."

"You expect my employer to believe that you just shrugged off what happened at the auction? Come on, Geminus. That's not your style."

"Of course I didn't."

"Then what did you do?"

He sighed and kicked back against the wall, one foot propped up on the desk.

"After Cheung did his fiddle with the auction, I was . . . annoyed. It was obvious that he'd never intended to give the stone to anyone but Ming-de. I don't like being played, so I had my servants to do some checking. They discovered who the sellers usually used for authentication. And fortunately for me, the little bastard was swimming in debt."

"You're talking about the luduan."

"Yes. I offered him a deal. I'd pay his debts if he switched the rune for a fake when he examined it."

"And once the fey found out and tracked him down?"

"That was his problem. But he could always deny it. There was no way anyone was going to know where, exactly, it went missing."

"Why were you at Ray's, if you already had a plan in place?"

This time, he didn't budge. "I wanted to make sure he didn't double-cross me. The stone was worth considerably more than I was paying on his debts. I didn't trust him."

"What happened?"

"My men and I surrounded the building, and the luduan went in. He was supposed to bring me the rune, but he never came back. I finally sent one of my boys in to check on things, and he found the luduan gone and Raymond screaming about a dead fey. I decided it might be prudent to leave at that point."

"You're telling me a luduan killed a fey warrior?"

"They're both fey, and the guard might not have been expecting it."

"If I were him, and I had something worth a king's ransom, I'd have been expecting it."

"Yet someone managed to do it." He had a point there. "I don't know if he killed the guard. I don't know that he has the rune. I only know I don't. You can tell your lady that."

"I will. And she may even believe you; Claire's the trusting type," I said, standing up and tucking my card under a corner of his blotter. "Unfortunately, her family isn't, and they'll be here tomorrow. Knowing Caedmon, he may decide to find the rune in the most efficient way possible."

"And what would that be?"

I shrugged. "Attack everyone who was at the auction and see who doesn't die."

Chapter Thirty-three

Five minutes later, I hit the sidewalk in front of Geminus's building. Not literally, this time; he hadn't thrown me out, but he also hadn't admitted a damn thing. Leaving me hours away from the trial and fresh out of ideas.

Two silent shadows peeled off the bricks and followed me as I headed down the street. They didn't say anything, including asking about what had happened upstairs. Of course, my cursing had probably already told them it wasn't good.

I leaned against the side of a building a few blocks over and lit the crumpled old joint I found in my jacket. Sucking in a long breath, I held it for a second before letting it out. Drugs don't do a lot for me thanks to my revved-up metabolism, but they're better than nothing. And this was excellent weed.

After a moment the wave hit, lifting my bones away from one another and loosening the joints in sequence— neck, shoulders, wrists, fingers—leaving me feeling like I was floating on the tide. The tension washed out of me from spine to fingertips before coursing away, leaving me calmer, if not any happier.

Not that I needed to be calmer. That little scene with Geminus had disturbed me, but probably not for the reason he'd intended. It wasn't the first time I'd been assaulted; it was, however, one of only two times in my life I could remember really wanting to fall into a dhampir rage and being unable to do so.

The other had been yesterday, when Æsubrand attacked.

I should have been able to break Geminus's hold, at least long enough to give me a chance to get my weapons. And when I stabbed Æsubrand, it should have been somewhere vital. Instead, they'd both made me look like a fool, and I strongly suspected I knew why.

The fey wine had seemed like a godsend, but I should have known better. Everything that came out of Faerie looked better, prettier, more enticing than it really was. It glittered like gold, but scratch the surface and what was revealed was a lot darker. So I was left with a choice: take the wine and put up with memories I didn't want and a substantial power loss, or don't take it and suffer homicidal blackouts.

Wonderful.

The clock ticking steadily inside my head wasn't helping my mood, either. Geminus had my number, but he hadn't used it. Either he really didn't have the stone or he was cocky enough to believe he could take on the fey. That left no one on the party list who wasn't dead or buttoned down tight. At least as far as I was concerned. Caedmon might have more luck, but he wasn't here. And by the time he arrived, Louis-Cesare would have been sentenced and possibly executed.

Marlowe had been right: something needed to shake loose, and it needed to happen now.

I hailed a cab. There was one person who hadn't been on the list who might know something. I'd already had my daily quota of ancient vampires with attitude problems who weren't going to tell me shit. But talking to Anthony beat doing nothing.

Although not by much.

A yellow taxi slid to a stop in front of me, and the silent duo got inside. I started to do the same when my phone rang. "Yeah?"

"Who the hell taught you how to answer the phone?" a brisk voice asked.

I wasn't sure I recognized it; the weather was overcast and the signal was lousy. "Fin?"

"The one and only. You still interested in that dead-beat?"

"Yeah, why?"

"Because he just showed up at his apartment. My boys are downstairs. If you want to talk to him before they take him apart, now would be the time.

"Now's good," I said fervently. "Thanks, Fin."

"Where to?" the cabbie asked.

"Chinatown."

A body hit the dirt at my feet, hard enough to send a gout of blood splashing up onto my face. I wiped it away and stared upward. I hate it when that happens.

"You will die a worse death if you do not leave my domain," a voice thundered down from the third story of the old tenement. "I am a servant of the Sacred Fire, the wielder of the flame of Arnor—"

"So I should call you Gandalf?" I asked, getting the toe of my boot into a crack in the wall.

There was silence for a long moment, except for the sound of brick flaking off under my boots as I scrabbled for purchase. I got a hand on the lowest rusty rung of the fire escape just as my toehold gave way. A wiggle and a heave got me up to the first landing, where a feral-looking cat hissed at me before jumping up to the next level.

I'd have preferred to use the door, but we were trying to cover all exits. Fin's boys were in the lobby, and Frick and Frack were watching the sides. This was the only way out left, and I wasn't about to let him use it.

"Aw, fudge," floated down to me, as a couple of golden eyes peered over a third-floor window ledge. "You're a freaking dhampir. Why are you reading Tolkien?"

I shrugged, then had to dodge the potted geranium he threw at me. "After five hundred years, you've read just about everything. Besides, he had hella world-building skills."

"You're five hundred?" A head with small, curved horns came into view. "No way."

"Yep." I followed the cat up the trembling staircase. Flakes of rust clung to my skin and ate into my palms as I hefted myself over a couple missing stairs and up another floor.

"Well, you don't look a day over four," I was told, as a ceramic lamp exploded on the railings right beside me.

One of the shards must have hit the cat, which sent up a mewl of distress. Suddenly, my objective's entire head stuck out of the window, regardless of the danger. "Oh, no! Pooky!"

"Pooky?" I demanded, as a squat creature crawled out onto the window ledge and held out a pawlike appendage beseechingly.

"Come to Daddy," it crooned, but the cat was having none of it. It hissed at both of us and tried to run between my legs, but I scooped it up, careful to keep those sharp, little claws out of my flesh.

"You have a cat?" I asked, one brow raised, as the fur ball in my arms spit and hissed.

"Why shouldn't I?" The creature's face wasn't real expressive, but its voice was defensive.

"You're a *dog*."

"I'm a luduan!" it said huffily.

I looked it over. It would be maybe three feet tall in its stocking feet, if it had feet, which it didn't, or was designed to walk standing up, which it wasn't. The body covered in golden brown fur looked a lot like a dog's, except for the too-large lionlike head with a curly brown mane. To further confuse the issue, it had a unicorn-type horn in the center of its forehead.

"Dog-ish," I corrected.

"Give me my cat!" it demanded.

"Or what? You'll smite me like a Balrog?"

The golden eyes narrowed. "I quote Tolkien because he puts it better. But I can still open a can of whup ass all over you."

"You're right," I told him. "He does put it better."

The creature used its horn to snag a radio by the handle, preparing to launch it at me. I dangled the kitty over the long drop. "Just try it."

His face crumpled. "Oh, come on. Don't do that. You'll scare her!"

"Maybe we can work something out," I offered.

He sighed in resignation. "I don't have any money, okay? So you can tell whichever one of those sharks you're working for that he's wasting his time."

"I don't want money."

"And you're not getting a pound of flesh, either!"

"I'm not here to beat you up."

The big head tilted. "Then why are you here?"

I pulled the cat back in. She didn't look particularly scared to me. Maybe because the "body" down below had vanished like the cut-rate illusion it was. "I just want to talk to you."

"About what?"

"About what happened at Ray's place last night."

He blinked those enormous eyes at me. "Come again?"

"You heard me."

"No, I didn't. That's the kind of talk that could get my horn ground up." He petted it nervously. "It's supposed to be an aphrodisiac, you know? Not that it's done me any good lately. Do you know how few lady luduans are in existence?"

"Not really."

"Neither do I," he said miserably. "I just know there's none around here."

"That's a bitch. Now are you going to help me or not?"

"Not!"

"Here, kitty, kitty."

"Cut that out!"

"Look, you can talk to me, or you can talk to Fin's boys. They're waiting downstairs. But I'm nicer." He shot me a look. "Okay, that was a lie. But I can help you out."

"How?"

"Tell me what you know, and I get you off the hook

with Fin." I couldn't afford it, but if it helped Louis-Cesare, I didn't think Mircea was going to quibble about the expense account.

He looked at me for a long moment, those lamp-lit eyes brighter than the streetlight across the road. "Touch the horn," he finally said.

It was my turn to look wary. "Is this something kinky?"

"As if." He sniffed. "You're not my type."

Thank God for small mercies. "If you poison me, I can't help you with Fin," I pointed out.

He yawned, showing a mouth full of needle-sharp teeth. They matched the talons at the end of its paws. "Relax. All that was just good propaganda. Not that I don't know a few tricks, mind you."

"Like the flame of—"

"Shut up."

I decided I didn't have time to be cautious, hiked up to the third-floor landing and touched the horn. And no sooner had my finger brushed the tip than he rammed it into my skin. "Ouch!"

"Don't be such a baby," he told me, as my blood sank into the apparently porous bone. His eyes rolled up in his head, and he sat there, humming and making these weird faces. I let him get away with it for maybe a minute, and then I gave the kitty a little squeeze. The spoiled thing mewed, and his eyes shot open. "You're a piece of work—you know that?" he demanded.

"I told you this had better not be kinky."

"It isn't!"

"Could have fooled me."

"Like that's hard," he sneered. "And you may as well let Pooky go. I know you won't drop her."

"Wanna bet?"

He sighed. "Lady—or may I call you Dorina?"

"No!"

"Okay, Dorina, it's like this. I'm a luduan. I taste your blood, and I know what kind of person you are, whether you're lying to me, yadda yadda." He waved a paw. "You know the score, or you wouldn't be here. Don't waste my time."

I sighed and pulled a gun. "You're right. I can't kill an innocent creature just for sport. You, on the other hand . . ."

"Hey!" Those bright eyes narrowed. "No need to get nasty. Did I say we couldn't do business?"

"Then what was all that about with the blood?"

"Establishing some guidelines. It saves time. Otherwise, people try to lie to me and it gives me a real headache"—he tapped the space above the horn with his paw—"right here."

"So do we have a deal?"

"I don't know. What exactly do you want to know?"

"Well, for starters, you could tell me who killed Jókell."

The creature's small ears went back, and its eyes widened before it started beckoning frantically with a paw. "Get in here!"

It could have been a trap, but I didn't think so. He looked genuinely panicked. Before I could move, the horn snagged my jacket and dragged me inside. The door slammed shut behind me, and I found myself in a narrow hallway smelling of mildew, urine and spices.

I didn't get a chance to look around, because I was dragged into an apartment before my eyes had even adjusted, and another door slammed shut behind me. "He's dead? Are you sure? What happened?" The luduan's tail was twitching excitedly back and forth as he prowled across the floor. He looked freaked.

"Yes, yes, and someone gutted him," I said, looking around for a chair and not finding one.

"But he had protection!" The little thing looked genuinely upset.

"You mean Naudiz?"

"That thing!" He wrinkled up his features in what I guess was a scowl. "I wish I'd never heard of it!"

"That seems to be the consensus. So what happened?"

He sighed and sat back on his haunches, but that still left his head too low for his liking. "Sit down, can't you?"

"Where?" The apartment was clearly set up for non-human use. The weak streetlight angling in through gaps in the blinds striped a nest of blankets on the floor, a large rawhide chew bone with one end gnawed off and a couple food dishes. I assumed these were for the cat, because a wash of junk-food wrappers had collected in the corners.

"It's over there," he said, reading my body language. "I keep one for bipedal clients."

He used the horn to point to a stack of folding chairs in the dining room area and I fetched one, bringing us closer to eye level. "Tell me."

"Worst night of my life; I thought I was dead for sure."

"You were there? You were in the office when he was attacked?"

"Yeah. I'd been there maybe a minute. I was late because I had to wait for that vampire who owns the club to leave. There was supposed to be a diversion to get him out of the office, but it wasn't needed. He left on his own and I walked up. And a few seconds later the attack came."

"You were working for Geminus."

"I didn't want to do it, but I needed the cash. I was in debt to him, big-time. Fin's boys will just beat me up; he would have killed me."

"In debt? For what?"

He blinked those massive eyes at me. "You're kidding, right? Geminus owns half the illegal fights around here. Between fey and humans, fey and fey, humans and humans—anything, really, as long as someone will pay money to see it. Or to bet on it."

I stared at him, a few things sliding into place. Along with drugs and weapons, no-holds-barred fights were another illegal import from Faerie. Ironically, it was the sort of thing the Dark Fey, who were treated like animals by some of their light counterparts, were fleeing Faerie to try to escape. But, once here, they had few contacts and fewer choices.

The authorities shut the matches down when they

stumbled across them, but it wasn't a priority. They weren't a factor in the war, and that was all anyone cared about right now. Or maybe there was another reason.

"You're telling me a senator was involved in a smuggling ring?"

"Involved in it? He runs it. He's been smuggling for longer than anybody. He started bringing people over for the fights, and then branched out. He's into a little of everything now."

I sat there, growing quietly furious. No wonder we'd had so much hell stopping the smugglers. Geminus must have been tipping them off to our every move. Leaving us to clean up his competition—like Vleck or Ray— while he grabbed a bigger and bigger share of the pie.

I guess he'd been telling the truth when he said he wasn't interested in politics.

"Why did he want the rune?"

"He didn't give me the details. But I guess so he could control the fights. Give the stone to the fighter he wanted to win, and he could determine the outcome of every bout. And clean up even more than he already does. My debts were nothing compared to that."

"You agreed to make the switch."

"I thought it would be easy: a little sleight of hand, and no harm done. Jókell would get his money, I would get out of hock to all the people I owe and Geminus would get off my back. But I didn't expect to be attacked!"

"What happened?"

"I'd barely gotten in the door. Jókell had taken the rune out of its carrier and was about to hand it to me, when the door burst open and someone threw me across the room."

"Who attacked you?"

"I don't know. I didn't see."

"What do you mean, you didn't see? You were right there!"

"Right there and almost unconscious. I hit the wall and all but cracked my skull open. I heard the fight going on behind me, realized something had gone wrong and knew I had to get out of there. But the only window was bricked up, and the fight was between me and the door."

"What did you do?"

He shrugged glossy shoulders—withers—whatever. "The only thing I could do. I went through the portal into Faerie. But time's running a little slower there, so it took me this long to get back."

I'd said it was like he'd fallen off the face of the Earth. I just hadn't realized it was literally true. "You didn't see *anything*?"

"I glanced back just as I crawled through the portal, to see if anybody was coming after me. And I glimpsed somebody in a dark cloak. But I didn't see the face."

"So tell me what you did see. Was he heavyset or skinny? Tall or short? Did you see hair color?"

"I saw the back of a cloak and it had the hood up; I couldn't tell. And you all look tall to me." He mumbled something that sounded like "planet of mutants."

"Scent, then—what did he smell like? Or sound—did he say anything?" At this point, I'd take what I could get.

"I don't have senses as acute as yours, and that club was too smelly and too noisy to make much out. Besides, I don't think he said anything."

I regarded him in utter frustration. I had an eyewitness who hadn't bothered to use his eyes—or anything else. Perfect.

"You knew I was dhampir before I even opened my mouth," I reminded him. "You must have sensed something."

"I can tell species, even under a glamourie. It's the whole truth thing." He waved a paw.

"Then what was it?"

He started to open his mouth, and then stopped, frowning. "You know, that's weird."

"What is?"

"I hadn't thought about it. But if I didn't know better, I'd swear it was a human."

Chapter Thirty-four

The luduan's evidence hadn't helped as much as I'd hoped, since the only human involved in the case was dead. But vamps had human servants, even mages on occasion. And he had provided one tasty little nugget.

I had my phone out before I'd reached the bottom floor. "Geminus," I told it.

"The master is—"

"Going to be really sorry if he doesn't take this call. I can talk to him, or I can talk to Marlowe about the smuggling ring he's been running. His choice."

Geminus was on the phone in less than a minute, which told me a lot on its own. SOP was to let people like me hang, but then, he was probably afraid I'd do the same to him. One call to the Senate, and Geminus was going to be a very unhappy boy.

"What do you want?" The question was snapped in my ear before I'd even had a chance to say hello.

"I already told you that."

"I don't have it!"

"That's too bad. I'm sure you've managed to cover your tracks pretty well up until now. But that was because no one was looking too closely at you. Once that changes, I don't think the evidence for your smuggling operation will be hard to find. And that doesn't even count what the fey are likely to—"

"Where are you?" he asked abruptly.

"Chinatown. Why?"

"Stay there, and keep your phone with you."

"If this is a stalling tactic—"

"It isn't. I really don't have the damned stone. But I may know who does."

"Who?"

"You don't need to know that. I'll get it and meet you." The phone went dead.

I looked up to find Frick and Frack staring at me. "That was Senator Geminus," Frick said.

"You *do* talk."

"You're blackmailing him?"

I put my phone away. "We're reaching a mutually advantageous agreement."

"What about the smuggling?"

It looked like someone had been eavesdropping. Not too surprising—it was probably why Marlowe had sent them along. "I'll have to keep quiet about that, if he comes through. Of course, what you do is none of my business."

They smiled.

Half an hour later, I was rooting around in my bamboo dim sum tray, hoping for another little barbecue pork bun, while my eyes scanned the scene outside. Chinatown is always colorful, but tonight was something special. A river of glittering lapis scales flowed by the window in front of me, twisting and turning in the traditional dragon dance, the light of nearby neon signs scattering spots of color on its long snakelike back.

The impromptu parade had been by twice already, a crowd following the dancers like the tide and blocking the entrance to the small restaurant. It was making the owner scowl from his perch behind the cash register, but the waiters and patrons clearly loved their front row seats. The August Moon Festival was a big deal, and everyone was in good spirits.

Everyone but me. Geminus hadn't called, and his phone went automatically to his mailbox. I drank my beer to wash the anxious heartburn back down and watched the spectacle with everyone else.

My chopsticks rattled on bamboo. I added the dead

soldier to the tower across the table while my waiter watched with big eyes. He was clearly wondering where I was putting it all. "Metabolism," I explained.

I was trying to decide between more buns and the Mongolian barbecue when a static charge ruffled the hair on the back of my neck. My head jerked up to stare at a vampire walking down the street, flickering in between the line of glossy duck butts in the window. He paused on the corner, the shadows around him ebbing and flowing along with the overhead neon light.

It wasn't Geminus. I saw a pleasant face with generic features under a swath of dark hair, totally unremarkable except for the sense of power radiating off him like a small sun. I watched the figure brighten and fade, brighten and fade, until it seemed like the face itself was flowing instead of the light.

There weren't too many vamps with a power signature that strong, and most of them were at the Challenge. The traffic stopped, and he headed across the street. And my eyes narrowed.

Despite the stereotypes, there are plenty of tall Chinese. There are also quite a few who fill out a pair of jeans in interesting ways. But there are few people of any race who move through a crowd as gracefully as a dancer across a ballroom. I knew those moves.

More unmistakably, I knew that butt.

I swallowed the last of my Kirin, shoved a fifty at my waiter and burst out into the brilliantly colored night.

The vamp was already almost a block ahead, moving fast through the mass of shopping-bag-carrying locals and camera-toting tourists. He hit a snag in the form of the crowd around the dragon dancers, and it let me get close enough to scent him—or it should have. I took a breath, but all I got was the acrid smell of gunpowder from teenagers setting off illegal fireworks. Then the wind shifted, blowing in my direction, and I fell back quickly.

And someone grabbed my arm.

I whirled, slamming my attacker back against the darkened window of a shop, a knife to his throat. "Y-your change?"

"Sorry," I mumbled, as I recognized the startled black eyes of my waiter. He thrust some bills into my hands and fled.

The distraction had been brief, but that's all it takes when chasing someone who can move like the wind. I ran across the street and into the alley, and found what I'd expected. The full moon hung low and fat and orange in the sky, glowing like a lantern through the crack between buildings. It lit up four- and five-story brick structures, garbage, and the ribbon of water down the center of the passageway. And nothing else.

Damn it!

I forged ahead anyway, pausing every few yards to sniff the air. I hadn't managed to get a whiff of him, but it didn't matter. That particular scent was already cemented in my brain. But all I smelled were dog droppings, gasoline and garbage, the latter redolent of the reek of rotting fish. That was probably because there was a fish market at the end of the alley, its bright electric lights piercing the dark like a beacon.

The vamp had come that way. I finally caught him on the air, a thin thread of scent interwoven with the cleaner the proprietors used, the chlorine in the water and the smell of fresher sea life. But he was nowhere in sight.

But someone else was.

I stepped back into shadow as a tall figure in a black coat and hood came down the alley. New York in August does not require outerwear unless you're hiding something. In my case, that something was weapons. I didn't think that was the reason here.

The asphalt under the coat was splashed with a delicate white light. The person wearing it was outlined by a narrow halo as well, as if the coat's fibers weren't thick enough to contain the radiance within. It probably hadn't been obvious on a street washed with light and color of its own, but in the gloom of the alley, it glowed.

I felt Frick and Frack come up to bracket me on either side. "Fey," one of them said unnecessarily.

A dark shape flickered into view up ahead, under a streetlight, then passed out of view around a corner. The vampire emerged from the night to follow, and the fey ghosted behind him. With us bringing up the rear, it was like a small parade. It would have been funny, if I hadn't thought it was about to get a lot more crowded.

"Can you distract him?" I asked Frick.

"We have no orders to engage the fey."

"I'm not asking you to engage him, just to distract him. Make sure he loses his target." They didn't bother to respond, and neither moved. "What exactly were your orders?"

"To assist and protect you."

"God, Marlowe must be desperate." Frick remained impassive, but Frack's lips quirked slightly. I saw them. "Look, I don't have time to explain. But if there's one fey, there's probably more—maybe a lot more. And they don't have any problem with engaging."

Frick still didn't say anything, but Frack stirred slightly. "If they spot her tracking them, we will have no choice but to defend her. And if there are others, the odds in that event might not be favorable."

Frick didn't respond, but after a moment, he sighed. The next second, they melted into the night after the fey. I gave them a brief head start and did likewise.

Away from the market's dazzling glare, the street was a half-perceived tangle of tumbled shapes and awkward angles. The coat was barely a glimmer, its radiance swallowed by the shadows crowding thick and suffocating on all sides, and the vampire was just a slightly different texture of night.

I didn't see what happened, exactly. One minute, the coat was gaining on the vampire, and the next, it had simply disappeared. It might have been jerked into an alley or side street, but it hadn't looked that way. From back where I was standing, it appeared to simply vanish.

Marlowe's boys were good. I wondered what they planned to do with him. I decided I didn't care.

I emerged onto a busy cross street in time to see the vampire pass into a pot noodle place on a corner. I followed and found it jam-packed with waiters shouting orders, people standing three and four deep at the counter and crowding the small tables. But a quick glance around told me that my two weren't among them.

I headed through the swinging door to the kitchen. I'd expected to be called on it, but I merited no more than a disinterested glance from the staff, who were sweating bullets trying to keep up with all the orders. I crossed to the back door, which was propped open to help with ventilation.

Outside, a graffiti-covered wall loomed over a small space filled with a stone table, a lot of cigarette butts and a heap of garbage bags. A tattered awning fluttered overhead on a small breeze. The remains of someone's dinner sat on the table, being nosed at by a few flies.

It was dark. It was quiet. It was utterly boring.

I glanced back at the kitchen, where the staff were still scurrying around, ignoring me. They seemed way too comfortable with guests roaming around their private preserve. I had the feeling a lot of people came this way. The question was, where did they go then?

I paused beside the table. Despite the utter normalcy of the scene, something was wrong. It took me a minute to realize it was the garbage.

The flies buzzing about the half-eaten meal were totally ignoring the bounty in the trash bags nearby. I walked over to the pile, my nose twitching. Not at what I smelled, but at what I didn't.

I'd expected the pungent odor of soured beer, the sharp acid of wilting vegetables, the stench of rotting meat. I'd expected it to smell bad. But it didn't. It didn't smell like much of anything, which was fair because it wasn't actually there.

It's never a good idea to stick anything you'd mind losing through an opaque ward. I went back to the kitchen, where a mountain of real garbage bags had been piled in a corner. The third one I tried yielded an empty industrial-sized aluminum foil container. In the center was a long cardboard tube, which I fished out and took back to the ward.

It wasn't fancy, but my makeshift periscope allowed me to peek beneath without risking my head. The tube didn't immediately catch fire or get chopped in two, which I counted as a plus. Of course, that didn't mean that there were no booby traps, just that any that existed were farther down.

The tube showed me a flight of steps leading down to a safety door. Light radiated through the ornate grille casting black traceries of shadow over the stairs. It also cast the silhouette of someone in the room beyond the door, tipped back against the wall, with what looked suspiciously like a rifle in the crook of one elbow. I couldn't get a scent reading on him, but not because of the ward. The sweet pungency of high-quality weed drifted up the stairs, filling my nose to the exclusion of anything else.

The fact that he had a rifle didn't mean he wasn't a vamp, but the weed probably did. Drugs had no effect on the vampire lack of a metabolism and so were uninteresting to them. They had plenty of other vices to compensate.

I stood up, tucked the tube inside my jacket and jumped through the ward. Any lingering doubt I'd had as to the type of doorkeeper I was facing wore off when there was no immediate response to the small tone the ward sent out at my entry. By the time the shadow's bootheels hit the cracked cement underfoot, I was already at the bottom of the stairs and reaching through the iron cage to grab him by the shirt. A quick slam of his head against the unyielding doors knocked him out and the keys were in his pocket.

Simple.

What wasn't so simple was what was reverberating off the walls. It sounded like drums or too many hearts beating too fast. I couldn't pin it down, but it was doing bad things to my blood pressure. I stepped through the door and over the inert guard, taking a second to attach him to the grille with the cuffs he'd thoughtfully had in his back pocket.

A couple of small red dots had stuck to my jeans. I peeled one off with a thumb. It said "forty-two." I flicked off a few more, and they had numbers, too. They were spilling out of a box with a lot of red, fewer orange and a couple of bright yellow circles. All had numbers, except for the yellow ones.

I took one of each, appropriated the guard's flashlight and headed down the corridor. It sloped away on a sharp incline, not quite as steep as the stairs but close, and the thrumming sound got worse the farther I went, echoing strangely in the enclosed space. There was something familiar about it, something I'd heard before, I just couldn't place it.

And then I didn't have to wonder anymore.

A door slammed open at the end of the corridor, and a guy staggered out, obviously inebriated. A wash of light, noise and strong smells spilled out along with him. I caught the door before it closed and found myself in the back of a large room lined with sloping stadium-style seats and packed with people. I couldn't see much else, because a couple of hulking shapes blocked my view.

The two vamps looked at me, one bored, the other just plain mean. The bored one said something, but I couldn't tell what. My hearing is better than good, but the noise level was incredible. The commotion going on behind them had reached a fever pitch, and the crowd was chanting and stomping their feet.

That was the weird sound I'd heard: the collective pounding of hundreds of feet on a dirt floor. The place looked like it had once been a cellar, one of the mass of old structures undergirding Chinatown. They and the tunnels that connect them were once used by the tongs as escape routes in their constant feuds, but these days, they'd mostly been converted to underground shopping malls and storage areas for smuggled Gucci knockoffs.

This one appeared to have been appropriated for another purpose.

Golden graffiti traced along one grimy wall, but unlike Fin's, it wasn't scrolling. Instead, a running outline of abstract shapes girdled a list of names, with numbers scrawled alongside them. They were odds, I realized, recognizing the formula.

The bored guard pointed at the yellow dot on my clothes and hiked a thumb to the left. I didn't know what that meant, but he moved out of the way, letting me pass, so I went in the specified direction.

I stayed near the wall, and edged around the crowd, trying to search for a familiar figure in the crush. It wasn't easy, as it was standing room only in the back, and my head only came up to the shoulders of a lot of the people. But here and there I caught glimpses of what looked like a live-action version of Olga's chess set.

A powerfully built male ogre in a leather loincloth was jabbing a long spear at an equally minimally attired troll. The troll had a club, but he wasn't using it. It lay ignored on the ground, the heavy wood a poor substitute for his own stonelike hands.

He appeared to be trying to crack the ogre's head between them like a nut. The ogre didn't seem in favor of this idea and kept jabbing the spear at the troll's small eyes. Considering how useless troll eyes are anyway, this seemed a bad strategy to me, and it had the double effect of pissing the troll off.

Luckily for the ogre, who was maybe half the troll's size, mountains of troll flesh do not move quickly. He was just keeping ahead of the massive hands, one of which smashed down into the floor with a bone-shaking thud. The troll was becoming frustrated, and the ogre was growing tired. This wasn't going to last much longer.

I spied a kind of box seats overhead, in the form of a platform jutting out of the wall. It looked like it had been built over the entrance to another tunnel. A rickety-looking set of wooden stairs went up to it and the back disappeared into darkness.

I headed for it, hoping that the stairs would give me a better vantage point from which to scan the room. There was a vamp at the bottom of the steps, which had a rope stretched across them, but he caught sight of the yellow tag on my shirt and let me through. I was halfway up when the stairs, which had been vibrating slightly to the enthusiastic stomping of the crowd, jittered more violently.

A man staggered out of the darkness at the top, a spill of bright red blood cascading down the front of his white dress shirt. I had a few seconds to recognize Geminus as he teetered on the edge of the platform, along with the gaping wound in his throat, the knife in his back and the disbelief on his features. Then he was falling, hitting the ground in the middle of the two combatants, his blood leeching out to stain the arena sands.

It looked like that ancient seer had been right, after all.

Chapter Thirty-five

For a moment, I could see the warm glow of Geminus's power melting through his skin like sunlight through gauze. It turned everything white and gold, the entire room bathed in flickering fox fire. It was strangely beautiful, but unlike the rest of the room, I didn't waste time staring. I'd seen enough dead vampires to know what was coming.

The young aren't too showy in death, having little power to expend. But Geminus had two thousand years of pent-up energy, and it had to go somewhere. And unlike with Elyas, his masters weren't around to absorb any of it.

My foot hit the top stair as a sudden burst of brightness flared at my back. I glanced behind me to see white-hot tendrils snaking around the body on the floor, and then a flash—and for a moment, Geminus became a human torch of impossible brilliance. I put on a burst of speed as something huge lashed through the room, an unseen current that trembled on the air, shaking a rain of dust from the rafters. And then the world fell away in a clash of thunder.

I was halfway down a sloping corridor, but the backlash was enough to pick me up and throw me half a dozen yards. I landed on my side and rolled, wincing away from the sheer brightness of it, shielding my eyes with my hands. I don't know if the stairs collapsed as Geminus's death released his power, or if everybody panicked and headed for the main exit. But nothing followed me down into the depths of the tunnel except for a billowing wash of dust and a lot of screams.

I lay on the floor, bruised and dust-covered for a second, breathing heavy. Until part of the roof collapsed, sending me scuttling down the tunnel on all fours, trying to stay ahead of the rain of dirt and moldy bricks. It felt like a dozen fists pummeling me, and I could see cracks in the round ceiling above, spreading rapidly.

There was a side tunnel up ahead, and I dove for it, afraid I was about to become a permanent resident of Chinatown. But the expected destruction never came. These tunnels had been here since the nineteenth century; I guess they'd withstood worse.

I hugged the wall anyway, my breathing labored in my ears. I don't like dark places. I really don't like dark, enclosed, underground places. And the fact that this one just happened to have a murderer running around in it wasn't helping my phobia.

I pulled a flashlight out of my jacket. My eyesight is good enough that I don't always need one, but I carried it just in case. The steel body did double duty as a club, and it felt reassuringly solid in my hand as I clicked it on.

At first, all I saw was tumbled brick, dirt and dust in the main corridor, and dark stone laced with cobwebs on the side. But then the light glinted off a dark smear on the floor. Blood; fresh.

I crouched, listening intently, and heard some faint cursing from somewhere deeper in the labyrinth. It could have been anything or anyone. I was sure plenty of people used these tunnels, and murderers wouldn't be likely to call attention to themselves by swearing up a storm. But I didn't have a trail at all in the other direction, and no knowledge whatsoever of the maze down here. I followed the blood.

It wasn't hard. Along with the spattered trail, there was a wide swath of slightly cleaner floor, near one wall, with some odd marks around it. They didn't look like they'd been left by shoes or boots, more like something had been dragged through the grime. Something that might have been struggling, because some of those markings looked a lot like handprints.

And then there was the blood. I could have prob- ably followed it without the flashlight, the smell was so strong. Stronger than it should have been, for such a thin trail.

I knelt and ran a finger through the century's worth of muck on the floor, bringing a small sample to my nose. And flinched away, an electric charge shooting up my spine. Vampire blood. From an old one, based on the feel. It was rich and dark, closer to black than red, with a strange, almost velvety texture. Very old, I decided, looking up.

The thought made me hesitate. I didn't think of my- self as particularly cowardly, and for once I had plenty of weapons and no compunction at all about using them. But a wounded master could drain me of the blood he des- perately needed to heal before I even got close enough to spot him. And no weapon would help me then.

But he had to know I was here; this close, he could smell every breath, hear every heartbeat. And he wasn't feeding yet. He was, however, cursing a lot more. But not in English. I listened, frowning, as I inched forward, and figured out what language he was corrupting about the same time I rounded a bend and saw him.

He was slouched on the filthy floor, inching along on his elbows, his back legs dragging through the grime. His once-white tunic was drenched in blood, much of it still wet. The dampness had picked up the furred gray cover of dust that had collected near the walls, like foam on the sea, as he dragged himself forward. The result was so startlingly like an enormous dust bunny that I just stared at him for a second, frozen in shock.

"Anthony?"

The esteemed consul of the powerful European Senate looked back over his grubby shoulder. And an expression of profound relief chased away the almost panic on his features. "Oh, thank the gods!"

I blinked. That wasn't the reception I usually received from vampires, much less master ones. I moved forward, and he grasped my hand, already babbling before I could so much as get a word out.

"We've got to get out of here. We've got to get out of here *now*."

"It's okay," I told him, trying to struggle out of a grip that was about to crush my fingers. "The roof held. I don't think we're in danger of a—"

"Oh, we're in danger, all right." He gave an almost giggle that had me doing a double take. Consuls did not giggle. I hadn't even thought they knew how.

"From what?" I asked cautiously. "Geminus is dead."

"Geminus." He hissed the name through his teeth. "I'd like to kill him for getting me into this."

"Didn't you?" There weren't a lot of people who could have sent a first-level master reeling into that arena, but I was looking at one of them. It seemed like Louis-Cesare might have been right, after all.

But Anthony merely shot me an exasperated glance. "Don't be ridiculous!"

"Then what did?"

His eyes darted here and there, the whites showing all the way around the iris. I wasn't sure if that was due to nervousness, or because of the way the skin seemed to have pulled back from his bones a little. Old Anthony wasn't looking too good.

"It was that *thing*," he whispered.

"What thing?" I asked, as he tried to struggle to his feet. He failed.

"The thing that killed him! It's still down here, and it's going to get us, too. Oh, yes, and don't think you'll be spared." He wagged a finger at me. "You're half vampire, aren't you?"

I had no idea what the hell he was talking about, or if he even did; he looked a little crazed. But at the moment, I was less concerned over some possibly mythical monster than over why he couldn't stand. It takes a lot to put a master vamp on his ass, and Anthony was clearly hurting.

"What happened to you?" I asked, drawing back the folds of the toga he still had half draped around himself. And sucked in a breath.

I knew where the blood came from, I thought dizzily. Anthony didn't have one stake in him, or even one dozen. His body was riddled by them, like a human porcupine. They didn't look like regulation stakes, now that I focused past the gore that covered them. More like shards of some kind of boards. But they'd done the trick. Some of the longer ones had passed completely through his body and were tenting the back of his toga.

And one had nailed him straight through the heart.

"Why haven't you pulled these out?" I asked, bewildered and a little sickened.

"Don't touch them!" he said savagely. "It was bad enough putting them in the first time!"

It took me a second, but I got it. Or I thought I did. "You stabbed *yourself*?"

"I had no choice. The stake through my heart is coated in wax. I had to drain myself so my body temperature would lower. Otherwise, I'd have melted the damn thing already."

"And vamp bodies don't bleed much from a single wound, so . . ."

"I had to keep on stabbing myself! If I hadn't been left near some old wooden crates, I'd be dead now."

"You bought yourself time for your neck to heal," I said, impressed in spite of myself. I'd killed a lot of vamps, and never once had any of them thought of that. Of course, most of them were pretty much paralyzed with a stake through the heart. I wondered how much power Anthony had to have to still be somewhat mobile in spite of the stake and the massive blood loss.

And then I wondered what would happen if he didn't make it. Geminus had almost brought down the roof, and Anthony was at least as old and a good deal more powerful. "We need to get out of here," I said, trying to get him up.

"Now, why didn't I think of that?" he asked, with vicious sarcasm.

Considering the circumstances, I decided to let that go and concentrated on where to grab him. There wasn't a lot of free space left, but I finally managed to get an arm around his waist. A heave got him to his somewhat shaky legs. It would have been nice to have been able to lean him against a wall, but that would only have done more damage. And it didn't look like he could take much more.

"Do you know these tunnels?" I asked him, wondering which way out was closest.

"Don't you?"

"Why would I have asked if I did?" I demanded, trying not to snap. Anthony weighed a ton, and he was bearing almost none of his own weight. "I've never been down here before."

"You live here. Don't you ever go exploring?"

"Underground? No."

"Underground is where all the interesting things happen."

"Underground is where the monsters live."

Anthony's surprisingly high-pitched laughter echoed off the walls. "You aren't kidding, sister."

Anthony, I decided, might have lost a little too much blood. He was getting punchy. "Come on," I told him, heading back for the main hall. Bad as it was, it beat wandering around lost for hours.

I'd started to get up a head of steam when Anthony suddenly jerked to a stop and stumbled over to the nearest wall. He clutched it, muttering another rude phrase in Latin. Mine's not too good, but I think it had something to do with someone's grandmother and a one-legged donkey.

"Are you all right?" I asked, feeling a little stupid even as I said it. Because obviously not. But his health didn't seem to be uppermost in Anthony's mind.

"It's back!" he hissed, staring around fearfully.

"What's back?"

"That thing! Gods! I thought it had left!"

I stared at him, wondering how I was supposed to get a seriously wounded consul out of this underground maze when the man was clearly not in his right mind.

And then I heard it, too: a distant, far-off echo, just a sigh on the air. "Anthoneee."

My breath caught.

"Don't tell me you didn't hear that!" Anthony said, looking at me wildly.

"I heard something." I paused, trying to listen past the thud of my heart slamming into my rib cage—Anthony's distress was contagious. But the sound didn't come again.

"Where is it? Which way did it come from?" he demanded.

"I don't know."

"Oh, gods!"

Master vamps hate to be seen losing their cool, and consuls are supposed to be above such human things. But Anthony was clearly terrified. I decided I didn't want to know what could frighten a guy who could stab himself a couple dozen times without flinching.

"Let's go."

I pulled him down the corridor, a little faster than his feet wanted to work. He kept wobbling over to one side or another, almost forcing me headfirst into a wall more than once. I finally pulled him into a fireman's carry, since most of the stakes along his torso had already been pushed through to the back, thanks to his dragging crawl along the floor.

We hit the main corridor again a few minutes later, Anthony lolling like an old drunk and me swearing. I propped my hand on the wall for a moment, trying to get my breath back. And when I moved it, I left a sweaty outline behind. I stared at it resentfully, breathing hard, and wondering why I never got the skinny villains. And then I heard that sound again. And unless I was very much mistaken, it was closer.

But I still couldn't tell the direction. There were too many side tunnels, too many echoes. Even our own voices sounded strangely like they were coming from several places at once.

"Come on, come on, what are you waiting for?" Anthony demanded anxiously.

To decide whether or not to leave your ass here, I didn't say.

"We have to move it!" he said, poking me.

I pushed off the wall, and slung him back over my shoulders. "I'll move it. As long as you tell me what you're doing here."

"Geminus called me up in a fearful panic, raving about the fey and retribution and Zeus knows what all. Turns out someone was trying to blackmail him for that damned rune and he'd gotten it into his head that I had it. He threatened to go to the Senate unless I handed it over."

"And did you?"

"I couldn't give him what I don't have," Anthony said testily.

"Then why did he think you did?"

"Who can say? You know these gladiator types. A little thick in the skull."

"Unlike these Senate types," I said, stopping. "A little slippery of the tongue."

Anthony waited me out for maybe half a minute, and then he cracked. "You would leave me here? A wounded man?"

"You're not a man, and in a heartbeat."

He expanded my vocabulary of ancient Roman curses for another moment, while I just stood there. "Oh, very well!" he said resentfully. "He saw me going into Elyas's study last night, moments before he died."

"So Louis-Cesare was right. You did kill him."

"I may have my flaws, but I am loyal to those who are loyal to me. And Elyas was an old supporter. I didn't go there to kill the man!"

"Then why did you go?"

"For Christine. Louis-Cesare has been looking for her for a century; he has some strange obsession with the woman. I thought if she was under my control, I would hold him. I went there to strike a bargain with Elyas. I would protect him from any retribution from Alejandro, but I wanted the girl."

"But you didn't get her," I said as I started staggering

back toward the arena. I just hoped like hell that the stairs were still there.

"No, thank the gods!"

"What happened?"

"I arrived to see Elyas and was told he'd retired to his study. I went along and knocked, but there was no answer. I went in and found him, trussed up like a Christmas goose."

"Why didn't you do something? You could have saved him—"

"I could have done nothing of the kind. I'd seen this trick a time or two, and one look was enough. The wax was already soft. Removing the blade would have dislodged it and merely killed him sooner."

"You could have tried to heal him, then."

He made an exasperated sound. "That sort of thing may run in your line, but mine isn't so gifted! And even had it been, it is doubtful I could have helped him. You saw his throat—it wasn't slit; it was bisected. He was seconds away from death, and there was nothing to be done about it."

"So that's what you did? Nothing?"

"I attempted to question him, to find out who was responsible, but he was groggy. I couldn't get anything useful out of the man and was about to summon his second when Louis-Cesare showed up."

"The study was soundproofed," I pointed out. "You couldn't have heard him."

"The charm doesn't work when the door isn't fully closed, and in my surprise, I hadn't bothered to pull it shut."

I tried to think back, and it seemed to me that he was telling the truth—about that much, anyway. The study door had been partly open when I arrived, sending a wedge of light out into the hall. That was how I'd known where to go.

"I heard the servant conducting him down the corridor," Anthony continued. "And . . . an idea presented itself."

"You left him there, knowing he would die and that Louis-Cesare would be blamed."

"And that I would get him off. He was never in any danger, other than to his pride. Which could stand a prick or two, I might say."

"You planned to force him to remain under your control, practically as a slave!"

Anthony sighed wistfully. "It was perfect. I should have known; the Fates have always hated me."

I stopped because we'd reached the door to the arena, or at least I assumed it was behind there somewhere. A massive fall of dirt, bricks and rock blocked the way. The whole damn thing might have caved in, or it could be a localized fall caused by a weak spot in the tunnel. And there was only one way to tell.

I swore under my breath, letting the flashlight play over the rough ceiling, or as much of it as I could see through the hanging cloud of dust. I could see where the old bricks had given way, letting through a ton of dirt and a cascade of long white roots. In the flickering light, they looked almost like grasping fingers, reaching out—

Okay, yeah. Enough of that. I'd been down here a little too long, listening to Anthony's ravings. I needed to get us both out of here, although it wasn't looking promising. The only way through the fall, assuming there was one, was going to be at the very top. I had a sudden vision of myself having to shimmy through on my back, the rock inches from my nose, another cave-in just waiting to happen ...

Have I mentioned that I really, really hate little dark places?

But there wasn't much choice in this case. I tucked the flashlight in my belt to leave both hands free. "I'm going to check it out," I told Anthony. "Stay here."

"As opposed to?" he asked wryly.

"I'll be right back," I promised. I wasn't sure who I was reassuring: him or me. From Anthony's expression, I think he figured that out, but he didn't say anything. I started to climb.

It was about as fun as I'd expected. It was pitch-dark except for the bouncing beam of the flashlight, which never seemed to be pointed where I needed it to be. And even when it was, it mostly highlighted the choking dust cloud, which wasn't helping me see or breathe. I misjudged the distance and cracked my head on the rough ceiling, and then my foot fell through a gap in the loose earth, causing a mini-avalanche.

My feet managed to find purchase at the last second on a section of brick that had all come down in a piece. I held on, hiding my face in my jacket and trying not to breathe as a few hundred pounds of dirt flowed over me. It finally stopped, and I looked up, blinking dirt and dust out of my eyes.

I was practically buried, with only my head sticking out of the fall. I coughed, got my bearings and started trying to fight my way free, causing the load of debris around me to shift. Unfortunately it mostly shifted back onto me. I scrambled to try to compensate, thinking I saw a gap up ahead, but a sudden cascade sent me sliding back down the mound on my stomach, getting pummeled by rocks, roots and sharp-edged bricks the whole way.

I slid to a stop at Anthony's feet, gasping and choking on the new wash of dirt in the air. "Now what?" he demanded. It didn't look like patience was the consul's strong suit.

I scowled up at him, bruised and filthy. "Now we're going to have to find another—"

"No!" He was starting to look panicked again. "There's no time. We have to go out here."

"I don't have a backhoe in my pocket," I snapped, struggling to my feet and vainly trying to dust off my clothes. But my sweat and his blood had caked the dirt onto them; all I was doing was smearing it around. I decided it could wait and looked up to find Anthony staring at me.

He wasn't going to plead, wasn't about to beg. But his face was doing it for him. The heatless flame of the flashlight flickered over drawn features and colorless flesh. Around his many wounds, dark rings glistened like hungry mouths, smearing his clothes and staining his skin.

But it didn't look like any more was flowing. I suspected that might be because there wasn't much left.

Anthony was running out of time.

I stared into the blackness of the corridor behind us, seeing nothing. But my brain supplied an image of the dark, unknown passageway, which probably opened onto more caverns and then more passageways . . . endless regressions into deeper and more silent darkness. I could find my way out, eventually, of that I had no doubt. But I couldn't do it and carry Anthony, and I wasn't sure what I'd find when I got back.

"I'll give it another try," I said reluctantly, and he nodded, looking slightly relieved. He got a hand to my backside and pushed, and I scrambled up the slippery slope once again.

I don't know if the previous avalanche had sloughed off most of the looser debris, or if I was just getting the hang of things. But I made it to the top this time with little difficulty, putting out a cautious hand to the ceiling so as to spare my head. I wedged myself into a some-what secure-feeling space between the ceiling and wall, and sent a pale tongue of light through the small space I'd previously noticed.

It was a definite gap. But I couldn't see anything on the other side, either because the flashlight's beam didn't extend that far, or because there wasn't anything to see. I could slither in there only to find another wall of dirt and rock. Or another avalanche waiting to come down on my head.

My fingers were aching from gripping the flashlight so hard, and it wasn't going to be much use anyway. I tucked it back in my belt and started crawling, before I could talk myself out of this. The gap at the top of the mountain was claustrophobically small, and the air was almost unbreathable. It also got smaller as I went along, to the point that my elbows were brushing it on either side, and my chin was carving through the dirt like a plough.

It was almost impossible to imagine dragging Anthony through this, even if there was an opening on the other side. The smart thing would be to turn around, to find another way out as fast as possible, and to send help back for him. He was as tough as nails, as he'd more than proven; maybe another hour or two wouldn't make a—

My head popped out into open air on a little cloud of dust. It was so unexpected that it caught me off guard, and I didn't stop my forward momentum fast enough. I found myself tumbling down another steep slope, head over heels into darkness.

I smashed into the pile of very hard debris at the bottom and just lay there for a moment, trying to breathe. It didn't go so well, at first because the wind had been knocked out of me. And then what little breath I had caught at the sight of someone standing just inside the shadow of the main door.

He was sliced diagonally by bands of ruddy light from some source behind him. I vaguely recognized it as the graffiti marquee, its dim glow filtered through a haze of dust. I couldn't make out much even with the light; there was too much crap in the air. But a monstrous shadow sprawled on the floor beside him.

I watched, out of breath and momentarily helpless, trying to get back to my feet. But my left foot was caught on something, and before I could figure out on what, the indistinct shape moved forward. Its hand lifted and the shadow appendage moved along with it, rippling, giant, and terrifying.

And reaching out for me.

Chapter Thirty-six

Panic caused me to jerked my trapped foot hard enough to crack the heavy old root it had become wedged under. I ignored a bright searing pain from my ankle and scrambled to my feet, gun in hand. Only to have it caught in an iron grip.

I twisted but couldn't break the hold, so I did the next-best thing and threw my attacker against the wall. He hit with a thud that had more dirt dropping down on top of us, but he still didn't let go. Instead, he spun me into his arms, and somehow got a grip on both wrists. So I stomped on his foot, trying to get enough leverage to—

"Please do not hit me below the belt again," a man said, sounding heartfelt. "I have not yet recovered from the last time."

"What are you doing here?" I asked, relaxing back into Louis-Cesare's arms.

"I followed Anthony. I wanted to know what was important enough to keep him away from the challenge of the century. Why are you here?"

"I followed you." I twisted in his grasp, and he let me go, a little reluctantly, I thought. Or maybe that was just wishful thinking. "Everyone is looking for you. The consul's about to have a fit, Marlowe's tearing his hair out and Mircea . . ."

"I know. I called him an hour ago, informing him that I will return for the trial. I never intended to do otherwise, but I had to be free to gather evidence, if such existed."

"I think Marlowe is already doing that."

"Yes, but there are places even he cannot go."

"Such as?"

"Such as Anthony's private rooms. I wished to search them for the stone—"

"You searched my rooms?" The outraged voice drifted faintly through the rubble.

Louis-Cesare's head jerked up. "What was—"

"Anthony," I said sourly. "I found him a little while ago."

"You found—" He looked at me incredulously. "But he could drain you from here! If he is the killer—"

"I don't think he is." I wanted to ask how Louis-Cesare had managed to search Anthony's rooms when Marlowe himself couldn't do it. But I decided it could wait. "Did you find anything?"

"No." He looked frustrated. "But he is dangerous nonetheless!"

"Not so much at the moment," I said drily.

"He killed Geminus!"

"He says not."

"I saw the body, Dorina. There are very few opponents who could have done that to a fighter of Geminus's caliber." It was the same thing I'd been thinking, but it still didn't make sense.

"He was attacked, too."

"By Geminus, no doubt attempting to defend himself."

"I'd think the same, but those weren't defensive wounds. Anthony said something killed Geminus and then attacked him."

"Some*thing*?" Louis-Cesare's expression spoke volumes.

"That's what he said, but he isn't completely coherent at the—"

The scream that tore the stillness caused us to jump as one, tensing against attack. But it wasn't on our side of the fall. "Anthony!" Louis-Cesare called, as I scrambled back up the slope.

There was no answer, but an odd scent suddenly flooded

the air, sweetness on the verge of putrefaction, hard and sharp-edged. I'd smelled it somewhere before, but I couldn't place it. But there was something off about it, something *wrong*.

The tiny tunnel at the top of the landslide was even harder to get through quickly. By the time I'd managed it, I'd lost what skin remained on both my elbows and cracked my head on the ceiling a few more times. Which was why I just stared at the scene on the other side. For a moment, I thought maybe I'd hit my head a little too hard.

Anthony was slumped against the wall, staring upward with an expression of stark terror. Half a dozen stakes had been pulled out of his chest, and lay scattered on the floor, their bloody tips pointing at the creature stroking red hands over Anthony's torso. The tiny, delicate fingers slid through slippery blood, teasing the edges of mortal wounds almost playfully.

But they were stronger than they looked. One of them suddenly backhanded Anthony, the manicured nails tearing into his cheek and snapping his head around, smashing his face into the rough wall. He forced his head back up, working his jaw absently. A trickle of blood made its way down his cheek before he began sluggishly to heal.

This seemed to enrage his tormenter, who gave another of those unearthly screams. Another slash of nails laid open his chest, but although he jerked against the pain, he kept his teeth clenched on a scream. With a digging twist the nails gouged deeper, until he twitched helplessly against their merciless grip, his head tossing back and cracking against the unforgiving bricks.

"Rotting carrion. How many times do I have to kill you?" his tormenter hissed.

"A few more, it would seem," Anthony said, grimacing. And then he had to grit his teeth again as those knifelike nails started tearing downward in sharp, hard tugs.

The movement galvanized me out of my shock. A moment later, I was slip-sliding down the tumbled mass of dirt as Anthony's nightmare looked up, snarling. I tensed, gun in one hand and heavy-duty flashlight in the other. But then the lips that had been pulled back in a rictus softened into a smile, and the glittering hate in the eyes melted away, as if it had never been there at all. If it hadn't been for the blood smearing her pale blue gown, she would have looked completely normal.

"*Christine*?"

"Hello, Dory." Her voice was calm, even, friendly. If I hadn't been watching, I'd have never known that her fingers were still tracking the furrowed paths of Anthony's wounds, slick with his blood.

I'd ended up teetering precariously on a pile of fallen bricks, so I stepped cautiously to the side. She didn't noticeably react. "Uh. What are you doing?" I asked, equally carefully.

"What does it look like?" Anthony asked hoarsely.

I thought he might be wise to stop drawing her attention. The hate returned to her eyes as she looked at him, so focused that I could feel it pulsing between them. Then her hand tightened on the stake in his heart, and before I could stop her, she had jerked it out.

Anthony choked back a scream, while Christine crouched over him, holding the bloody spike. She held it up, examining it with a puzzled frown. "Why isn't he dead?" she asked me.

I was wondering the same thing, until I saw his neck. There was a stuttering, puckered line where, until very recently, a gaping wound had been. He'd healed, I realized in disbelief. The stubborn son of a bitch had healed a mortal neck injury with a stake through his heart. I wouldn't have believed it was possible without seeing it myself.

It was a damn impressive trick, but I didn't think he had another one. The resignation on his face said that clearly enough. Anthony had given up; he thought this was it. And I had no clue why.

He should have been able to snap Christine like a twig, drain her, defend himself a hundred different ways from someone with little more power than a human. But he wasn't. And that couldn't be good.

"The wood is showing through," Christine complained, before I could figure it out. She proffered the gory stake. "I don't understand. It worked last time."

"Last time being?"

"Elyas," she said impatiently.

I walked over to take the stake, shedding dirt with every step and fighting to keep my breathing slow and steady. I didn't understand what was going on here, and that was bad. But the unmistakable flicker of madness in Christine's eyes was worse. If she wasn't running on all cylinders, even a minor slipup could get me in trouble.

And Anthony dead.

I took the stake and examined it, crouching down beside Christine and her prey. I turned it over in my hands. "It looks okay to me," I said. "Did you use the same type on Elyas?"

"Yes," she said fretfully. "I had them made to my specifications in Zurich by a silversmith. The shaft is apple wood, but I had him inlay a little silver tip, you see?" She pointed out the razor-sharp end with a nicely manicured nail. It would have been pretty if it hadn't had part of Anthony caught underneath it. "It makes it go in easier."

"I bet it's not as easily deflected by a rib, either," I said, because she obviously expected me to say something.

She nodded. "It isn't as good as a knife, of course, but at least it doesn't splinter."

"I tried iron banding once," I told her, "quite a while ago, but I found that—" I broke off at a painful jab in my right calf. I glanced down to find Anthony's hand gripping me. Right.

"Uh, so. Why did you kill Elyas again?"

She raised those lovely eyes from the stake to mine. "I'm sorry. Did you want him?" she asked politely.

"Not particularly, no."

"I don't blame you. He wasn't much of a challenge."

"Unlike Geminus?"

"Oh, no. He would have been interesting, but he wasn't expecting it, you see. They rarely do."

No, I didn't suppose so. I was standing in front of her,

watching Anthony's blood drip from her hands, and I was still having a hard time picturing her as the murderer. Her scent was off, but she looked the same as always: sweetly innocent and beautiful enough to turn heads.

And then she plunged the stake back into Anthony's chest, and it became a little easier.

He did scream that time—a pathetic, mewling sound that had me grabbing Christine's wrist before I thought about it. But she only crouched there, looking at me inquiringly. "Uh. You can't kill him," I said weakly, after a short hesitation.

Her head tilted curiously. "Why not?"

My mind raced, trying to come up with a reason, any reason, to save Anthony. It was a little difficult since I didn't know why she wanted him dead in the first place. And then a voice spoke calmly behind me. "His death energy would bring down the ceiling on our heads. We would all die."

Christine frowned, and let go of the stake. She slowly rose to her feet, bloody hands smoothing her crumpled skirt. "Louis-Cesare."

"Christine."

I glanced between the two of them. Louis-Cesare looked vaguely sick, regarding the tableau with a terrible sadness. But he did not look shocked.

He did not look *surprised*.

"What the hell?" I demanded, standing up.

He glanced at me and hesitated. But then his spine stiffened and he answered, "When I made Christine, it was as I told you. She had been drained of most of her magic, and with it, her life. She was close to death—so close, in fact, that I did not know if the process would take." He paused to lick his lips. "When she awoke, it became rapidly obvious that . . . there was something wrong. She was lucid enough. She knew me, but she was . . . troubled."

"Troubled as in . . ."

"She was violent. Disturbed. I put her to sleep, hoping it was merely the trauma of what she had been through. But the next night, when I went to check on her, she was gone. I tracked her to the abbey where she had been a novice and where she had once been whipped. I found it burned to the ground, and the abbess . . ."

I suddenly remembered a vision of a burned-out building, piles of ash and a desiccated corpse, as delicate and fragile as an insect's exoskeleton. "Christine?"

He nodded, swallowing. "Others had been fed upon. I tracked Christine for miles, and finally found her with a group of pilgrims. Or . . . what remained of them."

"Oh, gods." That was Anthony. I wasn't sure if it was a cry of pain, or because he was slowly reaching the same conclusion I was.

"She hasn't done anything like that since," Louis-Cesare said quickly, seeing the dawning horror in my eyes. "I kept watch over her, and she is easily enough restrained. Her power is minimal; she is only a danger to humans and she is not allowed—"

"Minimal?" Anthony coughed, a harsh, wet sound. "She's a goddamned first-level master. I should know!"

Christine casually put a delicate little patent leather shoe through his chest. I heard ribs crunch, and he cursed. "You do not wish to kill him, Christine. Remember?" Louis-Cesare said sharply.

"Oh. Oh, yes. I'm sorry." She meekly withdrew the foot, leaving Anthony writhing on the floor.

I stood there, feeling dizzy. "She's a revenant," I said numbly. Louis-Cesare didn't confirm it, but he didn't deny it either. He just stared at me, his face blank and pale like that of a man about to face the gallows.

Or like a man who had sired a monster.

It didn't happen often, but occasionally a young master would feed off the same person too many times in close succession, thereby passing on the metaphysical virus that was at the core of vampirism. But because the feedings weren't intended to be a Change, the master's blood wasn't also shared with the child. And thereby the link that power created was missing.

Revenants also occurred when something went wrong with the Change, either because of a mistake on the master's part or because of a problem with the subject selected—generally illness or age. If the subject was weak, the link formed was as well, and never provided the control needed to steer the new vampire's development.

However they were created, the newborn revenant was a problem from the start. They craved that connection with their master and the power it should have brought them. Without it, they went mad with hunger, attacking everything in sight, blindly searching for something they would never find.

Occasionally, one would survive for a few months, maybe as long as a year if he was in a relatively isolated place, like a mountain range with plenty of hiding places. But I'd never heard of one lasting longer than that. Certainly not long enough to rise in power. It had never even occurred to me—or to anyone I suspected—that a revenant *could* rise in power.

I guess the assumption always was that they were flawed mentally, so they must be flawed physically as well. And that was often true. The pale, hunchbacked, salivating vamp of legend, with fangs too large for his mouth and an unquenchable lust for blood, possibly came from sightings of revenants.

But what if one did live, because she had a powerful protector? A protector so ridden with guilt that he couldn't bear to follow the law and have her destroyed? And what if that revenant was highly functioning, enough so that, with careful supervision, she would appear merely eccentric rather than mad? And what if this farce had continued for three hundred years?

What could a first-level master revenant do? Other than manage to camouflage her abilities, even from her own maker. Who, after all, hadn't seen her for more than a century.

I glanced at Anthony. I guess I knew.

"She is not . . . She does not have to be a danger," Louis-Cesare said desperately. "She can be—"

"She's a fucking revenant," Anthony coughed. "She's a danger to everyone—you know this! Why the hell didn't you have her put down when you realized it?"

"How could I? I had already killed her twice! First

when I handed her over to that bastard of a mage, and then when I made her into a vampire. How many times am I supposed to kill this one poor woman? How much damage am I to do?"

I didn't think that was the question. I thought it was: how much *could* he do? Like human children, baby vamps tended to take attributes from their sire. So much so that family lines often became known for having certain gifts. Mircea's, for instance, was better than normal with healing, both themselves and others. Louis-Cesare had gained that advantage from Radu, but when he became a master, it was his own special gifts and interests that were passed to his children.

And, as everyone knew, his strongest ability was in combat.

Chapter Thirty-seven

I watched as red lightning started to flicker across Christine's palms and to coil up her arms. I didn't think she liked being talked about as if she wasn't in the room. I didn't think she liked being given orders, either. She kept glancing at Anthony, and the hunger on her face was startling.

Anthony didn't notice, having let his head droop down to his mutilated chest. I couldn't tell if that was deliberate—to hide the fact that his neck had healed—or if he was merely too tired to hold it up anymore. But looking at the way his skin was starting to shrink up against the bones, I was voting for the latter.

Anthony had to get out of here and back to his family, and he had to do it now. But no way was he managing that on his own. I glanced at Louis-Cesare to see if he got it, and found him staring intently back at me.

"Dorina?"

I almost jumped out of my skin when the word echoed softly through my brain. *"What?"* I thought back instinctively, and felt a surge of profound relief that I knew wasn't mine. I didn't feel relieved. I felt creeped the hell out. *"How long have you been able to—"*

"Can you do it?" he asked silently, cutting me off in my own head.

"Can I do what?"

He looked pointedly at Anthony. *"I will not leave you here with her."*

"You left me with her last night!"

"It was almost dawn, and I thought she had the power of a child then. You cannot hold her."

No, I thought bitterly, I didn't suppose so. I'd been getting my ass handed to me by vampires all day, and after seeing her with Anthony, I doubted this would be any different. But I also couldn't drag an almost-deadweight through the landslide, across a debris-filled room and up a lengthy tunnel. And then fog the minds of the people on the other side when I was through.

I thought that at him as hard as I could, and saw him wince. It had probably had the force of a shout behind it, but I didn't have centuries of practice at this. The only other times we'd had any kind of mental link, I'd been too distracted to worry about it.

I was plenty worried now, but other things took precedence. Like what I'd die of first, if Anthony went—the fire of his energy storm or being crushed to death as the tunnel collapsed. It wasn't a palatable choice.

"If Anthony dies, I'm dead anyway. And he'll die if he stays here. Get him out!" I sent.

"If she hurts you—"

"She won't. I'm her good vamp-killing buddy, remember? Just hurry back."

He sent me a slurry of emotions, intentionally or not, that had my eyes widening. *"Do. Not. Die."*

Yeah, well, that was the plan.

"Christine!" My voice caused her to start slightly. "You're draining Anthony. And if he dies, we do, too. Remember?"

She stared at me, dark eyes bright, for a long moment. And then she slowly nodded. "I can't die yet," she agreed. "I'm not done."

It was amazing how three small words could cause gooseflesh to break out all over my body. "Not done?"

"You asked why I killed Elyas. This is why," she said, obscurely.

"Because he was an evil vampire?"

"Well, of course," she agreed, pushing back a stray

lock of hair. The heel of her hand brushed her cheek, leaving a red streak behind, like badly placed rouge. "But I could have killed him at any time for that."

"So why now? To avoid Alejandro's executioner?" I knew before she answered that that wasn't right. Whoever Alejandro sent would have had a rude awakening.

"No. It was the rune."

"The rune."

"Yes. I knew Elyas had it." She frowned. "Or I thought he did. I didn't know about the necklace, you see, when I killed the fey. I checked his pockets, but I never thought to look there. And then I felt Elyas nearby and had to flee before I could look anymore. I couldn't let him see me. I couldn't be discovered. It was too soon. But then I saw him coming out with the necklace in his hand, and I realized my mistake."

"How did you know about the rune? You weren't at the auction."

I wanted to know, but I also wanted to keep her attention on me. Louis-Cesare had circled around behind her while we'd been talking.

"Elyas could talk of nothing else. All day he was on the telephone to Lord Cheung, all but begging him for it. He was afraid that once Louis-Cesare left the European Senate, he would no longer be able to retain his seat without help. I overheard enough to realize what it was, and what it could do."

"So that's why you picked up the carrier in the office."

She nodded. "I'd searched it when I killed Elyas. I'd remembered about the knives, not to touch them directly. But I'd thought the necklace wouldn't show fingerprints because of all the ridges. I'd forgotten about clairvoyants." She looked annoyed.

"How did you learn to kill vampires that way? It isn't common knowledge."

"I have had to learn many new methods in order to hunt." She looked frustrated. "Louis-Cesare was so careful; it was almost impossible for me to do anything. And Alejandro wasn't much better. He watched me all the time, afraid that I would run away. It was easier when I went to Elyas. He never noticed me."

Neither had anyone else, I thought grimly.

"Why wait until the party to kill Elyas?" I asked. "You could have killed him at any time."

"But if I did it before the party, only the family would have been home," she said reasonably. "There had to be other suspects, or everyone would have started to look at me."

"So you waited until the apartment was filled with people, and you could get Elyas alone."

"Yes. I didn't mean for Louis-Cesare to be blamed. I knew he had an appointment for that night; I had heard Elyas telling the doorman about it. But it was for earlier that evening. I waited to kill him until I thought the master would have come and gone."

"But Louis-Cesare was delayed." She nodded. "Is that why you killed Lutkin? To throw suspicion off Louis-Cesare?"

"No, the mage was at Elyas's party. I saw them talking together. It might have meant nothing; Elyas liked the races and Lutkin was a champion. But I thought there was a chance that a powerful mage could have stolen it."

I spared a thought for poor Lutkin, who had died because Christine thought there was an outside chance he had the stone. He'd probably never even seen it.

"But Lutkin was killed in daylight."

"I have been a daywalker for two centuries."

Daywalker was the old term for anything above a third-level master, because they were the only ones who could stand direct sunlight for any length of time. It looked like Anthony had known what he was talking about.

"How did you get in? The consul's security is pretty tight."

"They let me in. Louis-Cesare's name was still on the guest list, and I am his servant." She shrugged.

"So that left Geminus."

"Yes. I was sure he had the stone. He was at the night-club that night. I saw him when I was leaving, but I didn't think anything of it at the time. And Geminus was at the party. But he didn't have it, either."

"That's why you used the wax-covered knife on him." I had wondered. There were more efficient ways to kill people.

"I wanted to be able to search him before he died and the reaction set in. And then Anthony came, and so of course I had to kill him, too. I didn't mean to use a wax blade on him, but that was the one I grabbed first."

I made a mental note to tell Anthony: maybe the Fates didn't hate him as much as he thought.

"You killed him because he could have named you as the guilty party."

"Yes. I tied him and stabbed him and left, but when I didn't hear a second death rumble, I knew something had gone wrong."

"Clever."

"I can be clever." She glanced behind her, where the guys had disappeared through the fall. "I know they are leaving. It is all right. Anthony needed to go. I might have made a mistake with him here, and I can't afford that. Not tonight."

"What's special about tonight?"

"But haven't you realized? That is why it doesn't matter if they stay or go. Tonight is when I kill them. Tonight is when I kill all of them."

"Kill who?" I asked slowly.

Christine didn't answer. Her gaze had fallen to her watch, and her eyes widened. "I didn't know it was so late! I must go."

I caught her arm as she whirled and headed down the corridor, away from the landslide. I didn't so much as slow her down; it was more like I got towed along for the ride. "Wait! You haven't told me why you wanted the rune. It isn't as if you need the protection."

"Oh, but I do. That is why I came here tonight. One last chance . . ." Her voice faded, but then came back stronger, more resolute. "But then, perhaps this is God's way of telling me that it is enough. That once this is done, I will have redeemed myself at last."

"Once what is done?"

"I prayed so long for a miracle, and there was nothing. For years I thought that God had abandoned me, now that I was tainted. Unclean." She looked down at her blood-streaked clothes, her nose wrinkling in distaste. "But then He sent you to me, and all became clear."

"I made things clear?" I asked, panting in an effort to keep up.

"It has been your life's work, removing their stain from humanity. But there are too few of you. Too few dhampirs and so very many of them. And they reproduce at will, constantly making more and more. You need help."

"And you are going to help me?"

"I'm going to do more than that. After tonight, the vampire world will be in chaos, families feeding on one another as they once did, master against master, line against line. They will destroy themselves, and those who are left will be annihilated in the war. And you will be able to sit back and watch it all happen. I only wish I could be with you."

"Why can't you?"

She shot me a puzzled look. "Because I'll be dead. The rune was my last chance to survive what lies ahead. But I am beginning to see that perhaps I was not meant to survive it. Now that the work is done, I can shed this horrible skin, these baseless cravings. . . ."

"If you tell me a little more about what you plan to do, maybe I can help," I offered as bricklined nineteenth-century work blurred into modern concrete.

"You have already helped. You gave me the key."

Christine ducked into a side tunnel and I scurried to keep up. "You'd think I'd remember something like that."

"For a long time, I could not understand why God had allowed this to happen, why I of all people should be chosen for this fate," she told me. "But over many years, it slowly became clear: in order to destroy them, I had to be one of them. Only one who knew them intimately could devise a way to bring them down."

"You've been planning this for a while."

"Something like this," she agreed. "But I was missing a key element. Killing one or two vampires, here and there, does nothing. Killing masters is better, for then an entire line is weakened. And killing senators is truly useful, for it undermines the political structure and starts the process toward anarchy. But one or two senators will not do. They are merely replaced. To truly destroy their society, I needed a way to kill a great many leaders, all at once, from a great many Senates. But it seemed hopeless. When were they ever together?"

"For the Challenge," I said, starting to feel a little cold.

"I realized the opportunity the Challenge presented at once, but I did not know how to capitalize on it. I should have known that God would not let me come so far and fail to provide."

"He provided the rune?"

"No, Dory." She laughed. "He provided *you*. The task seemed impossible, but you showed me the way."

The darkness up ahead fractured, pierced by a dozen tiny shafts of light. It turned out to be a manhole cover, with a ladder leading up. I grabbed her sleeve with both hands. "How did I do that, exactly?"

Her head tilted. "But don't you see? If we had not gone through the park that night, I would never have thought about using the portal."

"What portal?"

"The one in the East Coast headquarters. I had been trying to think of a way to smuggle a bomb into the Challenge, but I knew it would be impossible. The wards would detect it immediately and detonate it inside a force field. It would all be for nothing."

"But then you met me," I said, feeling sick.

"And you showed me that I didn't have to get a bomb into headquarters. One was already there, in the form of their portal." She reached into a pocket in her skirt and came out with a small gray ball. I recognized the remains of my explosive putty.

"That's why you insisted on coming home with me," I said dully. "You wanted to take it from my bag."

"I am sorry for that," she said, apparently sincere. "I would have asked, but I did not think you would trust me with it. I *am* a vampire, after all."

"But you could have taken it at Elyas's," I said, desperately trying to stall. I couldn't catch Christine on the open streets, and headquarters was too close. By the time I made a call, she'd already be there. "You were alone with my duffel in the office while I talked to Mircea."

"No, Raymond was there. He would have seen. But in the confusion after the fey attacked, it was easy."

Yeah, easy. Like walking into the East Coast headquarters would be easy. Christine wasn't a dirty dhampir or a wanted criminal. She probably wouldn't even be challenged. And a mass of explosive like that in a large active portal—

She was right: she was clever.

There was a cascade of images in front of my eyes, and this time, they were my own. Radu in his ridiculous dressing gown; my mother, glimpsed through Mircea's eyes, the scene suffused with a love I had never believed existed; Louis-Cesare, head thrown back in passion, fingers gripping my arms like he never wanted to let go.

And Christine, off to destroy all of it.

There was only one solution left, and it meant I was about to disappoint Louis-Cesare. But there was no other choice. If I let her leave, it was over.

I pulled a gun out of my coat; Christine didn't even notice. She was halfway up the ladder, reaching for the manhole cover, happy and confident in her newfound purpose. And still carrying the putty in her right hand.

I didn't even try to take cover; there was no point. If the blast didn't kill me, Christine's death energy would. Or the tunnel would collapse and crush me. Any way I looked at it, I wasn't getting out of here. But at least this was something I could do. For once, I didn't need to be stronger or faster or have better weapons in order to compete. I just had to pull a trigger.

So I did.

Epilogue

"I told you she was evil," someone said as I blinked open my eyes.

I was in my bedroom. A wash of afternoon sunshine cascaded over the old sheets, turning the off-white cotton faintly yellow. A vampire sat beside my bed, and he was in yellow, too. And before my eyes focused on the face, I knew who it was. There aren't many people, even in the vampire world, who think that daffodil-colored satin is appropriate day wear.

Radu crossed his legs and flipped over another page in the magazine he was reading—*Car and Driver*, ominously enough—while I checked myself out. The parts I could see poking out of a faded blue T-shirt all appeared to be functional, although most were trying to decide between a livid red and a blue-black color scheme. But I'd looked worse, and I'd certainly felt worse. And, frankly, I was grateful to be feeling anything at all.

Even if I didn't understand it.

I pushed the extra pillow behind me and sat up. "Maybe you can clear something up for me that I've always wondered about," I said, meeting those famous turquoise eyes.

"Yes?"

"Why do you insist on dressing like freaking D'Artagnan when you were born two hundred years before that?"

Radu frowned. "Formal wear in my day was robes, Dory."

"And?"

"Nasty, long, hot, smothering robes. Good in winter, of course, but the rest of the time . . ."

"Vampires don't sweat."

"Yes, but knee pants are so much more flattering. You can see my legs."

"You want people to see your legs?"

"I have very nice legs!" We both paused to admire them for a moment.

"Are you here to shake me down for the car?" I asked, getting it over with. "Because I don't have three hundred thousand dollars."

'Du's eyes flicked over the well-worn furnishings and faded quilts. "I never would have guessed."

"I'm not likely to have it in the future, either."

His frown grew. "I'm not here about the car, Dory! I bought it for Gunther, in any case. I don't drive."

"Gunther? Your *bodyguard*?"

"He's a very good bodyguard."

I looked at him severely. " 'Du, you're not falling for a human, are you? You know how tacky that is."

"Certainly not." He shook out a sleeve. "Anyway, I bought him another one."

I grinned.

"Stop that."

"If you're not here over the car, why are you here?" I asked curiously. Radu was certainly strong enough to withstand daylight, but that didn't mean it was comfortable.

He poured me a glass of water from a bedside carafe and settled back with a disgruntled look. "Oh, I don't know, I'm sure. Perhaps I thought you might want to know how the trial went."

I sat up a little more. "They still had it?"

"Well, of course they still had it. Elyas is still dead, isn't he?"

"As far as I know. What happened?"

"Louis-Cesare was acquitted of murdering that sniveling creature." I felt my spine relax slightly into the pillow. "And convicted of mass endangerment by knowingly concealing a revenant."

I sat back up again. "What?"

"Well, what did you expect? She almost butchered Anthony."

"What's the sentence?" I asked, feeling my stomach drop.

"Death."

"Death?"

"But since Christine was under Elyas's care—and supposed supervision—while committing the murders, Mircea managed to successfully argue that the sentence should be carried out on him."

"On Elyas?"

"Mmm-hmm."

"But he's already dead."

"Yes. Quite the time-saver, that."

"So . . . they're just going to let Louis-Cesare walk?" That didn't sound like the Senate.

"Not entirely. He did sire her, after all, and failed to deal with the problem. He's lucky they didn't do worse."

"Radu! *What did they do?*"

"Threw him off the Senate—both of them. And he is banned from taking Senatorial office again for at least a century." He crossed his legs to get them out of a creeping patch of sunlight. "Of course, that's a lot of tosh. It was really the only compromise anyone could think of to the problem of which Senate should get him. Neither was willing to back down, and we can't very well afford a conflict when we're already in one. . . ."

"So Louis-Cesare had to fall on his sword?"

"In a manner of speaking. For my part, I think he should be pleased. It's going to be hell in the senate until all the new members settle in."

"So the challenges went off without a hitch?"

"Thus far. Of course, tonight was merely round one, and no one truly expected a problem yet."

"I assume Ming-de's candidates are cleaning up?"

"No. In fact, she had a rather poor showing. The only candidates to move on to the finals from the Chinese delegation were Zheng-ze and Lord Cheung, although it's early days."

"Zheng-ze?"

"Very odd sort. Believe it or not, he fought the whole night with a severed head tied to his belt!"

So Scarface was on his way to a Senate seat, after all. I grinned. "I believe it."

There was a knock on the door and a hairy little head poked in. Big gray eyes regarded me silently for a moment before Stinky scrambled up the bedpost and plopped down beside me. He had something wet and dripping in his hand, and before I could stop him, he slapped it to my forehead.

"Thank you," I told him as icy water dribbled down my neck.

"I'm sorry," Claire said, coming in with Aiden on her hip and a blond at her back. Her hair was extra bouncy today. I guess because of the curlers. "But he insisted. He seems to believe it's some sort of magic cure-all."

I surreptitiously passed the dripping offering to Radu, who put it on the nightstand. "I seem to be doing okay without it, although I'm not sure why."

"I am," the gorgeous blond man behind her said. He had a chair in each hand, both of which he put down in order to give me a kiss. "Hello, Dory."

"Caedmon. When did you get here?"

"Last night, as soon as our time streams caught up with one another," the fey king said.

"Heidar's here, too," Claire told me, "along with about fifty guards. It's a madhouse downstairs."

"It could be worse. Heidar wanted to bring half the army," Caedmon said drily.

"We could have used them," I told him. "How the hell did Æsubrand get loose? Claire said he was secure."

"It was clever," Caedmon admitted. "My sister wrote to me, begging to be allowed to see her son. Foolishly, as it turns out, I agreed."

"Why foolishly?"

"Efridís is adept at glamourie—good enough to fool even our own people. She paid Æsubrand a visit, they spoke for a time, and she left. At least that was what my guards believed."

"You're saying she took his place?" He nodded. "But how? If you knew Æsubrand had her ability—"

"On the contrary. Glamourie has always been difficult for him; he takes after his father in that regard. But my sister was veiled when she arrived, and through the gauze, the roughness in his assumed features was not obvious. And due to her rank, the guards did not check her too closely. Meanwhile, their prisoner's appearance was flawless."

"Then you have your *sister* in jail?"

"At present, yes. She resumed her old form once her son was safely away. It is an untenable situation, however. I cannot detain the Svarestri queen indefinitely, a fact she well knows."

"So she's sitting around your hunting lodge, playing cards or whatever, while that son of a bitch tries to kill Aiden?"

"But from what Claire tells me, Æsubrand was not trying to kill Aiden during the attacks. In fact, he never so much as looked for him. Both times he went directly after you. He even waited to attack the second time until he knew you had returned home."

"He wanted me to tell him where Aiden was."

"Did he say so directly?"

I tried to think back. It wasn't easy. My brain felt fuzzy and my tongue was as dry as sandpaper. I sipped some of the water Radu had poured. "Not in so many words, no. But that was the idea."

"But do you not think it is significant that he did not focus his attention on Claire? She was a double threat. Her null abilities allowed her to destroy the wards that made the constructs possible, and her Dark Fey heritage made her a formidable opponent, particularly when protecting her child."

"Maybe he knew she'd never give up her son's location and believed I'd be an easier target."

"Perhaps. But he had fought you before and had not managed to break you. In his situation, I would have concentrated on killing Claire, then you, and then searched at my leisure for the child."

Claire stared at him, horrified. "You would what?"

"I am merely telling you proper military procedure," he told her patiently. "And Æsubrand was trained as I was, to be logical in the choice of adversaries. Yet his actions here were not—*if* Aiden was his target."

"You don't think the Svarestri want him dead?" I demanded.

"Oh, they wish that, certainly. But I do not think they feel a sense of urgency. It will be decades, probably centuries, before he is powerful enough to pose a real threat."

"They tried to kill him before," Claire said angrily.

"Yes, but as a postscript, if you will, to an attempt to kill me. He became a priority only once they believed I was dead. Then he was the only thing standing between Æsubrand and the throne. As long as I live, that is not the case."

"Then you think the attack at the castle had nothing to do with Æsubrand?" Claire asked skeptically.

"Yes and no. I do not think he ordered it, but the main conspirator was the father of Ölvir, one of the traitors I was forced to execute after his recent coup attempt. The man committed suicide before we could lay our hands on him, but he left a letter. He said that as I had deprived him of a son, he would deprive me of a grandson."

Claire shivered.

"Æsubrand has been preoccupied with the search for Naudiz, in any case. Having an invincible commander could sway many to his cause, and it is a powerful symbol. It is only given to the heir to the throne."

"But you just said he was after me," I pointed out.

"Yes."

It took me a second, but it finally clicked. "I don't have it, Caedmon!"

"Not anymore," he agreed, holding something up. It was a crudely cut stone, off-white in color and about the size of my thumb. A few scratches on one side formed a crude glyph.

I pounced on it. "Where did you get this?"

"That vampire found it."

"Louis-Cesare?"

"Yes. I knew it was some ridiculous hyphenated name."

"It was discovered under your body when he pulled you out of the wreckage," Radu said, shooting Caedmon a less than friendly look.

"What was it doing there?" I asked, bewildered.

Caedmon shrugged. "It fell off your skin after its energy was expended, deflecting the blast."

"Off my *skin*?"

"Naudiz is meant to be worn into battle. When cast, it melts into the skin so that it cannot be dislodged."

"Like a tattoo?"

"No. The magical tattoos your mages wear are visible on the body. One of the advantages of Naudiz is that it is not. An enemy can therefore never be certain when the wearer is protected, and must assume that any attack made upon him will be very risky."

"That is why everyone wanted it for the challenges," Radu said. "Most magical aids would be detected. But Naudiz was specifically designed not to be."

I stared down at the small thing on my palm, my head reeling. "*I* had it? The whole time I was running all over the city, going crazy searching for it, it was on my damn skin?"

"And fortunately so. Had it not been, you would most certainly be dead."

"But . . . how did it get there?"

"We got a theory about that," a familiar voice said. It took me a second to recognize the guy who stood in the doorway. Because, for once, all his parts were where they were supposed to be.

"Ray. They put you back together already?"

"Good as new." He walked over and bent down to show me his scar. "Better, really," he said in a low voice. "The Senate's got some good bokors on their payroll. When they finished with my neck, I had them look at . . . other stuff."

"So no more Mr. Lumpy?"

"Naw. I'm a stallion, baby!"

"I'll take your word for it," I told him as he settled off to the side, well out of the sun.

I looked at Caedmon. "How did I end up with Naudiz? I wasn't at the auction and I never met Jókell."

"But I did," Ray said.

"What difference does that make?"

Ray leaned back against the wall, getting comfortable. "We think it went down something like this. Jókell's in the office, waiting on the luduan to authenticate the stone so he can get his money. The door opens, but he doesn't sense anything dangerous, just some human looking for the john or something."

"Because Christine's power signature was deceptive," I said. "She was one of those rare vampires able to hide her true strength."

"Right. So he's not worried. No human is gonna be a problem for him. So he gets caught flat-footed and she guts him."

"That's not speculation," I said. "I talked to the luduan yesterday, and that's what happened."

"Yeah, we talked to him, too, this morning. He said Jókell had the rune in his hand and was about to hand it to him to verify when Christine showed up."

I nodded. "He told me that, too."

"Okay, so there's Christine, who must have heard about the rune from eavesdropping on Elyas. She knows he's coming to do his own snatch and grab any minute, so she doesn't have much time. She checks Jókell's clothes, turns out his pockets, but doesn't find the rune. And then she senses Elyas approaching and has to leave or blow her cover too early."

"Following you so far."

"Then Elyas comes in. He sees Jókell lying there, all but dead, with the carrier he'd seen at the auction around his neck. He grabs the carrier, assuming it has the stone, and hurries off before anyone spots him. Leaving Jókell behind with the rune still in his hand."

"But if he had it at that point, why didn't he cast it?" I asked. "He had to know how it worked or he wouldn't have been able to sell it. Any buyer was going to need that information."

"He did cast it."

"Then why is he dead?"

"Because he made a mistake. Naudiz takes a few seconds to activate once the incantation is said. He was half unconscious with blood loss and in a lot of pain. When I came back, all he could think about was getting my attention, to let me know he needed help."

Light dawned. "H grabbed your ankle." I remembered Ray mentioning that, but it hadn't seemed important.

"With the hand holding Naudiz," Ray agreed. "It transferred to me and the next second, Jókell was dead."

"That still doesn't explain how I got it."

"Naudiz is designed to sustain life," Caedmon said. "It cannot function properly on a creature that, by its definition of the term, is already dead. It lent him some additional energy while it searched for a living body to fulfill its function, but it could do no more."

"The bokors said that's why I came through the whole dismemberment thing so good," Ray added. "According to them, I should have been pretty out of it."

Come to think of it, Ray had seemed remarkably . . . resilient. "But why transfer to me?"

"No reason other than you were the first living body with which Raymond had extensive contact," Caedmon explained.

"Yeah, your hands were all over me," Ray said with a cheerful leer. "And at some point—boom! It transferred. Probably during that crazy pursuit. I mean, who would notice, right?"

"But I've been hurt since," I protested. "Æsubrand broke my wrist!"

"Naudiz isn't a shield, Dorina," Caedmon told me. "It does not protect you against all injuries. It does ensure that those injuries are not life-threatening."

I nodded and started to ask something else when a huge yawn interrupted me. "She's tired," Claire said, getting up. "We should go."

"I'm okay," I protested, only to have her look at me severely.

"The healers said you'll need lots of rest, probably for the next week. The rune may have kept you alive, but you took a beating down there."

"It couldn't have been that bad. I—"

"Louis-Cesare had to pry your body out of the brickwork!"

I was suddenly grateful not to be able to remember anything. "Okay, but one more thing," I said as everyone else got up. "How did Æsubrand know I had the rune? I didn't even know."

"The most likely explanation is that he tracked the fey to the nightclub and saw Christine leaving the office," Caedmon said. "By the luduan's description, she was heavily muffled up, and from what I understand, she did bear a superficial resemblance to you."

I hadn't really thought about it, but I guess, from a distance, we would look something alike: dark hair, dark eyes, pale skin and roughly the same height. Of course, her hair had been long, but she'd usually worn it up. And the luduan had said she had a hood. I decided it was feasible. It also seemed irrelevant.

"There must be thousands of people in this city who look like me," I pointed out.

"Yes, but there are not thousands who could take on a fey warrior and hope to survive. Æsubrand saw a small, dark-haired woman with no discernable power signature leaving the office shortly before Jókell was found murdered. He does not know many humans, and therefore his thoughts must have immediately gone to you. He had his spies check your home and discovered that Claire was here. His logical conclusion was that she had asked you to retrieve the stone, and that you had done so."

"Son of a bitch."

"My people tell me that he has returned to Faerie for the present, no doubt realizing once we arrived that the rune was lost to him." He looked at me soberly. "But you should be careful, Dory. Æsubrand is not the type to forget a defeat, and you have bested him twice now in front of his men. I think you may see him again."

I remembered the fey I had seen following Louis-Cesare. Had Æsubrand hoped he would lead him to me? I decided I owed Marlowe's boys a drink.

Claire bent over to retrieve Stinky. "Get well soon," she told me. "I want to go see some movies, eat some greasy human food, go shopping. . . ."

"So you're not headed right back?"

She shook her head. "I know it doesn't sound like it from the way I've been talking, but there are things I love about Faerie. But I'm half human, too. And I think I've been away too long."

"Maybe you need to visit more often, then."

She grinned. "Maybe I do."

Radu was the last one remaining. He settled beside me on the bed, looking sober. "Louis-Cesare is downstairs. He's been here since he brought you back."

"Why didn't he come up?"

"He doesn't think you want to see him. I told him he was being ridiculous, but you know how he is."

"I'm learning."

"Should I tell him to come up?"

"Yeah." I had a few questions for him.

Radu nodded, but he didn't leave. "You know, even if she hadn't been an evil mutant, she was always quite bad for him. Not that I meddle."

"Of course not."

"But she was. He needs a nice, levelheaded girl. You're levelheaded, Dory."

"I'm insane, 'Du."

"Well, not all the time. And when you're not, you're quite lovely . . . in your own odd little way."

"Uh, thank you?"

Radu patted my arm. "You're welcome."

I closed my eyes for what felt like a brief moment after he left, and when I opened them again it was dark. Moonlight poured through the window onto the bed, tracing Louis-Cesare's face with a slender outline of silver. "I guess Claire was right," I murmured. "I must have been tired."

"With cause," he said softly.

"You didn't have to stay."

He brushed sweaty hair out of my eyes. "I have left you twice, and each time, you were almost killed."

"Perhaps you shouldn't leave, then."

He let his fingers, soft and featherlight, trail over the skin of my face. "I'm not going anywhere. But you need to sleep."

"Un-uh. You don't get off that easy." I didn't feel like getting up, so I bunched a fist in his pretty blue shirt and pulled him down beside me. His chest made a good pillow, I decided; my eyes were already trying to slip closed.

I forced them back open, because there were a couple of things I wanted to know. I decided to get the big one out of the way first. "Was Christine really your mistress?"

"For a brief time, before the Change. But afterwards . . . even had I been inclined to continue our affair, she hated vampires. She would never have been involved with one of us."

"Then why tell people that?"

"She required constant supervision and it was not a task I could trust to another. Had she managed to get away, any deaths she caused would have been my fault. I had to keep her constantly with me, and I had to have a believable reason for doing so."

"So you let everyone think you were just too smitten to let her out of your sight?"

"Essentially. But it backfired when Alejandro decided that kidnapping my beloved mistress would be a perfect way to force me to deal with Tomas."

"That's why you were so crazy to get her back. You knew how dangerous she could be."

"I had no idea how dangerous she could be," he said drily. "She kept her abilities very well hidden. I was more concerned with the possibility that she would give herself away. Christine was quite lucid much of the time, but at others . . ."

"I saw." That image of her playing in Anthony's mutilated chest would stay with me a while. She'd seemed so . . . happy.

"But at Alejandro's court, eccentricity is the order of the day. Apparently no one noticed. And Alejandro kept her closely confined; he knew that I would be looking for any way to steal her back."

"But Elyas wasn't so careful."

"No. Alejandro transferred Christine to him once he discovered that Tomas was missing, fearing that his threat to kill her might lead me to desperate measures. Elyas agreed to take her, but it seems that his only concession to security was to tell the doorman not to allow her egress! She appeared timid and powerless to him—not someone to worry about. Not someone to fear."

"Which is one reason she was able to kill so easily. Everyone else thought the same."

"Fortunately she appears to have concluded that killing single vampires would do little good in her quest to eradicate the breed. And it might lead to her discovery and execution before she could put a larger plan in place. At least, Marlowe can find no reports of mysterious deaths, either here or near Elyas's estate. We do not know what occurred at Alejandro's, but I assume it was the same."

"She was saving it up for one big blowout."

"It would seem so."

I rolled over so I could see his face. "Okay, end of the easy questions. What were you doing in my head?"

"Mind speak is part of your legacy, from your vampire half. I assume the wine you have been drinking allowed it to manifest."

Fey wine—a curse and a blessing, I thought. And then my eyes narrowed. "But how did you know that? I haven't been mind speaking to you, or to anyone."

He looked away, and his tongue swept over his lips again. "There may have been a few instances when I picked up . . . thoughts."

"Thoughts?"

"Feelings, mostly."

"Good feelings?"

His eyes flicked back to mine, and a faint smile tugged at his lips. "Very good."

Considering the kind of things I'd been picking up from him, I decided to let it drop. For the moment. "All right. But why tell me all that crap about you and Christine? You let me believe that you two were going to pick up where you left off."

"How could I do otherwise? You have spent a lifetime killing revenants. How could I tell you that I was harboring one?"

"You were afraid I'd kill her?"

"That, yes. But there was also your reaction. I knew you would be shocked, disgusted, horrified—everything I saw on your face in the tunnels. I did not want you to think less of me and I knew ..."

"Knew what?"

"That there was no chance for us!" His face was serious, passionate. It made me want to thump him.

"Why? Because Marlowe disapproves and the Senate won't like it? Personally I think that's kind of a bonus.'"

He looked at me in disbelief. "I stole from you. I lied to you about Christine. I left you with a madwoman—"

"Twice."

"You have every right to wish to never see me again!"

"Yes. But then, you also helped me fight off a bunch of crazy fey, ran out on your murder trial because you thought I might need help and, from what I hear, pried me out of a wall."

I yawned, and when I looked up again, Louis-Cesare had that same mix of hope, uncertainty and fear on his face that I'd seen once before. "What are you saying?" he asked carefully.

"I'm saying ..." I paused. What was I saying? Was I actually thinking about this? Was I actually *doing* this? Because out of a lifetime of crazy things, this had to take the prize. Dhampirs didn't have relationships—not long-term ones, at least. And certainly not with the creatures we were supposed to be hunting. I didn't know what the hell I was doing, and this was probably going to end in disaster. Everyone knew, there was no such thing as happy endings, and princes didn't end up with the family pariah.

But now it seems that I am a pariah, too, drifted through my head.

"Stop it," I said, leaning back against him. His arms were tight around me, but his hands were gentle. I could hear a heartbeat in my ear, and it sounded natural, soothing. "What are you saying? That I can't corrupt you?"

He brushed his lips over mine, the faintest of touches, his breath warm against my skin. "I intend to give you every opportunity to try."

I smiled as I drifted back to sleep. Okay. That could work.

KAREN CHANCE

If you enjoyed this book, there are several ways you can read more by the same author and make sure you get the inside track on all Penguin books.

Order any of the following titles direct:

The Cassandra Palmer series:

9780451460936	TOUCH THE DARK	£6.99
9780451461520	CLAIMED BY SHADOW	£6.99
9780141037752	EMBRACE THE NIGHT	£7.99

The Dorina Basarab series:

9780141039510	MIDNIGHT'S DAUGHTER	£6.99

Visit www.penguin.com and find out first about forthcoming titles, read exclusive material and author interviews, and enter exciting competitions. You can also browse through thousands of Penguin books and buy online.

IT'S NEVER BEEN EASIER TO READ MORE WITH PENGUIN

Frustrated by the quality of books available at Exeter station for his journey back to London one day in 1935, Allen Lane decided to do something about it. The Penguin paperback was born that day, and with it first-class writing became available to a mass audience for the very first time. This book is a direct descendant of those original Penguins and Lane's momentous vision. What will you read next?

He just wanted a decent book to read ...

Not too much to ask, is it? It was in 1935 when Allen Lane, Managing Director of Bodley Head Publishers, stood on a platform at Exeter railway station looking for something good to read on his journey back to London. His choice was limited to popular magazines and poor-quality paperbacks – the same choice faced every day by the vast majority of readers, few of whom could afford hardbacks. Lane's disappointment and subsequent anger at the range of books generally available led him to found a company – and change the world.

'We believed in the existence in this country of a vast reading public for intelligent books at a low price, and staked everything on it'
Sir Allen Lane, 1902–1970, founder of Penguin Books

The quality paperback had arrived – and not just in bookshops. Lane was adamant that his Penguins should appear in chain stores and tobacconists, and should cost no more than a packet of cigarettes.

Reading habits (and cigarette prices) have changed since 1935, but Penguin still believes in publishing the best books for everybody to enjoy. We still believe that good design costs no more than bad design, and we still believe that quality books published passionately and responsibly make the world a better place.

So wherever you see the little bird – whether it's on a piece of prize-winning literary fiction or a celebrity autobiography, political tour de force or historical masterpiece, a serial-killer thriller, reference book, world classic or a piece of pure escapism – you can bet that it represents the very best that the genre has to offer.

Whatever you like to read – trust Penguin.